19/3

FIGURES IN SILK

Also by Vanora Bennett

Portrait of an Unknown Woman

VANORA BENNETT

Figures in Silk

HarperCollins*Publishers*

HarperCollins*Publishers*
77–85 Fulham Palace Road,
Hammersmith, London W6 8JB

www.harpercollins.co.uk

Published by HarperCollins*Publishers* 2008

1

A catalogue record for this book
is available from the British Library

ISBN: 978 00 0 722494 4

While some characters are based on historical figures,
this novel is entirely a work of fiction.
The names, characters and incidents portrayed in it are
the work of the author's imagination. Any resemblance to
actual persons, living or dead, events or localities is
entirely coincidental.

Typeset in Sabon by Palimpsest Book Production Limited,
Grangemouth, Stirlingshire

Printed and bound in Great Britain by
Clays Ltd, St Ives plc

Mixed Sources
Product group from well-managed
forests and other controlled sources
www.fsc.org Cert no. SW-COC-1806
© 1996 Forest Stewardship Council
FSC

FSC is a non-profit international organisation established
to promote the responsible management of the world's forests.
Products carrying the FSC label are independently certified
to assure consumers that they come from forests that are managed
to meet the social, economic and ecological needs
of present and future generations.

Find out more about HarperCollins and the environment at
www.harpercollins.co.uk/green

For Luke and Joe

Warmest thanks to everyone who helped me write this book, from Susan Watt and her colleagues at HarperCollins and Tif Loehnis and hers at Janklow & Nesbit, to Lodovico Pizzati for linguistic advice on the finer points of Venetian, and of course to Chris McWatters, my husband, for his ideas, advice, patience and encouragement.

Contents

Silk

1

Isabel knelt. She didn't know the church, but she was aware of shadowy people moving round, or kneeling in corners. Not many, though. It was too late for Sext and too early for None. Most people would be out working. She put her hands up to her face, palmer fashion, staring down at the long, undecorated fingers in front of her eyes, shutting everything else out until even her eye's memory of the candle haloes in front of her had faded. Her father couldn't really mean to marry her to Thomas Claver, could he?

Her lips began to form the Latin words of prayer. She tried to ignore the picture in her mind, of Thomas Claver's thighs spreading on a window bench at the Tumbling Bear, and his mouth forming that slack, leering grin as he and her uncle both lifted their tankards to an embarrassed serving-girl (trying to ignore them, as all servants did) and nudged each other obscenely. She shivered, but perhaps that was just because the prayer that had come to her mind was so sombre. 'O most sweet lord Jesus Christ, true God,' she muttered, fixing her eyes on the calluses and

3

needle pricks on her fingers, proof that she, unlike Thomas Claver, wasn't so spoiled by coming from a wealthy family that she wouldn't deign to learn the family business, 'who was sent from the bosom of the almighty Father into the world to forgive sins, to comfort afflicted sinners, ransom captives, set free those in prison, bring together those who are scattered, lead travellers back to their native land, minister to the contrite in heart, comfort the sad, and to console those in grief and distress, deign to release me from the affliction, temptation, grief, sickness, need and danger in which I stand, and give me counsel.'

But however hard she concentrated on her fingertips and the movements of her mouth, she couldn't retreat into the muzz of incense and contemplation she was seeking. In her mind's eye, Thomas Claver was coming toward her, with his hands stretched out to grab her. She was frozen into the stillness of panic as he loomed over her; no point in shrinking back, as every fibre of her body was screaming to, because the door was locked and there was no escape.

Wisps of voices came unbidden into her head. Her father's: 'an honour for the family . . .' and '. . . important for the family to have Alice Claver's goodwill . . .' and '. . . an excellent businesswoman; she's well-connected, you know; she'll introduce you to people who can help you in life . . .' and '. . . it's not what you know, it's who you know . . .' and '. . . I'm relying on you to do the right thing for the family.' Her nurse's hurried, worried whispering, trying to make peace: 'at your age you think it's all about love . . . but all men are the same really . . . I know he's a bit wild now, but you'll set him right in no time, get him working . . . the important thing is to be in a good family; once you have babies you'll understand that children are all that matter in life anyway.' Jane, resigned but still giggling under the bedclothes, somehow managing to be philosophical even in this misery: '. . . well, at least you know your one likes girls. What am *I* going to do with that old stick Will Shore and his all-night ledgers? Just imagine trying to kiss *him*!'

It wasn't half so bad for Jane, Isabel thought furiously, trying to fight back the hot prickle behind her eyelids as she remembered her elder sister's bewitching face, all pale blonde hair and flirtatiously downturned green eyes and charm, breaking into that rueful smile at the idea of having to marry Will Shore. Will might be a walking cadaver with no chin and no conversation except for what was on his books, but at least he was a man set on his path in the world. He was a freeman and a citizen; he had an honourable apprenticeship behind him and a business already set up. He'd bore Jane to death, but he'd keep her in the silken idleness she liked so much too, lolling on cushions and reading romances and planning her next gown. And she knew it. What did she have to complain about?

Her shoulders heaved. The lump in her chest swelled to bursting. And before she knew where she was, she found herself holding her head in her hands, squeezing helplessly at her closed eyes to stop the tears coming out, with her fingers salty and wet and her breath as fast and anguished as if she were running for her life. I'm crying, she thought, with the calm part of her mind; observing herself, somewhere below that thought, hug her own shoulders with both arms and curl up so low that her head was almost touching the stone floor. But she was sobbing too hard to be surprised.

A shadow moved nearby. Footsteps stopped a few paces away. She heard the faint click of spurs. She didn't care any more. Now that she'd abandoned herself to the angry helplessness of her emotions, she couldn't have stopped the storm inside herself even if she'd wanted to.

The footsteps moved away. But not far enough to forget them. She didn't want to be aware of a new candle flame sputtering into life in the unfocused blaze around the Virgin. Yet it was enough to still her heaving chest for a moment and she fell silent, aware of the tears still coming through her fingers and the smeary mess her face must be, trying to breathe deep to control her sobs and what might be hiccups, pulling at her skin to try to dry it off, waiting for the unwanted fellow-worshipper with the spurs that clinked to go away.

But he didn't. He came back and stood right next to her. Peeping out from between her fingers, she could see the spurs and the mud on his boots. She kept her head determinedly down. He'd go, she thought, in an agony of impatience; she just had to keep quiet.

There was a silence the length of a long-held breath. Then, with dread, she felt a hand on the tight curved agony of her back: a warm hand; a deep, comforting, heel-of-the-hand caress. She burrowed lower into herself to escape; but not before she'd felt the solid reassurance of it. When the surprisingly beautiful bass voice murmured, from just above her head: 'Forgive me, but are you all right?' the memory of that silken male touch, the like of which she might never feel in the future closing in around her, was enough to dispel her irritation at being interrupted in her private grief.

Miserably, resignedly, she raised her head. The face she could half-see looking down at her was thin and dark and hard. But it was softened by an expression of concern. He couldn't have been more than a few years older than she was: eighteen or nineteen, maybe, like Thomas Claver. But he was an adult, with a shadowed jaw and the wiry strength of a man in the neat movement of his arms as he leaned further towards her, with enough delicacy of understanding to realise he shouldn't touch her, clasping his hands together as if to stop himself. She was strangely warmed by the kindness in those narrow eyes.

'Just praying,' she said, with what shreds of dignity she could muster, looking straight back at him, daring him to give her the lie – how was he to know she wasn't a hungry mystic, in the grip of a tearful vision? – but suddenly aware too of how she must look, with her kerchief pushed back and straggles of hair catching in her streaked wet face and her eyes all puffy and pink and swollen and her skin probably hideously blotched.

He didn't respond except to go on looking unblinkingly at her, and there was something quizzical on a face she could see was used to weighing up new situations quickly. She raised a hand and wiped firmly at both cheeks, trying to master herself and surprised at finding that gaze was enough to quell her sobs. She even managed a watery smile as she uncurled herself and sat up on her knees, feeling the darkness inside shrink as her back muscles straightened. 'Well, I *was* praying,' she added defensively. 'I was just crying too, that's all.'

He smiled, now, and although he had thin lips it was an attractive, straightforward smile; she found her own lips curling briefly up in response, aware of her hands busying themselves in their own ritual of patting and tidying her face and head, trying to restore order to herself.

He didn't comment on her appearance. She supposed there was nothing he could say without being either gallant, which would have been wrong, or discourteous, which would have been worse. He just carried on looking into her eyes, with the memory of a smile in his and with his body taut and still. She liked the stillness of him. She was aware of the sword buckled to his belt, the plain travelling cloak. He must have something to do with the troop movements, she thought, be a gentleman in someone's entourage. But his presence was so encouraging that she found herself hoping he wouldn't hurry away soon.

He didn't. Eventually he murmured, 'I'm forgetting that I came here to pray too.' And he glimmered at her, with the beginning of another smile. 'Like you. Sometimes your troubles seem so great that nothing but God's guidance will be enough. And even that . . .' He broke off and looked away, and she felt the sadness in him, a helplessness that seemed as great as hers, without needing to understand it. 'May I pray with you?' he said, a whisper of velvet bass.

She gestured, caught up in the moment, happy to have him near. He knelt beside her, in one fluid movement, and bent his head over his hands, and closed his eyes.

Isabel shut her eyes too and steepled her own hands, but she had stopped doing more than imitate the appearance of prayer; what she really wanted now was to hear the muttered words coming from the stranger's lips. She wanted to know what he was praying for. 'Even so, Lord Jesus Christ, son of the living God, deign to free me from every tribulation, sorrow and trouble in which I am placed and from the plots of my enemies,' he was murmuring, a prayer as sombre as hers but not one to enlighten her; 'and deign to send Michael the Archangel to my aid against them, and deign, Lord Jesus Christ, to bring to nothing the evil plans that they are making or wish to make against me, even as you brought to nothing the counsel of Achitophel who incited Absalom against King David . . .'

And his voice dropped to a drone of Latin, and then fell altogether silent. When she stole a sideways look at him, his lips were still moving; she thought she saw a tear glistening on his cheek too. He didn't seem to be aware of it. He was lost to the world.

She went on watching. He was visibly reaching a resolution. His jaw tightened. Then, without warning, he dropped his hands, raised his head and looked round at

Isabel, so quickly that she didn't have time to lower her own curious eyes. Without reproach, his bright gaze held hers; she felt it as a shock right through her body.

'So shall we both trust God to provide for us?' he said, and grinned, a bit wolfishly, suddenly looking cheerful and eager to be on the move. He was on his feet, holding a hand out to her. Without thinking, she took it and scrambled up too. His hand was warm and dry with strong fingers. She found herself walking with him. To her surprise, they headed towards the bright arch to the street, feet in step.

As long as I'm out I don't have to go home, Isabel thought, as the wind flapped at her skirts, with the fuzzy, fleeting contentment born of being caught up in an unexpected adventure. As long as no one sees me here I don't have to decide what to do. So she followed the stranger obediently into the Bush tavern, a few steps away down Aldersgate, where he headed straight for a table in a vaulted alcove under a window where someone else's meal, and the game of chess abandoned on a stool, hadn't yet been cleared away, ordering a jug of claret and whatever cold meat the landlord had as he passed. He stood looking down at the checkered wood, absent-mindedly fingering the pieces left at the side of the board, while a serving girl piled up tankards on one of the greasy boards covered in pork rinds. Isabel edged round the tables and stools towards him, suddenly breathless at her own strange boldness in sitting down to eat with a stranger. But if he was aware of her discomfort he didn't betray it. He was grinning at some thought of his own; he held one of the carved pieces out to her as she approached, and said lightly: 'After all, perhaps none of the moves that worry us so much in life are as important as we think'. He popped the piece into its bag. 'We all end up equal at the bottom of a bag, don't we?'

Isabel's nervousness vanished with the chess pieces he was whisking into their leathery resting place. She laughed and sat down. 'I just don't want to wait till I die before my problems get solved,' she answered, wishing she could achieve the same resigned tone. 'I'm hoping something will sort them out now.'

She wasn't made to be philosophical. Nor could she quite find it in herself to do what she wanted to – find out more about her vis-à-vis. As soon as the maid had dumped two wooden platters in front of them, and even before he had finished pouring out the wine, Isabel found herself pouring out the whole story of her own troubles instead.

She told him how her father had fallen from grace at the Guildhall for losing his temper at a meeting – so badly he began shouting and blaspheming – while he was trying, unsuccessfully, to persuade the City to support King Edward and his Yorkist army in the wars. John Lambert had thought the rest of the merchants were being hypo-critical to give in to the rival Lancastrian army – mad, pitiful King Henry, brought back to fight his last battles after ten years in forced retirement by the Earl of Warwick, who'd been King Edward's closest friend until they'd fallen out and he'd turned rebel. John Lambert didn't like the sight of the fierce, treacherous earl masterminding the feeble-minded Henry's every move. Nor did he have much stomach for Edward's younger brother, the Duke of Clarence, also in rebellion against his own blood; a lesser traitor hanging on Warwick's coat-tails, hoping in vain that he might get to be Yorkist king of the Lancastrian rebels. John Lambert had been right, really. It had been ugly. And London was Yorkist to a man, had been for years. Every merchant knew King Edward, who was strong and young and intelligent, and had been on the throne for ten years already, was a better king for supporting their trade than Henry, who had let lawlessness rule the land for more than twenty years before Edward first seized the throne. But the Lancastrian army had been here at the gates, and the consensus of the meeting had been 'anything for a quiet life'. So John Lambert's outburst had not only been disregarded but had turned the rest of the merchants against him. They set such store by dignified agreement, they couldn't forgive a man who could rail and rant the way he had.

She found herself describing her father's stricken look when the mayor's men came and took away the striped pole outside the Lambert house – his alderman's post, his treasured symbol of office, the pole on which aldermen posted their proclamations. She told him how her father had then fixed on the idea of mending his quarrel with the City's great men by marrying off her and her sister; the way he'd suddenly announced she and Jane were to be betrothed to the outlandish suitors he'd picked for them, as soon as he'd heard King Edward's army was winning and moving on London, as soon as he could be reasonably sure that the merchants would bow to circumstances and remember they'd been Yorkist all along and open the gates to King Edward; as soon as they might be persuaded to think John Lambert hadn't been so wrong after all.

Isabel thought her father had been rubbing his nose in his storeroom and plotting the whole thing for months beforehand. Bitterly, she told the stranger how she and her sister were being sacrificed for her father's ambition. It wasn't fair, she said. He'd promised his daughters all their lives that, within reason, they'd have the freedom to marry as they chose. But when it came to it, he was breaking that promise.

'I know it makes sense to him,' she finished. 'Half his old friends in the City are coming after him with court cases. They think he's finished. They're kicking him while he's down. And he wants to show them he's still got the power to make good alliances. He's imagining a wedding banquet that will put every trading company's summer feast into the shade – he loves parties; I just know he's already envisioning those tables groaning with honeyed peacocks and blancmanges of asses' milk. He wants to try and impress everyone with the idea that the Lamberts are still on top of the world. He thinks a couple of weddings will win them all back.

'But he doesn't seem to see it won't help him. They'll still remember him as the man who shouted at the mayor. And we'll be married to those clowns forever. It's wrong. I'm too young to be married. I'm only fourteen. And anyway, the last person I'd choose, ever, would be Thomas Claver.'

The dark man from the church was easy to talk to. He kept steady eyes on her throughout her passionate monologue. He nodded understandingly when she looked sad and his eyes crinkled in amusement when, in the hope of entertaining him, she started using fanciful turns of phrase she wouldn't normally have attempted. Yet when she came to a halt, Isabel had the uneasy feeling she'd got it wrong. He didn't look fired up with any of her indignation. He just looked thoughtful.

He'd been cutting up bits of meat with his knife while she was talking. He looked down at the red squares on his board now she'd fallen silent and seemed almost surprised they were all still there. He speared one and began chewing on it, looking at her again, still reflecting, until, in an agony of self-consciousness, she began to wish she'd kept quiet, or at least asked him more about himself before telling all her woes.

'I can see why you're unhappy,' he said in the end, and she glowed at the warmth in his voice. He wasn't

12

good-looking, quite. His thin features weren't as bold and regular and noble as her father's, say, or the godlike, golden Lynom boys'. This man's face was thin and serious; made to be worried. If he hadn't sat so straight and used his wiry body so fluidly, if he wasn't gazing at her with such unwavering attention, she might have found him rat-like. Mean-looking. But the richness of his voice vibrated through her, making him magical. 'You're in a difficult position,' he was saying. 'You think your father is making a bad judgement.'

She nodded, and took a sip from her cup of wine to hide the gratitude she could feel staining her face pink.

He leaned forward. Put his elbows on the table. She thought he might be going to touch her, comfort her. She blushed deeper and bent in on herself.

He didn't. He just joined his hands together, steepling them thoughtfully under his chin, leaning on his thumbs, and went on looking calmly at her. 'May I offer some advice?' he asked. His dignified simplicity made her feel ashamed of her own blurting.

Attempting to match his formality, she nodded again, trying not to let the hope shine too obviously on her face that he would hit on some easy way out for her.

'You have to marry as your circumstances demand,' he said, so gently she could hardly bear it. 'I think from what you've told me that you know your father loves you. He's saying he's trying to do what's best for your family. And it's a father's job to make good alliances for his children. Even if he hasn't fully understood your feelings, perhaps he knows more about your family's circumstances than you do.'

'But,' she stammered, lost in disappointment. 'But . . .'

'I know,' he said sadly, 'it's not what you wanted to hear.'

He lowered his eyes. So did she; concentrating furiously

13

on the new batch of pork rinds and pink shards of flesh on their own platters; willing away the hotness in her eyes.

'It can destroy a family if a father *doesn't* think about how to marry his children, you know,' he was saying, somewhere behind the redness of her eyelids. 'It nearly did mine.' She glanced up, surprised. His eyes were still on her, though they were unfocused now, far away, not so much looking into her soul as lost in a dark part of his own. 'He spent his whole life at the war, my father, and he was a good soldier. But when we heard he'd been killed, there we were: a brood of orphans scattered around the country, without a single marriage that would have given us a new protector among the six of us. He never realised that making alliances for his family was just as important as winning battles; that you need friends to defeat your enemies – a strategy for living, not just for dying.'

He laughed, with a tinge of real bitterness. Isabel kept quiet, less because she was artfully drawing him out at last, as she'd imagined she would, than because she didn't know how to respond. She was realising uncomfortably how little she knew of the world outside the Mercery, of the world where the war was. Trying to imagine what it would be like for your father to die, all that came to her mind was sounds: the snuffles of women weeping; the banging of a hammer, nailing down a coffin lid, nailing shut the door of her home; the chilly quiet of Cheapside by night, for those with nowhere to go; the scuttling of rats. Her mother had died too long ago for Isabel to remember her. But she couldn't form a picture of a life in which her father wasn't fretting in the silkroom, nagging a bit more work out of some sunken-eyed shepster, smiling even as he picked at a minutely off-kilter seam with his obsessively clean fingernails; or drawing in a noble client by singing out the beauty of his stock with his green eyes glowing; or counting out his piles of coin later with a sly laugh at how envious the noble client would be if she only realised by how much the servile merchant's silk profits outweighed her rents and rolling acres. Isabel couldn't imagine waiting, in some half-closed house in a field, for the rumour, or letter, or servant limping home in bandages, bringing word; *those* words, whatever this man must have heard. Yet even failing to envision it brought it closer. It had always been enough to know that the war happened to other people; but now she was talking to someone who had been touched by it she felt herself, for the first time, weighed down with nameless possibilities. She didn't know what the weak flexing in her gut was called, or the darkness seeping through her veins; but she thought it might be fear.

She crossed herself. Filled with a sudden longing to be wiser and older, she thought: it's ignorant to live in a city that's about to be entered by a conquering army (King Edward's army was at St Albans, people said; it would be here any day, and the mayor had already given the order to let the soldiers in) yet be so innocent of disaster. Pig ignorant. I've grown up in a land where two families of kings have been fighting each other for the throne for as long as anyone can remember, and I know nothing about it. You don't if you're a Londoner. We hardly see it. Still, he'd think me a child if he knew.

He didn't notice her gesture. 'Well, we survived. But we've been unlucky ever since with our marriage choices,' he was saying, with a twist to his mouth that made his face look pinched and hard. 'My eldest brother ran away with a war widow, the stupidest possible love match, just when what family we still had was finally arranging a proper alliance for him. We're only just seeing the end of the years of hatred that brought. And then a second brother married to spite the eldest brother, deliberately going against his wishes. And that's meant more trouble . . .'

He sighed and looked down at the neat meat squares his hands had been cutting as he talked, and pushed one gently towards himself with his knife. Then he stabbed it. Isabel took another sip of rough dark wine as it disappeared into his mouth, wondering which brother he'd been thinking of when he'd made that stabbing movement. 'I'm glad it's over now,' she ventured, glancing up, 'your family trouble, I mean.'

Perhaps it was the smallness of her voice that made his eyes gentle again.

'Almost over,' he corrected, looking properly at her once more. 'There's still my marriage to arrange.'

For a second, his voice was so tender that her heart leapt. She caught her breath, leaning eagerly forward behind her cup. Then she felt a sigh ebb out of her as he went on, more harshly: 'And now it's my turn there's nothing I want more than to make a marriage that will be good for my family – but my second brother's trying to stop me. He's fighting it so hard that I think even my trying to do the right thing might turn out to be the wrong thing. I've found myself thinking I should pull back . . . to satisfy him.' His jaw tightened, as it had in church. 'I'm not going to, though,' he added firmly. 'That wouldn't help either. But I sometimes wonder if we'll ever stop being orphans at war, wilful children in men's bodies, destroying each other while we try to sort out the things our father should have decided.' He sighed. 'You can see why I believe there's nothing more important than marrying in the best interests of your family, can't you?' he added with more energy. 'You have to work together, do your duty; or you're lost.'

'Oh,' Isabel muttered lamely. There was another long silence, broken from somewhere behind by a roar of male

16

laughter. The girl cleared away their boards. Isabel noticed that the light was failing. The window was still bright, but his face was falling into shadow. She hadn't heard the bell; but the markets must be closing.

He was sitting very straight and apparently still on his stool. She felt, rather than saw, the tiny movement of his hand twitching at his sword hilt. She remembered peeping sideways at his hands in the church: they'd been brown and well-made, with thin fingers, with bitten nails.

She wanted to ask: 'Do you love her?' But she sensed that was a question girls giggling in silkrooms might ask, and not for him. Instead, she faltered, 'But don't you ever wish . . . ?' and left the question hanging. She didn't know herself how she'd have finished it.

When his voice came out of the gloom again, it was wistful and there was no flash of eyes; he must be looking down.

'Ah, wishes . . .' he whispered back. 'If we could live by our wishes . . . please ourselves: live at peace, kill nothing but dragons . . . eat buttercups . . . ride unicorns . . . who knows what any of us would do?'

She heard a quiet rumble of laughter. She could see the ghost of the evening star through a smeared window pane. She put her cup down and left her hands spread on the table. She looked at the two pale shadows on the dark wood: fingers long and lovely enough to embroider church vestments with, as her father liked to say. The question flashed through her mind – was he looking at them too? – as she thought, all I want is to go on sitting here in this darkness; not to talk; not to think; not to go home.

'Of course, you don't have to take my advice,' he said in the end. When she looked up his eyes were gleaming quizzically at her again over steepled fingers, his long eyes the only clearly visible part of his shadowed form. 'If you have choices, that is.'

'Choices?' she repeated dully, as reality came back like a sour taste in the mouth. Knowing that her father wouldn't let her run away from marrying Thomas Claver by paying her dowry to a nunnery instead, since she'd never shown the least sign of having a vocation; wondering if she'd have the nerve to risk walking out of his great place, where she'd always been Miss Isabel, daintily perched on wallows of silk, sewing altar cloths, to become a withered, unregarded, unmarried housekeeper in the household of the kind of wealthy wife Jane would become. Knowing she wouldn't. Aware too that there were other, worse possibilities that her imagination was shying away from. 'What choices?'

He glanced over at the chessboard and grinned. 'Strategic choices,' he said, with a return of the wolfish energy she'd glimpsed as they left the church. 'You mustn't think life is a romance; that some knight errant will come along and slay the dragon for you. Knights don't really sit and pine at lovely ladies' gates. They fight. That's reality. War. Chess. All you can do is plan as many steps ahead as you can and position yourself for a good move next time. Know what your powers are and what you can do.'

Briskly, he shook out a couple of pieces. 'Look. Say I'm a king: I can move in several directions. If the way I want is blocked, there are others open to me. But let's call you a pawn. You don't have so many choices. All you can do is move forward, one step at a time. And I'd imagine your only forward movement now is to say yes.'

She glanced up; down, at her fingers, plucking at each other; up again through her eyelashes, seeking his eyes but hiding hers when she met them; not wanting to acquiesce. How could he look so soft, but be so hard? Was that what the war had done to him, or just his nature? She didn't want to accept that her dilemma could be reduced to this ruthless balancing of possible outcomes; this cold-blooded comparison of disadvantage. All she wanted was to come up with some way of talking her father out of his foolishness, she thought; ready to toss her head like an impatient pony, but restraining herself just in time, with the dawning awareness that there was no place left in her life for petulance. Her father wasn't going to change his mind.

'Well?' the man in front of her murmured. His voice might be soft, but there was no ignoring the challenge in it. 'Do you have any other choices?'

She shook her head, filling up inside with a darkness that crawled and churned.

'You're young,' she heard him add. She thought she heard sympathy. 'Take the long view. This is only your first move. You'll get more chances later.'

The serving girl was lighting candles in the back vaults; people were crowding in from the markets. She couldn't bring herself even to nod. Forever yawned ahead of her fourteen-year-old mind like a pit. She got up. Wished she had a cloak to wrap carefully around herself. It would be cold outside. There was nowhere to go but home.

'Thank you for your company,' she muttered, staring at her feet, and turned to the door.

He was on his feet in a dark whirl; beside her, a hand on her back. 'It's not easy, I know,' he whispered. 'I was lucky we met today: you've helped me see what I should do. So thank you. And good luck. I hope I've helped you do the right thing too.'

She was aware of his downturned face just above hers. From very close, she became conscious of his arm stretching around behind her; of long lean muscle and the dizzy moving together of bodies. Or did she misunderstand? Before she quite knew what was happening, it wasn't happening any more. He was striding off very fast towards the serving girl, in her pool of candlelight, feeling down his leg for a purse; glancing briefly back at her, still with those half-closed, intent eyes; muttering, 'Goodbye, Isabel.'

She stood there for a moment more. Astonished; still feeling the heat of his hand on her skin. Watching his retreating back. Then she braced herself for the evening chill, and walked out into the starlight. She thought she glimpsed him turning back round to watch the door swing shut behind her, but she couldn't be sure.

Every step she took back towards her home felt harder. Every dutiful footfall was heavier. That last moment was still with her, mixed up with the wind flapping at her skirts. It stayed with her like the eye's long memory of flame: the man with the soft eyes and the hard mind looking back at her over a lean shoulder, then moving away so fast that the candles silhouetting his form shrank back as if a dark wind was blowing at them, murmuring goodbye in his black velvet voice. His hand on her back. She didn't even know his name. She'd never see him again. It would have to be enough that for an instant they'd drawn so close she'd almost felt the heat of his body on hers. Even the possibility of one day feeling that radiance again, of being transformed like a wisp of silk lit up by the sun, might help to sustain her through the drab future her father was planning for her.

2

Isabel married Thomas Claver a week later, on a bright April morning, on the steps of St Thomas of Acre. The little people squinting across Cheapside to the church door smiled at the sight while they filled up their buckets at the water conduit, or popping heads out from one of the many covered markets behind the Mercers' thoroughfare and the cramped stalls lining the road, where low-ranking silkwomen doing needlework or weaving or throwing or twisting threads craned their failing eyes to watch the world go by as they worked. A couple of crones poked each other and cheered the little procession on to the door, with the mocking laughs of the old. But all they probably noticed was John Lambert, in his mercer's blue velvet livery robes trimmed with fur, looking as magnificent and proud as a prince between the two young female forms whose future he was settling.

Isabel's heart was beating so loud she was breathless with the boom and thud of blood in her ears. It was all she could do to stop her own small, unimpressive, down-covered limbs, so like her dead mother's had been, from trembling, and her freckled face from showing fear. When she'd looked into her mother's beaten copper mirror before

21

leaving, the dark blue eyes in the face that had stared back from it had been wiped of their usual intent, good-humoured look. There was no sign in that face that its owner was usually chatty and bright and asked inquisitive questions about everything she saw. There was none of the charm in those neat, symmetrical features that often made people look at her with the beginning of a shared smile, even if she wasn't trying to beguile them. The face looking back at her now didn't seem pretty: just quiet, even placid. Her red-gold hair was smoothed neatly away under her veil. It was the best display she could manage in the circumstances.

She couldn't look at Jane, as slender and golden as ever. Jane was dressed exactly like Isabel in one of the yellow gowns embroidered with silk flowers in which John Lambert had displayed them on his retail stall in the biggest market, the Crown Seld, whenever he made them sit there, embroidering the heavy orphreys that would later border extravagant church vestments. (The sight of the two girls, so fresh and pretty, was supposed to draw in passing trade; Isabel had spent her life complaining that she wanted to do more than just sew while she was working in the seld, but her father had always been adamant – embroidering church vestments was the only suitable part of the mercer's trade for a young lady of her stature.) Jane was her father's daughter even now, down to the emerald-green eyes and noble profile and air of perfect composure under pressure. Isabel shrank into herself as she peeped at her sister, wished she could look so self-assured. Isabel couldn't look at the bridegrooms – Will Shore, somewhere over there on the edge of her field of vision, behind Jane, a shy beanpole in violet hose, and Thomas Claver, thick-set and reddish-haired, next to her. In Thomas's case, though, she was at least aware of his eyes darting between the watchers and her father and his own tub of a mother, whose reddish face was cheerful above her serviceable dark clothes. John Lambert had wondered aloud more than once in the past few days whether Alice Claver – who was famously not one for ceremony – would have the decency to dress appropriately for the occasion. She'd lived down to his expectations, wearing only her usual market clothes with a bright blue cloak wrapped over them, as if she'd hastily borrowed some of her stock for the day, or was expecting rain. If anything in the assembly of people Isabel couldn't look at now gave her comfort, it was Alice Claver looking scratchy and uncomfortable in that dressed-up cloak.

There hadn't been much time for Isabel to get used to her situation, what with King Edward's army entering the City and the curfew being moved to before sunset, just in case, and her father being called on to head one of the city patrols watching the soldiers to prevent outrages against the citizens. At the end of the first day, when people had begun to relax a little, as they saw this army, now mostly camped outside the walls in Moorfields (with just a few hundred lodged in Baynard's Castle, the river-side family home of the dukes of York), was not going to make trouble, and as eager vintners and fishmongers rushed to make contracts to supply the soldiers until they left to march north again, an agitated John Lambert had got the call to join the King and his generals at the thanks-giving Mass they were holding at St Paul's. His delight at that almost compensated for being left out of the farewell banquet at Baynard's Castle last night, at which the mayor had been allowed to serve the King's wine. And his preparations for being briefly in sight of the court had overshadowed the planning for the weddings.

With so much going on, John Lambert had only had time to take Isabel once to the Claver house on Catte

Street, a great place whose airy halls and parlours put to shame even the substantial Lambert family home round the corner on Milk Street, even if it wasn't decorated with half so many tapestries and carpets as the Lambert house. It was in the morning of the day the gates were opened to the army. He was already in his harness ready to ride out with the patrol. He'd hastily sorted out the business side of the marriage with Alice Claver, at one end of the great hall, in the space of an hour, while the betrothed couple had been given a brief chance to get to know each other, sitting awkwardly on benches drawn up across from each other, at the other end of the room.

It had taken Isabel what seemed an eternity to find the strength to raise her eyes. When she did, she'd been astonished by the picture the young man opposite her presented. He wasn't slurping at the cup of wine his mother had left by his side before tactfully drawing away. He was slumped on his bench, with his pink face in shadow under hair that wouldn't lie down. He was staring at his feet, pulling at the purse dangling down his leg with busy fingers, and biting his lip.

He looks scared to death, Isabel had thought suddenly, sitting up straighter with the realisation. More scared than me. He'd probably never succeeded in touching any of the tavern girls she'd seen him leering over in the Tumbling Bear and the Lion, she realised with a flash of intuition. This indulged only child of a rich widow, who'd never been sent to start an apprenticeship in another household, who'd been allowed to avoid learning his mother's trade in her own house, was looking like a large child on the brink of tears. He'd almost certainly never been alone with a female of his own age. And now it was all catching up with him. She'd been surprised to find herself feeling something close to pity.

She'd leaned forward, wanting so much to comfort him

that she very nearly patted his hand. But the only subject she could think of to break the ice was business. Her father had said Alice Claver was planning to buy her son into the livery and give him one thousand pounds' worth of goods so he could bypass apprenticeship altogether – the ten years of study most boys did – and start trading on his own account as soon as he was married. They'd still have to live with his mother while he was setting himself up; but Alice Claver's home contained so many leagues of rooms and halls that it would be no hardship. Perhaps Thomas Claver would be reassured by being reminded of his prospects, so glorious compared to the ten pounds here and five pounds there that so many young bachelors cadged from wherever they could to scrape together the stock they needed to start trading for themselves. It might make him feel in control of his destiny. 'You must be pleased about getting into the livery,' she'd ventured hesitantly, trying to form an alliance, doing her best at an encouraging smile.

But he'd only scuffed his feet against each other and scowled. 'Oh, that. It's just my ma pulling strings,' he'd said sullenly. 'It doesn't mean anything. Doesn't mean I'll actually get to do what I want. She'll have her fingers all over my business from day one, just you wait and see. "Thomas, do this; Thomas, do that; Thomas, don't do that."' He peered up at last, but only to fix her with a look of gloomy malice before turning back down to his scuffing and scowling. 'And it won't be long before she starts in on you either.'

Isabel only knew Alice Claver by reputation. In the markets, the silkwoman was respected and mostly liked as a force of nature; a solid woman in her middle years with a wide face and a wider smile, when she chose, though she wasn't scared of scowling or talking sharply either. Alice Claver whisked through the covered markets where she kept half a dozen retail stalls and booths and chests, selling whole silk cloths from Italy and silk threads from all over the world and the piecework ribbons and small goods that were made by her workers in London, jollying her own people relentlessly along, sweet-talking the mercers, and selling to clients with such down-to-earth persuasiveness that they hardly knew where they were before they were parting with their money. She hadn't married again after her husband died, years ago. But she'd kept his business going. And she'd made enough money from carrying on Richard Claver's trade in luxury goods to go on leasing the palatial great place they'd lived in together from the Mercers for what every silkwoman in the Crown Seld knew to be the princely annual rent of £8 13s 4d. She'd registered to trade in her own name, as a femme sole, taking responsibility for her own debts. She didn't have John Lambert's disdain for training girls – she trained younger silkwomen as if they were proper male apprentices, teaching them everything about how trade was conducted. The only thing the trained silkwomen couldn't do was to join the Mercers' Company; that was for the men; but they could set themselves up and, if things went well for them, keep themselves in style without depending on a husband. Things had gone well for Alice Claver. She sold fine silk goods to the King's Wardrobe. She visited textile markets in the Low Countries and bought the finest cloths in quantities that were the envy of many merchants. She'd even organised the other wives of the silk business, and some of the most influential of their mercer husbands, to join her and the unmarried silk-women in petitioning parliament to protect their trade from foreign competition. And she was the centre of charity around her home. She might not have much physical grace, but she had more energy than most women half her age – enough energy, Isabel thought with another surprised stab of compassion, to overwhelm a son with no great appetite for work.

So Isabel persevered with her smile. 'Oh well,' she said brightly, reminding herself that a soft answer turns away wrath, 'we'll see her off, don't worry.' She sounded more confident than she felt. Alice Claver would be hard to see off. 'You'll soon learn how to run things for yourself. And I can help. At least,' she corrected herself, smiling a bit ruefully at the thought, 'I can a bit. My father's always refused to let the women in his family learn the business. He says it's because he has his position to think of, and there's no need now he's so rich, though we know it's really because my mother never knew enough about silk-work to teach us herself or hold her own in the selds, and after she died it would have meant losing face to change his ways and let us start learning. Anyway, he doesn't like training girls too much. So all he's ever let me do is embroidery. But I'm good at that.'

She kept her eyes on his face. She felt, rather than saw, him begin to look less lugubrious when she started to laugh gently at her own family.

So she persisted, willing him to laugh with her: 'He says, "Lovely ladies with long fingers should embroider church vestments,"' and she imitated her father's rolling, mellifluous voice well enough that the corners of his mouth lifted up. 'It's the only thing he thinks ladylike enough for us.'

Suddenly he looked up and stared into her eyes, so straight and so hard and so long that she thought she'd said something to offend. She stared back, astonished. What could it have been? But then she realised he wasn't offended, just overcoming shyness. Slowly, his face soft-ened. She could see sweetness in his relieved grin. 'You're not half as grand as I thought you'd be,' he'd said. Isabel thought they'd both briefly sensed the possibility of forming an alliance: the young and powerless against the families who controlled them.

Whether Thomas Claver still felt well-disposed towards her now, at the church door, Isabel couldn't say. Her eyes were fixed on the nails on the door while the priest mumbled.

Her father had to nudge her when the time came to exchange rings. She pulled hers off her finger and held it out, still staring at the doornails through the drumbeats in her ears. Her fingers were damp and she could feel prickles on her back. But she didn't hesitate.

Thomas was less lucky. She could feel him tug. Nothing happened. He tugged again. This time the ring came off, glittered in the corner of her eye, and flew down towards the cobbles. It bounced twice. It turned like a tiny hoop. She heard, rather than saw, it come to rest at her feet.

Everyone went quiet. Her father drew in his breath. His mother hissed, 'Thomas!' Isabel glanced sideways at him from under her veil. He'd gone bright red. His mortified face was wet, his eyes appalled at his own clumsiness. Alice Claver was poking him in the ribs, pointing down, miming instructions for him to lean forward and pick the ring up. But he was rooted to the spot. Everyone else was frozen too.

Isabel's heart swelled with something that made her forget her fear. She bent down, picked up the offending ring herself, and put it on her own finger; then she reached for Thomas Claver's unresponsive hand, drew it to her, and slipped her ring onto his finger. The group still seemed to have stopped breathing. Taking a deep breath, she raised her eyes slowly along Thomas Claver's arm until she was looking into his face, and watched his eyes move from an awed consideration of the hand she'd dressed with her ring, up her arm to her face. Behind his obvious

terror, whether it was at having broken the forward movement of the ceremony in a way that would be chewed
over in the selds as a possible bad omen, or just at having
embarrassed his mother with his clumsiness, she could see
the dawn of a quiet, desperate hope in those white-ringed
eyes, a hope that she might somehow save him.

Hardly knowing what she was doing, she lifted her face
to his, pre-empting the moment in the ceremony when
bride and groom were invited to kiss. And when he only
stared back at her, as if he had no idea what to do next,
she boldly stretched out the hand that now wore his ring
to touch the back of his head, stood on tiptoe and kissed
him firmly on the lips.

There was a screech of approving laughter from one
of the beldames by the water conduit. Then, even from
within that awkward embrace, with her eyes shut and her
body held apart from the big, hot frame of her husband,
Isabel could feel the Lamberts and Clavers and Shores all
relax; breath expelled; bodies moving; little murmurs and
eddies of happy sound. When she opened her eyes and
stepped back, Thomas Claver went on looking at her in
a kind of amazement. He was still pink about the face,
and still damp. But he was smiling.

Isabel danced at the feast. She danced with Thomas,
suddenly shy again and avoiding his eyes; aware of the
dampness of his hands; holding herself nervously back
from his large body. She danced more freely with every
mercer who was her father's or her new mother-in-law's
friend, until the blood came back to her cheeks with the
sheer pleasure of movement. She whirled her skirts and
flashed her ankles; sufficient unto the day, she thought,
with sudden hectic gaiety, draining her cup of wine.
Suddenly it felt like an easing of her burden in life to be
free of her father. She was nervous about what would

come after the dancing, of course; but there'd be time to worry about tonight when tonight came. When the third course was brought in, giant pyramids of blancmanges wobbling in the heat, she let her partner, a bright-eyed old friend of Alice Claver's called William Pratte, lead her back to his place on the trestles and courteously pass sweet dainties her way.

Thomas brought William Pratte's wife, Anne, back to the table, then left the room. He half-glanced at Isabel. She caught the nervous look, but was too shy to smile back. It was only after he'd turned uncertainly towards the door that her lips started to curve up. She sat breathlessly quiet among his mother's friends, feeling grown-up. She couldn't be unaware of Alice Claver and the plump, knowing, eager Prattes gossiping beside her. They talked in low voices, darting cautious glances all around; but they clearly weren't trying to hide what they were saying from her.

'Well of course they fight dirty,' William Pratte was saying, with a mischievous gleam in his eye. 'The nobility have never been half as noble as they like to make out. They say King Edward didn't so much win the last battle as chase the other lot into the millpond and drown them.'

Alice Claver snorted irreverently. 'Like kittens,' she said. 'Well, all I can say is good riddance.'

'Still. It's not exactly Camelot, is it?'

John Lambert was leading Jane down the row of raised arms in the centre of the room. He was radiating happiness at having pulled off his plan, skittishly kicking up his heels and smiling at everyone whose eyes he met. Yet he must be able to see the room was only half-full, and mostly with the Clavers' and Shores' family connections, not the great and good of the City he'd wanted to attract. Isabel thought: if they'd really forgiven him, the mayor

30

would be here. The aldermen. Her relief at having got the ordeal of the wedding over was so great that the thought almost made her feel sorry for him.

'Do you think it's true what they say?' Anne Pratte was half-whispering, her eyes batting flirtatiously up and down. These people seemed to be much more disrespectful and sharp-tongued than her father, Isabel thought, with a flicker of interest. She'd only ever heard the York royal family discussed in tones of hushed reverence at home. Did they always talk like this? 'About the youngest brother; the Duke of Gloucester; how he killed . . .'

She dropped her voice. Isabel sensed she'd hear the same stories again. But for now a movement at the other end of the room was distracting her; a flurry at the door. Thomas? She glanced up.

A crowd was forming over there. She could hear the sounds of hooves and metal outside. There were new people sliding into the room, round the edge of the group; and she could see one of them was Alderman John Brown. At the centre of the crowd was a tawny uncovered head, taller than the rest, with bobbing and bowing going on all around it.

William Pratte was still whispering conspiratorially, getting back to the meaty talk, lifting one hand off his plump knees; including Isabel, to her slight alarm, in his bright-eyed gaze. It was almost as if these middle-aged people, with their knowing ways and cheerfully treasonous talk, hadn't realised how young and inexperienced Isabel was; if she hadn't known such a thing to be impossible, she might have thought they were deliberately trying to include her; trying to be friends.

The crowd by the door shifted and cleared, like clouds blown by the wind. For a second, Isabel could see over the three grey heads bent in front of her, and what she seemed to be seeing was her father, down on his knees, grinning like a lunatic at the floor and being patted on the back by a tall man in clothes that seemed to shimmer gold in the heavy afternoon light.

'Look,' she said. Her voice was hoarse with surprise.

William Pratte followed her finger. 'Good God,' he said. 'Alice, look.'

Alice Claver's head turned, and stayed stuck in a stare directed at the doorway. But Anne Pratte was still caught up in the whispering.

'But Alice, that's exactly what they are saying,' she was muttering happily. And then she looked up, too, saw Alice Claver rising slowly to her feet, still staring, and began to gape like an astonished fish. 'It's the King!' Anne Pratte said foolishly – foolishly, because others were dropping to their knees too now, crowding in: the mayor, suddenly and miraculously present; Will Shore's parents; the Prattes; Alice Claver (how had she got there so fast?). Now John Lambert was scrambling to his feet to get out of the crush of kneelers, dancing backwards in something close to panic to create a place of honour for the monarch who was gracing his table with this extraordinary visit, and startled apprentices and serving girls, getting the message, were rushing to and fro clearing away the dishes from the tabletop and whisking in fresh dishes and strewing the boards with rose petals. And every bare head was bowed, but every pair of eyes was raised, fixed on King Edward, drinking him in.

'Well,' said the King, casually moving through the room towards Isabel's father and patting him on the back again, and every mouth opened in adoring appreciation of his words, 'how could I let my best friend in the City of London marry his daughters without coming to wish them well?'

John Lambert was pink with gratification; his smile almost cracking his face in half. He didn't look handsome and distinguished, for once; his bowed posture and that smile reduced him to servility. He looked as though he was thanking God for having given him the opportunity, over the years, to lend King Edward £1,052 10s, the sum he so often liked to remind his daughters was as much as the Duke of Gloucester himself could hope for in rents in a year and more than most knights could hope to lay their hands on in a lifetime; he looked as though he was thinking that the reward of the King's presence here, now, was enough to repay those debts even if he never saw a penny of the money again (which he might easily not). Still, no one could look handsome next to this King, whatever they were thinking, Isabel realised. Edward's golden presence would always diminish everyone else.

The King and his friend – a dark, laughing nobleman almost Edward's height, who would have been the most striking person in the room if he'd come alone, and whom Anne Pratte identified for Isabel, in a piercing whisper, as Thomas, Lord Hastings, the King's dearest friend – looked as though they were here to stay. The King ate a slice of beef. He drank a cup of claret. He smiled at Jane till she blushed. He congratulated Will Shore on his bride. He asked the groom's permission to dance with her. He led Jane, floating like thistledown, through an entire basse dance. Why her, not me? Isabel thought, without really understanding the thought; she knew really that she'd have been terrified to touch the King's person. But everyone turned to Jane first. 'There, you see,' Anne Pratte burbled to Isabel, her face glowing, her disrespectful gossip of a few moments before entirely forgotten, blotted out by the majesty of majesty, 'your father's in the good graces of the King, all right . . . what an honour . . . can you imagine? I've never heard of anything like this before . . . you'd never have got King Henry mixing with merchants, that sad sack . . . I've always said loyalty deserves to be rewarded.'

Now John Lambert was rushing to Isabel to present her to the King. She was embarrassed by the look of triumph on her father's face, but she let him take her hand. However fast her heart was beating, she kept her eyes turned down as he pulled her along the side of the table and began muttering 'Sire' and 'May it please your grace', and bowing and scraping. She made her deepest curtsey and rose, with her eyes still down. She didn't want to be drawn into the excitement. But it was infectious. 'Aha, another Lambert beauty,' the King said. And his voice was so deep and rich and full of unexpected beauty that it surprised her into looking up; for a second it had reminded her of the voice of the stranger she'd met in the church. For a second, as she met this stranger's eyes, she was disappointed to see a bigger face, fleshier and hand-somer. But something kept her gazing into these eyes, full of lazy laughter; aware of his sensual mouth, twitching up at one corner as if starting to laugh at some secret joke he was about to share with her. Perhaps it was the long gold of the afternoon, but in the warmth of that gaze she felt time was suspended. The crowded scene faded. All she was aware of was the man's eyes holding hers until she felt her own cheeks tingle with pleasure and her mouth widen into a smile. Until, to her surprise, she found she was laughing; a laugh of pure, animal joy.

They were lighting candles at the back of the room, she noticed, coming to, wondering where this immense happiness had come from so suddenly.

Then it was over. No dancing. The King waved his congratulations to Thomas, just coming back into the room, who looked even more startled than everyone else, then alarmed, then scared when he saw his mother's frown, then almost fell over himself falling to his knees. And John Lambert rushed Isabel away to her table again, still bowing and grinning. All that was left was her exhilaration.

As John Lambert settled her back on her stool, fussing around her, unable to contain his excitement, he couldn't stop muttering: 'a wonderful man; a king to be proud of; we're living in fortunate times; you've been honoured . . . honoured . . .' As she reached for her cup, she noticed, with a small pang of a sourness she wouldn't admit might be jealousy, that the King was dancing with Jane again.

'One thing's for sure. No one will ever remember about the ring now,' Thomas said happily, stroking her fine fair hair with one hand, pulling himself up on his other elbow so he could look at her face on the pillow in the morning light. He wasn't fat, as she'd thought; she knew now that his ox-like body, twice the size of hers, was all heavy muscle and power.

She murmured something indistinct, trying to put aside her embarrassed, happy, sticky memories of the over-whelming things she and he had done in this bed in the dark, to the truly astonishing event of yesterday, the only thing about her wedding that every gossip in the selds would now be discussing – the King's presence at the feast.

The King of England at her wedding, she thought with sleepy wonder. The newly returned King Edward – who a year ago had been a terrified runaway, chased out of the country by King Henry's army, forced to take ship for the Low Countries after being routed in some battle at, she thought, Doncaster; and walking through the night, with his brother and his closest friends, across the Wash, while the tide came in and pulled his men, screaming, into the sea they hoped would save them, if they could only reach a port to escape abroad from. No wonder the other merchants had thought, back then, that it would be best to accept King Henry's army; even if they'd enjoyed the ten years of Edward's reign before that; even if they remembered the earlier decades of King Henry's

35

aimless rule as a slide into anarchy, when nothing could stop the pirates and the robber barons, when the wine fleet stopped coming and it was dangerous to cross the Channel with their cargoes. King Edward hadn't seemed to have a chance, a year ago. But he was a lucky man; a man with skill. He'd never lost a battle. He'd found funds and raised another army and fought his way back to London. And now he was showing how he planned to rule, if he finally defeated the Lancastrian armies still in the Midlands – as a friend of merchants. He'd come to her wedding.

No one had ever heard of such a thing. No other king had ever done anything like coming to a merchant's feast. But then no other king had had to borrow so much from the City to pay his way in the war he'd seemed fated, until recently, to lose. And there was no one he'd borrowed more from than John Lambert. Isabel thought back to the frantic bobbing and scraping that had taken over the party when King Edward walked through the door. The reverence. The fawning laughter. 'Oh . . . my father's face . . .' she recalled, and laughed; not the polite tinkle with which she met the pleasantries of grown-up mercers and their wives, but one of the big deep snorts of mirth she and Jane indulged themselves in, in the Lambert children's bed, when no one else was listening.

Thomas Claver guffawed with her. 'And my mother,' he picked up cheerfully. 'I could just see her wishing she'd dressed up properly for once. She wasn't the only one, either. I'd say every woman in that room would have done anything to catch his eye.' He pulled himself over her, planting a big elbow beside each of her ears, grinning down at her with a confidence that looked new and unfamiliar on him. 'Even you, maybe. Hmm?' She shut her eyes, shy at looking at him so close, in daylight, and breathless now his chest was squashing down on her again, his legs pushing between hers. He brushed a strand of her hair mischievously across her eyelids. 'Tell me. Was the King the man of your dreams?'

She shook her head with her eyes still shut, smiling at the soft brush of hair on skin and the gruff gentleness of his voice. If they were going to go on being this kind to each other it would be easy to stay absorbed in the moment, this one and perhaps many more; to feel lucky at being granted the new pleasure of being with someone who would never criticise her or demand anything of her beyond physical affection and answers to the kind of excitable, puppyish questions he'd been pounding her with since before dawn – 'What are your three favourite colours?' '... your favourite food?' '... your worst memory?' '... your patron saint?' But his question reawakened a part of her that was separate from Thomas Claver; a part that knew that this easy sprawl of limbs, and even the first pulses of excitement in her body as he pushed his weight closer, didn't fill her senses and change the colours of the air in the way they'd been changed, for a few magical seconds, by the man in the tavern who'd told her she had no choice but to marry.

'No,' she whispered, laughing, 'of course he wasn't.' And she arched her aching body up invitingly under Thomas Claver's, and met his lips with hers, and tried to banish that other face – the piercing black eyes, the raised eyebrows like a cross, the dark velvet voice – back to the limbo it belonged in. I'm blessed to have found this much happiness, she told herself; it would be a sin to ask for more.

'So who is?' Thomas Claver's voice interrupted, as he moved his lips across her face to her ear, sounding hoarse now as desire gripped him in earnest, and she breathed the answer he wanted to hear, and almost meant it:

'You.'

Afterwards, stretching back on the pillows, she shook

her head lazily when Thomas said, with a sudden return of anxiety, 'We should go to breakfast soon; there's hell to pay if you're not down by dawn.'

'We don't have to do everything they want today; they'll understand,' she murmured back, stroking his shoulder, 'they'd be disappointed if we rushed out to eat this morning.'

She was pleased when his face relaxed back into its previous expression of joy – and then suddenly struck by what might have been the very oddest part of the whole strange day she'd just lived through.

It was Jane. Jane, who was never anything but perfectly sunny as she did the right thing and kept everyone satisfied; Jane, who always looked for something to be happy about in the most miserable of situations; Jane, who'd accepted her father's choice of husband with so much less fuss than Isabel ('It can't be that bad – at least we'll never have to sit on those horrible stools in the Crown again, blinding ourselves just to trim some old bishop's robe, with every market boy gawping at us as though they'd never seen a girl before'). Jane, whom she'd expected to become the perfect wife instantly: laughing in the kitchen with the servants and the children; laughing more elegantly at the mayor's table; charming her husband into high office; magicking contracts out of customers with her wit and lovely limbs.

Jane hadn't been so graciously dutiful last night. As soon as the King had bowed and asked her husband's permission to take her as partner in the basse dance, she'd got up, without even waiting for Will Shore's stammered consent, and swayed off across the room with the King, looking radiant.

An hour later, when Isabel and Thomas left, Jane was still sitting with the King in a pool of golden light, ignoring her husband, deep in a serene conversation quite unrelated to the hubbub of dancing and shadows all around. And, in the darkness beyond their conversation, Isabel now remembered an uneasy play of eyes. John Lambert's eyes, fixed adoringly on the King. The eyes of the King's friend, Lord Hastings, fixed hungrily on Jane. And Will Shore's eyes, dazed and puzzled, looking from one golden head to the other, as if he were wondering whether to feel awestruck by the King's attention to his new wife, or just left out.

In the end, they only got up in time to join Alice Claver for dinner after eleven in the morning. There was a simple dish of beef and bread and beer, all anyone could manage after yesterday's excesses. William and Anne Pratte were there with Alice – had they even gone away? Alice wondered. They seemed as familiar with this house as if they lived here, though she knew they had their own home near Jane's new one on Old Jewry. They were gossiping and grinning, like they had been yesterday, and Anne, on seeing the young couple, immediately launched into a story for them about the excitements they'd missed later last night. About how more courtiers had come to join the king after the couple had left, including the King's brother, the Duke of Gloucester, small and dark, ill-favoured and bad-tempered, and about how Jane had danced with the King practically till the candles had burned down.

Perhaps it was sharing work, in the way of so many Mercery families – the husband doing the wholesale trading while the wives made luxury retail products from their husbands' silk purchases, sold them, and minded the apprentices – that had made this couple look so like twins. They were both small and tubby and cheerful. William Pratte's hair was thin and grey, and both pairs of eyes were grey too, but as lively and inquisitive as those of squirrels. They finished each other's sentences, and Alice

Claver's too. That would never have happened at the decorous, often silent Lambert table; but no one here seemed to mind.

The three of them made such a point of courteously including the newlyweds in their grown-up conversation, and so strenuously avoided reference, even by the smallest untoward smirk or movement of an eyebrow, to the pleasures of the marriage bed, that Isabel spent the entire meal going alternately hot with shame and cold with dread, just in case they were about to start.

Her stomach churned so badly at times that she could only half-hear the harmless gossip they were chewing over from the wedding feast. John Brown, her father's replacement as alderman: going bald; looking fat; should take more exercise. Her father: looking indecently handsome; what had his robes cost him? (Here three bright pairs of adult eyes turned cautiously towards her, then away.) Gratefully, she felt Thomas's hand cover hers under the table and squeeze. His hand was damp; his face hangdog; he must feel as nervous as her.

'You'd never have got King Henry turning up like that at a merchant's wedding,' little Anne Pratte whispered confidingly, turning to Alice Claver. Isabel waited for Alice Claver, the head of this household, to look forbiddingly at her; it didn't do to gossip about kings. But the larger woman just snickered encouragingly and replied, with a disrespect Isabel found startling: 'No, never; give me a big handsome hero for a king any day, especially if he's going to take a proper interest in us . . .'

'. . . And stop the Italians cheating us,' William Pratte butted in hopefully. 'And knock some sense into the Hanse. Maybe even get the French pirates while he's about it. I'll be for the House of York, all right, if King Edward's going to really stir himself to help the City. No more loafing around while every lord in the land runs wild and our

40

business goes to rack and ruin. I tell you, it'll be 'God Save the King' and 'Hallelujah!' every morning at my table if Edward goes on doing better than that . . .' He screwed up his face and stuck his tongue out of his mouth, letting it loll like a lunatic's. The street-boy code for half-wit King Henry.

Isabel stared. She should have been scared of what her father would definitely have called treasonous talk. But there was something about the casual mischief flickering round the table that she thought she was going to like, once she'd had time to get used to it.

'Well, let's hope he wins, then,' Alice Claver said briskly. 'He still has to catch Warwick.'

'Now,' she swept on, turning so suddenly to Isabel and Thomas that the bride hardly had time for her heart to leap into her mouth. 'You two. Talking of our business going to rack and ruin, isn't it time to get you to work?'

Alice Claver's manner might have been brusque, but her eyes twinkled so merrily that Isabel didn't feel offended. For a moment, at least. Then she realised Thomas, at her side, was bristling with resentment, and thought, falteringly, that perhaps she'd misunderstood the mood.

'Get your lovely legs into the storeroom, eh, Thomas?' Alice Claver went on prodding, with the beginning of a rough growl of laughter in her voice. 'Show Isabel the ropes?'

Isabel looked down at the table, but not before she saw the Prattes giving each other another of their sharp, bird-like looks – enough to show her it wasn't the first time they'd heard Alice Claver say this sort of thing to her son, and that they didn't expect a positive outcome. Isabel squeezed Thomas's hand back. If he felt bullied, she wanted to show her support.

'Aw, Ma,' she heard Thomas answer. It was a child's whine, and there was a cunning look in his eye that she

41

could see meant he had no intention of working today and would say anything to avoid it. Isabel let her hand go soft again. 'We only got married yesterday.'

Alice Claver looked unimpressed. 'Well, you've had all morning to loll about, haven't you?' she said, and there was more roughness and less laughter in her voice now. Isabel blushed. The Prattes glanced at each other again. Visibly restraining her impatience, Alice Claver continued: 'You know William's very kindly offering to take you round the selds. Showing you the kind of range of goods you might think of buying to set yourself up. Introducing you to the kind of people at Guildhall who can advise you.'

She paused, as if this would jog Thomas's memory. But Thomas stayed mulishly quiet.

Anne Pratte piped up, in her fluting little voice: 'You don't need to worry about Isabel, Thomas. I'll look after her for the afternoon. I'm going round Alice's embroidery suppliers; it would be useful for Isabel to meet them. She can come with me . . .'

Isabel could see both offers would be helpful if Thomas were to start buying in enough stock to get going as a merchant in his own right, and she needed to learn the names and faces of the silkwomen she'd soon, perhaps, need to commission work from. She squeezed his hand again and looked encouragingly at him from under her lashes, trying to convey that she'd like him to say yes. But Thomas just scowled harder.

'Ma,' he repeated, with the elaborate patience of a man talking to an idiot. 'I just said. We've just got married. And Isabel wants to go and see off the King's army. We were going to take a picnic.'

The eyes all turned on Isabel, making her face burn. She'd been acutely embarrassed by Thomas's tone of voice. However informal people were in this household, it surely

42

couldn't be right to talk back to your mother like that. Besides, she'd made no plan for a picnic or a trip to see the army leave Moorfields; if anyone had asked her, she'd have said no. She knew nothing about soldiers except that they were dangerous. Why court trouble? And she certainly didn't want to be Thomas's alibi for shirking an arrangement his mother had made for him. It would only make Alice Claver dislike her, and she didn't want that either.

But she was Thomas's wife now. It was her duty to stand by him. And she didn't like the way Alice Claver was using the Prattes as an audience to try to shame Thomas publicly. She'd have to find a way to sweet-talk him into doing what his mother wanted, privately, later. For now, all she could do was brazen out Alice Claver's accusing stare, try to smile light-heartedly, as if nothing were amiss, and pray that the hot tide of blood staining her face red right to the roots of her hair would recede.

There was a long, frustrated pause.

'Well, if that's what *Isabel* wants,' Alice Claver said coldly, turning away. She didn't finish the sentence. No one else finished it for her this time, either.

'Come on, Isabel,' Thomas said, getting up and pulling her along behind him.

Isabel glanced back from the doorway. The Prattes were quietly shaking their heads at each other. But Alice Claver was still staring straight at her, and there was a cold anger in her eyes. With a sinking heart, Isabel realised she'd made an enemy.

Like every other Londoner who'd gone to gawp gratefully at the soldiers who'd come into their city without robbing or raping them, when it came to it, Isabel and Thomas Claver were too nervous of the men at arms camping outside the walls to go very near. Instead they joined the crowd lurking cautiously under the fruit trees that the city people grew on their vegetable patches, munching bread, trampling people's beans and peas, knocking over archery butts – enjoying the muted thrill of threat from the peace of the dappled shade, but not wanting to enter that vast, gleaming, sunlit tapestry of horsemen and sharp blades. We're like cows chewing our cud, she thought, lulled into a half-dream by the drone of insects and the buzz of the crowd and the warmth of Thomas Claver's arm around her waist, not knowing whether to feel proud or ashamed of the prudence of her own city sort. And, watching the fighters clean their harnesses and weapons – the word was that all these knights and squires and countrymen and cut-throats would be marching north tomorrow to find the Earl of Warwick and finish him off – she also thought, and they're like wolves.

She and Thomas hadn't spoken since leaving the house, just walked with the sun on their backs in companionable silence. The rhythm of the walk had helped diminish Isabel's sense of unease. Once Thomas had calmed down, she thought, she'd find a way to talk about work and make it easy for him to agree to do as his mother asked. But not just yet.

'You're so tiny,' Thomas Claver muttered suddenly, pulling her round into his arms, staring softly down at her. She hardly reached his big shoulders.

He nuzzled her ear with his lips.

'Thomas,' she murmured, turning her face up to his, but not knowing quite how to go on; wishing she'd had more practice at persuading people to do things.

He put his lips above her eyes. 'Kissing away your frown,' he whispered.

She smiled uncertainly. Then, not able to think of a clever way of raising the subject, she plunged ahead. Better to get it over, she told herself. 'We will start work tomorrow, won't we?' she said anxiously. 'I don't want your mother to think I'm a bad influence on you.'

He smiled back, but his eyes shifted sideways.

'I just want a few days alone with you,' he said softly. 'That's not too much to ask, is it?' Then, with a show of what he clearly hoped was nonchalance, he went on: 'We'll get that out of my ma without too much trouble. Don't worry about her. She's a tough old bird, but I know how to handle her.' He put his lips on hers. She closed her eyes and let him sweep her up almost off her feet into a kiss.

But even as her body responded her mind was filling with difficult questions. Was this kiss just his way of stopping her from talking? And how long was he planning to spin out those 'few days' of idleness?

'We'll start after May Day,' Thomas said. 'That's quite soon enough.' He shut his mouth as tight as a trap. He'd said the same thing every day, at every meal, for a week.

The Prattes eyed each other.

Alice Claver gave Isabel her by now habitual look of loathing. When she was angry her round face went a duller red. Her eyes went almost black. Her lips became a sneering slit.

Isabel eyed her defiantly back. What's the point of you all blaming me? she thought helplessly. He's never worked. You've never made him. It's not my fault if he won't now.

She could hardly remember the gossipy charm of that first dinner. The atmosphere in the house had become so poisonous that she was almost relieved to be out with Thomas after every morning row. Boating. Fishing. Watching him at the archery butts. Dining in taverns farther from the Mercery than she'd ever been: in Westminster, in riverside villages as far away as Kew, or in the wilds of Haringey Park. She'd learned so minutely in these days of startling physical closeness how his face and hair and thickly muscled limbs would move at any given moment, that she felt they'd become close. She'd almost stopped comparing his body with her memory of the man in the church; that quick darkness. But these trips, in which aspects of Thomas's life that she'd never have seen in Catte Street were revealed every day, were an unsettling reminder of how little she really knew him. It seemed as though Thomas must know tavern keepers and shifty drunks across half of England. Everywhere they went, men sidled up to him, grinning. 'My wife,' he'd say, proudly; and they'd give her the kind of measuring looks that made her blush, or they'd guffaw and nudge him. 'Making good, are you, Tommy boy?' one old villain with a broken nose asked him merrily. 'Well, it's high time you settled down.'

Whatever Thomas said, she didn't for a moment believe he would knuckle down to learning his trade after May Day. He'd find another excuse to postpone it. She thought he must be scared of admitting how much he had to learn; she also thought his mother wasn't making it any easier by bullying him in front of the Prattes, who were always dropping in because Anne Pratte worked with Alice. It can't go on like this, Isabel thought sometimes. Thomas will have to start work soon. But she'd begun to accept her dreamlike, aimless new existence. She was feeling more defiant every time Alice Claver froze her with one of her stares. Anything was better than being at Catte Street with those frightening looks.

When Isabel was woken up at dawn on May Day by the door of her chamber banging open, and Alice Claver's familiar, heavy footsteps storming in, her first sleepy, confused thought was that her mother-in-law must finally have got so angry that she'd resolved to pull them out of bed by force and put the pair of them to work right now, feast day or not.

Quickly, she pulled the sheet over her head and prodded Thomas into muttering wakefulness. Luckily the bed curtains were drawn. They lay in each other's arms in the hot darkness, hardly breathing, listening for clues; bracing for invasion.

But the footsteps went thudding right past the bed, straight to the window, then fell silent. Alice Claver must be leaning out listening to the street talk, Isabel thought; she wouldn't hear it from her own room, which looked out on the garden. But why? All she'd hear would be a lot of people setting up their stalls and talking about the maypole dancing later. Thomas raised an eyebrow, giving Isabel the kind of rueful look that she now knew to be an invitation to giggle at his mother's infuriating ways. She grinned back.

Yet when Alice Claver did finally stalk over to the bed and twitch back their curtains, her face was so drained of colour and her eyes so full of fear that the sight of it wiped away their guilty smiles in an instant.

Alice Claver said, in a monotone, 'They say there are ships attacking from the river,' and, after a long, expressionless stare at both of them, 'Get up; quick; we must lock up.' And she half-ran from the room.

As the door clapped shut, Isabel and Thomas pulled themselves up on their elbows, both wide awake now, and stared at each other. He looks excited, Isabel thought, and knew his face was reflecting her own expression. Neither of them was really scared. The memory of King Edward's chivalrous soldiers was too recent for that, and they'd never seen any others.

'I should go out,' he said, drinking her in hungrily. 'Join the patrols.'

'No,' she replied quickly. She put a hand on his arm.

I don't want him doing anything dangerous, she thought. But she also knew she didn't want to be left alone in this house.

'I must,' he said, and for the first time she saw what he might look like once his youth had passed: calm and decisive, as if he'd been relieved of all the uncertainties of his youth. It took her breath away. Feeling almost giddy with what she thought must be the first pang of real love, she looked down, feeling ashamed, listening in silence as he went on: 'I'm a good marksman.' He looked at her, almost pleadingly. 'I want you to be proud of me.'

She nodded, reluctantly accepting his choice. Very tenderly, he raised her face to his.

He'd gone before she realised she hadn't remembered to say a prayer over him or whisper a word of love. She set off downstairs alone to face Alice Claver.

The first rush of closing shutters and barring doors and dragging chests in front of them and drawing water and bringing in all the loaves and cured meat they could lay hands on in the pantries left them breathless and hot. It was only after that, while they sat in the half-dark they were to stay in for the best part of the next two weeks, that the fear set in and they got cold. First it was just Isabel and Alice Claver and three serving girls in the parlour, shivering and hugging themselves despite the summer swelter; but then, a few hours later, Anne Pratte came too, banging at the door to be let in with none of her usual timidity, bringing life back into the room.

William Pratte was in charge of the Old Jewry patrol. He'd dropped his wife at Catte Street as he set off for the riverside with his muster of amateur archers. 'Thomas will have joined him, don't you fret,' Anne Pratte said comfortably to both Alice Claver and Isabel, settling herself down on a bench with her sewing. Isabel was relieved to see that, just as Thomas's stock had risen because he'd been so eager to go out and defend his women and his city, her own enemy status was becoming fuzzy in this artificial twilight.

Anne Pratte's calm astonished Isabel. Even from the relative safety of Catte Street, well back from the Thames, you could hear the explosions and the crash of riverside buildings falling. The Bastard of Fauconberg's Lancastrian troops were trying to rescue King Henry from the Tower; the pirates from Kent and Essex with him just wanted to run riot through London with their clubs and pitchforks. Every thudding footstep outside might be the first of them, and you could do nothing about it except pray. Each booming hit sent a shudder through the nearby streets. Not just because of the windows cracking, or the falling pewterware, but because of the dirty black tide of dread that comes over all human flesh at the realisation that it is soft and pink and defenceless against death. Yet even when one of the serving girls began whimpering, and Alice Claver, grey-faced in the grey light, was muttering prayers under her breath, and Isabel had her eyes tight shut, willing herself not to lose her dignity but feeling the dark tide coming close to overwhelming her, Anne Pratte carried on sewing and grumbling. Isabel admired her for it. It somehow helped keep the fear at bay.

'Knights in shining armour indeed,' Anne Pratte said crossly, early on, biting off a thread as though it were an advancing Lancastrian's head, so fiercely that her floppy turkey neck quivered. 'The laws of chivalry, my foot. I don't care what they say about warfare being a noble art. This is just fighting. Bullies with weapons, and us caught in the middle.'

Naturally, in the circumstances she spent a lot of those twilit days complaining about the Lancastrians. But she was catholic in her dislikes. She had bad things to say

49

about the Yorks too. King Edward's womanising got short shrift. So did his grasping queen, Elizabeth Woodville, ('not a drop of royal blood in her body, that one; but more than enough pure ambition to make up for it . . . a beauty, of course, but harder than diamonds') who enjoyed the exercise of power so much that she kept every princess of the blood royal standing for three silent hours at every meal. 'Just because she can,' Anne Pratte finished triumphantly.

She didn't have much time for King Edward's brothers either. The Duke of Clarence, who'd gone over to the Earl of Warwick's side and married his daughter, Isabel Neville, in the misguided hope Warwick would think that reason enough to make him king, was an opportunist and, worse, a 'nasty little traitor who's no better than he ought to be'.

As for the younger brother, the Duke of Gloucester (an eighteen-year-old veteran whom Isabel remembered John Lambert describing with awestruck reverence after seeing him at King Edward's Mass in April), in Anne Pratte's view he was an out-and-out thief. He'd kidnapped an elderly noblewoman and forced her to sign away her lands. Anne Pratte had heard the story from Sir John Risley, a Knight of the Body for whom she was making some silk pieces. 'Sir John says the old countess thought the duke would kill her if she refused. So she did it. Wept a lot, of course. But she had no choice. She's got nothing any more, Sir John says; she's taking in sewing to pay the nuns. And when Sir John asked the King the other day whether he thought it would be a good investment for him to buy the house from Gloucester, he said the King just squirmed with embarrassment. "Don't touch it, Risley," he said. "Don't touch it." He knows his brother stole it all right.'

She leaned forward to catch Isabel's eye. She was enjoying the younger woman's attention. Isabel was imagining the

Duke of Gloucester bullying the old countess, and in her mind's eye the duke was dark and thin, with a scowling face as hard as the man's she'd met in the church might, perhaps, sometimes be, while the old lady looked like a frightened, thin Alice Claver. Isabel had her sewing with her – a piece of embroidery she planned to turn into a purse for Thomas when he got back, with hearts and flowers in blues and greens, and their initials twined together – though it was so dark in here that she'd hardly touched it. Still, a truce between Isabel and Anne was definitely taking shape on the bench they were sharing, even if Alice Claver, in her own corner, was doing no more than grunt every now and then in response to her friend's non-stop talk. Isabel knew Alice Claver must be too frightened to reply. She couldn't feel sorry for her mother-in-law, not after all those rows and glares; even now, even here. But she could see Anne Pratte wanted, tactfully, to comfort her friend.

Over in the other corner, a throat was cleared. Then Alice Claver's voice boomed out of the darkness, so loud and so ordinary that Isabel almost jumped: 'Disgraceful. Almost makes you proud not to be one of them, doesn't it? Men of honour, my eye.'

There was triumph in Anne Pratte's eyes at having brought her friend back from the darkness. 'Yes, indeed, dear,' she answered gently. 'I always say all the fighting these great lords enjoy so much is really just an excuse to go out and grab someone else's land, isn't it?'

Alice Claver began to laugh. A single hoot at first, then more hoots; then gales of relief. It was infectious. Before Isabel knew where she was, she and the others had joined in too. When she turned round somewhere in the middle of a gust of laughter, and met Alice Claver's creased, weeping eyes for the first time in a long time, she realised the black, hateful look had gone from them. From relief

51

as much as anything else, she started laughing even harder, until she, like Alice Claver, was holding her sides and groaning with it.

'Ooh,' Alice Claver said, what seemed like much later; sounding almost her usual self. Anne Pratte was watching her from over her flashing needle with quiet satisfaction. 'It hurts. I tell you what, Anne. You'd better give us all some of your sewing to do. It's keeping you calmer than the rest of us put together.'

All Anne Pratte had in her pile was sheets for turning. Nothing you needed strong light to see. Alice Claver got up, took one off the pile and sat down again to thread a needle.

She turned and looked at Isabel with triumph, as if she'd hit on a new reason to find fault with her. 'Don't just sit there,' she snapped. 'Get yourself a sheet too. Do some work. Go on.'

She must be feeling better. She was turning nasty again. Isabel blinked away the tears prickling behind her eyes. Hadn't Alice Claver seen she already had work in her lap? Silently, with as much dignity as she could muster, she held up her little rectangle of silk embroidery in self-defence.

Alice Claver got up and with a single dark swoop snatched it away and pushed a sheet at her instead. 'Waste of silk,' she said gruffly. 'You'll only make a mess of it in this light.'

Isabel lowered her head. Without comment, as if she were also a little frightened of her friend's rage, Anne Pratte passed Isabel a needle.

But, as Alice Claver sat down, Isabel was aware of her mother-in-law looking closely at the confiscated piece of embroidery as if to find something in it to sneer at; then peering closer, then holding it up to the light. She could almost swear Alice Claver looked surprised. Well, she was

52

good at embroidery. Everyone had always said so. She kept her eyes firmly on the needle she was threading, her back tense, waiting for a new attack once Alice Claver had worked out what to say. But it didn't come. They sewed in silence.

'He wasn't with me,' William Pratte said. 'I never saw him.'

William Pratte was filthier than Isabel could have imagined. But he looked happy and healthy too, leaner and more muscled than he'd been a fortnight before, with his bald patch freckled a pinky brown and the sun still warm on his cheeks.

The relief of knowing it was over, and the Bastard's head, along with those of the Mayor of Canterbury and the pirate captains, was safely on London Bridge, was making everyone feel drunk with the pleasure of being alive. The serving girls were opening the shutters, letting air and sun in with a series of joyful bangs. After a twirling embrace with her husband, Anne Pratte had rushed straight out to the garden to see what salad leaves there were. 'I've been thinking for days, I could murder a nice dish of sorrel,' she'd shrilled, waving her arms.

'Perhaps he went with your father,' William Pratte said, scratching himself. Isabel breathed: 'Did you see *him*?' He nodded kindly. 'Oh yes, don't worry about him, I saw him on Tower Hill just yesterday. He had Will Shore with him. Hugh Wyche. The Chigwells. I didn't see Thomas. Then again, I didn't stop to ask. Just waved. But Thomas will be somewhere.'

Alice Claver was beaming so hard at being let out of the darkness that nothing could dash her spirits. 'Well, all I can say is thank God we have the daylight back,' she said happily, including Isabel in her smile. 'Thomas has always been a law unto himself. He'll turn up in his own good time. And we'd better get you bathed before he does, William. I've never seen so much dirt on one body.'

No one worried too much when Thomas didn't show up that night either. Half the patrols were still out celebrating. The taverns were heaving.

A little hesitantly, Isabel went along when, just before sunset, William Pratte took the two silkwomen to explore the damaged riverside zone beyond Cordwainer Lane. She didn't want to be out when Thomas arrived, but Alice Claver gave her a warmish look and said, 'We'll get back before he does,' and she gave in. Women were walking along the Strand through summer clouds of gnats, looking in astonishment at the fallen masonry and the burn marks or listening to their dirty, proud men gabbling, very fast and excited, 'This is where we were when they started shooting', or 'This is where I hid from the wildfire'.

The pirates had been beaten back from London Bridge. They'd gone downriver to Kew and tried to land there. They'd come back. But the defences had held. There was drunken singing everywhere, and a lot of woozy yelling: 'God Save King Edward!'

Seeing Isabel glancing around in case Thomas suddenly came out from some corner, Alice Claver told her: 'It would be unusual for Thomas to come straight home', and laughed, not unkindly, in the direction of the Tumbling Bear. Isabel tried not to feel disappointed that her husband hadn't rushed back to her side. But, since no one had word of him being hurt, and William Pratte said there'd been surprisingly few men killed, he must just be out drinking somewhere. For the first time, the memory of all those shady men he knew in all those taverns came back to her, replacing the pictures she'd called to mind so often in the darkness that they now seemed thread-bare and soiled from overuse: his soft look back at her as he'd slipped out of the door on the day the ships came in; his parting murmur of 'I want you to be proud of me.'

'I love you,' she muttered under her breath, to keep her spirits up, as she'd done a million times during the siege. 'I love you.' But she could feel doubt creeping in. She knew Thomas found home difficult and work difficult. Perhaps, now he'd discovered the pleasures of fighting, he'd seen a more exciting way of keeping out of his mother's hair than sheltering behind his new wife? Perhaps her novelty had worn off?

Isabel felt suddenly so alone that she shivered. The heat was going out of the evening air. It was nearly curfew. He wouldn't come tonight. Anne Pratte put her shawl round Isabel's shoulders without comment; Isabel looked gratefully at her.

'We kept our spirits up by turning sheets while you were out there fighting,' Alice Claver boomed at William Pratte, back at Catte Street, over the evening meal. 'And Anne kept our spirits up with gossip.' She turned to Isabel for confirmation. 'Didn't she?'

And, seeing those eyes on her again with this new expression of wary near-warmth, it was suddenly clear to Isabel what she had to do before Thomas got home. She didn't want to be enemies with Alice Claver. And tonight, Alice Claver didn't look as though she wanted to be enemies either. There was no need. The half-truce that had set in might just hold if she helped it along. It was Thomas's stubbornness that had made things go wrong. Now was her chance to put things right. If she wanted to be happy as a Claver, she was going to have to get up at dawn and offer to start working for her mother-in-law.

3

Alice Claver had the same idea. When she saw Isabel in the morning, she didn't even comment on Thomas's non-appearance. She just said: 'Shall I show you the storeroom?'

Isabel nodded, trying to match that matter-of-factness. She'd hardly ever been in her own father's storeroom. It was his holy of holies; too precious for children, he said.

She padded down the corridor behind her mother-in-law, secretly impressed; willing Alice Claver, now fiddling with keys at the door, to learn to like her.

Alice Claver's warehouse stretched all the way along the side of her house: a vast barn of a place, its high rafters lit up by slanting early sunlight from window slits.

It took a few moments for Isabel's eyes to adjust. Then she gasped.

She'd never seen so much luxury in one place. It was as if she was in the middle of a snowfall, but an unimaginably lovely and costly snowfall that gleamed and glowed in every rich colour possible. There were wafts and drifts of it wherever she looked, piled up against walls, soft on the stone floor. She glided forward, swept away by the magic of it, to touch as well as look. She'd seen plenty of velvets like these, in the dark colours of Lucca or the brighter hues of Siena; but never anything like the piece glittering stiffly with gold embroidery under her hand, or the green silk cloth underneath it, figured with peacocks shimmering blue and purple, or the unicorns and leaping harts prancing across the red and gold satins and damasks and taffetas. Nothing like this.

She twirled and turned in the dusty shafts of light, pulling at one bale, holding up another. Lost in the moment. Astonished.

She only remembered Alice Claver was there when she became aware of the older woman looking at her, with a slow half-smile on her lips, as if she understood Isabel's enchantment. She must feel it herself. In this shadow world, lit up by one of the sideways rays of light from on high, with the ground around her a tumbling mass of scarlets and purples and silvers, Alice Claver had stopped looking as barrel-like and brutally commonsensical as she did elsewhere; she seemed suddenly taller and more mysterious, like an angel in a halo of gold, or a rustic wise woman summoning spirits from the woods.

Now Alice Claver was sweeping Isabel around, poking into corners, pulling things out, energetically talking. The silkwoman poured out information at a speed Isabel could hardly keep up with, giving her stern looks if she felt Isabel's attention flagging. Isabel nodded, and tried to absorb as much of the flood of knowledge as she could. She was learning more in her first hour in this storeroom than she had in a lifetime as John Lambert's daughter. It was exhausting. But it was exhilarating too; so absorbing it kept her returning thud of anxiety – 'Where is Thomas?' – at bay.

Alice started with reels and skeins and loops of silk threads: dyed, twined, thrown, boiled, raw; all glowing with the sun and scents of faraway places Isabel could hardly imagine. She learned that Persian silk came from the mysterious regions near the Caspian Sea: Ghilan, Shilan, Azerbaijan; that since Constantinople had fallen to the Turks Venetian merchants hadn't been able to buy in their old Black Sea markets, but that the Persians were sending more and more silk – both cloth and threads – by caravan to Syria, outside the control of the Turks, and that the Venetians were now getting their Persian silk supplies in from the markets of Damascus and Aleppo. She saw Persian silk threads called *ablaca*, *ardassa*, and *rasbar*. She saw Syrian silk threads called *castrovana*, *decara*, and *safetina*. She saw Romanian silk threads called *belgrado*, *belladonna* and *fior di morea*. ('Most of my supplies come from Venice,' Alice Claver said by way of explanation of the Lombard-sounding names, 'it's still the greatest centre in the world, where East meets West . . . and the quickest way for you to pick up some Italian, which you'll need to do – and Flemish, of course, that's vital too – is going to be by learning these Venetian names.') She rolled the names on her tongue as though they were poems; Isabel imitated her as best she could. Spanish silk threads: *spagnola*, *cattalana*. Threads from southern Italy: *napoletana*, *abruzzese*, *pugliese*, *calabrese*, *messinese*. The home-grown silks from the forests of mulberry trees cultivated by old ladies in black in Tuscany: *nostrale*. The home-grown silks from the forests of mulberry trees cultivated by old ladies in black in Venice's own Terraferma hinterland: *nostrane*.

They were both so absorbed that they jumped when Anne Pratte's round face came into view at the door. She was illuminated by the sunlight, too, but she had none of the skittish cheerfulness of yesterday. She looked grey; stricken. 'Alice,' she said quietly to her friend. She didn't even seem to notice Isabel. 'Alice. I'm sorry. They've found Thomas.'

Isabel didn't understand the look, but she felt faint with foreboding. She stole a timid glance at Alice, looking for guidance. Alice was clutching very hard at the skein of stuff she'd been showing her daughter-in-law. It was indigo-coloured, Isabel remembered afterwards, the darkness of widow's weeds, and now it had tightened painfully against Alice's blotchy hands. Alice wasn't one to waste words, and she could see that Anne's face made it pointless to ask whether Thomas was alive.

'Where?' Alice asked.

He hadn't gone far. He'd been trapped under what must have been one of the first falls of masonry on Thames Street on his way to find the fighting. The men digging him out had just seen his name stitched into his purse and come to the house to bring word. When they'd arrived at the door, Anne had already been walking in. She'd rushed straight back to Alice to break the news more gently than they could.

Wordlessly, Alice held her hand out for the purse. Feel the goods for yourself; take nothing on trust: market laws. The indigo silk dropped away, leaving a red weal across her index finger and palm. But Anne shook her head, and now even Isabel, whose mother had died before she remembered, who hadn't known death, could understand that there was no comfort in that look, no possibility of error. 'It's his,' Anne said gently; bleakly. 'I saw it.'

'I sewed that purse myself,' Alice Claver said with unnatural calm. 'I thought it would help if he passed out in a tavern somewhere. Having his name so clear on it.' Then her body began to heave. The sound that started coming from her was not unlike her laughter in the dark parlour a few days earlier: a harsh, dry sucking in of breath; a snort of something loud and unmelodious. It took Isabel – standing utterly still at her mother-in-law's side as if she'd been turned to stone – what felt like an eternity to realise that this strange braying noise must be crying.

'There, dear, there,' Anne Pratte was murmuring, as her larger friend heaved towards her in an ungainly mess of arms.

No one acknowledged Isabel's presence. It was as if she wasn't there; didn't exist; hadn't been married to Alice Claver's son; hadn't just been trying to learn Alice Claver's work. Neither of the older women even saw her leave.

'You're well-provided for, at least,' Anne Pratte said, dabbing at Isabel's face. 'You won't have to worry. You get half the thousand pounds Alice settled on Thomas for the marriage. Quite a dower. Your father will welcome you back with open arms with all that.'

Why would I go back to my father? Isabel wondered, but she kept the thought to herself.

Anne Pratte had come up as dusk fell with a bowl of water. She'd murmured, 'Oh, your poor eyes' and 'Alice is sitting with him; they've laid him out in the hall; would you like to join her?' and just sighed when Isabel shook her head. She appreciated being remembered by Anne Pratte, who had a kind heart. But she'd wait. She couldn't face Alice Claver now.

'I know. It hasn't been easy,' Anne Pratte had said sadly. She'd had the grace to stop there.

She'd waited a few more moments, patting and dabbing at eyes and shoulders, before clearing her throat and asking, 'Forgive me, dear, but I know you'll understand why I . . .' and giving Isabel something like her usual bright, inquisitive look. Isabel had stared back, not understanding. Anne Pratte had looked harder at her and raised her eyebrows. Her expression was encouraging, as if she were trying, wordlessly, to discover some secret only Isabel knew. Isabel knew she must be being stupid not to understand. She looked down at the bowl of water with the cloth sticking out. Anne Pratte composed her features into an expression of still greater patience. 'Are you . . . by any chance . . . ?' She'd nodded her head. Then she'd paused delicately.

'Oh,' Isabel had said flatly. 'With child, you mean. No.'

Anne had sighed. There was a silence. Then she'd nodded again.

'Shall I send for your sister?' she'd asked a moment later. 'Or your father?'

Isabel could see what Anne Pratte was feeling towards: nudging her back to the Lamberts to save her friend Alice Claver from having to go on sharing her home with an irritant, a girl who'd never settled in and never worked, and whose continued presence now would only remind her of the son she'd lost. If Isabel had been expecting a baby, or if they'd become close, it might have been different. But it was too late to think like that. This was how it was.

She shook her head again. Stubbornly. Refusing the possibility of sinking back into her childhood life as if this time with Thomas had never been, because what went with that would be waiting to be found a new husband and sent off again like a parcel of cloth. She didn't want Jane's smug pity or the servants' anxious, helpless eyes; not yet. She didn't want her father rushing to find a new plan. She didn't want to have to face up to a choice between being a burden on the Lamberts or a burden on Alice Claver. There'd be time for that tomorrow, after the funeral. She just wanted to be alone and, later, to sneak downstairs and be alone with Thomas.

She was grateful when Anne Pratte patted her shoulder and left.

*　*　*

61

Alice Claver was asleep on a chair drawn up near Thomas. Her face was ravaged. She was snoring softly. The candles at his head were low. It was nearly dawn.

Isabel tiptoed round her and put a stool quietly down on the other side of the two benches they'd laid Thomas on.

They'd wiped the dust off him, but the smell of death was so strong it turned her stomach. His body was wrapped in sheets. They'd left his face uncovered. It was so perfectly still that it seemed somehow flatter and wider than she remembered. She leaned forward, trying not to be frightened; trying to stop retching. She touched his cold cheek, then crouched down over his face and kissed it until it was as wet as hers. But it stayed empty. 'I love you,' she muttered, so panicked by the finality of it she couldn't think of a prayer.

Alice Claver stirred. Isabel froze into her crouch, hardly breathing, willing her mother-in-law back to sleep.

But Alice Claver opened swollen eyes and said: 'I used to swing him round in the garden until I was dizzy.'

Isabel wasn't sure Alice Claver was talking to her. 'When he was little,' Alice Claver went on in the same dreamy monotone, 'he couldn't get enough of it. Lay on the grass howling with laughter.'

She nodded, up and down; remembering. 'While Richard was alive . . .' she murmured. 'When I still had time.'

A shadow passed across her face. 'I should have made more time.'

She closed her eyes again. But Isabel could see she hadn't gone back to sleep. Her face was too alive for that: terrible with grief; twitching with memories.

Isabel hadn't imagined Alice Claver would feel guilty.

Wishing she had the courage to show the compassion sweeping through her – to go over and put her arms round the older woman, or pray with her – but knowing she didn't, Isabel put a last tentative kiss on the lips of the husk of Thomas instead, and slipped away.

Her last thought before her own twitchy, uneasy sleep took her over was, 'I'll go home.'

It was only after the funeral the next day that she realised she couldn't go home.

Not because of her father's irritating calculations at the plain meal of bread and cheese and beer that the Prattes organised in Alice Claver's house after the burial – 'You'll be out of mourning in a year; you could marry again at sixteen. With that dower you'll be able to choose whoever you want' – as if she was really supposed to believe that John Lambert would keep his word and let Isabel choose, any more than he had the first time. Not even because he'd said, with what she thought supreme tactlessness, as if discussing possibilities for her next marriage at her husband's graveside might cheer her up, 'One of the Lynom boys, even. Now *that* would be a good match.'

It was the other guests who shut the door home to her: Thomas's friends from outside the Mercery. One red-nosed shabby man after another; some vaguely familiar, some perfect strangers, but all avoiding her eyes and Alice Claver's. All shuffling up to William Pratte instead, taking him off into corners for their private chats, searching through pockets and pouches and purses for dirty bits of paper to present to him. They wanted to talk to a man.

William Pratte was well-known as an administrator. He was on the merchant venturers' committee at the Guildhall. He knew how to be correct. Isabel watched him out of the corner of her eye as he gravely thanked each guest for the paper, and folded it away. But his plump face, already sad, got longer every time a new hand tapped him on the shoulder.

He waited for everyone to leave before he took Isabel into Alice Claver's accounting parlour and told her. She could see the pity in his eyes; hear it in the gentleness of his voice. Thomas had debts. Over the past four years, he'd pledged away every penny and more of the money his mother had settled on him. 'I had no idea,' William Pratte said sadly. 'I just thought he was sowing his wild oats in the taverns.' He showed her the documents on which Thomas's many half-baked hopes of instant wealth had been set out: a half-share in a failed brewery here; £100 to an absconding Southampton shipper there; £85 for a consignment of Cyprus gold thread that had never materialised; deeds for a tenement in Southwark that had caught fire; and dogs, bears, and tavern bills mounting up to dizzying amounts. He'd even bought Uncle Alexander Marshall a horse. Everyone knew Thomas had expectations; it seemed he'd been easy meat for every trickster in town. William Pratte finished sombrely: 'This might not be all, either. We'll just have to wait and see what other bills come in.'

'But,' Isabel stammered, her head reeling, unable to take it in, 'he can't have spent that much. It's a king's ransom.'

'He must have thought it would be easy to make back the kind of money that would make Alice sit up and take notice,' William Pratte said, shaking his mild head. 'At first, anyway. And later he must have realised they'd come after him for payment as soon as word got out that Alice had set him up to start trading properly. No wonder he kept putting off the day, poor boy. I don't like to think how he must have worried.'

Suddenly Isabel remembered the calm, cleansed look Thomas had given her when he decided to go and fight. 'I want you to be proud of me,' he'd said. Pity hit her in the chest like a stab wound. Was this why he'd gone?

Equally suddenly, she found herself blurting a question she only realised she needed to ask as she heard her own words: 'My inheritance?'

But she already knew the answer. Thomas had spent her inheritance.

'I'll call Alice in now,' William Pratte said, avoiding the question. 'I wanted to tell you first.'

When Alice swept in, knowing, as Isabel herself had known a short while before, that William Pratte could only have bad news, Isabel's face was as set as her mother-in-law's. It was so obvious in advance that Alice was going to blame her for Thomas Claver's transgressions that she wasn't even surprised at the narrowing of the older woman's eyes; the furious, accusing glances her way; the white flared nostrils; the horse-snorts of breath. Isabel just stared at her feet and tried not to hear Alice Claver growl, at first disbelievingly, then with a rage she didn't want to see, 'Thomas was an innocent for his own good', and then, 'He'd never have thought of any of that by himself'. If Alice Claver chose to think the question of Thomas's debts through, she'd realise it would have been impossible for him to have spent that vast fortune in the few short weeks of his marriage. But Isabel could see that Thomas's thrifty mother couldn't bring herself to consider how a sum of money equivalent to the King's loans from John Lambert could possibly have been lost so lightly. It happened all the time; the sons of the rich didn't always value the hard-earned wealth their parents had amassed. But facts were too difficult for her right now. Easier to look at the bowed girl's head in front of her and puff and glare; easier to say to herself, 'She led him astray.'

The unfairness of it cut at Isabel's heart. The child in her wanted to wail, as she'd always wailed when Jane got off without punishment while she was beaten for some shared misdemeanour, that the grown-ups had got it terribly wrong. But she was grown up herself now. She scuffed one toe against another and pursed her lips.

She stayed in her room that evening. The Prattes stayed downstairs with Alice Claver.

She sat very straight, not moving, intent on working out what to do and how. Even when she remembered Thomas, lying on the bed watching her think something out before, laughing and saying, 'You've gone like a cat watching a mouse; are you going to pounce?' she wouldn't let the thought in or the tears out. This wasn't the time for crying.

He'd wanted her to be proud of him. And if he hadn't been killed he'd have sorted his troubles out somehow, so she could have been. But she could still protect his memory.

So much of what was on her mind was so painful that it was a relief, from time to time, to let her thoughts wander back to the dark man in the church, with his soft eyes and hard-nosed advice. There was no point in dreaming of that man; no point in taking refuge in girlish musings about how, if she'd been married to someone with that man's capacity for clearly understanding a problem, she'd never have been in this trouble in the first place. She just had to take the best from that memory. He'd had more foresight than she'd realised when he'd said, 'This is just your first move. There'll be others later.' She hadn't expected the next move to come within weeks. But now it was here. And she had to make it a good one. She had to think it through as carefully as a general planning a battle.

By morning, she'd worked out the best thing to do in the circumstances. It wasn't going to be easy. But it would be right. She thought the man in the church would approve.

She rose early enough to clean her face of its stains,

dress soberly, and catch her mother-in-law alone, heading out to Mass with a terrible loneliness on her face.

Lonely or not, she could see Alice Claver would rather go without her. But she didn't give her the opportunity. 'May I come with you?' she asked, and determinedly linked arms. After a moment's rigid surprise, she felt her mother-in-law's arm relax.

Alice Claver didn't seem to notice the tears running down Isabel's cheeks in the chapel. She came out calm and quiet; cleansed. But she didn't say a word to Isabel.

Isabel waited till they'd got back into the great hall. She settled Alice Claver onto a bench. Fetched her left-over bread and cheese. Set it out neatly. Her heart was thumping.

Alice Claver was staring unseeingly out of the window. Her expression wasn't promising.

'I wanted to ask,' Isabel began, hesitantly.

Those dark eyes came reluctantly to rest on her. It struck Isabel, for the first time, that Alice Claver was too uneasy with her. She couldn't really go on choosing to blame Isabel for leading her son astray; not for long. It was just possible, instead, that Alice Claver was feeling embarrassed at Isabel being left a penniless widow as a result of marrying a Claver. The thought gave her courage.

'. . . I want to stay here,' she finished. 'Live with you.'

Now she had Alice Claver's attention. Hostile attention, perhaps; but that was better than nothing.

'Why?' the older woman barked.

'I can't go home,' Isabel said, rushing into her argument. 'My father will want to marry me again. But I won't have a dower now. And I don't want them to find out why.'

She paused to let the idea sink in. The older woman turned away. Isabel could see her thinking. Alice Claver didn't want the Lamberts to find out there was no dower either. They could both imagine the destructive buzz in the markets. It would ruin Isabel's chances of marrying again, if she ever wanted to, but it would also blacken Thomas's name forever. It wouldn't be good for Alice's business, either.

'I don't want people to think badly of Thomas,' Isabel went on, as persuasively as she knew how. 'And if I stayed with you, there'd be no need for anyone to know what he left me. Not unless I were to get married again, anyway.'

She could feel Alice Claver softening. She knew the woman was a swift weigher-up of realities, so must understand that Isabel was offering her a chance to save face. The next answer, another bark, was less fierce. 'You'd have to work, you know. There's no room for merry widows here. You can't just sit around having picnics all your life.'

Isabel nodded, refusing to be nettled; she knew she was winning. 'Oh, I'll work all right,' she replied, with all the enthusiasm she could muster. 'You know I will. I'll need to, now; I have a dower to earn back', and although she kept her voice soft she felt a quiver from the older woman that she hoped might be shame at her own ungraciousness. 'I've thought it all out. You don't even have to take my word for it. We could make a contract if you'd rather. You could take me on as a proper apprentice.'

Alice Claver nearly stared. An apprentice? She'd be getting ten years of unpaid labour out of a deal like that.

Isabel knew it was a good offer. But Alice Claver was too canny a market woman to show surprise. Raising a hand to her mouth to cover her expression, she said, deadpan: 'I could.' And, several seconds later, 'I suppose.'

Isabel could hardly contain her impatience.

'So . . . will you?' she said.

Alice Claver dragged out her pause for longer than Isabel would have thought possible. But when, finally,

making a show of reluctance, she did nod agreement –
then leaned forward, with a shadow of her usual market
manner, and shook Isabel's hand as if to close the deal –
Isabel thought she could see a gleam of satisfaction in
those puffy dark eyes.

4

'But I want to stay with her,' Isabel said wearily. The conversation seemed to have gone on for hours.

'But you can't,' her father said again. 'Not as an apprentice.'

She knew his style of argument. It was merchant style: repeating himself, without raising his voice, until the sheer boredom of the discussion wore whoever he was arguing with into reluctant agreement. He called it consensus. And what he'd been saying today was: You could marry anyone in the City with your dower. And: No daughter of mine need ever work; I've given you the best opportunities in life; what will people think? And: Just look at your hands; lady's hands; think what they're going to look like once your new (eyebrows raised, shoulders raised) *mistress* gets you throwing raw silk or dunking yarn into pots of dye.

John Lambert glanced round his great hall, as if trying to draw inspiration from his lavish tapestries and his cupboard full of gleaming silverware. He was visibly longing to go back to their more pleasurable earlier conversation, in which he'd been able to boast that Lord Hastings and the Duke of Gloucester had paid him a personal visit at the Crown Seld that morning – 'Just sauntered in; His

70

Grace was gracious enough to remember me from the Lord Mayor's banquet; two of the greatest men in the land . . .' – and they'd looked at his imported Italian silk cloths, and Hastings had ended up shaking hands on a promise to buy a length of green figured velvet. He poked at the remains of his meal.

'Look,' Isabel said impatiently, 'I didn't want to marry a Claver in the first place, but you insisted. You said it would be good for your business to make a relationship with the Clavers. Now I want to stay; but you're saying I shouldn't. It's only a month later. Tell me this: what's changed?'

'That was a marriage,' her father said, sounding impatient at last. 'This is . . .' he wrinkled his nose, 'business. And an unsuitable business for a young lady of your accomplishments, if I may say so. A waste of your French . . . your Latin . . . your lute playing.'

Isabel bared her teeth at him in a grin so angry it felt almost like a snarl. 'Well, why shouldn't I learn the business?' she said. 'You do it; and a lot of girls I know learn it too. We Lamberts are the only ones who think we're too grand. But what's wrong with doing something useful? What if I actually want to be a silkwoman? What if I want to be', she lingered, 'independent? Of other people's whims?'

'You can't do it,' he said hotly. Both hands clutched at the table edge.

'Why?' she replied, eyeing him insolently back.

'Because I forbid you to!' he yelled, startling her as he leapt to his feet. 'I forbid you to humiliate the Lamberts, and drag our family name down!'

'You can't forbid me to!' she cried back, standing up too. 'I don't have to obey you any more! I'm a widow! Widows are legally responsible for themselves! I'm not a Lambert now – I'm a Claver! And I can choose my own future!'

71

They eyeballed each other like fighting dogs. There was a long, ominous silence. She'd never disobeyed him before; not like this. He didn't look as though he'd forgive her easily for betraying him into this undignified shouting match – for losing his temper again, like he had at the Guildhall.

He turned and walked out, without a backwards glance.

Isabel had thought Jane would be contemptuous of the idea of working in the markets. But when she first told her older sister, Jane was endearingly practical. 'Ten years,' she said gently, wrinkling her nose but trying to understand; not sneering. 'That's a long time. What if you hate it in a month?'

Isabel nearly cried at her sister's sympathetic tone. She was moments away from confiding in Jane; but she couldn't. She didn't know if Jane – who was glowing even more beautifully than before now she was married – would tell her husband; if word would get out. So she shrugged and tried to look unconcerned.

'There'd be no going back,' she said laconically.

Jane tried again. She put a hand on Isabel's arm and looked very sweetly into her eyes.

'I know you're in mourning,' she murmured. 'I can imagine how terrible it must feel . . .'

Isabel nodded mutely, looking away; looking down; willing herself not to weep.

'But, Isabel,' Jane went on, in the same sweetly reasonable voice. 'It was just an arranged marriage. Don't you remember? A month ago, you didn't want Thomas Claver for a husband. You can't really believe you're heartbroken enough now to sign away half your life to his mother.'

Isabel flinched. She'd known, really, that Jane wouldn't understand.

'Even if you really do think now that you'll always feel

like this, you must know it will pass,' Jane said, and now Isabel could hear the familiar patronising big-sister note creeping into the voice in her ears. 'What if a year goes by and you want to marry again? If you're an apprentice you'll have to wait till you're twenty-four. And you'll be even older before you can have a baby.'

Twenty-four, Isabel thought, before her defences came up against that tone of voice. An eternity. Then, with startling simplicity, it came to her that she didn't want to marry again and become a hostage to someone else's fortune. It wasn't just something to say defiantly to her father. It wasn't just that she had no choice but to apprentice herself to Alice Claver if she were to protect Thomas's memory. This future might actually be for the best. Widows were legally free; their fathers couldn't control them; they could make their own money and spend it as they chose. Alice Claver was robust. She'd used the freedom of widowhood to make a good life. Maybe she'd teach Isabel to do the same thing. With a flash of defiance, Isabel thought: 'I won't marry again. Not unless I'm free to choose someone who makes me feel . . .' She didn't know what she would want to feel; the nearest she could come to it was something like that brief moment, before all this, in the tavern, when the touch of a man who was not Thomas Claver had sparked through her like lightning. So she smiled, tightly, and crossed her arms against her sister, and repeated: 'No going back.'

Jane sighed. 'Well,' she said, rather sadly, 'I suppose we all find our own escapes.'

Isabel could see her sister had given in. She thought, suddenly, that she might have judged Jane's intervention too harshly. Jane was only doing her best in uncertain circumstances. She hadn't meant to give offence.

Jane started pinning a dark gown from the wardrobe against Isabel. 'You've lost weight,' she said, with a mouthful of pins. Then: 'You must have found something better than you expected in Thomas Claver . . .' There was a question in her eyes.

Isabel pressed her lips together and nodded. She felt tears near. To stave them off, she answered with her own question: 'Doesn't everyone?' She hadn't even asked Jane how things were turning out with Will Shore, she realised. Hastily, she added: 'Isn't living with Will better than you expected?'

It seemed a safe question. Jane had given no sign of being unhappy. If anything, she was more radiantly beautiful than ever; her skin glowed gold.

Jane laughed. It was such a joyful laugh that Isabel thought she must be agreeing. It was only later, going back to Catte Street, with one dark gown on her back and another in a basket, that Isabel realised she hadn't paid attention to what Jane Shore's words had been: 'Will is exactly what I expected.'

It wasn't the glowing endorsement of life with a husband that Jane's air of barely suppressed pleasure in living led you to expect.

Lord Hastings and the Duke of Gloucester were strolling through the Broad Seld after the leisurely meal they'd taken at the Tumbling Bear. They were side by side, talking quietly and occasionally laughing at remarks no one else could hear. Unlike most strangers, who tend to think themselves unobserved when on unfamiliar terrain, not realising how sharply they stood out to everyone else, these two noblemen – soldiers by instinct and experience – were aware of the eyes on their backs; on their swords and spurs. But they didn't mind.

Hastings was saying, with a touch of self-mockery: 'blonde . . . sings like a nightingale . . . witty, too . . . and dances like thistledown. You should see her dance. And her eyes . . .' Then: 'The same green as that velvet. She'll look beautiful in it. I'll send it to her as soon as I get it.'

His long limbs were made for war, but the troubadour words made his voice sound made for love. The thought of Jane Shore's skin and smile had filled him with sunshine for weeks. He looked cheerfully down at his companion, a few inches shorter than him and twenty years younger: his battle companion, his dearest friend's brother, a boy now grown to manhood and fast becoming a friend in his own right. He wanted them to share the irony of buying a rich cloth from a merchant and giving it to the merchant's lovely daughter.

But Dickon wasn't really listening or meeting Hastings' eyes. There was a polite half-smile on the younger man's thin, sallow face, but his eyes were wandering: from stall to stall, from one white-fingered embroiderer to the next, as if he were looking for someone.

'Looking for someone?' Hastings asked lightly; a question not meant to be taken seriously.

Dickon came to; for a moment he looked almost startled. Then he grinned his wolf-grin and shook his head. 'We're not all hankering after merchants' daughters, Will,' he said breezily. Then, with his grin turning into a laugh, 'though enough people seem to be hankering after your one.'

He looked around again (for a second, William Hastings thought he glimpsed the questing look in those narrow dark eyes again), and added, even more breezily: 'And there are plenty of pretty girls here, of course.'

Dickon's eyes never looked lost. Dickon's decisiveness was one of the qualities Hastings admired in the Duke. Hastings knew there was a fatal softness in his own soul that might, one day, do for him; it made him appreciate the cheerful ruthlessness of Dickon's approach to life even more. Dickon's flintiness had saved him once already, on that night they'd been half-walking, half-running across the Wash after everything had gone so wrong at Doncaster; when the tide had come rushing treacherously in on them and some of his men, with mud and sand gluing their wet boots down, hadn't had the strength to pull up their exhausted legs to sprint to the tussocks of grass that suddenly meant safety. It was the knight right behind Hastings who'd been swept back into the boiling water – Thomas de Teffont, a Wiltshireman; Hastings still remembered the young man's look of terror as he was pulled back, wide eyes and mouth open in a soundless scream, teeth glittering in the moonlight. Hastings had been about to release his own hold on the grasses to stretch back for Teffont, who was hardly more than a boy; who shouldn't die there, when Dickon had stopped him. Dickon, one hand grabbing into the heart of a spindly bush, the other hand hard on Hastings' soaking brigandine. Dickon: a voice as cold as Hell frozen over, grating: 'Leave him. It's more important to save yourself.'

So Hastings was surprised to find he didn't completely believe in Dickon's breeziness today. The voice of the man who never dissembled didn't, for once, ring quite true; it carried a different message from the one in his eyes. Hastings listened with the beginning of curiosity as the duke went on, still casually, but with hungry eyes: 'Wasn't Lambert marrying off two daughters, anyway? The blonde one we've been hearing so much about ever since, but another one too – a redhead?'

Hastings nodded, suddenly swept away by the memory of his first sight of Jane Shore in Lambert's great hall at that wedding feast: Edward dancing with her until her cheeks flushed with roses and her teeth flashed in the smile that had swept him away.

Hastings had poured her a goblet of wine as Edward sat her down next to him. He'd leaned forward and given it to her himself, and she'd touched his hand for a fraction longer than she'd needed to, and looked at him with soft, shining eyes.

'Well,' Dickon's voice went on, with a hint of impatience, 'where is she now?'

'Who?' Hastings said blankly. Then, with slight embarrassment: 'Ah – the redhead.' He spread his arms wide in a parody of bewilderment and shook his head and let his courtier's smile – a smile of great charm – spread over his face. 'Married,' he replied, and shrugged a little more. 'So who can say?'

They walked out into Cheapside. Hastings could hear Dickon humming under his breath.

'Didn't you want to buy something too?' he said awkwardly, as they reached their horses. 'I thought you said . . .'

Dickon's eyes glinted at him with characteristic dry amusement over the knotted reins, as if relieved Hastings wasn't too love-struck to have noticed his friend had come away empty-handed. 'Nothing caught my fancy,' he answered easily.

Isabel wouldn't wait any longer. She knew her father would sulk for months. She was past caring. She called in a notary from Guildhall the very next morning to draw up the apprenticeship agreement, as soon as she'd taken in the two dark robes. She didn't want to be dissuaded. It would be too easy to give in and go home.

The young man who turned up at Catte Street was the younger of the two Lynom boys; the tall, clean-cut sons of Hugh Lynom, silk merchant of Old Jewry, the Prattes' and the Shores' closest neighbour; the boys every girl in the Mercery had always dreamed of marrying. They were twins: so alike Isabel had never been able to tell them apart, though she thought this one was called Robert.

But the sight of his eyes (topaz, she remembered Elizabeth Marchpane calling the colour of the Lynom boys' eyes; no, manticore, Anne Hagour had dreamily contradicted her: man-tiger) reminded her of the one definite thing she knew about them: that they'd both chosen not to go into their father's business but to train as lawyers instead. Their father had gone round telling people, with wistfulness in his voice and hurt in his eyes, 'they say there are opportunities I'm too old to understand in government; they'll see the world and better themselves faster outside the Mercery, they say.' Thomas had told his father that with all the redistribution of lands and estates that the wars had brought, he'd get richer faster if he went into drawing up property transfer agreements. Robert had told his father he'd get richer faster if he stayed in the City but went into representing City merchants and the Guildhall in negotiations with the Royal Wardrobe. They weren't the only young men to see new horizons beyond the City walls; and everyone knew their father was longing to amass a big enough fortune to buy his way into the gentry anyway; but the fact of both sons leaving the Mercery had aroused comment. The selds had buzzed with it for weeks.

Isabel gritted her teeth. It was just her luck. A Lynom wasn't going to sympathise with her decision to sign up for a ten-year silkworking apprenticeship. If she wasn't careful he might even delay things; let her father know before the papers were signed and sealed.

For once she was grateful for Alice Claver's warhorse ways. 'Sit down, young man, and take down the terms,' her mother-in-law rattled out, breaking through the visitor's formal regrets over the death in the family; and the Lynom boy sat obediently at the table and began unpacking his box of pens and parchment. If Isabel hadn't felt certain nothing could make Alice Claver nervous, she might have thought the silkwoman was in even more haste than she was. 'Term, ten years. Premium, five pounds.'

The Lynom boy's good-humoured eyes were laughing. He could feel her haste too. And he was intrigued. Isabel thought for a moment he must sense a story to tell the selds – at least until she remembered that he'd changed his own life to get away from the selds. Perhaps, she thought, reassured, he was the right person to be making this document after all.

As it turned out, he didn't try to delay. He'd become a lawyer through and through. He wrote the usual promises into the document: that Isabel would cherish her mistress's interests, not waste her goods or trade without her permission, behave well, and not withdraw unlawfully from her service; that Alice Claver would 'teach, take charge of, and instruct her apprentice' in her craft, chastise her in meet fashion, and find her footwear, clothing, a bed, and all other suitable necessities.

Alice Claver looked over his shoulder. 'What's this?' she said sharply as he carried on writing. He stopped, looking confused, and ran his hand through his tawny-blond hair. He'd started to add the final boilerplate phrase of contracts involving girl apprentices – that Isabel should be treated *pulchrior modo*, more kindly than a boy. 'She's my family,' Alice Claver said brusquely. 'How else would I treat her?' She barked with laughter. After a pause, Isabel laughed too. The Lynom boy looked from the older woman to the younger, both in their black gowns. Then he smiled and crossed out the offending line. But Isabel felt his gaze linger curiously on her as he packed up his pens.

'My fee for drawing up the indentures and registering them with the Mercers' Company clerk is one shilling,' the Lynom boy said, sanding what he'd written with fluid muscles.

Alice Claver nodded. 'Do it today,' she said.

*   *   *

The Lynom boy brought copies of the documents back two days later, duly registered. Isabel received him, wondering at the discreet sympathy in his eyes until he gave her the other letter he was also carrying for her.

It was a cold, brief letter from her father: formal notice that he was rewriting his will to leave his estate to Jane, 'my one dutiful daughter'. Isabel could see from Robert Lynom's expression that he knew what it said.

She glanced over it. Nodded curtly. Let the hand holding the letter flutter down to her side. Kept the anger and contempt and hurt boiling inside her tightly shut down. She knew what her father would want her to do, but she wasn't going to weep or run begging to him to change his mind. She wouldn't let herself be bullied. She was learning not to let her face show her feelings.

Alice Claver and Anne Pratte swept in. When Alice Claver saw the young lawyer, she held her hand out for the documents she was expecting. He smiled, bowed courteously, and passed them over. She gave them a careful reading, then grunted with satisfaction. She tucked them into her large purse. She didn't look at Isabel or ask what the letter still held loosely in her apprentice's hand was.

Alice fixed Robert Lynom with a sudden, fierce smile. Now the business was done, she had time for conversation. 'I hear Lord Hastings has been buying in the selds. In person. From', she gestured sideways at Isabel without catching her eye, 'my new apprentice's father.'

Isabel looked away; perhaps she should have told Alice Claver about Lord Hastings' visit herself, but her quarrel with her father had made her forget it. However, Robert Lynom knew enough to satisfy the silkwoman. He nodded easily. 'He has indeed,' he said, including Isabel in his answering smile, putting away his papers in his box. 'A cloth of green figured velvet. From Lucca, if I remember rightly. They say he paid a good price for it too.'

It was natural to discuss this new phenomenon. It was unusual for noblemen to visit the markets themselves. If they were of the blood royal, they usually placed orders through the King's Wardrobe in Old Jewry, and administrators such as Robert Lynom would find merchants to meet their requirements. Otherwise lords might send representatives to the markets to bargain for luxury goods in their place.

But unusual things had been happening since King Edward came back, and Lord Hastings, his closest adviser, was an unusual nobleman anyway. He'd survived the times of exile and poverty by living on his considerable wits; he'd gradually turned the meagre estates of his inheritance into a magnate's fabulous wealth. Now that his lord was back on the throne, Hastings was showing he wasn't the kind to stand grandly on his aristocratic dignity, willing only to live by the sword. As a mark of the King's trust, he'd recently been named Governor of Calais, and the markets were full of the rumour that he planned not just to run the garrison there but to take a personal interest in the port's trade as well. There was even talk that Lord Hastings was courting the staplers of Calais, who controlled all the exports of raw wool from England, by becoming a merchant of the staple himself. They said he had the wit and imagination to find common ground with anyone, noble or not. Remembering his merry, kindly eyes from the wedding feast (before he started staring so hungrily at Jane, at least), Isabel could believe it.

Alice Claver wanted to know more, but she didn't want to show her envy of John Lambert's deal too openly. She didn't ask the price her competitor had charged for his cloth. Instead, she asked casually: 'And did his lordship say what he was going to do with the velvet?'

Isabel was trying to think of nothing more than enjoying the story. She would have time enough later to fret about

81

her father; there was nothing she could do about him anyway. She leaned encouragingly towards Robert Lynom.

'He didn't,' the Lynom boy said briefly.

But Anne Pratte knew more. She always did. She'd quietly taken up a seat on a little footstool by the window; she had a piece of work in her hands; but she was following everything like a small bloodhound. She picked up the narrative by piping up, with gusto: 'But there's talk, of course. They say he sent it as a gift to a lady, don't they?'

At her voice, Robert Lynom suddenly started to look excruciatingly uncomfortable. He stopped; bit his tongue; blushed. Isabel couldn't understand what was going through his head. 'Well,' Alice said impatiently. 'Who to? You must know. You'll have done the paperwork, won't you? Spit it out, man.'

He mumbled something. Even his scalp was on fire. He picked up his box.

Alice Claver planted herself one step in front of him, her smile half a threat.

'Don't leave us hanging,' she said, more command than plea. 'Who was the cloth for?'

He composed himself. Decided upon his choice of who to offend, and made himself smile at Alice Claver. Turning sharply away from Anne Pratte and slightly away from Isabel, he said: 'They say – though I can't be sure they're right – to your new apprentice's sister, Mistress Shore.'

Alice Claver almost choked. 'No,' she said, with a mixture of shock, disbelief, envy and amusement. 'Really?' Then, as if remembering Isabel's presence, she clapped a friendly hand on Robert Lynom's back and ushered him out towards the door. Twittering excitedly, Anne Pratte followed; she wasn't an unkind woman usually, but the thrill of that story had eclipsed any worries she might otherwise have had about Isabel's feelings.

Isabel thought he wouldn't dare even glance back at

her. He disliked market gossip, and he'd known what was in the letter her father had written her; he'd be miserably aware of having added to her worries about her family with the story they'd bullied out of him.

But he did look back, from the doorway. 'Good day, Mistress Claver,' he said bravely; and, in a rush, 'My apologies. I shouldn't have . . .'

She met his eyes and nodded, forgiving him. And it was the memory of that moment of mutual bravery, and the gratefulness on his face, that gave her the courage to decide, once she was alone with the letter, not to think about it any more, or rage against her father, or envy Jane's beauty or aristocratic admirers. She was a Claver now. Her life was here.

If Isabel thought she'd be taken straight back to Alice Claver's inner sanctum, the silk storeroom, as soon as she'd apprenticed herself, she was undeceived that night over dinner.

The apprenticeship timetable Alice Claver outlined, with a hard look, had no space in it for musing over the finest luxuries of civilisation, or for planning vast wholesale purchase strategies. It involved mastering all the eye-straining, low-grade, repetitive, menial tasks of retail silkwork first – the jobs Alice Claver put out to the wrinkled, skinny shepster and throwster women who worked from five-foot-wide stalls huddled outside the biggest selling markets, the Crown and Broad Selds, along their frontages on Cheapside and down their side doors on Soper Lane. Not just twisting imported raw silk into threads; but throwing it into yarns ready for use, and spinning, and dyeing, and turning seams. She was to learn every stage of the process from taking the strands of raw silk gathered by Italian reelers from silkworm cocoons to selling manufactured silk, on the street, by the ounce or the pound, as sewing silk, open silk, twine silk or rough web silk, the stuff used to make loops on which to attach warp threads while weaving, so they could be separated into two sets to let the weft thread pass between them. And she wasn't just to learn these humble jobs, but to sit outside in all weathers with the hunched shepsters and throwsters and dyers, learning from them, and about them.

The Prattes sneaked a look at each other. Isabel knew it was a test. Alice Claver must be doing this deliberately. She could imagine her mother-in-law's voice saying, with grim satisfaction, 'Let's knock the nonsense out of her'. She must think Isabel would protest. Isabel wasn't going to. She kept her eyes humbly down on her untouched food and nodded.

'It's only for a year,' Anne Pratte said reassuringly, in her papery little voice, as if trying to soften Alice Claver's blow. 'The next stage is embroidery. But we already know how good you are at that. So it won't be long before you can move on to the real thing and start learning weaving. Narrow-loom work. Ribbons. Cauls. Laces. London's glory. The finest silk piecework in Christendom. And,' daringly, flinching from Alice Claver's cold gaze, she leaned forward and patted Isabel's hand, 'I've asked Alice if I can teach you that.'

Isabel looked up, surprised and touched. Four Pratte eyes were on her, brimming with kindness. The Prattes were both ignoring Alice Claver, still glowering behind them.

She rose in the dark all winter. She went to work holding a candle in chapped, raw hands, like all the other poor girls in brown and grey woollens working in the selds, whose existence she'd never been more than half-aware of until now. Like them, in those clothes, she'd become invisible to everyone from the Mercery's richer, gayer families – even her own father. He walked straight at her in the street – she sometimes felt, as she jumped out of his way, that if she didn't move he'd walk straight through her. The pretty merchants' daughters she'd grown up with didn't mean to snub her. They just wafted by the quiet dun mouse of a girl on their way to sit embroidering at their fathers' stalls in their spring-coloured puffs of satin. They couldn't see her.

Sometimes she felt like a living ghost – transparent to everyone she'd ever known. No one minded nowadays if, while she was throwing or twisting silk or turning a seam, her eyes filled with hot tears that crept down her face until, in the autumn winds, her cheeks became as raw and chapped as her fingers. No one minded, because no one noticed, as long as she turned out the required number of threads or piles of fluffiness or bright twisted yarns, when she would be rewarded with a rough pat, or a grunt, from whichever shabby mistress she was being loaned to for the day. And she found the hotness of her own tears a comfort – a proof to herself that she was there, after all; not quite transparent and emptied of the fluids of life; not quite invisible.

The tears were for Thomas, she told herself. So was the shrivelling pain she always felt under her heart, always, as if her body were being drained away by a tide that was pulling her off into the darkness. But sometimes, as her hands moved through the silk, with a deft life that felt independent of her mind, she thought the tears, and the pain, might after all be just for herself.

She talked to Thomas in her head. Or she tried. Tried to keep him alive; tried to take comfort in remembering his look of fuzzy astonishment when he woke up to find her next to him, his delighted snugglings and the little kisses he'd place, shyly, like acts of worship, on her hands or forehead. But all she had to tell him, apart from how she missed him, missed the warmth of a time when someone needed her, was about the detail of her days drudging in the selds. And what would he have understood of any of that?

Sometimes, when it felt too hard to explain to Thomas why she'd kept submissively quiet when Alice Claver or one of her underlings pulled a piece of work apart and told her to start again, when she couldn't even begin to imagine the look on his face, she'd talk in her head to the man from the church instead. He'd have understood why she gritted her teeth through the cold that went into her bones; took the telling-off and the false starts so patiently. Gradually his became the face she conjured up to talk to in whatever corner she was working in; a stranger, really, but someone who knew about purposefulness, who could coolly plan ahead. 'He'd be proud of me if he saw me now,' she thought stoutly sometimes, 'doing the right thing by Thomas, and helping fate to bring me a better future into the bargain.' Though at other times, in the moments of despair when her guts felt full of ground glass, when she stopped believing she was anything but a pair of hands twitching outside a grey dress, when the darkness seemed to be going to last forever, she'd sometimes also think: 'No, he'd be horrified. I've taken the wrong way. I'm lost.'

She came home to Alice Claver's house most nights too tired to think. She was grateful for that. All she had energy to do was to curl up alone on her grand, empty marriage bed, stretching out her cramped muscles, whispering to Thomas as she rubbed warmth back into her blue-white fingers.

With time, though, she found there were consolations. Long after she'd lost one world she realised she'd somehow gained another: the busy, raucous, teeming world of the other hard-working women in browns and greys: the ones who did the jobs other people made fortunes from, the ones she herself had only just begun to notice.

Isabel had grown up at the smart northern end of the Mercery – the roads leading up to Catte Street and the Guildhall beyond: grand Milk Street and Honey Lane and Colechurch Lane; Old Jewry, to the east beyond St Thomas of Acre, where the Prattes and Lynoms and Shores lived, and where the Royal Wardrobe was, the depot for all royal cloth purchases. Now, running errands for Alice Claver taught her every inch of the industrial south side of Cheapside too: the sunless snakings of Popkirtle, Thenwend and Gropecunt Lanes, behind Cordwainer Street; every tenement, warehouse and patch of garden, and every jobbing mercer and silkwoman wife, stallkeeper, denizen, stranger and pieceworker living and working in them.

For anyone willing to listen, those lanes were alive with talk.

The silk workers she was farmed out to quickly forgot to be shy of her. Sometimes Isabel had her ear bent by the forbidding Katherine Dore, the throwster who was taking her ex-apprentice Joan Woulbarowe to court for stealing £12 13s 4d of silk. Sometimes she'd get caught, somewhere in Soper Lane, by gangling, wild-elbowed Joan Woulbarowe, out of jail now, preparing for her next appeal appearance at the Court of Arches while she stayed with her aunt, Rose Trapp, in a tenement in Lad Lane. Joan Woulbarowe said her mistress had wanted to keep her in service once her term was up, and had invented the whole tarradiddle as a way of trapping her to stay on as unpaid help. Isabel never got to the bottom of the story.

Sometimes Isabel learned things about her own Lambert family from the market talk. When Agnes Langton died at Stourbridge Fair, her terrifyingly overbearing mother, Jane Langton, the widow of a saddler, who knew nothing of the silk trade, had swept out from a hitherto un-suspected tenement behind St Benet Sherehog Church and completed Agnes's enormous transaction with two Genoese merchants for silk goods worth £300 15s – then sold the lot on to John Lambert for a cheeky £350, enough to keep her comfortably in her old age, and retired to Norfolk. 'He doesn't keep his ear to the ground, that John Lambert,' Agnes Brundyssch the throwster said comfort-ably. 'Never did.'

But no one on the street had a bad word to say about Alice Claver. She was the heroine of the markets. Alice Claver was the protector of the poor, because she wrote the petitions every market woman wanted: the *Stop the Italians* petitions. The grey and brown women hated the Italians, who tried to undercut the delicate small silk goods that they made in London by selling their own country-women's imported goods at cut price. Isabel knew that Alice Claver got William Pratte to help her draft the peti-tions that she and a gaggle of lesser silkwomen presented regularly to Parliament, using proper legal language. But they didn't care about him; he was invisible to them. They believed it was purely thanks to Alice Claver that they'd got four Acts of Parliament through, protecting them from the greedy Lombards, who as everyone knew were worse than the French and Hanse and Flemish put together. 'You have to be tough to stop the Italians,' Isabel Fremely said, nodding at Agnes Brundyssch. 'Mistress Claver's more than a woman. She's a force of nature.'

As winter turned to spring – every now and then a fresh breeze blowing through the stalls with a promise of blossom tomorrow – Isabel sometimes found herself breathing in deep and thinking, 'I'm still here' and 'I've done it.' And when she did, it was the face of the man in the church that creased into an encouraging wolf-smile in response. Quite what she'd done, beyond surviving the winter, wasn't clear even to herself. But sometimes she thought it was keeping quiet to the market women about her personal sorrows, her times of weakness; sticking with iron-hard determination to her pledge to become a good apprentice to Alice Claver, not to sink into peevish resentments. When she smelled spring coming, and heard the respect of the tough women around her for her mistress, she realised she agreed. She'd learned to share their grudging admiration for Alice Claver's limitless commitment to her work.

Isabel kept out of Jane's way all winter. She didn't know what to say to her. She was mastering the resentment she might have felt for Alice Claver; and she didn't want to have to start struggling to master resentment against her sister. Besides, it would have been excruciating if Jane had started trying to make peace between her and their father, charming him with a flick of golden blondeness or an alluring white hand on his sleeve.

She saw her sister on Sundays, at St Thomas of Acre, and every time Jane appeared in church she'd be dressed in something finer than the last time, and her honey skin would be softer and her eyes brighter than ever before. Throughout the prayers, Isabel would be aware of Jane looking shyly over, sweetly as ever, as if trying to meet her eye. But Isabel kept her own eyes down. And when they did stop to talk on the street afterwards it was hard to know how to take up the old companionship of children who'd shared a bed and squabbled over toys. Jane hardly mentioned Will Shore, who anyway was always off somewhere abroad – Bruges, or Cologne – building up his business. Isabel thought it might be because Jane didn't want to remind her of her own widowed state. If that was Jane's notion of delicacy, she was grateful for it; but she didn't enjoy the small talk about luxurious living that Jane chose to go in for instead. Jane had taken up hawking, she said. She was working on a tapestry of St George killing the dragon. John Lambert was going to take her as his partner to the hunt King Edward had invited him to at Eltham; she was going to have new sleeves made for her yellow silk for the occasion. And her eyes would seek Isabel's out, gently offering to share her pleasure at life, then lower themselves again, with a hint of disappointment, when Isabel failed to respond.

If Alice Claver was aware of the silence growing between Isabel and her sister, or of the breakdown in communications between Isabel and her father, she didn't show it, even though her eyes were always on Isabel, boring into her back in the selds or in the house. She never talked about Thomas, though Isabel longed painfully to hear someone else talking about him with love and pain. It was as if Alice Claver didn't want to share her memories of him with a girl she now treated as an outsider. But her animosity was gone. Isabel couldn't read what was in the quietness that had replaced it.

After church on Sundays, instead of visiting her family or going with Alice Claver to eat with the Prattes, Isabel filled her free hours by working on the embroidered purse she'd started making for Thomas during the siege. The delicate work brought her numb fingers back to life. She sat alone by her window, watching her needle flash up and down, sewing tiny stitches into his initials, trying to think of each stitch as a prayer for her husband's soul, an act of remembrance. She got Agnes Brundyssch to teach her how to make cord for the braid. She got Isabel Fremely to cadge her some leftover Cyprus gold thread from David Galganete, the sharp Genoese merchant she bought from, to make tassels.

She finished the purse in time for Thomas's obit, a year after his death. But by the June morning when she quietly laid her offering on the altar at St Thomas of Acre, under cover of a cloud of incense and the drone of the chantry priest, she knew Jane had been right to say her feelings for Thomas might fade. She was still full of pain, but it had become vague and cloudy, without a source. She could hardly recall his face or voice now. It was as if she'd sewn all her memories into the purse and had nothing left.

Even the purse, which had started as a love token, had become something else. For months now, she'd found herself taking pride in it as a sampler of the fine silkwork she hoped to master. What she wanted most in the world now was for Alice Claver to pick up her work from the altar and admire it enough to send her to Anne Pratte for lessons. Isabel bent her head in prayer as Alice Claver's hand strayed towards the purse.

5

A time for everything, and everything at the proper time. Alice Claver waited out Anne and William, with their regrets; Father Ignatius; the pompous, wordy, hand-wringing John Lambert, and his idle elder daughter, the long one with the flashing eyes and teeth and with breasts precariously laced into a bodice that might have been suitable for court but had no place at a sober City memorial service.

She knew exactly what she was going to say. She'd thought it out carefully. But that didn't stop her rehearsing it a few more times as she tapped her fingers on the table, willing Lambert to take himself and his family off home, impatiently tweaking off the heads of flame of any candles she could see that had burned down to anything like their last inch, and prodding at the platters of cheese whenever the boy passed, a gesture amounting to a broad hint to start clearing up even before the guests had gone.

Even so, when she was finally left alone with her charge, she didn't know how to begin. It wasn't that Isabel's modest gown, cautiously bowed shoulders and watchful eyes actually conveyed anything she could construe as reproach. It was more that the neat figure, slipping quietly in and out of the house, working in almost complete silence at home or in the selds, lowering her eyes whenever she felt Alice Claver looking at her to contemplate her own raw hands with their purple and yellow blotches from dye and their calluses and ridges from market work, had begun to remind Alice Claver uncomfortably of her own younger self.

Alice Claver was proud of that enterprising younger self. She'd been raised by an uncle in Derby, while her parents were living in France supplying cloth to the garrisons. She'd worked her fingers to the bone for her foster family, though they'd never been close; neither side had been sorry when, once she turned twelve, her silk skills were well-enough known that she'd been offered an apprenticeship with Robert Large in London. London had felt glamorous: bustling, big, busy, full of possibilities, and, best of all, safe. The walls and gates and patrols and carts and cheerful push and shove helped banish the memory of the empty Derbyshire countryside – the brambles and scrub advancing over what people said had once been fields; birdsong and the rustle of animals where there'd once been fires in hearths; the skeletons of manor houses abandoned after the Black Death long ago; her uncle kicking over a collapsed wall in the forest, one of a strangled collection of stones in ivy that must have once been a village, telling her, with gloomy relish, 'This is where we Boothes came from. Right here. If this was a hundred years ago, you'd have seen dozens of people here. Working, praying, eating, raising children. Our blood. And none of them with the least idea they were all about to be wiped out. God rest their souls.'

It was lucky for her, she'd been told, that people today still lived with those ghosts and that the gravestones in the churchyards danced with skeletons; that everyone still reminisced over the warmer, richer, safer days when the land was full of fields and the fields were full of people. It was because the world had shrunk into this modern twilight of spectres and memories – and later, within her own memory, because the war had also begun taking its toll on the young men of Derby – that so many girls were encouraged to train in the guilds. Looking back, Alice knew that getting a trade had saved her. Her parents, stubbornly struggling to live in Normandy while their daughter was raised at home, went missing during the fall of France. There was no way of knowing whether they'd become part of the army of vagrants that straggled back to England or begged in the streets of Calais, or survived, for a while, in the forests. But by then, in her twenties, she'd established herself as a Londoner. Her parents were shadowy half-memories. Her real family had become the Large establishment at Catte Street: the other apprentices her brothers and sisters, as proud as Alice to be part of one of the best businesses in the Mercery. If she hadn't been a trained silkwoman; if she hadn't married Richard Claver out of the Large household and worked with him on making their business even bigger than Robert Large's, she'd have been lost too.

No, I've never been afraid of hard work, and it's made me who I am, she thought complacently, letting her mind dwell with irritation on the lounging, indolent, grinning Shore girl, who'd have been lost if she'd ever been called on to do an honest day's labour. Who'd never had to do such a thing, like so many children of the London rich. They were all the same: spoiled and idle, thought they were too good for it . . .

Alice Claver pulled herself up, feeling those certainties fade as she tried not to think of Thomas. She looked at the smaller, browner sister of that girl, with her face carefully wiped clean of expression; at the scars of work on those younger hands. A girl who hadn't been brought up to fear the emptiness of birdsong. A girl who'd grown up with expectations of wealth and ease. A girl who'd lost all that and yet taken on Alice Claver's hard apprenticeship without complaining.

'You've learned all you need to know from the markets,' Alice Claver said, feeling her lower jaw clamped to her head so that it was hard for the words to come out.

Isabel looked carefully up.

'You can start with Anne tomorrow. It's time for you to learn to make manufactured goods. Do the skilled work.'

Isabel looked down again. But Alice Claver had seen the light gleam in her eyes.

'You'll meet my Venetian supplier this week. Goffredo D'Amico. It's an important relationship,' she went on. 'He and another old friend of mine are staying with the Prattes. They'll eat here. I'd like you to join us . . .'

Alice could see Isabel realise there was more to come. The girl looked up; trying to puzzle out what she'd be asked.

'I wanted to get Thomas's obit behind us before starting work with D'Amico,' Alice Claver said. 'But there's one thing I've already talked over with him. I've arranged a loan.'

She looked almost beseechingly at Isabel. She didn't want the girl to take this as some sort of apology. 'For five hundred pounds. The sum your dower would have been.'

Isabel's eyebrows were beginning to rise.

'It's time for us both to take stock.' Alice Claver hurried over the words. She didn't want to mention Thomas's name. Thomas would have sorted himself out if God hadn't taken him back. She knew that Isabel knew that. 'There's no room for shirkers in my house. I'll need someone who can become a partner, once they're trained.

95

So I want you to know now that you're provided for. I'm going to make over the five hundred pounds to you as a dower. If you want to go off to your family, get married, you're free to. You've got the money. I can dissolve our contract. But you can still', and now she was looking down at her own rough hands, 'choose to stay.'

There was a long silence. She plaited her fingers, waiting. 'And work,' she added gruffly. 'Hard.'

When she did dare raise her eyes, there were no embarrassing transports of joy on the little heart-shaped face in front of her. Isabel was looking up at her, very seriously, with her eyes slightly narrowed. It was the look Alice Claver put on her own face when she was considering an offer. With a shock of what she thought might be gratitude, Alice Claver realised Isabel must have learned that look from her.

She was almost surprised to see Isabel's lips form the words: 'I would like to stay.'

Alice Claver felt the wide grin she reserved for the Prattes and her other old friends break out on her face; she was suddenly strangely short of breath. I've got used to having her around, she told herself. That must be why. Somewhere in the confused back-clap that followed, the bustle of sitting down and pouring out two cups and starting to describe tomorrow's work in something much closer to an everyday voice, then the move to the silk storeroom, Alice Claver felt the beginning of the same comfort she'd drawn from making friends, back in those first days at Catte Street, with Anne and William and the others; the smoothing out of differences, mistakes, flaws in the weave; the tying of bonds that might be strong enough to take the place of family.

Isabel could see Alice Claver was reassured to be in her storeroom. The diagonals of pink and gold light from the

96

windows made her wares shimmer. They transformed her too. She lost her gruffness. Her eyes sparkled. There was love in her voice.

She set out a brisk timetable for the rest of Isabel's voluntary apprenticeship. Two years to learn to sew each of the delicate small items that made manufactured silk-work London's glory – from transparent cauls for the hair, decorated with jewels and gold thread, to the laces and points needed to fit together the elaborate items of clothing made by the vestment-makers, to tasselled and embroidered and jewelled purses pulled tight by drawstrings and tied to the belt by purse strings, to the heavy strips of glittering embroidery, to orphreys for edging ecclesiastical robes, to ribbons, woven on a miniature narrow-loom, a box so small you could clamp it to the edge of a table – the only piece of equipment more complicated than a needle in English silkwork.

During those two years Isabel would also accompany Alice Claver to meetings with foreign silk merchants and aristocratic clients; she would go to the Royal Wardrobe when Alice Claver had a contract to supply royalty, and learn how to tender for work and the formalities for delivering it. She would learn some of the faces and the names of the most powerful people in the business. Once the two years were up, she'd start going with Alice Claver to the trade fairs at Bruges and Antwerp. There, she would begin to see how to make the large-scale wholesale deals considered the pinnacle of achievement for a silk merchant – choosing and buying the trade's greatest luxury, the whole silk cloths woven in the East and in Italy on full-size broadlooms, a skill not known in England. She'd learn how to import these cloths, each worth a substantial portion of a prince's annual rents, to make garments for the richest people in England.

'Why do we have to go abroad to buy whole silk cloths?'

97

Isabel ventured, feeling ignorant. 'Or pay the margins the Italians here take? Can't they be made in London?'

Alice Claver darted a bright, intense look at her, as if Isabel had intuited something extraordinary.

'We don't have the knowledge,' she answered, after a pause.

'Why?' Isabel asked. 'Surely it's just the same as weaving wool?'

She felt as she said it that she must be saying something stupid. But her question seemed to have opened the way to Alice Claver's heart.

Alice Claver's eyes were full of enthusiasm, but she shook her head. 'Far more complicated,' she said decisively. 'Finer, for one thing. Venetian export damasks have 9,600 silk threads in a single arm's-width, a *braccio*. Even cloth of gold and plain velvets have 7,200 threads. And to get the patterns in the cloth, you need far more than one line of warp threads and one line of wefts; you might have half a dozen of each in a single cloth, each needing something different done to it. Considering what silk costs, no one could afford to just start experimenting. You'd need to know the secret before you even thought of trying to build, or thread up, a full-size loom – as long as two men and as wide as another – with good-quality silk. It would bankrupt a king to start working it out from scratch.

'And it's not just the number of threads. It's knowing how to mix the different imports. Look,' she went on. It was clear she'd thought about this many times. She started pulling out bolts of stuff to show Isabel how threads from different lands could be mixed together in the same piece of silk cloth; how a single bolt could be made of Spanish silk warp and Persian silk weft for a satin; or a Syrian silk warp and Greek silk weft for a damask; how two kinds of silk from different regions could be put together and thrown to form a single thread. She said some silks, such as *orsogli*, were especially suitable for warp threads; that all types of cloth could use weft threads of Persian *leggibenti*, *catangi* or *talani*; that velvet-like satins needed weft threads of the *calabrese*, the *catanzana*, and the *crespolina* productions; that the *siciliana* was right for heavy satins and that medium-thick silk threads, for slightly lighter cloths, were called *di donna* and *granegli*. Isabel learned that silk from Almeria was used for taffetas and satins, and silk from Abruzzi for *zetani*, fabrics made with a satin weave and sometimes with a velvety pile.

'These are just the odds and ends of knowledge I've picked up over the years from buying silk,' Alice Claver said modestly. 'But to weave a silk cloth that would be distinctive, and saleable, you'd need to have mastered all this and more. Much more.'

Isabel surprised a yearning look on her mistress's face.

'To have a hope of succeeding, you'd need a three-way deal on a scale no one has ever done in London,' Alice Claver went on.

She'd thought about it a lot, Isabel could see. Alice Claver couldn't shake off her longing to do this vast deal, however impossible she was making it sound. 'First, you'd need an Italian master willing to share his secrets with you,' she said briskly, lifting up one finger. 'And that's a rare beast, let me tell you. It would be easier to catch a unicorn.'

She lifted a second finger. 'Next, he'd need to get permission from his city government in Italy to import a full workshop of craftsmen here to set up. And the Venetian silk boards hate letting good people go. So you'd have to factor in years of bribing bureaucrats. Nothing happens fast in Italy.'

Isabel nodded, reluctantly. It did sound intimidating.

'But the biggest problem would be the third one,' Alice

said, looking gloomily at the third finger she was raising to wave in Isabel's face. 'Money. Even if you had the other parts of the deal in place, who would pay? You'd need a rich backer at the London end. A very rich backer. Someone willing to lose vast amounts of money every year for decades while an entire industry was set up. You might not see a return for twenty years. But there'd be wages and houses and materials and costs to cover all the while. Silk doesn't come cheap. It would be beyond the means of anyone I can think of, except the King, unless by some miracle the entire guild of mercers joined forces to back it instead.'

The silkwoman laughed mirthlessly. 'They certainly never would. They'd be too scared. The Lombards here make half their money out of importing silk cloths to sell to us; and the rest from banking for London merchants. They wouldn't take kindly to Londoners trying to set up a business that competed with theirs. And since our mercers do their banking with the London Italians, they couldn't cross them without having their trade accounts cut off,' she snapped her fingers, 'just like that. No one would run that risk. You might get rich in twenty years by weaving silk cloths, but how would you buy your ready-made silks at Antwerp and Bruges until then, without those accounts?'

She shrugged. She looked down at the silks she'd pulled out, tutted, and began resignedly to fold them away, as if she were packing away the impossible dream at the same time.

Then she stopped again; she couldn't quite bear to drop the subject. She gave Isabel a hard look. 'And while we're talking about impossible, there's this too,' she said. 'Gossip. Even if you did manage to find a way to get going, you'd have to spend all those years of setting up keeping your plans a complete secret from every Italian merchant in

London. But can you imagine starting something so big, which would employ so many people, without the markets being full of it?' She grunted. 'There'd always be talk. It's all impossible.'

She sighed. Looked at the greens and golds still spread around her, blazing in the sunset; the colours of dreams.

Isabel said stubbornly: 'The money's the real thing, though. Wouldn't the King pay?'

Alice Claver snorted. 'Him?' she answered succinctly. 'Broke. Too many wars.'

Isabel sighed. Alice was right, she realised; the King was always borrowing money from the City. 'Someone will work out how, sooner or later, though . . .' she said wistfully.

Her mistress's face brightened. 'Yes, and make a fortune,' she agreed robustly. 'At least I hope so. London silkwomen are the best in Christendom. It's against nature for us to let the Italians have the best of the market. There must be more for us in the future than fiddling around with tassels and braids and bits of ribbon!'

She guffawed as if she and Isabel were old friends. Astonished to have been given a glimpse of Alice Claver's heart's desire, Isabel hesitantly joined in.

6

'So is it true?' Anne Pratte asked, eyes coquettishly down on her flying fingers. 'What they're saying about your sister?'

Isabel had her fingers awkwardly up in the air, each with a bow of blue silk around them, and the other end of the blue threads tied, six feet away, to a nail in the wall. The braiding technique involved swapping bows from one finger to the next, using four fingers on each hand in a complicated chain of movements, each round of which created an elaborate knot that lengthened the fingerloop braid by a fraction. She'd been hoping to astonish her new teacher with her skill.

She had no idea what Anne Pratte could have heard about Jane. She should have known, though. She was coming to appreciate how important it was to know what people were saying. A rumour might mean a concealed truth; guessing a secret might give inside information that might then translate into a deal on advantageous terms. So the question made her drop one loop, then another. She hissed in a breath.

'Pick it up, dear, quickly,' Anne Pratte said calmly, taking in the tangle of threads and instantly understanding what was going on with them. 'You're on bow reversed; pick up the side below, not the side above; then lower the bows.' Without for a second pausing the lightning rhythm of her own hand movements, in and out, with a haze of blue loops whisking on and off her fingers, and the cord, which would be used as the drawstring for a purse, already at least a foot long, she went on, in the same meditative tone: 'They say Jane Shore is going to divorce her husband.'

'Oh dear,' Anne Pratte added fretfully a moment later, looking across again. 'Whatever have you done with that braid now?'

Anne Pratte let Isabel out early when Isabel said she wanted to visit her sister. She softened visibly when Isabel told her she'd been meaning to tell Jane she'd moved inside the Claver house to start learning fine silkwork.

There was no one at the Shore house on Old Jewry. It was shut up. Isabel found Jane in the garden of John Lambert's house instead, even though their father was away in the Low Countries. She was sitting on a bench, bareheaded, with the sun turning her waist-length blonde hair to a white-gold flame. She was reading a French romance; one of the new printed ones from Gutenberg. She was wearing a green velvet robe, with an emerald-in-the-heart pendant round her neck. There was a little smile on her face, and she was humming.

'You probably know more than I do,' she said coyly, in answer to Isabel's abrupt question. She didn't seem surprised by it, any more than she did by Isabel's sudden appearance at the Lambert house for the first time in months. It all seemed quite natural to her. She was used to people wanting to know her business. 'What are they saying?'

It took Isabel what seemed like hours to drag it out of

her sister, in a welter of embarrassment and euphemism. Will Shore had never beaten his wife, or neglected her (except for his ledgers), or been cruel in any worse way than to bore her. But he couldn't perform the act of love. 'We've never . . . never . . . you know,' Jane muttered, and Isabel first nodded, then shook her head, with the smell of Thomas's body suddenly filling her nostrils. She shut her mind to it; pursed her lips to keep memory away. Jane was giggling in what sounded like girlish embarrassment.

The four-year age gap between them used to mean that Jane always seemed grown-up and sophisticated to Isabel, whatever she did. But when Isabel heard that pretty tinkle of a laugh she suddenly felt older than her elder sister. Jane didn't seem to know the meaning of pain. A divorce would publicly shame Will Shore forever, Isabel thought. She hardly knew him, but he seemed harmless enough: skinny and hard-working and dull. And she could just imagine Katherine Dore and Agnes Brundyssch's response to the gossip. The delight. The catcalls. The gestures. He'd be destroyed.

'Why a divorce?' she asked. 'Why can't you just quietly get an annulment? If the marriage hasn't . . . hasn't really . . .' She collected herself. 'It seems cruel.'

Jane's answer was strangely light. 'Well, he's gone to Bruges to hide his blushes,' she said casually. 'Anyway, he refused to talk about an annulment. I did ask. I think he thought I'd just shut up if he said no. But I won't.' She tilted her chin up; Isabel thought she had all the confidence of an indulged child that things would go her way. She went on, a little defiantly: 'Why should I? Non-consummation of a marriage is grounds for divorce. It's the purpose of holy wedlock to allow women to bear children; to settle for less is to deny God's will.'

Isabel gaped. Those sounded like someone else's words. Jane wasn't usually hard. Whose advice was she taking?

'Who's paying for the hearing?' she asked, groping for the truth. Not Will, surely? And not their father. He must be furious, however gentle he'd always been with Jane. It would cost a fortune, and he'd be humiliating himself. He'd arranged the marriage in the first place.

The question made Jane shift in her seat, and pleat the cloth of her dress. Isabel looked hard at her. Jane wasn't good at secrets. She was definitely hiding something. 'Father,' Jane said eventually. But she blushed as she said it.

'Why?' Isabel asked blankly. Jane only looked demure and shrugged, like a cat getting a speck of dirt off its gleaming coat.

'Of course, he's not happy . . .' she offered. And she put her hand on Isabel's arm, cajolingly. 'I'm not either.'

Jane Shore didn't know how to sound serious. Everything always came out with a giggle and a shrug, as though she didn't quite believe in what she was saying. It had been like that since she'd grown so tall and men had started hanging on her every word, looking foolishly happy, then, equally inexplicably, getting angry with her. They all seemed to assume she must be deliberately exerting some sort of influence over them; that she was in control of the effect she had; when the reality was that she understood neither the open-mouthed, moonstruck beginnings of their overtures nor the bitterness that followed; she just felt guilty, as if she agreed with them that she must, in some way she didn't understand, be to blame. Which made her giggle, and shrug, as if she was perpetually excusing herself. Which she was. She could see from her sister's unsympathetic face now that she was failing to convey the miserable reality of her marriage. She couldn't blame Isabel for not understanding, exactly. She just wished she was better at explaining herself.

It had started with the wedding night. Will's big eyes, with the black smudges underneath, opened wide and accusing; his little mouth pursing up small and round and ugly. Like a cat's behind, she thought, with a miserable giggle. Sneering at her. The remarks. That first night it had all been about dancing with the King. 'If you could have seen yourself. No one knew where to put themselves. You were panting over him like a dog on heat.' But what else could she have done but dance with the King if he asked her? If he came to her wedding party? She didn't ask, and Will didn't offer an explanation. After all the happiness and energy of the party, she felt as shamed as if he'd poured dirty water on her.

After that, there was always something she seemed to be doing wrong, and whatever she did to try to put things right only seemed to make things worse. It wasn't that he couldn't make love to her; the problem was that he wouldn't. When she'd first tried to kiss him, twining her legs through his, he'd pushed her away. She'd felt like a whore. When she'd tried to sleep quietly at his side and not disturb him, he'd woken her up, repeatedly, through the night; shaking her spitefully; mouthing at her, 'You're snoring!'

'But Isabel never told me I snored,' she'd stammered, trying to defend herself but not knowing how. He only pursed his mouth up again and took himself, wrapped in a sheet, off to another room.

She felt uglier every time he moved his arms or legs another fastidious inch away from her, as if she smelled or her breath were rank; there was a pained look his face took on at the sight of her that cut her to the quick. Once he'd brought home a basket of pomegranates and she'd burst into delighted laughter. It must be a peace token, she'd thought.

'Are those for me?' she'd asked, looking at him with hope. 'Shall we share them? Shall I peel you one?'

And he'd smiled like cold steel before answering: 'Well,

dear wife, I don't know that you've done anything to deserve treats,' and, laughing, had taken the basket away.

Sometimes he'd end a conversation in which she was trying to suggest a visit or a dinner or an outing with the casual line, 'That might be good – if I loved you'; sometimes he'd tell her she broke her bread too aggressively, or cut her meat like a peasant; or that she walked clumsily, or drank too much, or was a slattern in the house; or he'd just remark on how different the two of them were, as if inviting her to ask in what way (she quickly learned not to, if she wanted to avoid being hurt). And sometimes he'd give a long-suffering sigh and ask her to stop caterwauling, and she'd realise she must have been singing under her breath while she sewed.

She had tried; she really had. At least for a while. But it had so quickly all come to seem hopeless. And when her father had asked her to go with him to one or two of the court functions he'd started being invited to she'd been thrilled to discover how easy it was, as soon as she got out of the poisonous atmosphere of her new house in Old Jewry (she couldn't think of it as a home), to sparkle and laugh again.

But even that had only made things worse. When her husband got it into his head that she was sleeping with the King there was no appeasing him. 'You slut, you whore, you dog,' he'd say conversationally – it was the chatty ordinariness of his voice that most frightened her, 'have you no shame?' It made no difference what words she used to deny it; how many times she widened her eyes, put a pleading hand on his arm, and said, 'But it was just a hunt', or, 'I was with my father all day.'

So Jane was grateful beyond belief that the hearing at the Court of Arches was set for just two weeks hence. Will would be back from Bruges by then. She could only pray that he would actually turn up.

She was desperate for it to be properly over. She didn't want to have to giggle and shrug apologetically and submit to any more hard stares from people who seemed to think it must be all her fault. Even Isabel, who she knew had a kind heart, but whose way of listening to news was so unnerving; who was sitting now as Jane remembered her always having done while she thought about things: tucked up on herself like a little ginger cat, knees under chin, hands round knees. Her eyes, looking hard and cold. Not blinking. Not touching. Not saying a word.

'Isn't there anything else?' Isabel asked in the end. She still didn't understand. 'Anything you've forgotten to tell me?' It was Jane's way sometimes to forget things.

Jane ran long fingers through messy blonde hair. There was a tiny frown threatening between her perfect eyebrows. But fretfulness only made her look more adorable.

'Oh . . .' she said disconsolately. 'So many things; I don't know where to begin. I don't want to complain about him, you know. I just want it to be finished.'

And she looked so imploring that Isabel found herself feeling sorry for her, and melting, and smiling, and doing what she knew Jane would want: opening her arms to offer comfort. But even in the tangle of arms and blondeness and prettily tearful smiles that ensued, Isabel went on worrying over whether there wasn't more to this than met the eye. It didn't add up.

Isabel could feel the story taking on its own life in the markets, even on her brief walk home. Speculative eyes burned into her back. On the corner of Milk Street and Catte Street, two boys who caught sight of her started rhythmically grinding their pelvises and wrapping their arms round invisible women, then looking down, miming horrified disappointment, and bursting into comical boo-hoos. She speeded up, with her cheeks burning.

More gales of laughter met her inside the Claver door. Male laughter. She stared. There were two strangers in the hall. They were sitting on the two benches with a chessboard laid out between them on the little chest, but they weren't looking at the board. They didn't look at Isabel either, shrinking back in the doorway, hoping they weren't also enjoying the market story about Jane. They were too busy slapping their thighs and holding their stomachs and groaning with mirth to see anyone. They had tears running down their cheeks.

'Whatever's got into you?' Isabel heard Alice Claver say from the kitchen end of the hall. She had a servant behind her, with a platter of meat and pastry and a jug of wine.

They straightened up, a bit guiltily, when they heard her voice. Alice Claver was used to respect. But neither of these men – one a tall, sandy-haired, stooping man of middle years, in blue velvet mercer's robes; the other of similar age, a well-knit fellow with the blue-black hair and dark eyes of an Italian, who must be Goffredo D'Amico – could stop himself. The dark man looked down, but he couldn't stop his lips twitching. The sandy one wiped his eyes, tried to straighten his face, then began helplessly guffawing again.

'Will,' Alice Claver said forbiddingly. 'Goffredo.' Isabel, feeling invisible, thought she was about to bring them to order. But then, to her astonishment, Alice Claver's mouth also began to lift at the corners. 'Come on, tell me,' she said, as skittish as the girl she must once have been. Isabel could swear she was about to join in the laughter.

'You must remember, Alice . . .' the sandy one, who must be Will, said through his laughter, showing no fear at all. 'Master Large's face when he got his first delivery from Venice.' Alice Claver's face was definitely creasing up now. She sat heavily down, leaned forward on her elbows, and joined in the story for the Italian guest with such gusto that soon Isabel could hardly tell who was spluttering out which choked phrase. 'Crimson purple silk.' 'Supposed to be for the French Queen's coronation robe.' 'When he realised it wasn't dyed with the proper expensive kermes he'd paid for . . .' '. . . because all the cheap brazilwood and indigo they'd doctored it with in Venice started leaking into the wash he'd got us to do . . .' '. . . and he was so angry . . .' '. . . he stormed out of the storeroom to tell Mistress Large . . .' '. . . with his hands dripping with fraud's purple . . .' '. . . and put his foot . . .' '. . . right into her bucket of chicken food!' And all three of them put back their heads and howled at the long-ago memory. 'Ha ha ha!'

Isabel was smiling in her corner, almost with them, in the quiet way of someone not sure whether they're invited to join in. This display of back-slapping camaraderie that clearly stretched back half a lifetime – she was almost sure now that the man called Will must be Will Caxton, who she knew was now a merchant venturer based in the Low Countries or maybe Cologne, and who'd once been a mercer's apprentice with Alice in this house – was making her feel left out of life, in just the same way that her creeping feeling that Jane must only be telling her half of what had been going on with her husband had. She despised herself for the prickle of self-pity she suddenly felt; the sense that her own life had become small, dull, lonely and closed. But she couldn't help herself. She found herself longing for eyes to light up with glee when they saw her face, for girls to twitch maypole ribbons round her while she kicked up her heels, for men to pull her

110

excitedly into groups of laughing friends and buy her lengths of green velvet.

'Ahhh . . .' Alice Claver sighed, putting her head in her hands. The laughter was fading.

Isabel shifted a foot. She shrank shyly back as the Venetian turned a surprised head towards her, clearly only just becoming aware of her. He must be forty, like his friends, but he was so tall and muscled that he seemed in the prime of life. Under his black, rumpled hair she could see a powerful face, with laugh lines running from hooked nose to strong mouth. And there were more laugh lines at the edges of the dark, thickly fringed, dramatic eyes that were now fastening on her. But perhaps that was just because he was crinkling his eyes again in the beginning of a delighted smile. At her.

'So,' he said, holding her eyes for so long she could see the tiger flecks in his; so long that she felt warmth wash right through her at the slow, glowing happiness the sight of her seemed to be giving him; not looking away even though his question, in rolling, flirtatious, lustrously foreign English, was for Alice, '*who* have we here?'

And before she knew where she was, he'd paced over to her, taken her hand, bowed over it so close she could feel his breath on her fingers, and, straightening up, put his other hand round her waist and propelled her forward to join Alice and Will. Isabel looked up at him; he was close enough to kiss her as he looked merrily back down. She'd never been looked at like this before. 'Please, join us,' she heard him saying, and he gave a playful half-bow. 'I can guess who you are. Alice's new apprentice; we're waiting for you. She's told us all about you.' He stopped and corrected himself. 'Not quite all.' He grinned; she liked the impudence of it. 'She never once mentioned your eyes.'

*   *   *

111

'Well, why not spend time with a beautiful woman?' Dickon was saying. He swung himself into his saddle. 'Nothing wrong with that, if it makes you happy.'

Still on foot, with his hands grasping his own saddle, ready to mount, William Hastings looked searchingly up. But Dickon was a black silhouette against the sharp morning sun. He couldn't make out the expression in the younger man's eyes. He shrugged. It didn't really matter what Dickon thought, anyway.

It was only once the horses were walking at a slow clop out of the Westminster gate, with the knights and squires all clattering along behind, that Dickon spoke again.

'Though of course it would make more sense if the beautiful woman you loved so much could actually be your mistress,' he added prosaically. 'Otherwise, what's the point?'

Hastings sighed. He'd known, right through the previous day's feasting, that Dickon wasn't warming to Jane. He'd danced with her, once; he'd listened to her play the viol and sing, and had smiled, coolly; he'd admired the green velvet gown; and he'd laughed in approximately the right places when she made her heart-stoppingly innocent little comments, so full of wit for those who knew how to appreciate them. Yet Hastings had been aware that Dickon's eyes hadn't ever filled with the soft fire he felt in himself when he looked at Jane, and saw in the face of the King or Thomas Dorset. Dickon had no finer feelings, Hastings thought regretfully. He was a fighter without equal; a resourceful planner; a tireless campaigner; an entertaining, cheerful, unpretentious companion; and faultlessly loyal. But all his virtues were warrior virtues. He was made for war. He just didn't understand the softer joys of peace and music and love.

As if confirming Hastings' unspoken judgement,

Dickon's deep voice broke into his reverie. 'Knights pining for the unattainable lady in the ivory tower – crossing forests and slaying giants to give her a token of their devotion, and all the rest of it – it's just stories; romances,' the voice said, with ruthless cheerfulness. 'You know that. Let's face it, Will. She's spoken for. You'll never have her.'

Suddenly relieved, Hastings laughed and raised his hands in mock-surrender. Dickon's certainty was catching, and he was right, after all. Hastings knew himself to be trapped in moonbeams. He wasn't the kind of man who couldn't laugh at the foolishness he'd got himself into; he'd always been a clear-headed man of war too, until now.

'Seriously,' he said; for it was hard to stop talking about her. 'What did you think of her?'

Dickon paused to marshal his thoughts. Hastings' mind flashed back to the one snippet of conversation he'd heard between Jane Shore and the duke. Dickon had asked after the sister who'd got married at the same time, and Jane had dimpled exquisitely and replied, with a hint of mischief: 'Ah, my serious sister! She's widowed now.' He remembered Dickon's head leaning towards hers; his faultlessly courteous condolences. And he remembered Jane going on, with mockery beginning to twist her face; it must have embarrassed her to have to explain what had become of her sister. 'Well, it was only an arranged marriage . . . though she's gone a bit odd since he died. Apprenticed herself to her mother-in-law – terrible woman – fire-breathing dragon. Insisted on it. My father was furious. So now she's spending her life winding threads in markets . . . poor thing . . .' Perhaps she'd realised she sounded spiteful. She'd dimpled again; but not sweetly enough to take away the sting. Hastings had felt sorry for her; but he'd been aware of Dickon drawing quietly back, with a look of distaste.

Dickon had the same look on his face now, remembering her. 'Pretty,' he said briefly. It wasn't altogether a compliment. He added: 'But not as soft as she likes to seem.' After a silence, broken only by the creak of leather in sunlight and the jingle of metal and the breath of horses, he spoke again. He said, 'My honest opinion?' and Hastings nodded. Dickon said: 'Well then. Too fond of being the centre of men's attention. And too many men.'

'Immoral, you mean?' Hastings queried; but Dickon was too good a companion to be drawn too far into insulting a friend's love. He only laughed, and spurred his horse on.

'You know there's no harm in Goffredo,' Anne Pratte said, following Alice's baleful stare. 'Let him be.'

Goffredo D'Amico had been coming to the house for a week, sweeping his cloak, flashing his eyes, and clasping Isabel too close as he guided her from room to room, house to garden, and back again, along paths which, in Alice Claver's view, Isabel knew quite well enough for Goffredo to be able to refrain from putting one hand on hers and the other round her waist and practically dancing her along the corridors. Especially when there was no need anyway for all those tête-à-têtes that were now so closely spaced that they were in danger of becoming one long murmuring tiger-smile conversation. Now, the house had sprouted all kinds of unlikely dainties. There were so many baskets of figs, raisins, prunes, capers, pomegranates, oranges, spices and lampreys in the kitchen that someone was almost bound to end up with a foot in one of them. There were bunches of flowers on every table. Isabel had a new lawn coif and Holland cloth for kerchiefs. Goffredo, twinkling cheerfully as he paid his lavish but not quite improper compliments in the full gaze of all his friends, had taken to mixing up hippocras and coming to the house with a boy trotting along behind, trying not to spill from the jug. 'Sweets to the sweet,' he'd say, flamboyantly offering round the next bowl of almonds or dates, or, 'homage to beauty' or 'eyes like dewdrops'.

'It's all very well,' Alice Claver said grumpily. 'And the turtle doves do sound lovely in the orchard. But what in the name of God are we going to do with this popinjay he's bought?'

Anne Pratte ignored the rhetorical question. 'He's enjoying himself,' she answered unflappably. 'It's a game, Alice. And it's about time that girl had a bit of fun. It's not stopping her doing well at her work with me. And you can't deny you wanted her to start making a relationship of her own with him . . .'

Alice Claver harrumphed. 'A *trade* relationship! Not a great overblown rrroses-and-a-moonlight-and-a-can-a-you-hear-a-da-nightingales flirtation!' she said indignantly.

But when she saw Anne Pratte put her hands on her hips she stopped. It was true, she thought, deflating suddenly. Venetians might be sly; but handsome Goffredo's charm was so practised and inoffensive that she really didn't think he would risk damning his immortal soul, and damaging his best partnership in London into the bargain, by trying to seduce her apprentice. Not really. Not that that would stop her keeping a careful eye on his carryings-on, of course. You couldn't ever really be sure with an Italian.

Dusk. Roses swooning on the windowsill. Gnats dancing near the flame. The two Williams on their bench, going through Goffredo's hippocras and oranges while William Pratte brought Will Caxton up to date on London gossip. The story he was telling was the one in which King Edward's brother, the Duke of Gloucester, had – perhaps – secretly killed old King Henry in the Tower last year.

'We'll never know, of course. All we can say for sure is that the official explanation wasn't half good enough. Who would be naïve enough to believe Henry died of "pure melancholy and displeasure"?' William Pratte was saying. 'Do they take us for fools?'

There was an answering gleam of mischief from Will Caxton. Alice was out of the room, closing up the workshop. Anne Pratte, reluctant substitute chaperone, was keeping her eyes studiously on her work and shutting her ears to every subversive bit of gossip and flirting Alice Claver might have been listening out for.

Goffredo was setting out the chess board with long, brown fingers and a lazy smile. 'Chess: a game for lovers, they say,' he murmured, looking at Isabel through hooded eyes.

She half-closed her eyes back, feeling quietly irritated, as she did more and more often with Goffredo, but trying not to let it show. His attention was welcome in one way – it had gained her admittance to the charmed circle of evening visits by Alice's mercer friends. No one was surprised to see her at this table any more. For the first time, she belonged with the powerful; and she was grateful. But did he have to be quite so intrusive – constantly touching her as he drew her from one sight to the next; laying his hand on hers, for too long, at every opportunity; whispering at her, too close, and laughing if she drew her face back? It wasn't just that she could see it irritated Alice Claver almost to snapping point whenever he sidled up. The sight of him, the knowledge that he'd be whispering and winking and stroking her before she knew where she was, made her uncomfortable on her own account. She didn't know how to respond.

Here he went again: turning Will Caxton's neglected chess board into an instrument of flirtation. As he passed her the ivory pieces – as if he thought she knew how to play or could set up the board – his fingers were brushing against hers. She blushed and moved her hand back a fraction; then felt foolish when she saw Will Caxton glance up from his conversation and notice her flustered look. Goffredo was unabashed by her small rejection; he just murmured: 'If the Lady plays her Beauty, the Lover counters with his Regard.' Will Caxton was looking at them properly now. Ignoring him, Goffredo murmured persuasively: 'Or his Desire.'

'Venus and Mars,' Will Caxton chimed in, apparently following their conversation. 'Venus plays with honour, beauty, modesty, disdain; Mars with . . .' Isabel was impressed by the way he was outdoing Goffredo at thinking of fanciful bookish allusions. But Goffredo began shuffling sheepishly. Will Caxton gave him an accusing look across the table and said: 'Goffredo, you're shameless. You've been reading my *Scachs d'Amor*. You're quoting.'

Could a man as swarthy as Goffredo blush? Isabel wondered, laughing at the deft way Will Caxton had discountenanced the Venetian without giving offence; smiling at the usually smooth Goffredo's embarrassment. His hands went up in defeat. 'I admit it,' he said. 'It caught my eye. It sounded impressive, though, didn't it, *cara*?' and his fingers brushed hers again, and his eyebrows danced. She didn't mind any more, now Will Caxton had his eye on him. She grinned back. There was nothing to be frightened of, she thought. It was just Goffredo's game.

She hadn't paid much attention to Will Caxton, mercer turned import–export venturer. She hadn't had a chance to, with the handsome Venetian laying such energetic siege to her. Will Caxton was the kind of man who faded into the background. She'd just been aware of him as a friendly, sandy presence; someone with clever eyes; a man soaking

117

up the endless talk of London town as though he felt homesick.

But she warmed to him now as he came up to their end of the table, sat down next to Goffredo, clapped the other man warmly on the back and, turning to her, said: 'You must think Goffredo a clown', then, turning to his old friend, adding, though so affectionately that there was no sting in the words, 'because you've been acting the clown, D'Amico, admit it.' Caxton kept his arm on Goffredo's shoulder, but turned back to Isabel and looked more seriously at her. 'But I hope you'll forgive him his Italian ways when you see more of him,' he added.

She liked the simplicity of that appeal, just as she liked Goffredo more now he was looking mildly ashamed of himself, not making the advances she'd found just a little threatening. She nodded and smiled, rather uncertainly. 'He's a better man than you'll have had a chance to see, so far,' Caxton said, and grinned at the Italian. 'The only reliable Italian in London, for one thing. Honest as the day is long. And he knows more about silk than anyone I've come across; a master.'

Pleased at being let down so lightly, Goffredo bowed his head. Caxton went on: 'He knows how to make money, too. Wooh!' He puffed air out through his pale lips, making them both laugh with relief. 'Hand over fist. I'm relying on him for money myself,' he added. But he didn't rush to explain. He just nodded at Isabel with what might be an offer of friendship in his eyes and began setting out the pieces on the chess board, quietly and neatly. When Goffredo's eyes began to sparkle, under their big dark brows, at the prospect of a game, Caxton clicked his tongue at the Venetian and said, 'Nothing I can teach you, my friend. But I think it's time our young colleague here . . .' and he nodded in avuncular fashion at Isabel, 'learned some strategy.'

'I'll teach her,' Goffredo offered, eager again. 'I was just about to.'

Caxton only laughed. Not unkindly, he answered: 'You? What, and let her end up thinking the pieces are called Regard, and Desire, and Disdain?'

Gracefully, Goffredo gave in. He laughed and got up. 'All right, all right,' he said, and Isabel liked the ease with which he accepted defeat more than anything she'd seen of him till now. 'I'll go and find Alice.'

She concentrated as hard as she could on Will Caxton's explanations. She wanted to please him, and he was easy to learn from. He seemed to be telling her more than the specific rules – that the auphin always moved sideways, for instance. ('The name means elephant, but think of it as a bishop, the kind of sneaky priest who can't tell the truth straight but approaches everything deviously, at an oblique angle, and you won't forget,' he twinkled.) She felt he was conveying general principles, too: how to think clearly, how to understand other people's stratagems, and how to get your own way – things she needed to know to succeed.

It was getting dark. As he leaned forward to light the nearest candle, she suddenly found herself remembering another twilight under the arches of a tavern, and the man in the church laughing to himself as he bagged up leftover chessmen.

'Someone once told me,' she said thoughtfully, and, although her voice was so quiet she might have been talking to herself, Will Caxton looked up at once. Encouraged, she went on: '. . . a joke about chess. Well, a kind of joke. He was putting the pieces away. And he said, "We all spend our lives trying to win, but we all end up equal in the bottom of the bag."'

The corners of Caxton's mouth turned up, though he

didn't look as amused as she'd hoped. 'Ah,' he said, 'true enough – though there's more to life than playing games.'

He sat down and looked at the board, but she could see from the pale blue distance in his eyes that he'd begun thinking of something else. She kept respectfully still.

'Mind you,' he said after a while, into the silence, 'there's plenty of writing about chess these days. It's not just a game of strategy for knights any more; a lot of people play it. When you're living overseas, you see a lot of books – like the one Goffredo was quoting just now – which draw on chess. It's an allegory for war; it's an allegory for love.' He was musing now. She held her breath. 'I could translate something . . . it might sell.'

Translate? Sell?

He laughed when he finally noticed her bewilderment. He patted her hand. 'There, I'm running on like an old fool,' he said ruefully. 'And you've no idea what the old fool's talking about, have you? Well, how could you? You should have stopped me and asked me what I meant. I wouldn't mind.'

Isabel grinned, and, feeling suddenly confident, said, with a pertness she judged he'd given permission to, 'Well then, what *did* you mean?'

Caxton had none of the tight-lipped caution of the common run of merchants, which surprised Isabel, since she'd found out, by careful listening in the past few days, that he'd once been the Governor of the English at Bruges, and was still an important mercer and venturer now he'd based himself at Cologne. There was no side to him. His crinkly eyes were full of hope; his mind full of a young man's big ideas.

Hugging her new knowledge of Goffredo's business acumen to herself, Isabel listened carefully as the sandy Kentishman began telling her his dream of setting up an entirely new business in London – a dream Goffredo had

120

helped to back. Ever since Bruges, where book-learning was fashionable and every knight and squire kept a library, Caxton had been fascinated by the printing machines he'd seen, invented by the German, Johannes Gutenberg. He'd bought his own printing machine, in Cologne, using Goffredo's loan, and learned how to put the tiny metal blocks of type, each containing a letter, into a composing stick; how to bolt completed lines together into a block that represented a page of writing; how to ink the formes and work the press and transfer inky copies of the block onto paper made of shredded, fermented rags. 'They call it the black art in Germany,' Caxton said with a resigned grin down at his hands – which she noticed, for the first time, were stained with shadowy blue, like a dyer's – 'it does for your hands.' He'd already started importing books to London, in the same barrels that carried the cloth purchases he resold in the Mercery. But he was itching to make his own books too: choose texts, translate them, print them, sell them. He wanted to come back to London soon, he said, and settle here again; bring his press and his workers. William Pratte was paving the way for him with the Guildhall; he was hoping to raise money from the City. His eyes widened joyfully at the idea.

Jane had three printed French romances, Isabel recalled: luxuries, each worth several years of her own apprentice's pay, but still many times cheaper than a hand-copied book in the old style. 'You'll be richer than ever, soon enough, then,' she said, in as sophisticated a tone as she could, half-wondering why a man so established in his trade would want to throw it all away to chase moonbeams, but half-admiring his courage.

But Caxton only shook his head. 'Rich would be good,' he said, but without the answering enthusiasm she'd been expecting, 'but I don't know if it's realistic. Gutenberg never made much from his press. And it would take years to get going here. Anyway, that's not really why . . .' His voice trailed away; he was thinking again. 'It's just that I've seen so many extraordinary books on my travels. Extraordinary stories; extraordinary ideas; the sheer *beauty* of them . . .' He shook his head, as if knowing he'd never manage to convey his feelings. 'I think there are many more people who'd be as impressed as I am, if only they could see them . . .' Another shake of the head. Then, suddenly, he grinned. 'You must forgive me. I'm off again. I get carried away too easily. That's the trouble with dreams – they're so prone to making a fool of you.'

Isabel was daydreaming as her fingers passed expertly over the fingerloop braid. She'd mastered the technique now. She could let her thoughts wander as the braid grew in length and she shuffled her stool gradually further and further back from the nail on the wall to which its first end was attached.

Where her thoughts were wandering to was Goffredo's description of the foreign noblemen and princes who sent the agents to Venice to buy large amounts of the most expensive types of the finest silk fabrics in Europe for their wardrobes and palaces at silent, dignified, street exhibitions known as *parangons*. She was fascinated by the procedure: as remarkably elaborate and dignified as the cloths themselves.

The finest cloths, which in Venice and Genoa were those velvets most intricately interwoven with gold and silver, those judged by six Silk Supervisors to be worthy of export to the rest of the world, were displayed once a week near the Silk Office and the shops of the wealthiest *setaioli*, or silk merchants, at the Capella dei Veruzzi in the Parish of San Bartolomeo, and were called *drappi da parangon*. (All other cloths were coarser and cheaper, whether they were classified as *drappi domestici* for the hangings and clothing of Venice's own families, or *mezzani* for sale in city shops, sealed with the lion of St Mark, or inferior cloths woven specially for trade with particular areas – *da navegar* for the Levant and *da fontego* for German merchants.)

After the *parangon* cloths had been pre-selected for exhibition because of their exquisite design and pure dyes, their selvages were wiredrawn with gold and they were marked at each end with a seal bearing the symbol of a crown by the Venetian Senate's permanent commission of experts in the silk craft. Any fraud uncovered by these experts would mean the silk-maker was fined by the city government and his cloths confiscated. Then, once every fabric had been labelled with a number and the name of its maker, the exhibitors would withdraw to one side of the *parangon* – the name came from the Venetian word for exhibiting; the cloths were, literally, 'show-off' cloths – and wait silently for customers. (Isabel couldn't imagine a market in which the organisers managed to stop the salesmen shouting the virtues of their wares; but Goffredo said that in Venice these *cridori* were considered *modi disonesti* of selling. The virtue of the fabric should speak for itself. The buyers would pass through the two rows of stalls, with the *parangon* supervisors, a train of advisers, brokers, tailors and artisans, to judge the cloth. When they'd chosen what to buy, the supervisor would identify the name of the producer from the numbers attached to the bolts of cloth and call them, one by one, to negotiate a sale price with the customers. As soon as a deal was cut, the advisers were asked to leave and the cutting of the cloths began under the eye of the supervisor. Once the buyers finished, they left too. The exhibitors, standing back in silence, could collect merchandise and dismantle the *parangon* until the next week.

Now that, with Will Caxton's help, Isabel had got

Goffredo's flirtatiousness under control, she was enjoying asking the Venetian about his business world more than she ever had receiving his lavish compliments. He knew so many things that would be useful to her; she wanted to be able to find out about them without worrying about whether he'd try to hold her hand as he told her. She thought he might be secretly relieved, too, now he'd stopped plying her with hippocras and dates; he must be realising what a fortune he'd been frittering away on them. And why bother, now he could see that it was his stories about the way the silk trade operated at its European heart that could be relied on to make her eyes open wide in wonder? He was working that out; telling her more and more; enjoying her appreciation. He rolled his eyes and his R's and exaggerated every gesture as he talked up the virtues of silk.

'Is it not clear that silk adorns everything?' he'd said last night. 'Is it not silk that adorns the coaches, the carriages, the litters, the maritime gondolas, the horses of the Princes, with trappings, with outfits, with tassels, with fringes, with cords, with cushions, with cloths, and a thousand other beautiful things? Does not silk adorn the banners, the standards, the insignia, the halberds trimmed with brocaded velvet and fringes, the sheathed pikes, the bandoleers, the trumpets, the uniforms of the soldiers at war? Does not silk adorn the umbrellas, the canopies, the chasubles, the copes, the pictures, the palliums, the sandals, the cassocks, the dalmatics, the gloves, the maniples, the stoles, the burses, the veils for chalices, the lining of tabernacles, the cushions, the pulpits, and all other things of the Church?'

If he was parodying the importance of his trade, and his own adoration of it, it was only a slight exaggeration. Even here in London, she knew silk to be the ultimate measure of wealth: silk clothes for well-off families, or silk hung on walls with the family coat of arms embroidered on it in gold and silver, or silk cloths sewn together to form baldachins, mosquito curtains, coverlets, sheets, or used as linings and covers for cases, chests, books, chairs, mirrors. She was falling in love; but it wasn't the kind that Alice Claver had briefly worried about. The passion growing in her was the same love that consumed Alice Claver, the Prattes, Will Caxton and Goffredo: the love of the glowing, magical stuff that symbolised success and dignity and order and happiness and civilisation; men's (and women's) ability to create the highest forms of beauty from something as humble as the thread spun by a worm.

The excitement of it was almost enough to make her forget her lowly place in the household, but not quite. Goffredo might have brought her into Alice Claver's evening circle; and her own resourcefulness – as well as Will Caxton's help – might have tamed the Italian and consolidated her own hold on these powerful allies, but by day she was still just an apprentice, and a very junior one at that. She'd seen Alice Claver's wary glances in the past few days – her mistress didn't look altogether happy about Isabel's growing camaraderie with the most respected silk merchants in London. So, when Alice was in the room, Isabel kept her eyes down and did everything she could to show, mutely, that she wasn't getting above herself. Alice, in her turn, did everything she could to remind her apprentice that she was good with her fingers but too junior to be noticed unless she was being taught something or an errand needed running.

Now, for instance: Goffredo was flinging open the store-room door and bowing Alice into her domain. Alice knew that Anne had been showing Isabel braiding there all morning, but all she said, before moving away to her table, was a single expressionless word of greeting, and it was: 'Anne.'

Goffredo glanced over at Isabel. He winked, but only over his shoulder. Then he too moved off to start staring at Alice's ledgers.

Isabel always tried to hear what they talked about when they talked big business. But they always seemed to be murmuring just too softly for her to catch the words.

Anne Pratte was looking approvingly over at Isabel's braid and nodding. In the sing-song, rhythmic voice of someone half-hypnotised by the drawing together of threads, she said: 'Yes . . . you just needed time. The tension was all wrong at first. Much too tight. But you've got the hang of it now.'

Isabel nodded, but she wasn't really listening. Behind Anne Pratte, she could see Goffredo standing; leaning over the table, holding the edges with his hands. He was towering over Alice Claver. He looked more serious than usual. And he was speaking more forcefully. 'We should do it too,' he was saying. 'You know we should. It can't be *that* hard to import looms, teachers. The *Provveditori* would give me permission. I'm sure they would. If they can do it in Tours, why not here?'

But Isabel could see from Alice Claver's shoulders what her face must be like. Even if setting up a silk-weaving manufacture like the Italian venture in Tours was her heart's desire, she wasn't one to rush into anything foolhardy. Isabel strained her ears, and heard bits of the exasperated answer: 'Can't be done' and 'Would cost a fortune' and, rather louder, '. . . need big backing, and where on earth do you think that's going to come from?' She saw Goffredo shush Alice Claver with gentling downward hand movements and his most charming smiles. But Alice Claver overrode him: '. . . and you'd be a fool to think you'll get any help from the Mercers' Company. You'd

126

be astonished at how short on vision and foresight they can be if they think you're planning to do anything that might annoy their favourite Lombards.' Another calming baritone rumble, broken by her strident laugh. 'Straight to the Borromei? Now you really *are* being a fool. You think they'd lend to you so you could put every other Italian in town out of business? I'm telling you: if you give just one Italian in London just one hint that you want to set up silk looms here, they'll all want to eat you alive.'

Out of the corner of her eye, Isabel could see Goffredo looking crestfallen.

'That braid's long enough now,' Anne Pratte said from close up, bringing her out of her daydream. 'You can knot it up; I'll start showing you how to make tassels today.'

She held out a knife. As Isabel carefully transferred the loops to the fingers of one hand, and Anne Pratte showed her how to complete the braid so it wouldn't unravel, then cut each tied bow neatly into the finished product, she looked brightly up at the apprentice silkwoman.

'You remember what they've been saying about the King's three mistresses?' she began. It was a story Anne herself had energetically spread through the markets as soon as she'd heard it at her last fitting with Sir John Risley, the newish Knight of the Body she'd got so friendly with. The King had apparently told Risley he had three mistresses: one the wisest, one the merriest, and one the holiest harlot in the land. It had kept Anne and half the women in the selds happy for days attaching names to those descriptions.

Isabel enjoyed Anne's gossipiness. She nodded. 'Mmm,' she said, admiring her finished braid; aware of Goffredo's and Alice's heads bent over the books. 'So, have you worked out who all three of the ladies are yet?'

'Oh, yes dear,' Anne said. 'Well, mostly. Eleanor Butler's

the holy one, of course; that's not hard to guess. And they say Elizabeth Lucy is the wise one, though frankly . . .' She shook her head, as if she knew these court ladies personally and her experience made her doubt Elizabeth Lucy's claim.

She gave Isabel another bright, inquiring look. 'And of course, no one really knows about the third one, the merry one,' she added, with just the right amount of doubt creeping into her voice, 'but I've heard people saying . . . it might be your sister . . . ?'

Coup

7

Jane only giggled ruefully when Isabel sneaked another illicit hour off work to ask whether the King was helping her pay to take her now-rejected divorce suit to Rome.

'It's supposed to be a secret,' she murmured. But her blush said it all.

Isabel didn't even ask whether the rest of the rumour was true. It explained everything, from Jane's expensive new wardrobe to the way Jane had said, when Isabel had first taken it into her head to apprentice herself to Alice Claver rather than go home to her parents, 'everyone chooses their own way of escape', to their father's complaisance. Isabel tried not to feel angry with John Lambert for accepting Jane's way of escape from marriage so much more easily than he had his younger daughter's (the sin of adultery must seem less sinful when it brought a monarch into the family; and anyway it was hard to think of sin and Jane's breathy, laughing innocence at the same time). If Isabel tried, she could see why her father would quietly prize a king's favour more highly than her own virtuous industry. But she couldn't turn the other cheek, and forgive. After all, she'd been disinherited.

Apparently vaguely aware of a need to make up for

having been economical with the truth earlier, Jane put a soft hand confidingly on Isabel's sleeve. 'He's so . . .' she whispered, and though her voice trailed away without completing the sentence, Isabel could tell, from the blissful expression on her sister's face, that she was not referring to her husband. 'It's all so . . .' she went on, in the same breathy, wondering tone. 'Sometimes I'm at court and I look around and I just don't believe it's all really happening to me . . .' She smiled down at her toes. With a hint of defiance strengthening this wispy performance, she added: 'And he: so kind, so gracious.'

Isabel was struggling to be pleased for her sister. She remembered how the King's charisma had overwhelmed her, too, when he'd looked into her eyes. How could Jane have resisted? And Jane couldn't know how foolish Isabel had felt confronting the near-reproach in Anne Pratte's gaze. Jane had no idea how it would have helped establish Isabel's reputation to have been better informed. So she turned her lips up, dutifully, trying to smile. But she couldn't help also saying, rather sourly, 'I just wish you'd told me sooner.' Then, a split second later, the beginning of a thought flashed through her head which put a real smile on her face. 'Jane,' she breathed, suddenly excited, 'would you take me with you to court, one day?'

Jane was no fool. She knew there must be some reason why her sister, who'd only wanted to twist threads on market stalls a few months before, suddenly wanted to go to court. 'Just to see,' Isabel said innocently. She didn't quite know herself, yet; she just knew that even if she hadn't been the first to discover her sister's relation with the King, she could at least be the first to explore the God-sent advantages it might offer. She didn't think her sister was quite convinced of her innocence. But the subject lapsed.

Instead, Isabel started praising Jane's tan velvet gown. 'Lucchese,' Jane simpered, pirouetting for her. Jane loved compliments. 'Not cheap.'

'If only we could make velvet here in London,' Isabel went on, letting a note of genuine wistfulness into her voice. 'And other silks. At half the price the Italians charge . . . if only someone, the Mercers maybe, would put up the money to try . . .'

But Jane just wrinkled her nose. 'What money?' she said with a hint of scorn in her smile. 'The King's had it all off them in benevolences. Their pockets are empty. Anyway, I'm very happy with Lucchese velvet . . .' Lovingly, she smoothed down her glowing skirts. Isabel sighed.

Isabel didn't mean to do what she did next, either, but on her way home she found her footsteps taking her by John Lambert's main stall in the selds. It was only when she was in sight of it, being jostled by boy apprentices, that she allowed herself to recognise what she was preparing to do: approach him and suggest he put up funds to set up a silk-weaving business, bringing in other wealthy mercers to help if need be.

She took a deep breath, already hearing the persuasive words in her head: 'This is how we could do it . . .' But, she thought, with her courage already ebbing, before she could say that she'd have to make peace; look him in the eye knowing he'd disinherited her; hope for softness in a face better suited to hardness. He'd be bound to say no. She could imagine him pronouncing unforgivable words: *you should stop worrying your head about business*. Or: *you should be more like Jane*. The stall was ten yards away, but there were too many people between her and it for her to see it clearly. It was almost a relief when, as the crowd thinned, she realised it was packed up. Her father was away.

Alice Claver had been right, she thought, turning disconsolately towards Catte Street, trying to banish the image of John Lambert's scornful face from her mind. They'd never get the Mercers of London to fund a silk-weaving industry.

Three weeks later, Jane and Isabel sat shaded from the sun in a lodge made of green boughs and hung with scarlet and blue silk flags. There was wine in front of them, and a flutter of pages rustling in and out to replace one dish of untouched refreshments with another. All around were dozens of other make-believe lodges, with the old royal palace of the Bower rearing up behind them, half-hidden by Waltham Forest. In each lodge sat more fairytale ladies with necklines plunging as low as their headdresses rose into the sky. Each lady had more impossibly white skin and pale, pampered hands and pink cheeks than the last. The picnic had gone on since six in the morning. It was nearly ten now, time for the hunt to return. Isabel could feel the cooking fires being lit, adding to the heat.

She was wearing a borrowed robe provided by Jane – a more magnificent piece of gold-shot green than she'd ever seen outside Alice Claver's storeroom, over a kirtle of the finest lawn, embroidered with tiny scarlet strawberries. She was trying her best not to look overawed. She was sweaty. There were prickles of moisture in her hair, and the inside of her bodice was soaked. She didn't know how Jane, wasp-waisted in a flowing scarlet ensemble so tight it must be unbearably hot, could manage to appear so composed and effortlessly cool. Only her fingers, quietly turning her rings round, as if to unstick them from her skin, suggested any kind of discomfort.

It had been beautiful to ride side-saddle through the coolness of the dawn, and a thrill to watch the falcons rise off the wrists of accomplished hunters, and later a pleasure to lie back on the cushions and listen to the horns and the hounds in the dense clouds of green that now hid the hunting party. Part of her felt hazily that she had somehow stepped inside a tapestry; that if she looked more carefully she might see the grass underfoot was scattered with pearls, or spot centaurs trotting by.

But Isabel was also stiff and bored; she was uncomfortably aware of being not nearly as elegant as the ladies of the court, and, except for Jane, alone. It hadn't been so bad before the men rode out. Jane had other admirers as well as the King, and the two most important of them had spent the first part of the morning vying for her attention. Lord Hastings (dark, bowing, fine-featured and supremely affable) had escorted them from the palace, laughing, picking buttercups for Jane to put in her hair, telling mischievous stories about the dog-fights in the kitchen when they'd changed the animals at the spit, and encouraging Jane to take his falcon. Then Lord Dorset (blond, bowing, fine-featured and also supremely affable) had brought them two jewelled cups of wine and plumped their cushions and amused them with a slightly crueller story about Lord Hastings being bucked off his new horse into a puddle in full sight of the Queen. It was only after the hunters had cantered off into the trees that Isabel had begun to feel really uneasy: when, every time they stepped outside their bower to try and create movement in the still, stifling air, they came across more of the perfect ladies, each one laughing and murmuring to a companion; each one, as far as she could tell, quite unable to see either her or Jane. It made her feel even more invisible than her first days of apprenticeship had; spectral. Jane squeezed her arm encouragingly when she saw Isabel look first surprised, then downcast, at the snubs. 'Don't pay any attention,' she whispered, and there was a brave edge to her smile. 'That's Elizabeth Lucy. She doesn't like me.'

And she drew Isabel further into the edges of the forest, where, if the air still didn't move, at least there was more shade; and pointed out the children playing nearby. 'The King's children,' she muttered. Nearest was a little girl of maybe five or six, with hair as startlingly copper-coloured as the Queen's, much redder than Isabel's gentle strawberry-blonde, though this flame hair graced an ordinary, round, solemn child's head that wasn't much like the extraordinary, bewitching, heart-shaped face of the beauty Isabel had glimpsed riding proudly ahead on the way to the forest. Three or four smaller girls, all with the same flaming hair and placid faces, sat quietly nearby, as if the heat had sapped their will to move. A toddler – a boy – was crawling towards a carved wooden horse on an enormous carpet so padded and plumped with cushions that Isabel couldn't imagine how he could make progress; and, watching him, sitting on a stool, nursing a baby, sat a strapping young woman in the Queen's colours. Jane smiled, as if fondly; but she didn't move any closer. Isabel saw that, after all, she hadn't really stepped inside the tapestry. Neither had Jane. They were still outside, watching, as if from behind glass.

Her spirits only lifted when she heard the thunder of hooves; when, after the cavalcade emerged from the trees followed by men carrying two bucks and several hares, the ladies swayed decorously to the purple-draped wooden platform to have the morning's sport re-enacted for them, with many blood-curdling cries, before being ushered, half-fainting from the heat, into the still hotter, enclosed space of the royal pavilion to toast the King's success and taste the meat that had been cooked while they watched.

Isabel's heart sank for a moment when Jane pulled her aside, not letting her into the pavilion with the first surge of the crowd. 'What?' she whispered. 'Why not?' But Jane just shushed her with an urgent shake of the head.

They scuffed their feet as ladies streamed past; but a minute or two later, to Isabel's relief, Jane let them join the forward movement after all. 'I saw the Duke of Gloucester up ahead,' Jane whispered, with more dislike than Isabel had seen her showing for anyone; as if she'd been humiliated by him. 'The King's brother. The one they say murdered the Duke of Clarence; the other brother. Let's give him a chance to get ahead. He gives me the shivers.' She shuddered eloquently. 'A horrible man. Rat face; cold eyes.'

But Jane smiled joyfully when Lord Hastings, tousled and sweaty and even handsomer than before, spurred towards them. She fumbled in her right sleeve as he drew up and pulled out a green kerchief; his token, which she must have accepted in private on the ride to the woods, and which she now handed back. She laughed at him, so invitingly and intimately that Isabel, relieved at a moment of real human contact, couldn't help joining in.

'I prayed for you to take the buck,' Jane dimpled, breathy and baby-voiced, 'and see how God answered me.'

He touched the kerchief to his lips, grinned, and trotted off.

So Isabel was confused when Lord Dorset, tousled and sweaty and also handsomer than before, spurred his horse towards them a few moments later, and Jane, smiling very sweetly at him, fumbled in her left sleeve and pulled out a mulberry kerchief, his token, which she handed back.

'I knew you'd get the hares,' she breathed at him. 'With your sharp eyes. I was praying for your success.'

And this time Isabel just watched, gape-mouthed, as Dorset put the mulberry kerchief to his lips in a gesture identical to Hastings', and trotted off back towards the King, straight-backed and successful.

'Jane,' she whispered, not knowing whether to be shocked.

Jane only giggled. 'Well, it made them both happy,' she whispered back. Jane never really felt guilty when caught in one of her pieces of guile. Her voice sounded pleading, but her smile was so merry and infectious that Isabel began to laugh again, out of sheer relief at this naughtiness amidst the dignity and blank stares. Jane added, through Isabel's laughter: 'And they hate each other so much; they'd have been miserable if I'd turned one of them down for the other. I couldn't have taken one token without taking the second, now, could I?'

So this was how Jane bore the lonely dullness, Isabel thought, feeling a little happier for her sister. If, that was, Jane even found this boring or lonely. Perhaps she didn't. Jane had always known how to amuse herself with some almost innocent bit of mischief. Isabel was less surprised this time, when, once they'd arranged themselves somewhere low down the table in the tent, and were eating in silence, and the big, casual King loped up to them, as golden and tousled as a lion, crunching at the piece of meat speared on the knife in his hand, Jane gave him a dewy look full of promise and pulled an embroidered crimson kerchief from her bodice. 'I knew you'd take the biggest buck,' she breathed invitingly. 'No one else can compare to the Sun in Splendour . . .'

He laughed; a long, lazy chuckle that suggested to Isabel he knew perfectly well what Jane had been up to, but didn't mind her minxiness in the least. After taking back the token, he leaned down and touched Jane affectionately on the tip of her nose with his finger, and murmured something in her ear.

Isabel politely looked away. She was expecting to be ignored. But the King, unlike his courtiers, wasn't a man for discourtesy.

'The second lovely Lambert daughter,' he said, startling her; lighting her up with a long gaze. It was the kind of look that made her feel he not only knew her well and admired her, but also that she was the loveliest and wittiest person in the room, and that he was about to laugh heartily when she made her next brilliant pleasantry. She'd heard he always had this illuminating effect. Anne Pratte, her guide to what people said, was clear on this point: King Edward could be relied on to know the title, acreage and rental income of every knight in every remote corner of the land. This might, Anne Pratte was careful to add, just be because he needed to know how much he could count on when he stung them for loans, which he often did. And the reason he was also said to know the name of every knight's and merchant's wife might be because he had slept with them all. But that was just gossip, Isabel thought, dazzled. He said: 'I was the unexpected guest at your wedding,' as if politely reminding her of something she might have forgotten. He continued, just as easily, 'I'm sorry for your loss, Mistress Claver. Your husband died with courage.'

She bowed her head. So, respectfully, did he. So, after a second, did Jane. 'Thank you, Sire,' Isabel whispered.

A pipe and viol started playing a jig behind them. Following the rhythm, the King waved a hand and raised merry eyebrows. The sad moment was over.

'If I may say so,' he went on, his eyes gleaming with the pleasure of the compliment he was clearly about to pay, 'that is a very beautiful silk you're wearing.' He leaned over to touch the green-and-gold overskirt Jane had lent Isabel. The gesture brought his face level with Isabel's and his big body so uncomfortably close that she nearly jumped back.

Grinning rather wolfishly at her, with his eyes now only a few inches from hers, he added, in a husky growl that, in someone else, might pass for a whisper: 'One of the Claver house's elegant imports from Italy, perhaps?'

He must know where it was from, she thought, in a daze. He must have bought it for Jane himself. It must have cost . . . Suddenly, she almost laughed at herself. Kings didn't have to notice details, or refrain from flirting with their mistresses' sisters, any more than Jane had to wear only one knight's token. Why was she being so solemn? Perhaps it was going to be easier than she'd realised to bring the conversation round to the subject she wanted to discuss.

She grinned cheekily back and shook her head. Somewhere in her head she could feel the first glimmer of an idea. She raised a storyteller's finger.

'Ahh, no; it's not from Italy,' she said playfully, making sure to catch the King's eyes and hold them. 'Not this cloth. But it is beautiful, isn't it? It's from the newest manufacture of Italian silk cloth in Europe – from Tours.'

Don't give me away, she silently prayed to Jane; she'd felt Jane startle at her lie. Then, gratefully, she sensed her sister's shoulders rise in acquiescence. Jane was always playing this sort of joke on people, after all. She'd give Isabel the benefit of the doubt for now; she'd go along with the story.

'Tours?' the King asked. 'They make silk in France now?'

'Oh yes,' she said, with an extraordinary external calm matched only by the extraordinary turmoil inside. 'In his wisdom, the King of France is doing all he can to encourage the weaving of silk cloths at Tours . . .'

She fixed him with her most persuasive gaze.

'You may wonder why?' she went on.

The King paused. Isabel was aware of Jane at her side, scarcely breathing.

She could imagine what Jane must be thinking. The King was good-natured, but how good-natured would even the most tolerant of kings go on being if he got bored? Then, to both girls' combined relief and terror, he smiled and began to look at least a little intrigued. 'Why?' he asked.

'Because,' Isabel continued, not missing a beat, 'he understands that establishing a silk industry in France is going to give an honest and profitable occupation to ten thousand people.'

She'd forgotten Jane now. But Jane's whole attention was still fixed, in utter astonishment, on her odd little sister. Isabel was almost singing, Jane was thinking; as if she were wooing him. She wasn't having a little joke, bending reality to amuse herself, as Jane might have; it looked for all the world as though she was about to start selling him something. 'Ten thousand people,' Isabel went on, 'all ranks and sorts of people, from clergymen to noblemen to religious women to others – all the people who'd sat idle before. Ten thousand people – imagine. That's a fifth of the population of London.'

Edward wasn't angry, in fact his eyes were glinting at Isabel with what Jane thought might be amusement at this thin young girl-widow's eloquence.

'That's why silk manufacture has been spreading out of Italy for twenty years. To Spain. To Flanders. To France. Because rulers of countries all over Christendom are coming to realise that establishing a silk industry helps everyone in a community,' Isabel intoned. Really, Jane thought, almost shocked, she was staring at him like a snake hypnotising its prey. But Edward seemed willing to be hypnotised. At least, he sat down on the bench and gestured Isabel to sit next to him.

'How so?' he asked. Jane was left standing.

'Because,' Isabel answered coolly, sitting down beside the King without for a moment letting her voice stop caressing his ears, 'there are so many crafts in silk. Children and women can raise the silkworms, and reel and wind the silk they produce. The poor and the old can sort the silk, dress it, weave it and dye it. Merchants can run silk shops. And any citizen can plant mulberry trees or make partnerships with merchants.'

She smiled confidently at Edward. 'And, of course, getting so many people into their honest and profitable new occupation can only be good for their king,' she went on. 'As Your Majesty will appreciate.'

He lifted an eyebrow and leaned closer. 'Go on,' he said seriously. Even Jane, whose fearful heartbeat was now slowing to a rate at which she could breathe almost normally, recognised this as an unambiguous signal to continue.

Isabel said purposefully: 'A new manufacture attracts more outsiders into the City – like the five thousand newcomers who have come to Tours. That means bigger revenues – from taxes on grain and wine and salt and food and clothing – and also from tolls on merchandise entering and leaving the City, which obviously all go up too, because all those new people need new houses and shops and looms and workshops built for them.' She was rattling her figures off with glib expertise. She was smiling more intently than ever at the hypnotised Edward. 'And don't forget that once the business is established, the king will also be able to earn much more than before in dues for exporting textiles – because there will be many more textiles to export.'

She paused for emphasis: 'It's hugely profitable, in fact,' she said, with magnificent assurance. 'That's why the wise king is willing to make the initial outlay. Of course, it's not cheap or quick to set up. But you'll reap many times the benefit later.'

How does she know all this? Jane wondered, lost in Isabel's argument. Then, did she just say, '*you* will reap many times the benefit later'? What did she mean by that?

Isabel's hands were trembling; but with her dawning sense of achievement, not with fear. The divine madness was ebbing. She couldn't believe what she'd been doing and saying. She finished: 'The great pity is that there's no English silk-weaving centre.' She lowered her eyes modestly, setting the King free at last. 'Yet,' she added.

A man standing behind Jane began to laugh and clap. Isabel turned to see who it was.

Lord Hastings was nodding at her. His feet were planted wide apart as if to steady himself. His dark face was split in the same kind of delighted grin she could see on King Edward's face. 'Do you know, Sire, I think she's got a point,' he said. 'It might work. It just might work.'

The King smiled at Hastings. 'Lord Hastings knows about trade,' he said comfortably, welcoming his friend into the circle with a gesture. 'You know that, don't you? He's a stapler when he's at Calais. One of you merchants: making fortunes out of cloth. If he thinks it could work, then . . .' He waved his hand again.

Lord Hastings passed Jane as if she wasn't there. 'Bravo, Mistress Claver,' he said, bowing as he squashed onto the bench with them. 'Who'd have thought you had a business head on your shoulders? And now – what can you tell us about this initial investment?'

She rode home at the back of a party of knights returning to London. Jane stayed behind. For a few moments, Isabel revelled quietly in her solitude; the first time all day she hadn't had to guard her expression. It was also the first time she'd had to consider the leering way the Marquess of Dorset, Jane's blond second admirer, had cornered her in the tent's shadows while Jane was dancing with Lord Hastings, after a lot of food and drink had been consumed by everyone present. Dorset had lurched his admittedly handsome body at her, and pressed beery lips down on hers, grinning. She'd pushed him away, but he'd just said: 'Oh come on, you know you want it', and, 'you're a beautiful woman, you know', with lust and contempt equally mixed on his face. She'd had to kick his leg quite hard, while trying not to let anyone see what she was doing, to make him pull back. He'd sworn and stepped away, but he'd gone off, shrugging, still with that drunken, leering, triumphant grin on his face. Thinking about it now, she let her face twist into open contempt for the first time. Why did Jane tolerate him?

But there were more important things to think about. It was only once she was alone on the road, up on her horse, that Isabel became yawningly, terrifyingly aware that she needed a real silk expert for the follow-up negotiations the King had suggested take place with Lord Hastings, tomorrow, at the Palace at Westminster. She'd already taken this deal as far as her own cheek and intuition and what scraps of knowledge she'd gleaned at Alice's would go. She didn't know what to ask for next.

She couldn't ask Alice. Alice would take all the credit for doing a deal with the King. She couldn't ask Anne Pratte, either, because Anne's first move would be to tell Alice. Isabel knew that without having to test it: Anne wouldn't be able to resist. Nor could Isabel ask William Pratte, for all his standing with the Mercers and loyalty to Alice – because he would tell Anne, and Anne would tell Alice.

She plaited the reins between her fingers, thinking. For a few moments she wondered about asking Goffredo. He knew everything. And he'd enjoy the adventure more than anyone. But then she imagined the overheated atmosphere that sharing a secret with him, even for a day or two, would produce; and shook her head. She'd just stopped him pawing her at every opportunity. She didn't want all that starting again.

That only left Will Caxton. His business in London wasn't with Alice, unlike Goffredo's, so if he suddenly absented himself the next morning, Alice wouldn't bother herself too much with where he was going. But he was so unassuming, so low-key. Her first instinct was to rely on someone whose expertise she could hide behind: someone more flamboyant, a showman. And yet, as the horse jolted her one way or another on its leisurely amble, she began hesitantly to grasp the reality that her own showmanship had got her this far. She didn't need someone else's flamboyance, after all; only some detailed knowledge and negotiating experience. And gingery, gentle Will – who'd done as much, really, to make her part of Alice Claver's circle as Goffredo ever had; who always behaved with respect, as if she were his friend – would provide all she needed of that, and more. He wouldn't try to steal her glory either.

She sat up straighter and kicked her horse out of its amble and into a smart trot. It was settled.

'Westminster? Whatever for?' Will Caxton said blankly, when she whispered her request to him that night. He didn't want to waste his precious last days in England on something unnecessary. He had business of his own to transact. 'Not something else to do with your sister?'

He hadn't met Jane. But all of Alice Claver's circle disapproved of her.

Cagily, Isabel replied, almost whispering: 'Not exactly . . . though I've told Alice it is. I wouldn't ask if it weren't important.'

He sighed.

'Well, I hope it is, that's all,' he said resignedly.

'Please, Will. I really need you,' she muttered, and sensed him softening. 'And please don't tell Alice you're coming, either. I'll explain once we're on the boat.'

Once they were both safely on the wherry seat, side by side, watching the other boats go by in the morning glitter, past the gnats and dragonflies dancing on the reeds, she started to whisper what she wanted of him. Will Caxton didn't believe her at first. He even got a little short with her. She sensed, from the slight colour around his sandy hairline, that he was as close as he ever got to being angry. 'I haven't got time for wild goose chases,' he said sternly, as if doubting he'd done right to be so friendly with this untested girl. 'Are you absolutely sure you're not just making this up?'

Even when she showed him the scrawled *laissez-passer* Lord Hastings had given her, to get her through the Palace guards, he wasn't sure. He screwed up his eyes and peered at it with undisguised scepticism.

'Why would he agree to see you?' he said, after a long silence.

She couldn't quite keep the note of exasperation out of her voice as she replied, more shrilly than she'd have liked, 'I've told you why; it's true.' Perhaps that almost convinced him. At any rate, he fell quiet. Looked thoughtfully at the paper again. And, as Westminster loomed up ahead – the double towers of the Abbey and the great arching roofs of the Palace, the fairytale homes of priests and princes – she could see him begin to work out negotiating points; whistling under his breath. Just in case.

The corridors they went through were no grander than those they were used to, but there were many more of them. The Palace seemed an entire city in stone. They didn't know where to go or what to say to soldiers, so they waited in silence at the gates while the soldiers conferred, and waited again, several more times, as they were shuffled along corridors by hesitant underlings.

Eventually a tall, dark, harassed-looking man who looked a little like Lord Hastings came out to their latest

146

stone corridor and bowed. A page piped out his titles: Ralph Hastings, Esquire of the Body, Master of the King's Horse, and Keeper of the King's Lions, Lionesses and Leopards. Isabel guessed this must be Lord Hastings' brother. Trying not to look overwhelmed, she dropped a curtsey as deep as Will Caxton's answering bow.

Ralph Hastings led them down yet more corridors to the Lord Chamberlain's rooms. He talked, very calmly and slowly, in his outlandish Midlands country voice, putting them at their ease. 'This is a good time to call on my brother,' he said, 'after his morning duties are over. It's the first moment in the day he gets time to think.'

Isabel knew Lord Hastings' duties as chamberlain ran from organising the household – ordering the King's meals and arranging audiences with him – to secretarial work, to intimate duties of the body: ensuring the fires were tended and candles lit in the royal bedroom, the bed aired, the chamberpot emptied, and dogs and cats driven out of the chamber; helping His Majesty dress, making sure his clean linen had been warmed at the fire, handing him his carefully brushed clothes, and preparing and supervising his rosewater baths.

Isabel wondered: how does Lord Hastings get time to run the Calais garrison and the King's Midland armies and mint new issues of coin if he has to do all that too every morning? Curiously she asked, 'Doesn't he get pages to do the morning duties for him?'

But Ralph Hastings shook his head, with a courtier's astonishment at this childlike outsider's ignorance in questioning Palace ways. 'Touch the King's person?' he asked, with raised eyebrows. He must mean 'no', Isabel decided, feeling abashed. Lord Hastings must do all that himself.

She was aware of Will Caxton, at her side, almost imperceptibly shaking his head. She wished he hadn't seen her make a fool of herself. 'Let me', he muttered, 'do the talking.' For a moment she was nettled by this. But mostly she felt relieved. This was why she'd brought Will, after all.

The chamber they entered was large and airy, but simple enough: a great mullioned window looking on to the river, water light reflected on the bare walls, a large table covered with papers set near the back wall, two scriveners sitting at it tidying the papers and making notes, and, by the window, Lord Hastings himself, splendid in blue velvet tunic and hose, with his hat already sweeping off his head and his laughing eyes on Isabel, beginning to bow as he said, with what she thought to be affectionate welcome: 'Ah, the young Mistress Claver! Come in, come in . . . we have business to settle, I believe.'

Lord Hastings knew Will Caxton's name (as he seemed to know everyone's). As soon as Will Caxton was formally announced by the page, he turned with great ease to the sandy, skinny merchant and said, 'We haven't met. But your work at Bruges was famous; of course I know of that. And we all admired the excellent agreement you struck with the Hanse merchants.' Then, to Isabel, with respect and courtesy combined: 'I see you've brought a colleague as talented as yourself. A good friend to have.'

Will was more self-possessed before nobility than Isabel had perhaps expected. He bowed and answered formally; took his place at the table with poise. It was easy to take her lead from him. It was only for a brief moment, as they settled themselves to talk, that she caught his eyes on hers. His head nodded, in quiet approval.

In the hour that followed, she was surprised many times by how adept Will Caxton was at the business at hand. He set out what would be needed to establish a silk-weaving industry, clearly and briefly; and, equally calmly, Lord Hastings agreed to everything. The contract (which named Isabel as an entrepreneur in her own right, along

148

with Alice Claver, Goffredo D'Amico and both Prattes, to be known collectively as the House of Claver) did not even include Will Caxton. 'I'm planning a different business,' he said, when Lord Hastings raised an inviting eyebrow at him. 'I'm just here to offer advice.'

Isabel couldn't believe how easily what she wanted was, thanks to Will, taking shape in the document one of the scriveners was composing as they talked. The contract specified that the silk industry they would set up would have the King's protection for twenty-five years. The scrivener's legal French, which she could only just follow, allowed the House of Claver to make contracts with a full workshop of Venetian dyers, spinners and weavers to immigrate to England.

Will Caxton raised the question of their safety – the City was prone to riots against greedy Lombards.

'Where would you like to establish yourselves?' Lord Hastings asked Isabel.

Will Caxton answered, as quickly as if they'd agreed this beforehand among themselves: 'Here – in Westminster. That would be safer.'

And down it went into the text: that the silk weavers would be lodged in a quiet, anonymous house in the precincts of the Abbey, far from the prying eyes of the merchants of London. Goffredo was to be offered English citizenship, in case he ran into trouble with the Venetian authorities or the Italians in London. The Venetian masters would use the workshop to teach a first group of English weavers how to produce a full range of satins, damasks, velvets and taffetas. No other foreigners would be permitted to set up a rival business in Westminster or London until this quarter-century contract expired. The Venetians would have a moratorium on repaying any debts incurred at home and any taxes due in London, just as they would have immunity from prosecution for crimes committed overseas. The workshop would be exempt from municipal levies and obligations. Nor would it have to pay for imports of any raw or spun silk, dyestuffs, gold or silver that the artisans would need for their work. The King would pay the ten-shillings-a-year rent on the house. He would advance money too for the food, clothes and thirty-ducat annual salaries of the foreign workers – a quarter-century interest-free loan. All the House of Claver would have to do would be to buy the equipment: twenty looms for high-quality cloths; spinning machines; mangles, vats and tools for the dye shop. 'We don't know how to calculate the price for the machinery,' Lord Hastings said apologetically. 'Best you keep that to yourselves.' But everything else would be paid for from the King's own purse.

A silence fell as Will Caxton considered whether any other points needed to be written into the contract. The scrivener was dropping sand on his paper, to blot the ink, and funnelling it back off into the sandbox. Lord Hastings grinned. He leaned forward and tapped Isabel on the shoulder, looking suddenly conspiratorial.

'You do know, don't you,' the King's friend said, 'that although it's the King's Grace who's happy to take formal responsibility for your costs, in practice the only way he'll have of getting the money for it is by borrowing from the merchants of the City of London? He's not a wealthy monarch in his own right . . .'

Isabel saw Will Caxton permit himself a small answering smile. He knew. She echoed it.

'Essentially,' Hastings went on, crossing one leg athletically over the other, 'your father and his friends will be paying for your venture – but won't know they are. Yet your House of Claver will enjoy all the profit if it succeeds, as I'm certain it will. You've done well, Mistress Claver. This is a sweet deal for you.'

Her smile deepened as that thought sunk in. Will Caxton looked modestly down, enjoying it too. Lord Hastings looked kindly at her, as if well aware of the greater complexity of her feelings – as if realising that the love of the beauty of silk that had started her down this path in life was now giving way to an appreciation of something she hadn't seen until now: the beauty of power, used with elegance. Slowly, he nodded. Then he got up, in another fluid movement. 'I think that's everything, isn't it?' he said gently. The audience was over.

Outside, walking back down the corridor, accompanied only by the page this time, Isabel, whose eyes were fixed straight ahead, whose head was full of the triumphant singing of heavenly choirs, slowly became aware of Will Caxton beside her, suddenly slightly sweaty with relief, rumpling his velvet hat in his hands, then running his hands through his thin hair before putting it back on. He started whistling again, very quietly, under his breath. She half-turned her head, ready to grin at him. He winked back, but his cautious body movements suggested to her that it wouldn't yet be appropriate to rejoice out loud. She fixed her eyes on the page's tunic ahead, and carried on walking.

Will waited until they'd got right past the last soldier and were standing on the jetty, waiting for their boat back to London, before he whooshed out a great sigh of pent-up happiness. 'We did it!' he said, putting a hand on her arm and jigging it up and down. 'We really did it!' His voice was high and cracked.

Excitement flooded through her as she beamed back at him, rejoicing at being allowed to show her feelings at last. He looked his normal self again now – unassuming and astonished by his success, with his pale eyebrows giving him his usual air of surprise. He wasn't half as impressive as he'd been in the Palace any more. She had to remind herself that it was this man who'd done all that; she'd chosen right. 'Will,' she cried warmly, 'that was unbelievable! You were . . . You were . . .' She was so overcome she couldn't even think of a strong enough expression of praise. 'You were so GOOD,' she ended, not caring.

He grinned, bashfully. He knew she meant the highest praise; and who didn't like praise? But his voice was calmer as he said modestly, 'Well, I've had years of experience, you know . . .' He nodded at her with equal warmth. 'And there was me, not even believing you this morning. Growling at you like an old bear. You've done an extraordinary thing yourself, to see this opportunity; to seize it.'

It was Isabel's turn to blush. Will Caxton took his eyes off her happy confusion. He looked around instead, approvingly, at the calm of the scene on the riverbanks: the gentle swell of the river plain; the rooftops covering priests and functionaries and contemplatives. 'And this really will be a good place to work out how to do something new; not too much fuss and bustle,' he said thoughtfully. 'Perhaps, when I come back, it's where I should settle, too . . .'

He stood for another minute, looking at the panorama, whistling through his teeth. Then he shook himself back into the moment, and smiled at Isabel. She could see the new respect in his gaze. 'You're an unusual young woman, Mistress Isabel Claver,' he said with determination, 'and you mustn't let anyone tell you any different. Alice should know it was you who set all this up. You deserve all the credit for it, not me. I've just been the adviser, nothing more. You don't need to mention my having been here. I won't say a word to Alice or Anne if you don't want me to.'

He was delighted with his offer; he knew how generous it was. As for Isabel, she was too overcome to speak.

*   *   *

152

They all looked surprised when a messenger turned up at the house a day or two later to deliver a document for Isabel. It wasn't her place to get documents. She was the girl learning purse-making. But no one asked who it was from when she rushed to the door to take receipt of it. They didn't ask even when she came back into the store-room a short while later, with her eyes down and pink cheeks and a bulge in her purse. They were merchants; they set store by good manners and privacy. They waited for her to tell.

Isabel couldn't speak all day. Her secret was like a vast bulge in her throat; keeping her apart. She waited till evening, after the day's work was done and they'd all left the storehouse, before presenting the contract to Alice as she took her place at the dining table. She even bowed her head submissively as Alice made a point of finishing tying the lace on her sleeve she'd noticed trailing before looking up.

Finally, Alice held out a hand for what Isabel had to offer her. She started to read. She must have noticed the weight of the document as soon as she picked it up. It was stiff with wax seals, and Alice would have been blind not to see the King's emblems on them: three blazing suns, and the royal motto, *Confort et Liesse*. Comfort and Joy. Still, Alice didn't say anything for a long while. She just stared at the words, as if they were dancing in front of her eyes.

Alice's face was perfectly still as Goffredo came into the room and sat down beside her at the table. The silkwoman passed the document to Goffredo, with just one word, 'Read'. She still hadn't deigned to look at her apprentice. But Isabel thought she'd spotted a gleam of satisfaction in the other woman's eyes.

Goffredo glanced down. He looked astonished. Then more astonished. Then he put the letter down and started

153

to laugh. As Anne Pratte wandered in, picked up the document and, wrinkling her nose, said fretfully to her husband, 'Tell me what it means, dear', and William Pratte started to translate for her, they too started to look astonished, then more astonished. Goffredo's laugh got louder and louder, until he was slapping his thighs and clutching his sides.

'Just like that,' he chortled. 'He gave it to us, just like that.'

They were all buzzing with it now; shifting and murmuring; unbelievable news. All looking at each other; all watching Goffredo's mirth; not quite believing it wasn't a joke.

'No corners cut,' William Pratte said.

Anne Pratte added: 'No expense spared.'

Then Goffredo stopped. Looked at Isabel without flirtatiousness – just with pure admiration.

'Your name is on this,' he said warmly. 'It was sent to you. Tell me. What did you do?'

She was blushing furiously. Staring at her feet. Suddenly so surprised to have succeeded beyond her wildest dreams that she didn't know where to put herself. She didn't want Alice to think her boastful. She almost wanted to tell them that Will Caxton had struck the deal on her behalf, to take the eyes off her; but she stopped herself just in time. Will had said she could take the credit, hadn't he? And it had been her daring that had got the deal, hadn't it?

'I was lucky,' she muttered. 'I met the King. Through Jane. I asked him.'

They all started laughing at that. Could life really be so simple? She looked hopefully up from under her lashes. They were beginning to believe it; passing the letter from hand to hand; shaking their heads in wonderment. 'But I didn't believe, until this came, that it had really worked,' she mumbled.

'Look at her,' Goffredo marvelled. 'Sitting there so shy and sweet, as if butter wouldn't melt in her mouth.' He leaned forward. Patted her on the knee. 'Look happier!' he commanded boisterously. 'You've just made the deal of all our lifetimes! You're allowed to celebrate, *cara!*'

And before she knew where she was he'd pulled her up and was dancing her up and down the room – she didn't mind his touch this time – and everyone else laughed, and the torches dipped and flickered, and even Alice's growl, 'Goffredo, please!' didn't sound half as grumpy as usual.

But Isabel still couldn't quite believe it herself; not even when the hippocras came out, and Goffredo's sweetmeats, and William Pratte had made the first toast of the evening to their future success. She only really knew she'd done something worth doing when Alice started smiling directly at her, as if she'd had an idea of her own, and said, with none of her usual gruffness, with a respect that sounded almost shy, 'Isabel – would you like to be the first to go and inspect the house at Westminster? You can have the day off. You deserve it.'

8

Isabel was walking past fields of pale green corn. She was too absorbed in her thoughts to look at the other people on the road. The smoke of London was behind her, even the forbidding Strand fortresses only a memory as long as she didn't turn round. She was as free as the silver stretch of river on her left; Westminster a magical village just ahead.

She was glad she'd walked. The exercise was clearing her head. She was almost beginning to believe her dream had come true. A part of her was already mentally hiring her favourite silkwomen, the ones who might, just possibly, be trusted with a secret on this scale.

Perhaps I'll hire away some of Father's silk apprentices, she thought with a flicker of mischief. I know they're well-trained. Isabel also knew, from growing up in the Lambert house herself, which women had the neatest fingers and the sparsest private lives. How angry it would make him if they were to leave his service and vanish to Westminster.

Mostly, though, it was Joan Woulbarowe she thought of. She couldn't stop herself imagining Joan Woulbarowe staring at her, eyes like plates, her mouth gradually widening into a grin that showed every one of her black stumps of teeth, then beginning to stammer out rough words of gratitude. Joan Woulbarowe deserved a fresh start after all those penniless years in the courts fighting her ex-mistress's accusations. Now, Isabel thought, feeling almost God-like in her generosity, I can give her that fresh start. She can start again here.

Isabel was slower to articulate the rest of her thought to herself, but a part of her was also aware that it wouldn't hurt, either, that the disgraced ex-apprentice throwster had no relatives (except a crazy aunt, Rose Trapp) and few friends among the silkwomen. By and large, they had prudently taken rich Katherine Dore's side in the Mercery's most public dispute. Joan Woulbarowe wouldn't be missed in Soper Lane. And she had quick fingers. She'd learn fast. She'd be so grateful she'd work all hours. Isabel also knew – with the hard-headed instinct of the career spinster she could feel herself becoming – that there wasn't much danger of Joan starting to dream of getting married or having children. Even if she was foolish enough to fall in love, she'd lived too hard for too long. Her ravaged face and ruined mouth would stop any nonsense. Someone like Joan would be a good worker for the rest of her days.

Even as she enjoyed her Joan Woulbarowe fantasy, Isabel was also thinking about the Italian end of the bargain. Goffredo would have to set off at once to cut his deal with the government of Venice and start recruiting workers. She knew that would take time. The Provveditori della Seta he talked about so much would need persuading. She imagined many palms would need greasing before he got his documents and permissions. And he'd have to find devious ways of smuggling the looms into England, bit by bit, in disguise, to stop the London Italians hearing what he was importing. Perhaps, she wondered light-headedly, Will Caxton would help after his London break?

She was so intoxicated with her success that she began to imagine Will, sitting in a warehouse somewhere in the German lands, wrapping each segment of wood painstakingly into one of his consignments of textiles with his own hands. Shaking his head of thinning sandy hair in comical despair at the undisguisable shape and size of them. Wondering if he could describe them to the Customs men as parts of a printing press. Then laughing in his boyish way when he'd solved the puzzle and vanished the bits into his ship's hold.

She realised she must have been smiling when she noticed the men at the gate fall silent and give each other meaningful looks as she passed into the streets between Palace and Abbey. One nodded, deadpan, and the other tapped a finger against the side of his head and pulled a lunatic face. She composed herself, hastily, and slowed to a more decorous pace over the cobbles. They probably didn't see many young ladies in yellow silk – she'd dressed in her best gown – coming from London on foot in the heat of midday, pink-faced and grinning like fools. She must stand out. Should she have dressed less conspicuously – faded into the background? She knew how. Then she grinned again and lifted a jaunty chin. She'd just been given her heart's desire, after all. She couldn't imagine being happier than on this perfect day. She could smile if she wanted. Wear yellow. Who cared if they stared, or thought she was mad?

She didn't know her way around Westminster. The Abbey precincts were bigger than she'd thought. And the tidy streets housing the craftsmen who serviced Benedictines and courtiers were quieter for this time of day than a Londoner would have expected.

She stopped, baffled.

'Which way is the Almonry?' she asked the first old

woman she came across. She was shy of accosting a strange man in this unfamiliar place, even if half of them were monks. But the crone just stared back in feeble-minded alarm, shook her head and shuffled hastily on.

Isabel shrugged. She looked around for someone who might give proper directions.

There was a horseman on the shady side of the road, giving his dusty mount a drink at the trough. He'd been fiddling with the horse's harness while she looked around: knotting the reins and loosening the saddle girth as if he was about to take a rest after a long ride. Now, with his back still to her, he dipped his hands into the water too, raised a handful to his head and splashed it onto his face. She saw drops gleam in the air. She heard him say a cheerful 'brrrr!' to his horse and saw him run both wet hands through his hair, then link his fingers and stretch his arms luxuriantly above his head.

He sounded young. The clothes on his wiry back were dark and plain enough to blend into the shadows, but the hat he'd let drop by the trough was of good-quality black velvet. Not a footpad's hat. He didn't look dangerous. Anyway, what could go wrong today?

'Sir,' she called boldly. 'Can you direct me to the sign of the Red Pale, at the Almonry?'

He turned round. There was water dripping off his hair into a drenched face; he was blinking it happily out of his eyes. He took two loping steps towards her, into the light. 'Can't see a thing,' he said, still shaking the water out of his head but now shading his eyes with his hand too. 'So bright.'

She knew that voice. It was as deep and soft and beautiful as the black velvet of his hat.

She stared. Sallow skin; black hair; a wiry, muscled body; and a mouth that might have looked hard, if it wasn't radiating such simple animal joy at being out of the saddle and dripping with cool water on a blazing summer's day. At the pleasure of stretching his arms and legs; at just being alive. She felt the hot air shimmer and change.

Suddenly she was fourteen again, listening to that voice in the darkness of the Bush tavern as she fretted over her father's choice of husband; feeling the deep warmth of his hand on her back. In that instant, everything that had happened to her since vanished; as if it had all been a loop she'd made in a braid; a stitch in time crafted with all the care it had needed while it was being furled and turned and knotted, but now cast off, with her braid just a fraction longer. She was back where she'd started; just better off.

She was still staring when his vision cleared enough for him to stop shading his eyes. He came to a halt beside her. He hadn't yet recognised her. He was so close now she could feel the heat of his body.

'The Red Pale,' he was saying. He put a hand on her shoulder-blade as if to whisk her round. She drew in breath; humbled by her pleasure. 'You're heading the wrong way.'

She hardly dared look him in the eye. What if he didn't remember her? But she couldn't stop herself slowly turning to face him fully, head first, neck second, shoulders third, with what she thought might be an imploring look, but she didn't really care. Her whole existence had shrunk, narrowed, shortened, until there was nothing but this moment: dazzling sunshine; the man in black beside her; his hand on her back. It was enough.

He stopped talking. His hand went still, but stayed where it was.

She loved the stillness of him.

'Isabel Lambert,' he said.

'Claver,' she replied quickly; relief making her grin and gabble. 'I took your advice.'

He held her gaze; shaking his head, beginning to smile too. Those soft, amused eyes.

'A widow now,' she added, wishing as the words came out that the sight of him – this extra blessing on a day when she had thought God had already granted her every wish – wasn't making her blurt like an over-eager child, the way she had before.

He moved. He raised his other hand, used it to cross himself politely, and murmured, 'God rest Master Claver's soul', with a formal heavenward glance, before moving his eyes back to find hers, as if the only peace he could know would come from locking gazes with her. This man would always see her, and know her, and seek comfort in her eyes, whatever she was wearing or doing; his look had nothing to do with status, or clothing, or the concerns of the world. It was simpler than that. And the extraordinary contentment that his stare brought her made her know for sure that all Goffredo's flirtatious plays of eyes this summer had been just meaningless games.

She couldn't bring herself to look sad, though she crossed herself. 'Some time ago,' she couldn't help herself saying, as her hand dropped. 'A year and more.' She gestured at her yellow silk, so glowing and celebratory. 'I'm out of mourning.'

He nodded, with the attentiveness she remembered. And kept nodding, and gazing. She realised, suddenly, with fear, that they had run out of pleasantries; that he would have to ride on now; that she might never see him again.

'I'm going through the Almonry myself,' he said. Smiling as if he'd warded off the darkness. 'I can show you the Red Pale.' And he strode back across the street, with those taut, economical movements, without breaking off his gaze, and unknotted his horse; and, before she knew where she was, they were walking down the street together, with the horse clopping along beside them, chomping on its bridle, blowing through its teeth, as happy with its memory of the glittering sunlit water as either of the humans it was with.

'Before . . . you know, last time,' she said, feeling her heart leap but speaking as casually as she dared over the easy rhythm of feet and hooves. 'I never once asked your name.'

She thought he paused before answering, though the rhythm of walking carried on. She watched her skirts billow out in front of her in what shade the midday sun allowed; felt warmth on her back. Waited.

'Dickon,' she heard him say at last, and she felt the pet name sink in with a soft thrill of discovery. She let herself begin to hope that there would be more.

She saw her house at once, over the road from the sign of the Red Pale, behind the well-made almoner's offices tacked on to the edge of the Abbey. It was shuttered and barred, but she could see even without reaching for the key in her purse that it was a more than respectable premises. From the pale-grey stone frontage, two solid storeys high, with a gate in the wall at the side, she could guess at the three spacious rooms on each floor and the light that would pour in through the solar windows above. The looms would go downstairs. The barn down the side of the courtyard would serve as a warehouse. The solars above would be sleeping quarters. She'd need to make lists of things to buy: beds, kitchen equipment, linens.

Dickon helped her pull open the shutters in the first empty room, letting a blast of sunshine in to dry the stale air and gild the dust. There were mildewed rags in one corner. Otherwise it was empty of all traces of the vestment-maker who, she'd been told, had lived here in old King Henry's time; empty of everything except the dreams she was already weaving. She showed him round, with her excitement at meeting him magnifying her pride at being the new householder, flattered by the way he followed the story pouring out of her. He was absorbing it all with a minimum of words; narrowing his long eyes; nodding intelligently. Once or twice he burst out laughing, in what struck her as a pure, joyous celebration of her success. When she explained how she'd come to meet the King, twice, he looked surprised for a second. 'Jane Shore,' he mused aloud, as if he might know her, 'she's your sister . . .' But he didn't ask any more. Jane was well-known now as the King's lover. People had started repeating Anne Pratte's story about the King, saying his three mistresses were the merriest, the wisest, and the holiest harlots in the land – and Jane the merriest. This man must have heard a story like that somewhere. She shrugged it off. Perhaps she was being reckless, talking so freely. It felt strange to go back to the girlish chattiness that must have been natural to her the last time they met; being Alice Claver's apprentice had taught her more caution than she'd realised. But she was sure it wouldn't matter what she told him. Not just because he wasn't from the Mercery, and wasn't a merchant, and so wouldn't know who to tell her trade secret to if he were minded to give it away – but because, instinctively, she trusted him.

'The King's done you proud,' Dickon said easily as she locked up. 'You deserve it.'

Was that the beginning of a farewell? She stiffened.

'Now, I've been on the road since dawn,' he went on; eyes finding hers, laughing into her soul, dispelling her fears. 'You probably don't know this, but there are no good taverns for miles up the Great North Road – just cheap bread and stinking cheese for farmers bringing their flocks to town. I couldn't face going in. So I'm hungry.'

She let herself begin to laugh. (Another question for

163

later, the hopeful part of her noted: Where's he been coming from? Why the Great North Road?)

'But this place', and he pointed at the sprawling tavern opposite, 'has the best cook in Westminster.'

She waited, trying not to hope too painfully.

'I often come here when I first reach Westminster. It's a good place to sit a while when you've been away. Find out what people are talking about. I like that,' he grinned mischievously. 'I sometimes even stay my first night here. Recover from the journey. They treat my horses well. And they have good beds. Clean straw. No fleas.'

He raised an eyebrow; an invitation. 'Aren't you hungry after your long walk?'

'No food for an hour,' the innkeeper said, wiping his hands on his trousers as he came out. His broad face was red. He grinned at Dickon. 'But it's your favourite: beef stew.'

From the kitchen, Isabel could smell onions frying. Dickon said easily, 'We can wait.'

She saw the badge on the purse he paid from. It was embroidered in silk: a white boar with a golden collar.

This tavern looked clean and bright. There was fresh sawdust on the floor. The windows were open and bunches of gillyflowers in cups on the tables caught the light. There were a few other customers – a monk in black, sitting morosely alone by the door, nursing some private grievance and a large ale; two ladies in their middle years, in the dark velvets of the respectably rich, chatting quietly at the back over a jug of ale and some slices of bread and cheese and cold meats. The hot food being prepared smelled inviting.

'I'll fetch something to do from my bag,' Dickon said. 'Cards; or a game.'

He slipped out into the street; the entrance to the bedchambers where he'd put up must be outside.

The innkeeper brought a jug of wine and cups while

164

Dickon was away; while Isabel was settling herself at a quiet table in a window. He half-looked at her as he poured, ready to talk if she did. It was her chance.

'So he's a regular,' she said tentatively. 'Dickon?'

'Mm.' The man set the jug down. 'He comes and goes.'

She tested: 'With the Duke of Gloucester . . .'

'That's right,' the man replied. 'Stays when the Duke's at the Palace. A night, sometimes two; till they find him quarters there. He says it's because my beef stew's so good.' He beamed and retreated.

Isabel thought about the expensive embroidery on Dickon's purse.

Dickon returned, a dark blur of energy, with a bag. He sat down at the table opposite her. A delicious tremulousness was coming over Isabel. What would they talk about, she and this stranger? Her tongue was sticking against the roof of her mouth; she couldn't meet his eyes. All the questions she'd been meaning to ask had flown out of her head.

Neither of them spoke for a moment. Then they both began at once.

She said: 'The flowers are pretty.'

He said: 'I so nearly kissed you last time.'

Unable to stop, she said: 'Though I like roses better.' Then, 'What?'

His eyes were glowing into hers like coals. 'I didn't want to spoil it. You had other things on your mind.' He grinned that wolfish grin. 'It was better just to go.'

Her cheeks were on fire. She should have looked away. But she didn't. She went on staring back, with the wondering start of a smile; knowing she was lost, but not caring.

Perhaps he'd embarrassed himself too. He drained his cup and shook out pieces from the bag. Chess, she saw, staring down now, catching her breath. It was lucky Will had taught her a bit.

It was a relief to have something to do with her hands. She moved one piece. Moved again. She was getting her breath back.

Then she stared. He'd just moved a fers; the weak vizier piece. She knew the rules: it could only go sideways, one square at a time. But he'd moved it right across the board.

'You're cheating!' she said, lifting her eyes to his, so delighted at the sight of his that catching him out seemed a pleasure. 'I saw you!'

But he only grinned and whistled through his teeth. 'Ahh,' he said easily, 'no, I'm not. I'm just playing the new game.'

She opened her eyes wider. 'Tell me,' she said, not sure if he was just teasing her, but too gloriously happy to care if he was. He did, sitting back, crossing one leg casually over the other knee; he knew all about it. In Spain, he said, after the fighting Queen of Castile had gone on her crusade against the Moors, they'd started playing a new game of chess, full of powerful women. The piece Isabel knew as the fers was called the Queen now, and had gained the most powerful moves on the board. A chess Queen could move anywhere – as far as she wanted, in any direction. Using the Queen well was a player's key to winning, and the best way to kill the other side's King – the aim of the game.

'It's all the rage, this new game,' Dickon said, showing her his move again.

'At court,' she replied innocuously; and he nodded, too absorbed to notice he was being drawn out.

Then he looked up, with more mischief curling his lips. 'Another new rule – you'll like this,' he said. Under his gleaming eyes his voice was a caress. 'I called you a pawn once, remember? Said you had no other choice but to move forward, one step at a time?'

She nodded. Remembering, fondly; thanking God that dilemma was over and she was here.

'Well,' he said, 'in the new game, a pawn that manages to move all the way across the board – eight spaces – and gets to journey's end at the other side, becomes a queen too.'

She grinned back, reflecting his pleasure. 'So, if I just keep going, I can be a Queen?' she said.

He nodded.

'Even if there's already a Queen or two on the board?'

He nodded again, baring his teeth and laughing down at her. 'There can be as many Queens as you like in this game,' he said cheerfully. 'As many Queens as there are pawns – as long as the pawns are ambitious enough, or lucky enough, to go the full distance.' He laughed. 'Just like life at the court of King Edward, really,' he added. 'Wouldn't you say? We only have one official Queen, if you don't count the captive Queen from the other side who's in the Tower – Henry's French Queen. Let's not. She's finished. But look at all the pawns rushing at the King now: all those mistresses, running round court, sucking up favours, new Queens and Queenlets in the making.' He twinkled at her. 'Your sister's one,' he added. 'The merry one, I believe.'

He seemed to know the court. Might he really know Jane? She found the thought distasteful. She tried not to let it show.

But she stopped thinking about Jane and everything else when he touched her hand; a butterfly brush. It could have been accidental. 'Now you're on your way too,' he whispered, and the smile softened. 'You'll be the Queen of Silk.'

She could feel his hand, almost; it was still resting just next to hers on the board. She could imagine the warmth of it; if she moved hers a fraction, they'd touch again.

Very softly, she sucked in air between her teeth. He'd knocked over a piece and not noticed. He'd stopped thinking about the game of chess too.

'Here we go!' the innkeeper warbled into the charged silence. 'Mind yourselves! Stew's up!' And he and his serving girl bore down on them with big bowls of stew and spoons, banging and clattering, ignoring the furtive retreat of hands, clearing off the game and arranging food in front of the diners.

Dickon just laughed. Isabel was flustered, but he didn't look in the least abashed. 'Best beef stew in town,' he said, and slipped the innkeeper another coin. 'Thank you, Hamo.'

They ate. The innkeeper retreated, but Isabel was now aware he would be somewhere nearby, waiting to come out and clear the platters. She kept her hands on her spoon and bowl or in her lap.

'I like it here,' Dickon said, breaking bread into his soup. 'No questions . . . no one snooping behind the tapestry. It's like being on the road. Free.' He laughed, and put steaming wet bread neatly in his mouth. 'Except that the food's better.'

She thought she understood. She started telling him about her year in the selds, as a girl in brown; how none of her wealthy friends (or her father) had seemed even to see her when she wasn't wearing the bright silk uniform of the rich; how becoming invisible to them had been lonely at first, but how putting on the clothes of a humble worker had shown her another life too. How she'd started liking the lively, mischievous tenement talk of the poorer silkwomen, whose world she'd never imagined while she lived at her father's, but who had been there under her nose all along. She said: 'So I know what you mean about being on the road, and free. I've found a way of feeling free myself.'

He nodded. She liked the absorption with which he

listened. 'A good lesson,' he said. 'I had my ups and downs during the war; it served me well to know how to fade into the background from time to time. It can save your life to be anonymous. Your Mistress Claver is an intelligent woman if she's taught you that.'

'I'm grateful,' she acquiesced, almost surprised at the word; at the affection in her voice. She wiped her bowl with bread. 'I suppose that's why my Mistress Claver is a better merchant than my father,' she finished thoughtfully. 'Even though she's a woman, and won't ever get to be a liveryman of the Mercers' Company, or alderman, or Mayor of London, or wear the uniforms and have the power my father wants. He only sees the display. But she looks beyond. Sees people's faces, their skills, their hopes, their souls. Sees what they can do, or could do if they got half a chance. Not many people do that in the City. No one else looks after the poor silkwomen like she does. You wouldn't get my father or his friends writing petitions to Parliament for them. So no one else gets the rewards either. You know, she's actually richer than my father; though you'd never guess it to look at her, all bundled up in her old gowns.'

He laughed comfortably.

There was a pause. He pushed his plate back. She felt braver now that they'd found things to talk about. In what she hoped was a casual voice, she asked: 'So did you marry the girl you told me about? The one your brother was against?'

She thought, from his stillness, that he didn't like the question. Every fibre of her being was willing him not to nod.

But when he nodded, she wasn't surprised. Not by his answer; the silence had told her already. Only by the quiet sadness stealing into her, as if a cloud had covered the sun.

She tried not to let it show. She made herself smile, and went bravely on. 'And was your brother angry?'

He looked up with a sudden flash of charm, as if grateful to be forgiven, and grinned. 'Yes,' he said. 'Very.'

She felt for her purse. She knew she should leave. He was married. The meal was over. But she couldn't quite make herself get up. Not yet.

'It worked out well,' he went on, perhaps sensing she was thinking of going, and trying to spin out the moment. 'She's an heiress. I've gained half her father's lands. I'm a big man in the North now. It's a good enough match not to worry what my brother thinks.'

She found the purse, clutched at it. 'Children?' she whispered, tensing, ready to rise.

He shook his head. 'Poor girl,' he said lightly. She thought he meant his wife. 'No.'

She stood up and bowed; smiled formally. 'Thank you for inviting me,' she said. 'I should be getting back.'

He looked downcast. Picked up the jug. 'There's still some wine?' he said, asking a wistful favour.

She shook her head and gave him the same regretful smile. Took a first step away.

A voice in her head was telling her there was no need to behave like a jilted bride. Nothing untoward had happened. She'd eaten; she'd enjoyed a conversation. She spent half her life talking with married men like William Pratte and widowers like Will Caxton. There was nothing wrong with that; it was the point of independence. And this was someone she'd wanted to meet again. A stranger she had struck up an instant friendship with. It was part of the strange good fortune of today that she'd found him now.

She paused. Felt radiant relief at the simplicity of it. This didn't have to be all. Turned back to where he was still sitting, still looking at her.

'I'll be here a lot,' she said. 'Perhaps we could have dinner again, next time you are?'

He nodded. 'I'd like that,' he said slowly, and she could hear the pleasure in his voice. 'Tell each other our stories . . . I'll walk you out.'

In half a dozen steps they were outside, blinking in the sunlight, standing next to the open side door, through which she could see a staircase. They paused; perhaps both thinking of how to say goodbye. It was Dickon who put a hand on her arm, but it was Isabel who acted. She felt a jolt like fire go through her flesh. She shivered. She couldn't stop herself. She whispered, 'Come,' and pulled him through the door, looking back at him and laughing, and he was laughing back at her, and before she knew what was happening they were in interior shadow again, behind the door, on bare boards, with stairs leading up and a shaft of light beaming down, and he was kissing her.

She was looking for her linen. The bare room – just a bed and plaster walls and pale oak beams and Dickon's bundle against the wall – had been neat an hour before. They'd turned it into a wild rumple of sheets. She could smell new straw in the mattress.

She smiled, remembering. The heat of it half-embarrassed her now. She'd had no idea, no idea, she thought tenderly; it hadn't been like this before. She picked her shift out of the mess and pulled it on. Dickon was asleep. She softened at the sight of him, loving the dark line of muscle and skin against the cloth.

'Soon, again,' he'd murmured, sliding off her. 'My kindred spirit.'

'You're married,' she'd whispered back, snuggling into him. 'We can't. I shouldn't have.'

They'd both known she meant yes.

Lives changed, she thought now, without being shocked at herself: people died; wives changed. No one need know for now. There was always hope for tomorrow.

She'd wake him up. She looked around. With delight she saw his knife lying on the floor, by the crucifix he'd found time to take off in the rush for the bed, on his open missal.

She lifted up the knife. The handle was metal and cold: metal inlaid on bone. She laid it flat on his forehead.

He came awake, startled; then, seeing her so close, leaning over him, pale red-gold hair falling over his face, laughing at his shock, his face melted into relieved happiness. He pulled her down on him. 'No surprises,' he muttered, kissing her ear as he whispered into it, 'you had me worried for a moment.' But he didn't sound angry to have been teased; and now he was too absorbed in touching her skin with his lips, sliding his mouth slowly down her neck, to talk at all.

She leaned over his head to drop the knife back, still laughing. His tongue was exploring her collarbone. She shivered in anticipation.

But she couldn't just let the knife go; not onto an open book. It was plain but it must be expensive. It would get damaged lying open. So she let the knife clatter onto the boards; she reached a hand down to shift the crucifix and close the book. And she saw the three words written on the open page: '*Loyaute Me Lie.*'

Loyalty Binds Me. She knew that motto. She embroidered regalia; she knew them all. Dickon's tongue was teasing at the edge of her shift now, but she pulled away. Sat up.

He looked surprised. 'I know,' he breathed, 'you have to go. But not just yet . . .'

'Your prayer book has the Duke of Gloucester's motto written in it,' she said baldly.

His eyes flickered. He sat up too.

'Yes,' he said, equally baldly. 'It would.'

He hadn't really hidden anything, she thought, with her head whirling. She'd seen the purse with the badge. She knew he was here, not at the Palace, enjoying a moment of anonymity. She knew he owned land in the North. She knew his name was Dickon. She just hadn't guessed that made him Richard of Gloucester. The King's brother.

He should have told me, she thought hotly. Then: Why? He didn't have time. I seduced him.

The next thought that came clear from the whirlpool in her head was pure sadness. It was only a few minutes since she'd been putting on her shift and hoping, sinfully, as she now realised, that his wife might die; that, having inherited her estates, Dickon might . . . She shook her head. She couldn't even finish the thought. The foolishness of that hope, remembered now, made her close her eyes and feel sick and hot.

Then came shame. She could hear his voice, when they'd been downstairs, and it was saying, mockingly, '. . . look at all the pawns rushing at the King now: all those mistresses, running round court, sucking up favours . . .' and 'Your sister's one . . . The merry one, I believe.'

She didn't want him to think she was one of them. However cringingly pleased her father might secretly be at his daughter's relationship with the King, Isabel despised the easy life it allowed Jane to lead. She always would. It had nothing to do with the Bible's strictures against fornication; it was more that Isabel couldn't respect or understand idleness. She didn't want to be known as a woman whose life's work was charming favours out of important people so she could go on prettily doing nothing. She didn't want to be like Jane.

To her horror, her eyes filled with tears. 'You'll think

I'm . . .' she muttered. She couldn't go on for a minute. 'I'm not a mistress,' she said, blinking blindly. 'I wasn't looking for a protector.'

She felt his hand on hers.

'I know,' he said; very soft, very low. 'You're an honest woman, with a plan in life. I admire it . . . and you. I understand.'

She stared at his hand; memorising it; she might never see it again.

'I do,' he went on. 'You wouldn't want to be hanging round on the fringes of court waiting for me, fretting, gossiping . . . being snubbed . . . begging for gowns and jewels . . . all the rest of it . . . any more than I'd want you to. We each have our lives. We can't change them.'

She looked up, partly comforted by his voice; partly waiting for the dismissal she could feel about to come. She managed a watery smile.

'But I want to see you again,' he went on, begging her with his eyes. 'When I can; when you can. And we could. Sometimes. No one need know. It could be here.'

The room's soft plaster and oak glowed again; the colour of happiness.

Weakly, she said: "But people would talk. It wouldn't be good, for me or for you."

'Who has to know?' he replied, and she could see laughter beginning in his eyes. 'Weren't we just talking about this? It's good to fade into the background from time to time, didn't we agree?"

'You didn't mean this to happen,' he went on, and his voice was stronger, deeper, more persuasive with every word. 'I didn't, either. But we couldn't help it. We're two of a kind. We recognised each other. I'm glad.'

She was drawing strength from his words. She recognised this. If he'd been a merchant she'd even have known what to call what she could hear him doing: striking a deal.

'You don't meet much honesty as a prince,' he said sombrely. 'And most of the ambition you see is ambition to do you harm. I don't trust many of the people around me.' He pulled her to him with both arms, pinioned her to him. 'But I trust you.'

He took a deep breath. He finished: 'So – will you trust me? Let me be just Dickon; just your love? And come to me again, when you can, here?'

She didn't hesitate; not for a moment; not even to savour the scent of him in her nostrils, the press of skin on skin, and know it wasn't the last time she'd feel this.

She knew. This was what she wanted. She nodded.

9

It was ten years since Isabel had last been inside the Palace of Westminster. Yet, however much of a queen of silk she knew herself to have become in that decade, she was still overawed on this cold February morning by the sheer size of the city in stone; by the waiting, and the corridors, and the slow whispers of the men-at-arms.

She tried to put all that aside as she knelt in front of the plump girl with the pallid face and swollen eyes and flaming red-gold hair whom she'd come to serve. In businesslike fashion, she lifted a flap of red cloth of gold from one side of the girl's gown, folding her lips round her mouthful of pins, trying to work out where best to cut.

Princess Elizabeth, King Edward's eldest daughter, was sixteen to Isabel's twenty-six. But she looked far younger. She was stiff and owlish; her dignity was indistinguishable from a child's awkward silence.

The child had good reason to look solemn, Isabel thought, without particular compassion – there hadn't been a trace of warmth yet from the young royal person in front of her, standing so on her dignity, and Isabel saw

176

no reason for personal sympathy. Princess Elizabeth had just failed to become the Queen of France. Her father's English alliance with France had collapsed now that the sly French King had decided not to bother with the English wedding and, instead, had married his son to the Duke of Burgundy's daughter. The Princess's glittering future had turned to dust in a day. King Edward was furious for many reasons, one being that the King of France had also stopped paying him the fat pension he'd been living on for years, and a king as poor as Edward couldn't easily handle any loss of income. So Isabel had been called in to unpick the Princess's trousseau, sewn in the now suddenly violently disliked French style, and to decide which silk pieces could be reworked in a fashion less painful to observers, which could be reused for more down-to-earth purpose later. That was King Edward's way of venting his anger and saving money at the same time. Jane Shore had suggested it to him, and, while he was laughing in his easygoing way at his mistress's idea, she'd also suggested Isabel be chosen to do the work.

It was Elizabeth who'd bravely said to Isabel that they should start with the wedding gown itself – a magnificent confection of cloth of gold embroidered with a latticework of gold thread and pearls so stiff it seemed to be standing up by itself. She was wearing it now. But, even with all that splendour on her back, she was nothing much to look at herself, Isabel thought; the red hair she'd inherited from her beautiful mother was lovely enough, but she'd also got her father's tight little rosebud lips, and a pair of green eyes that might, in happier times, have been pretty, but were puffy and pinkish today, probably from crying. In the quiet of the antechamber, she looked all set to cry again.

Isabel was trying not to look up at the Princess's trembling lower lip when she became aware of a small sound behind her. She froze. She'd heard this might happen: this creeping, no-warning, hackle-raising manifestation of a new presence in the room, right behind your back. It meant the Queen was here: King Edward's wife, Queen Elizabeth Woodville, the striking redhead hated by everyone in England, the woman whose pointy beauty hid the temper of the devil himself.

Isabel shifted on her knees. She was aware of the Queen only as a swish of colour somewhere behind her; a prickling down her spine. She guessed the Queen was pacing, on kid slippers that made no sound, along the thick arras of this small, hot room, which was so filled with valuable clothing of almost miraculous design that you could practically feel pearls and gold thread in the dust tickling your throat. The Princess had starting breathing shallowly, as if afraid, and she'd stopped moving. There was panic in her swollen eyes. Isabel was glad she'd been already on her knees when the Queen entered.

She'd heard the stories about the Queen, keeping the ladies of the court standing for three silent hours a day while she dined. It wasn't hard to see that England's only ever commoner Queen would be just as eager to impose humiliating rules on servants. Rules that emphasised the grandeur of a Queen who'd come from nowhere. Who'd come to the attention of the kingdom at large nineteen years ago, when the young King Edward – gloriously descended from Japhet, son of Noah, through the Kings of Troy, the founders of Rome, and Brutus, the first king of Britain – had sneaked off and secretly married her while out hunting. Back then, she'd just been the impoverished widow of Sir John Grey, a Lancastrian who'd been killed fighting on the wrong side at the second battle of St Albans; she'd had nothing but her red-gold hair to help her make her way. People said the King had drawn a dagger on her to force her into his bed; but she'd just stared him down with her cool green eyes and said, 'I might be too base to be a King's wife; but I'm too good to be your harlot.' So he'd married her instead, and she'd stayed Queen even though the marriage had caused another war.

King Edward's strongest lord, the Earl of Warwick, had been so furious he'd brought back old, defeated King Henry from the shadows, and tried, for a year, to be Lancastrian. But Edward had won through in the end, and returned to London after a year to reclaim his queen from sanctuary at Westminster. Queen Elizabeth Woodville had given birth to his son, little Prince Edward, at the Abbot's house there. She was fearless all right, but she'd never be royal enough to relax. She'd always need fantastical displays of obeisance to help her believe she'd risen so far in the world. Isabel wanted to avoid humiliation by staying safely out of her way.

The wildcat footsteps stopped. Isabel's head was bowed, so all she could see was her own torso and knees, but every fibre of her body could feel the eyes burning into her.

Suddenly a hand was thrust in front of her: white, elegant, glittering fingers. Isabel stared. She didn't know what to do with it. Then, gingerly, hoping she wouldn't wobble if she moved, she reached for it with her right hand and kissed the fingertips. She didn't dare raise her head. She wasn't invited to either.

'They say you have nimble fingers, Mistress Claver,' she heard. Isabel squinted up as far as she could without being impertinent enough to raise her head. The Queen – with the most perfectly beautiful cat-face over her perfectly beautiful cat-body – knew she was peeping. Isabel realised the other woman was looking straight back into her eyes, with one corner of her lovely mouth lifted. Isabel wouldn't call it a smile. But she did realise, from that look, that whatever it was that was making the Queen almost vibrate with suppressed rage, it wasn't Isabel. She breathed. Looked up more boldly.

The Queen flicked a dismissive hand towards the great armoury of clothing that had been designed to awe two kingdoms, and celebrate God's blessing of the Princess as His own anointed Queen of France. Said, with a twist of her lips so fastidious that she might have been looking at rotting corpses: 'Well, do what you can with *that*', and, turning away with lithe, liquid movements, stalked off to the door. From there, beside the guards, without turning round, she dropped three final words. 'You may stand.'

But both Isabel and the Princess stayed frozen where they were for a few more moments, listening to her departing footsteps. Isabel got the impression that everything inside this Palace would always be done with the same caution. She wondered if everyone who survived a possible mauling by the Queen felt the same surge of warmth for their fellow-survivors as she was now feeling for the miserable-looking lump of a girl slouched in front of the arras. Growing up with that tiger of a mother must be every bit as frightening as Isabel's first dealings with Alice Claver had been.

Finally, she raised her head and dared to look at the Princess. For the first time, Princess Elizabeth deigned to look directly back at her, and Isabel was surprised to see that there was, after all, nothing childish in the girl's eyes. Elizabeth was no stranger to the curdling effects of humiliation and didn't expect Isabel to be; for all her trappings of finery, the princess was someone who didn't expect much from life. The Princess nodded dejectedly. 'Let's go on,' she said. 'She won't be back for a while.'

Isabel pinned in silence for a few more minutes. But she couldn't get those eyes, as watchful as hers had been every moment of her year in the selds, out of her head, or shake off her new awareness of the Princess as someone as helpless as Isabel had once been: someone waiting, and soaking up knowledge that might be useful later, biding her time, living through her period of powerlessness, just waiting for her chance to strike out for herself. So the silence grew warmer.

Eventually, Isabel ventured to speak. 'This must be very strange for you,' she mumbled, through her pins, and she was rewarded with just the kind of careful look she herself might have given one of the silkwomen she'd eventually grown close to, at the first sign of warmth. Elizabeth nodded, cautiously. 'It seemed so definite, my wedding,' she said. 'For so long. We used to act it out in the nursery, even; my little brother Edward would play being the King of England, giving me away at the altar to become Queen of France.'

Her eyes slid away. 'And now . . . nothing,' she added. There was a hint of bitterness in her voice as she added, 'I mean, for me. Though Edward will still be King one day.'

There was nothing Isabel could safely say to that. Carefully, she took out the remaining pins from her mouth and put them back in her box; then, thanking God for pins, called the two guards. While Elizabeth stepped out of the gown in one room, she oversaw the men carrying out the separated sleeves and train that made up the rest of the ensemble, each in a different padded velvet bag, from the outer room. The valuable garments would be taken under escort to Catte Street. It was a good first day's work.

The men returned to take away the pinned gown. Elizabeth stood in the doorway in her kirtle, listlessly watching. Trying again to comfort her, Isabel said: 'I expect there'll be a new marriage arranged for you before we even have time to take any of these apart . . .'

The Princess smiled a wintry smile in return, acknowledging Isabel's efforts at optimism even if she didn't pretend to be reassured by them.

'If I may,' Isabel said, feeling sorrier than ever for the girl, though still not sure whether that was the same as enjoying her company, 'I'll take my leave now, until next week. I don't want to tire Your Highness out . . .' She raised an eyebrow, to signify, 'May I be dismissed?'

To her surprise, that gesture made Elizabeth smile properly for the first time, like the child she'd so recently been. 'You can lift one eyebrow by itself!' she said, with unexpected childish joy. 'Like my uncle! We're always trying; but none of us can.'

'Oh . . .' Isabel said, touched; suddenly able to imagine all those young princesses with time hanging so heavy on their hands, realising that their easiest refuge would, naturally, be in the innocence of childish games that kept dangerous adult eyes away from them. 'Well, I'll show you the secret next time, then. We can practise.'

Was that really all it took to break the ice? Maybe they'd begin to have a real working relationship from now on; one that would bring Isabel more jobs in the future.

Isabel was smiling inside at a private joke, too: at how much more truth there was in the Princess's words than she could know. Dickon *was* always comically lifting one eyebrow. Had Isabel copied the gesture from him? Or he from her? She didn't know. But just that chance reminder of Dickon's existence – the memory of the muscles of his lively face working; the texture of his skin; his smell on the sheets – was enough to touch her with grace. It reminded her that, if she got out of the Palace within the hour – and she would now – she'd catch him at the inn before he went back north tomorrow.

She kept her dignity right through the process of leaving the Palace – one corridor, then a wait with the guards, smoothing down her skirts; another corridor, another escort, another wait until the next keys and spurs began jangling; right to the gates. But once she got outside, onto the street, she couldn't stop herself rushing. The air suddenly felt warm and wild with the promise of spring. She picked up her blue satin skirts so she could move faster. By the time she reached the Abbey, she was running.

He was waiting in the street. The impatient wind was flapping his cloak around his ankles. It was nearly dark.

'Come on,' he said, rough-voiced over the bluster of air. His eyes were gleaming. 'We're not staying here. It's late. I'm going to take you back to London. Your Alice Claver will worry about you otherwise.'

She laughed. 'What do you mean?' she asked. She had to almost shout; the wind blew away her words. 'There's still an hour; more.' But he just began pulling her along, the way she'd come, grinning. He had an idea. There was nothing for her to do but go along with it. She could never be sure what Dickon would do next.

Last time he'd been south had been for Twelfth Night, a month or more earlier. They'd had a snatched, intent hour's walk along the river, in the dark of London, on a colder, frostier version of this evening. The streets had been still full of debris from the previous night's madness. He'd been on his way to the Tower, where Lord Hastings, his friend as well as Jane's, had been waiting to show him the latest coin he was in charge of minting, the new angelet. In their dark cloaks that night, she and Dickon had looked like any other couple who might have drunk too much in the revels the night before, clinging to each other, feeling each other's heat: lovers with nowhere to go. It had been too painful, that visit; so short, so unfulfilled. She'd plucked at the quiet cloak at his neck with both hands. 'Your cloak of invisibility,' she'd said sadly. 'Who'd ever think you were a prince, kicking at old bottles on the wharves?' And he'd looked at her with the same longing she felt. Said nothing; kissed her a last time in front of All Hallows by the Tower, and walked away briskly, whistling, but still looking lonely, with the horse he was leading jingling its harness and blowing great clouds of white behind him.

He must have thought of something better for this evening – though she couldn't imagine what could be better or easier than the warm quiet of his tavern room, a haven she so seldom managed to visit. At the jetty, with one hand holding his dark cap down on his hair and the other around Isabel's waist, Dickon pulled out a purse and gave the first boatman he saw a gold coin and a wink. The stubbly old man stared doubtfully at it as the first stars made their pinpoint appearances in the sky. His creaking six-seater rowboat wouldn't be worth that much if he sold it. Was the gentleman drunk?

'Pick your boat up from the moorings below the bridge in the morning,' Dickon said blithely. 'I'll take it till then.' The man began to protest. But Dickon cut through his wheezing *my-livelihood-my-dearest-possession-as-God-help-me-I'm-a-father-of-six* talk with another gold coin and a wave of the hand. 'Have a drink on me,' Dickon added.

The man's eyes opened very wide. As if scared Dickon might change his mind, he pocketed both coins and scuttled off, very quickly, up the jetty. Dickon threw his head back and laughed at the greed in those rheumy eyes. 'Like a crab,' he spluttered; 'he just couldn't believe it, could he?'

Taking her cue from him, Isabel laughed too. Dickon made everything so easy.

He kissed her forehead. She raised her face to his, but, still smiling at the enjoyable memory, Dickon stepped back unexpectedly, and said, in servile tones, 'Your vessel awaits, milady,' and handed her down into the old boat. The water gurgled wildly around her, already nearly black, as the boat rocked and righted itself. The lantern at the back of the boat flickered, as if it was winking too. She looked breathlessly around. Was this his surprise? 'And your boatman,' he added, stepping in after her. He took the oars.

She drew in a deep gulp of wind. It was always like this: despair or euphoria, with nothing in between. The more she knew him the more she realised it always would be. He enjoyed living by the skin of his teeth. She liked to think that was why she loved him with this desperate simplicity – with a pure need that still sucked the breath out of her body and left her awed by its power. He didn't live with the solemnity of other princes, she thought; maybe because he hadn't always been a prince. He'd been everything in the course of the wars: noble before he became royal, since Edward hadn't grown up expecting to be King. Poor as well as rich. A winner now, but, for years, a loser. The uncertainty had left its mark; he still liked danger. She knew now that when she'd first met Dickon he'd just spent a year in hiding overseas with his brother. They'd only managed to escape England by a miracle. Lord Hastings had fought off the Lancastrians at the front door of the house where they'd been cornered; the King and Dickon escaped out the back. They'd found a ship, but had no money to pay for their passage. 'We had no idea where we were going,' Dickon had told her once, stroking her face, but with his mind in the past, 'and we had nothing but the clothes we stood up in. Thank God, Edward had a cloak lined with marten fur; the skipper took it instead of money.' He stopped; looked properly down at her; smiled wickedly. 'Best argument I know for a good strong dark anonymous cloak, lined with something very expensive.'

The cloak he was wearing now was lined with marten, too. He took it off and put it across her shoulders, under a big sky, shot with wisps of flame-coloured cloud. She sat very still on the passengers' platform at the front of the boat, lined with mildewed cushions, snuggling into the heaviness of the cloak. It was still warm from the touch of his body. As he rowed them out into the current, she looked first at the sun sinking over the water, then, as he neatly turned the boat – wherever had he learned how to row? – at the muscles she could see working in his back and arms, through his plain shirt. The water gurgled around them. Dreamy and warm, she listened to his rhythmic, heavy breathing and the judder of oars against rowlocks. The light faded.

He stopped rowing. He looked back at her, or perhaps at the end of the sunset behind her, with an expression she couldn't read. 'Beautiful,' he said softly, in a voice that made her shiver. He laid the oars carefully to rest inside the boat and shifted himself, too, onto the passenger platform where she was sitting.

She leaned against him. There was a light sweat on his forehead; on his chest. There was hardly anyone else on the river this late. He pulled her to him in a suddenly tender embrace and let her mouth find his. 'I'm willing to bet,' he whispered, very low, very mischievous, 'that you've never done this before', and he pushed her gently backwards.

She sank against the cushions. He pulled the cloak over both of them; she muttered, 'You can't; not here, on the river!' But he ignored whatever confused words she was whispering – rightly, as the way she was pulling him down onto her made it clear to both of them she didn't mean them – and, under the cloak now covering both of them, began touching mouth to skin again.

'Black cloak. No one can see us under it,' she heard

him whisper; then, mischievously, 'I think.' But by then she was beyond caring.

By the time their rapid breathing had given way to laughter; by the time she'd sat up, pulling her clothes back together, with her hair streaming loose and a shamefaced smile, saying, in a breathless pretence at reproach that was nothing of the kind, 'You really are the most sinful man I can imagine', as he kissed the inside of her arm and answered, 'And you the most abandoned woman I know – so, a good match', they'd drifted half a mile downstream and darkness had fallen in earnest.

'O-o-oh,' he said quickly, assessing where they were; sitting back up at the rower's bench, taking up the oars and setting off back upstream. 'This is where I'd like the real boatman back. Pity he's off getting drunk on more money than he's ever seen in his life.' He was humming under his breath as he rowed. She could see a flash of teeth every now and then.

He looks mighty pleased with himself, she thought.

As if intuiting her thought, he said gleefully: 'Did you know, I've never done that before either?'

But she just gazed at him, without questions; committing to memory this sliver of happiness, like the sliver of moon now visible in the sky, to comfort her in all the times when he wasn't there.

There was no hope she'd ever see more of Dickon than she did now. He was still as knife-sharp and whip-hard as the youth she'd first known – her own god of war made flesh. It was only his brother the King who'd got fat and self-indulgent.

Isabel knew this as much from Jane as from Dickon. She liked the comfortable way Jane spoke of the King, who, over the years, had become more her friend than her lover. Jane's confidences didn't make Isabel think there'd be any point in revealing her own secret love to her sister.

187

It was obvious that Jane's cosy friendship had none of the perfect spare urgency of what Isabel felt for Dickon. Jane would never understand. Still, now Isabel had become so successful in the City that she didn't need to compare herself with Jane any more, she enjoyed laughing indulgently at her sister's wide-eyed stories. King Edward's gut wobbling when he laughed at something Jane said. King Edward relaxing away from his demanding, exhausting, sharp-faced harridan of a wife, or chomping on a chicken, or enjoying letting Jane beat him at backgammon.

Now that King Edward liked those simple pleasures too much to want to fight his own wars, he needed Dickon to do all his fighting for him. He knew his brother to be more than a hard-bodied fighter and inspired general. Dickon was loyal too. And that meant Dickon was always on the road, and always would be.

As a reward for Dickon's military successes in Scotland – the whole of last year an agony of ignorance for Isabel, while he was away campaigning – the King had just added to his brother's already vast northern territories by granting him the county of Cumberland. Dickon was King of the North in all but name. He was happy. He'd never leave and come south. It was as unthinkable as the idea he'd once suggested: that Isabel might go and set up business in York. She'd just laughed: 'What would I do in York?' Even if there hadn't been her ever-expanding business in London and the Low Countries to think about, they both knew she wouldn't want to live in the shadow of his wife and child. Not that she was jealous of his wife, but she hated him even to mention his son, Edward, who must be nine or ten. She felt the child, not the mother, to be her real rival; she didn't want to think of his existence. They both tried not to complain of the shortness of their time together. This was all they could hope for. It had to be enough.

Now the rumour was that the King would soon start another war on France. If he did, Dickon would certainly go. And Isabel would endure more of the helpless pain of waiting; knowing she'd only find out if he'd been hurt or killed through street talk, because no one would think to tell her; why would anyone think she wanted to know? But before that began, for the next few months, while the war thickened like smoke before taking shape, he'd be coming to court; there'd be times – nights; half-days only, sometimes, but moments, at least, moments like this – to snatch at any price now so they could be remembered in the long wait later. If it meant lying to Alice Claver – still her mistress, formally, although nowadays it was Isabel who really ran everything – then so be it. She had no qualms about that. The commission Jane had just got for her, to work personally for Princess Elizabeth, would be more useful than Jane could possibly have imagined. As long as Alice Claver believed her to be at the Palace, she'd have no questions, ever, about Isabel going off to Westminster at short notice – where she could quietly see Dickon too.

'Do you think', she said, fishing for information about the shape her future would take, watching his back move, trying to sound casual, 'you will be sent to France?'

He didn't answer at once. But an oar sliced wildly over the surface of the water, splashing both of them and jerking the boat sideways.

He pulled it round; then, once his stroke was established again, said seriously, 'I don't know. Hastings wants to go all right. Spring's almost here: the campaign season. But I can't tell what's on Edward's mind.'

She couldn't see his face. His voice was coming from the shadows.

'Of course, if I went and Hastings went, and we took a proper army, Edward would end up alone here with all his wife's relatives,' she could hear him saying lightly, as if he might laugh, between gulps of air. 'In a court crawling with Woodville woodlice.'

Isabel snickered encouragingly. No one liked the jumped-up Woodvilles, all the Queen's on-the-make relatives who'd crept and married and slunk into power along with the commoner Queen. Court was two factions: them, against everyone who hated them. Only Jane, prudently, kept in with both groups. One of Jane's long-term admirers was, as ever, Lord Hastings, a leading light of the true nobility at court. Her other admirer, still, was Hastings' bitterest Woodville rival, the pretty, pushy, blond Marquess of Dorset (Isabel wasn't sure he was as faithful to his chaste love of Jane as Hastings was). Dorset was Queen Elizabeth Woodville's son by her first marriage. His beery, bleary, insulting attempt to grope Isabel in a tent, long ago, had defined her feelings towards the entire Woodville clan. Now she wrinkled her face and muttered, 'Ugh. Like Dorset . . . Jane still sees him, you know . . .'

Dickon had laughed at the story of that fumble. And it was one of the pleasures of being with him – a childish pleasure, she knew, but one that went with letting herself be perfectly frank with her lover – that Isabel sometimes encouraged him to talk less than kindly about Jane. Jane's overdressing. Jane's idleness. Jane's wish to twist men round her little finger. Jane's belief that the world could run on nothing more than smiles and silliness. Isabel knew, deep down, that Dickon only joined in because she egged him on; and sometimes she was uncomfortably aware that he was more loyal to his brother than she to her sister. But then, his brother was the King; while her sister was . . . well, a royal mistress was still a whore, wasn't she?

Today, Dickon wasn't going to be drawn into a spiteful conversation about Jane. She could see his head up in front, shaking sympathetically. But all he said was, 'Ah, once a Woodville . . . you've heard Dorset told the King last week that Hastings was plotting to sell Calais to the French, haven't you?' She laughed with him. Then he went on with his own thought, excusing his brother's indecisiveness about whether to go to war on France: 'Being left alone with a palace full of vermin like that would give me pause, all right. If I were Edward. He's still weighing things up.'

His voice fell silent. The only sound was the oars on the water.

'I don't mind,' he said suddenly, through the rhythmic splashing. 'About France. I can't go yet anyway. There's something I've got to settle first, at home.'

She heard the tightness in his voice now. This was what he was really thinking about.

Ready to reassure, she asked: 'What?' She wanted to know; but she never knew if she would still want to know once she knew more. His problems so often just reminded her of the gulf between their two lives.

'A land problem,' he said. Voice hollow; oars steady. 'In a way.'

'What way?' she persisted, sharply now, sitting forward. It was important to her to understand him, however hard it sometimes was. She wanted to do what little was in her power to protect him. 'Tell me.'

As he began, she realised it wasn't what her merchant mind would call a land problem at all. Dickon's nephew, a child called George Neville, lived with Dickon at Middleham. And he was ill: fever; coughing blood; wasting. 'I'm taking a physician north in the morning,' Dickon said. 'It's why I can't stay longer. I'm worried he's dying.'

She murmured, neutrally. Sometimes it didn't do to show your ignorance. She'd find out in a minute why, to an aristocrat, this was a land problem. She just had to let him tell.

He did. George was the child of traitors. Because of the rebellion by his Neville father and uncle twelve years ago, the estates the boy might once have inherited had been confiscated. They'd been given instead to Dickon and his brother Clarence, because the King's two brothers had Neville wives, and (after Clarence died, and Dickon got the rest of the lands too) the Neville estates had become the heart of Dickon's northern domains. Dickon needed that land to keep the rest of the North under his control. But – and here was the rub – if little George Neville were now to die childless, the Act of Parliament that had given Dickon the lands also said that the lands would only be Dickon's for his lifetime. His son, Edward of Middleham, wouldn't inherit them. After Dickon's death, they would go back to the Nevilles.

'You see my problem,' Dickon said. He'd stopped rowing. He'd raised the oars out of the water, and was pushing down on them with taut arms. He was twisting his head back to look at her for guidance. 'He dies – and it weakens my authority throughout the North, and loses my child half his inheritance.' He grimaced. 'And he *is* dying. I can see.'

She nodded. Quickly, to herself, she flicked through possible forms of comfort or advice she might offer. There was no point in expressing sympathy for the Neville boy's suffering; she hadn't heard any note of regret in that low-pitched exposition that suggested Dickon might enjoy living with him or miss his company if he passed on. And she couldn't discuss Dickon's own son's prospects, even if she'd had anything useful to say. But she could hear her lover wanted a framework to plan by; he wanted her wits.

'Who's the doctor?' she said. As a Londoner, she knew physicians, at least.

'Gigli,' he said.

192

'The Venetian,' she replied thoughtfully. She knew Dr Gigli sometimes tutored the little Prince of Wales and his brother Richard, when they were at Westminster. She'd seen him at prayer at St Thomas of Acre: he was sleek, with glittering eyes and a smooth jowl. The London Lombards all took their illnesses to him. 'Well, he has a good reputation.'

Dickon carried on looking steadily at her. It was too dark to be able to see the puckered brow or the chewed lower lip: the expression he wore when the burdens of leadership outweighed the pleasures. All she could see was eyes. But she read quiet hope in them; the closest he ever came to vulnerability. It made her heart swell to be needed liked this.

She filled her voice with all the calm certainty she could. She leaned forward; she could just reach close enough to put a hand on his twisted near shoulder. He put his own hand on hers. 'Well, take Gigli to the boy. See how he does,' she said, feeling the comfort of skin on skin; hoping it comforted him too. 'Gigli may make a difference.'

She let the warmth vibrate in her voice and linger in the air for a moment. Then she pressed on. Dickon was too sharp-brained to be satisfied with just that. 'But if the boy really is dying, and there's nothing Gigli can do,' she said frankly, 'it's still not an insoluble problem.'

It was his turn to murmur, as if waiting for enlightenment.

'Look, the King's just granted you the whole palatinate of Cumberland,' she went on persuasively. 'He certainly doesn't want your estates broken up. You hold his kingdom together. He's going to need you even more soon – to fight in France. You'll have to use that need. Talk to him while he plans the campaign; while needing you is uppermost in his mind. And make him promise then – soon – to intervene to protect your son. He'll understand why.

He's your brother; he loves you. And he's the King. He'll find a way.'

Slowly, Dickon nodded. In the lantern light she could see clouds clearing from his eyes. 'Yesss,' he murmured, letting breath escape slowly from his chest, and already his voice was less tight. 'I can see how the French campaign will help concentrate his mind . . .'

He started rowing again; big, easy strokes, towards the shore. It was getting cold. Isabel pulled the cloak tighter about her, wishing she could get rid of the image behind her eyes: a child's bony white face and pitiful black-ringed eyes.

It was only when they were already at the jetty, and Dickon was leaning forward in the thickness of the night air, fiddling with the rope, that he spoke again. 'Edward will help,' the black velvet voice said; and it had borrowed Isabel's certainty.

Aware that a parting was coming, but not wanting to make much of it, they talked only about inconsequential things on the way through the dark streets, already nearly empty so close to curfew. Dickon asked about Isabel's meeting with the Princess ('They're good children, Edward's,' he said, without especial warmth). They laughed at the terrifying appearance Queen Elizabeth Woodville had made during the fitting. Dickon said he'd walk up to the Tower from Catte Street now, and ask Hastings for a bed rather than go to his family home in London, Baynard's Castle. Hastings would be amused to see him on foot, and to hear he'd rowed upriver like a boatman. Quelling her impossible wish to be able to follow him, Isabel told him about the deal she was proud of having made with Pieter Bruinvels of Antwerp for £45 of Lucchese black velvet for shipment next week.

'And how's your Venetian?' Dickon asked, as the Catte Street house came into view. 'Goffredo D'Amico?'

194

There was a trace of awkwardness in the question. He'd left it till last to ask about the silk-weaving business that was still her favourite commercial dream. He kept the scepticism off his face, too; he made a point of taking her work concerns as seriously as she took his; but she felt disbelief hiding in him somewhere.

She knew Dickon had long ago stopped taking this project seriously. She couldn't be surprised, either, after all these years of Goffredo coming and going from London, always with new stories about why his endlessly protracted negotiations with the Venetian authorities hadn't yet borne fruit, always with some new bureaucratic obstacle to be overcome; the excruciatingly slow pace at which she and Goffredo had exported from Venice and imported to England all the separately packed parts of all those looms and other machines and delivered them, under a variety of aliases, to the house at Westminster, which was supposed to be full of Venetian masters, working, but still wasn't. There were times when she didn't believe the workshop would ever start work, either; when all that filled her heart when she thought of Goffredo, composing his ruggedly handsome features into a mask of regret and wringing his elegant hands as he poured out his latest excuse, was frustration. There were times when only Alice Claver seemed to go on doggedly trusting Goffredo. She'd growl: 'Have faith', and, 'You may not realise it, but what he's achieving over there is really nothing short of a miracle.' Reality must be testing even Alice's faith to the utmost; still, Isabel knew it was important to go on trying to believe it would happen. So she suppressed the sigh that had almost escaped her lips, and said, with her best attempt at enthusiasm: 'Well, it's coming along! Goffredo went back to Venice last week to collect the weavers. He says they'll be here by Passiontide. The workshop could be up and running by May Day.'

Her voice sounded forced, even to herself; her smile was strained.

Dickon drew her into his arms and touched his nose to hers. She felt the whole length of his body against hers in the pause that followed. She never wanted him to go. 'Passiontide, eh?' he murmured, and the lopsided smile on his face was one of farewell. 'It would be good if you were in Westminster often by then. I might be, too.'

And he was off. A flash of eyes; then just a shadow flitting along the wall.

It always took a moment to shake off one world and enter another – a moment of dizziness. But she could hear women's conversation in the great hall, where there'd be a fire by now; where they would have eaten already. The old silkwomen were waiting for her.

Sometimes the sound of those voices stripped Isabel of all the sleek self-assurance she'd assumed as she learned to make trades with the greatest merchants of Europe; sometimes they made her feel, again, like a shy young apprentice. Tonight was like that.

Sighing, Isabel re-entered her own reality and pushed open the door.

Anne Pratte's lip quivered when Isabel reported back on her successful first encounter at the Palace, and told them plainly what she'd just decided at the front door – that if she was going to go back to Westminster once a week for the rest of the fittings, she'd stay a night there at the silk house once a week too. 'It will avoid this late return,' she said, as the curfew bell began ringing outside the window, 'in the dark.'

Alice Claver looked thunderous. But, as Isabel inspected her mistress's face to see how bad the impending storm might be and what protective measures she should take, she found herself caught instead in the regretful thought:

how old she looks. Iron-grey hair, so many tones darker than Anne Pratte's gentle white that Isabel, who looked at both women every day, had somehow not been aware of it until now. A heavily corded throat. Lines dragging her cheeks down past her mouth; more lines between nose and mouth from her habit of wrinkling her lips into a small, tight O at the same time as she narrowed her eyes. Blotched, heavily veined hands.

'But,' Anne Pratte faltered, 'you can't. You'll be away for half the working week.'

'Quite impossible!' Alice Claver barked. 'You spend far too much time gadding about as it is. We need you here.' She paused. Considered. Added, 'I', and nodded, more decisively, 'need you here.'

Touched, Isabel said: 'But I'll still be here.' It was a new idea to her that her formidable teachers might be lonely without her, but Alice Claver's jutting lower lip made it wrenchingly plain how much they must now depend on her to be their child, their hope, their entertainment. She made her voice gentle. 'It's only one night a week.'

In principle, they should have been excited; let her do what she needed to make the contract work. Most people in the Mercery would have killed for this contract. Once Isabel had been to the Palace for measurements and fittings, she could subcontract the agreed alterations through the Claver house. The money would be excellent. And the prestige of working directly for the royal family, without having to bow and scrape to the officials at the Royal Wardrobe in Old Jewry, was beyond price.

Suddenly Isabel recalled Jane's bright, encouraging gaze when she'd told her sister about the promised work. 'It's up to you', Jane had said kindly, 'to make yourself so indispensable that you go on being called back to Westminster to do more.' Remembering the kindness in those beautiful eyes made Isabel prickle uncomfortably; when she knew she was so often so uncharitable towards her sister. Thanks to Jane, there need be no more of the subterfuges she'd had to enter into until now, whenever Dickon sent word in his peculiar way – 'there'll be cured pork for sale at the Almonry tomorrow at noon', or 'firewood on Friday' – to signify he was on the road south.

It had always been so hard for her to get away from Alice and Anne; she'd run out of excuses. Once she'd had to return to London before Dickon even got to Westminster. He'd been delayed; she'd been pretending to equip the kitchen at the Westminster silk house with pans; to have stayed a second night would have meant worrying Alice. Another time, after another delay on the road from Middleham, she'd had to throw herself on Jane's incurious mercy and pretend to be staying with her sister, while, in reality, she was sneaking back to Westminster to wait again in the empty silk house; stuffing rags around the shutters so her candle flame wouldn't show; slinking into cook-shops, buying pies with her face half-covered by veils; or just going hungry, too consumed by the hope he was at the door, or would be soon, to care. Now, the work Jane had found her would make it possible for Isabel to be nearby when Dickon was there; Isabel's faith and planning would do the rest. Jane's done me a big favour, she thought guiltily.

'But, dear, you can't do the job properly anyway; you're not a real vestment-maker,' Anne Pratte was saying plaintively.

From behind her, her husband, sitting so quiet and still that Isabel had almost forgotten he was there, rumbled into life. Sympathetic life, Isabel was relieved to hear.

'But, dear, that doesn't matter,' William Pratte said, with exaggerated patience. 'It's not a problem to find craftswomen. That's not what we're talking about.

This is a great opportunity for Isabel. Of course she must do whatever she needs to make a good fist of it.'

'Well, what about the petition?' Anne Pratte wailed back at her husband. 'We can't finish that without her.'

Isabel smiled. That, at least, was clearly not true. William Pratte had the next draft petition to be presented to Parliament under his hand. They'd been discussing it before they ate. Even now the light had all but gone, Isabel could still make out phrases from the front-page preamble, written out in his crabby old-man's hand: '*Sylkewymmen and Throwestres of the Craftes and occupation of Silkewerk . . .*' '*. . . lyved full honourably, and therewith many good Householdes kept, and many Gentilwymmen and other in grete noumbre like as there nowe be more than a M, haue be drawen under theym in lernyng the same Craftes and occupation ful vertueusly . . .*' He could be long-winded on paper. But he wasn't now. He just picked up the papers and waved them at his wife. She looked damply down.

'Don't be a fool, Anne,' Alice Claver said. 'That's not the point.' She fixed Isabel with an accusing stare. 'It's Goffredo.'

Now they all turned to look at Isabel.

Goffredo's current trip to Venice was supposed to be the very last of the dozens he'd made, over the years, to set up the business. When he came back he'd have the Venetian master weavers he'd contracted with him: Gasparino di Costanzo, Alvise Bianco di Jacopo, and Marino da Cataponte. Their families would come too. Once they reached England, they'd need to be set up; brought to the Westminster house; have servants hired; be taught enough English to survive in the street; and be provided with food, firewood, silk thread, and the discreet, hand-picked apprentices from London whom Isabel had already sounded out. It would be pandemonium for months; the time they'd been waiting on for so long. It could start any day now. They were ready and waiting for Goffredo: debts settled; Venetian travel permits issued; bags practically packed.

At least, they were supposed to be. But Isabel surely wasn't the only person in the room to realise that, even if Goffredo didn't run into storms on the journey, there would be bound to be more last-minute hitches and hiccups once he was there. There was only a month and a half before Passiontide. 'Passiontide at the latest!' he'd promised, joyful and optimistic as ever. But they all also remembered that Isabel had raised an eyebrow at him over the table. And that he'd blushed; and shrugged as if she'd caught him out in a lie; and spread his big hands out so wide that the jewels on his fingers had glittered, and added, 'if I possibly can', in a shamed little-boy way. Personally, Isabel doubted he and his teams would get to England before the end of summer. Michaelmas. Or, just possibly, if things went unusually smoothly, by Lammastide in August. Meanwhile, she reasoned, there was no point in turning down lucrative work.

She hesitated, feeling her way into words that would persuade, not offend, Alice and Anne. Refusing to feel panic that this gift, this freedom that her sister had won her, could be snatched away. Wondering how Dickon would have handled the old women's resistance. Letting her tongue and her instinct take the lead.

In the end, staring at the expectant eyes, all Isabel did was to smile and spread her hands out wide. 'This is only for a few months,' she said firmly. 'It's a question of putting out the work, and getting it back in. It's a wonderful relationship to nurture; and, anyway, do we really know when Goffredo is coming?' She added, sarcastically: 'Passiontide at the latest!' Then: *Eef poss-ssible! May Day eef not a-poss-ssible! Or St John's Eve, or*

Lammastide! Or Michaelmas! Or Christmastide eef my ship a-sinks!'

She wasn't really that good at Goffredo's Venetian braggadoccio. But her imitation made William Pratte laugh – a big snort of relief. Then, with silent women on either side giving him their most terrifying stares, he snuffled and stopped. 'Well,' he said, looking hunted. 'She's right, you know. It will take him months. Venice always does.'

Two more deadly looks struck him. But he went defiantly on: 'Look, even if he does get here by Passiontide, or Lady Day, it's surely not a problem. Isabel will already be spending one night a week at Westminster. She'll be right where she's needed.'

There was another awful silence. Finally, slowly, reluctantly, Anne Pratte muttered: 'I suppose you're right, dear,' and turned up the corners of her mouth in something not far off a smile. The ice and fire went out of the spring air. And, although Alice Claver continued to say nothing, just to give William Pratte the kind of looks that Christ in His goodness had forborne to give Judas Iscariot, her furious distress at the planned change in their routine somehow didn't matter. The decision Isabel wanted had been taken without Alice Claver's consent: a sign of the shift in power in the household that they all, without speaking, recognised had happened. Full of relief and sunshine, Isabel found herself thinking of the older woman's thwarted rage with something like sympathy.

In the morning, Isabel went to Old Jewry to thank Jane. She knew it was right to visit her sister. And she was grateful to her. But there were butterflies in her stomach all the same.

She didn't know why she still found it so hard to be affectionate and gracious with her sister. She should feel easier with Jane, she thought, now that her own income

201

had become substantial enough to take the sting out of having been disinherited. Isabel's profits from trading had allowed her to invest about a third of her capital in three small rental houses, six shops in the Crown Seld, a block of stalls down Soper Lane and the tenement in which Joan Woulbarowe's old aunt Rose Trapp lived. Her rents alone must equal anything John Lambert's inheritance would bring Jane, especially now that he'd chosen the precarious route to wealth of relying on rents from country property; and since he had (foolishly, in Isabel's view) allowed the King to repay all those vast cash loans with manors of dubious provenance: estates confiscated from exiled Lancastrians and scattered around the West Country. John Lambert lived in Somerset now. Isabel didn't see him. Jane said he had aspirations to buy or earn himself a knighthood; enter the gentry. Still, he must worry: what if, one day, the Lancastrians he'd displaced out there came back to claim their lands? Jane had the house in Old Jewry that had been her portion after Will Shore had finally seen sense and accepted the annulment the King arranged. She had the King's gifts and jewels. Still, Isabel was certainly richer.

It didn't make any difference. Being with Jane still made her feel all thumbs and elbows. An afterthought. Second best.

It didn't help that as she turned the corner into Old Jewry, she bumped, literally, into Will Caxton, who'd stopped in the street to brush worriedly at himself before what must be an important meeting. As soon as they'd disentangled themselves, he went back to picking imaginary specks off his carefully brushed baldekin doublet, not seeming to realise his sleeves were so worn they'd gone threadbare at the elbow. 'Isabel, in London, what a pleasure,' he said at the same time, peering affectionately at her; then bowing with the dignified mercer's formality he'd maintained long after leaving the guild. 'I was just going to pay a call on your sister. Are you?'

She smiled a little sadly and nodded. 'I suppose I should have expected to find you heading this way too, Will,' she said, wishing Jane's magic didn't work so reliably on every man she met, even this one, Isabel's dearest old friend.

Ever since Caxton had come back to England, and really had set up his printshop, and his home, at Westminster, right next to Isabel's silk house, she was in and out all the time. She relied on him to keep an eye on her house, to light the occasional fire in winter and open the occasional window in summer. She turned to him for advice about how to store and stack the machines Goffredo was sending, and for keys and pans and the occasional loan of servants. But their friendship was closer than that. Will Caxton, with his new printing venture, was already living the dream Isabel had for her own future. She drank in every one of his stories about the ups and downs of his business. She kept his secrets. She sympathised with the loneliness and worry of his work. She trusted his judgement. She'd come to think of him like family; like a rather old brother.

But she couldn't quite respect his feelings for Jane. It had been five years since the elderly widower first declared his love for Jane Shore by dedicating to her one of the books he was now printing full-time on the presses he'd brought home. Not by name – he'd been too timid – but they'd all known who he had in mind when he'd prefaced his Chaucer translation of Boethius in 1478 with the coy phrase '*printed at the request of a singular frende & gossip of mine*'.

Isabel had seen him fall in love, two years before that, when he'd first come back to England. He was staying then with the Prattes while he organised his Westminster lease. Isabel thought: if he's setting up a new business too, he'll need powerful friendships. Will Caxton had never met Jane, or wanted to – Alice Claver's disapproval had been enough for him. But Jane was established as the King's mistress now; she might help Will as she'd helped Isabel. So, impulsively, Isabel had invited him and Jane on a picnic at Moorfields. But, instead of using this precious contact wisely, as she'd had every reason to expect, Will had taken one look at the tall blonde girl in yellow silk, coloured up beetroot-red under the fading ginger hair peeping out from the hat he hadn't set properly on his head, and begun to talk. Flirt. Pass her dainties with suggestive smiles. Bring her little gifts. Sing German love songs in a cracked voice. Tell her City gossip in his odd Kentish accent. Laugh too hard and fast at her court stories. Lurk in the street when he hoped she might pass by. Cadge invitations to her presence. Cringing like a dog that's always expecting to be kicked; but, because Jane was too happy-go-lucky, or lazy, to cause pain, never actually feeling her toe crack against his ribs. There was no hope for him; he knew that. But he'd always seemed happy to worship without hope.

Looking at his old face, addled and silly with love, Isabel thought: he may stay like this forever. 'Let's brush you up,' she added gently, dusting him off and tweaking at sleeves and seams until he went pink with pleasure. There was nothing to be done about his black fingers. 'Those elbows need fixing,' she chided affectionately, before, linking arms, they made their way together to Jane's door.

Jane was delighted to see them both. She'd already been hugging to herself her pleasure at having got Isabel such a good commission; hoping her sister would call. But now dear old Will was here too, with that bulging bag that no doubt meant he had some new book-printing favour to ask, and giving her one of his adorably imploring looks. She'd be able to tell him the good news she was saving up for him – and be able to show Isabel how well she was looking after her sister's friends, too.

'Come in, come in,' she said, scattering kisses and embraces and smiles and bows around with the extravagance of mannerism she'd learned by long association with courtiers, yet which still felt a little unnatural around her sister. Isabel sometimes courteously told her that being the King's mistress, or whatever it was that she was to Edward these days, suited her; that she grew more beautiful by the day, even at the advanced age of twenty-eight; but her silkwoman sister always said those things with an ironic gleam in her eye that suggested to Jane she didn't quite mean them.

Although Jane had kept some of her family ties to the City whose existence surrounded her, and had even gone to the trouble of having herself declared a Freewoman of the City of London at the same time as Isabel, on Isabel's twenty-first birthday, so that, in principle, both sisters now had the right to trade as well as to advantageous access to justice and London government, Isabel's sceptical expression when considering Jane's courtly ways sometimes made Jane feel an alien in her own home town. So now Jane tried to restrain the dance of her hair and veils and arms; the glitter of gold on silk; but at the same time she wasn't too worried if Isabel did find her affected today, because once Isabel found out what new miracles Jane had managed to arrange, she'd ... she'd ... Jane couldn't even quite imagine how her still-faced, watchful-eyed sister would express her extreme joy. But that she'd feel it there could be no doubt. She knew Isabel worried about Will too.

Will Caxton was always bothering Jane about his books.

He had an insatiable hunger for patrons. Jane had done her best. She'd got him the official title of King's printer, and, although his new calling earned him only a fraction of what his old Mercery dealings had brought him, he was as happy as a lark translating books and writing prefaces and running his print shop and messing about with his foreign foreman Wynkyn and their strange, clanking machines. (His print machines had been good cover for Isabel, now that the parts of the twenty silk looms, deviously imported in pieces over a period of several years, so that their purpose couldn't be guessed at in the port of London – Jane admired the way they'd done that – were all propped up along the walls of the silk-house workshop, ready to be assembled. Anyone not conversant with the silk trade, and in Westminster there was no one but Isabel who was, might just be fooled into thinking these were parts for more outlandish print machines at the Caxton house next door.)

But poor Will still worried all the time about money. Jane thought Isabel probably would, in the same way, if the Claver silk-weaving venture ever got going – even though silk was a more reliable source of income than the printed word. Worry was the price everyone would have to pay for putting their heart into promoting these risky new manufactures. Even now Will was back in England, where he'd thought buyers would flock to him for his books, it was often hard to shift stock. He still had piles of the early ones, for which he'd chosen such bad dedicatees; he didn't seem to have the knack of finding good protectors for himself.

The first book, the chess one, which he'd printed in Bruges, he'd been foolish enough to dedicate to the King's second brother, the Duke of Clarence – who, as any Londoner could have told him, if he'd bothered to ask, had no time for books anyway and was a petulant, unstable, vengeful, dangerous fool into the bargain. (And that was even before the Duke had gone mad with grief over the death of his wife and son, and ended up accused of treason over all the murky stories about witchcraft, poisoning, wax dolls and pins that began to attach to him; and was then found dead in the Tower, where he'd been imprisoned.) If it hadn't been for Jane's introductions and praise in the right quarters, Caxton's business might easily have got into serious trouble right at the start.

Once Jane had started helping him, Caxton had acquired some influential friends. Jane had had a word with Dorset. Within weeks, Caxton had been permitted to dedicate books to the most bookish of the Woodvilles, Dorset's uncle and Queen Elizabeth Woodville's brother, Earl Rivers. Rivers was now the governor of little Prince Edward and his brother and spent a lot of time with them at Ludlow, on the Welsh border, where the Prince of Wales' household was formally based. Caxton and the learned Earl Rivers had developed a book-lover's friendship, and Caxton had won several commissions to print the Earl's translations. He'd even been allowed to present a book to the little crown prince himself – he'd chosen the story of Jason, the boy king threatened by his Herod-like wicked uncle, Pelias, who usurped the throne while pretending to be Jason's protector. With a further nudge from Jane, Caxton had included both boy princes in the flowery dedication he'd been allowed to make to the King of his account of the crusade of Godfrey of Bouillon.

Just to be sure Will Caxton had friends among the Woodvilles' enemies, Jane had also made sure that Will Hastings received a book dedicated to him – a *Mirror of the World* ordered by Hugh Bryce, the goldsmith, Will Hastings' deputy at the Royal Mint. So Caxton should have been nicely set up.

But Jane knew he'd got stuck on the translation of *The*

207

Golden Legend that Earl Rivers had ordered from him back in the autumn. He'd spent too long on it: a labour of love he couldn't bear to hurry. She didn't like to imagine the poor man, running low on funds, too scared to ask for an advance, scratching himself all over, rumpling up his hair in that unattractive way he had whenever he got worried. So she'd found more help.

In her parlour, with its wonderful pearl-encrusted hanging showing Judgement Day (she wasn't superstitious; she refused to believe her understanding with Edward could mean she'd be among the damned being strangled on the wall by the little tapestry devils, or that God had cursed her, any more than he had Edward), Jane politely pressed exotic fruits and cups of wine on her guests, and listened with affectionate pride while Isabel told the story of meeting the Princess, and tittered at Isabel's account of the Queen's fearsome pacing, and bowed her head modestly and prettily when Isabel thanked her, less laconically than she usually did, before breaking her news.

'Will,' she breathed, her gaze as sweetly honeyed as her breath, enjoying his happy-to-drown look: 'I've got you two new commissions. Good ones. *Very* good.'

His eyes opened wide. So excited and relieved that she knew she'd guessed right about his being hard up.

'The Marquess of Dorset would like you to print him a curial,' she said, pleasurably drawing out the next phrase, 'he has the text ready.' She knew Will would be most thrilled of all to hear that; a prepared text meant this would be a quick job, probably even quick enough to pay whatever bills were pressing. Will began to burble something; his face was pink under hair that looked more salt than pepper these days – soon, Jane thought sadly, if inconsequentially, it would be quite white.

'And when you've done that, do you think', she continued with exquisite politeness, 'you would have time to translate the Book of the Knight of the Tower into English . . . and print it' – it was cruel to pause now, but she couldn't resist waiting so she could be absolutely sure she had both listeners' full attention – 'for Her Majesty the Queen?'

The reaction was just what she'd hoped. Will kissing her hand and laughing with such delight and relief that he was practically sobbing; and Isabel so astonished that Jane had done something so practical for Will, not to mention getting a commission from the woman who hated her most at court (though it should be obvious that she'd gone through Dorset, as usual), that she forgot to look half as quizzical as usual.

Jane found herself quietly watching her sister, as she often did, for some telltale sign of love. A token around her neck, perhaps; a mark on her skin. Or just a blush. But even today, when Isabel was smiling with more warmth than usual, there was nothing.

She'd never say this to Isabel, of course, but her most secret hope was that her little sister would be distracted from her money-making by falling in love and marrying, and give the whole thing up. She'd like to see her sister married and happy with children one day soon. She'd like to see Isabel lose her self-contained look; see her tired out with happiness instead. Sometimes she thought she'd like that for herself, too, one day; sometimes when she surprised other women gazing at the babies in their arms, two faces locked together in a look of shared, complete absorption, she'd feel a pang of loneliness she couldn't explain, even to herself. But it wasn't the time for her now. She was too well established as she was to think of changing her life. Edward needed his escapes to her; she couldn't imagine a life without his visits. And too many of her own people in the City needed her to be with Edward. Especially her father. Even if John Lambert had long ago given up hope of becoming Mayor of London, the greatest dream of his life, he'd consoled himself in recent years with his new ambition of dying a country gentleman. It had been a blow, of course, when his entire team of ex-apprentices left his silk house within days, each one implausibly claiming to be going home to the provinces to care for sick parents. Jane had felt indignant with Isabel for a while: there were so many other silk-women she could have chosen to hire away from their masters, after all; and their father had been so bewildered. Still, she could see why Isabel had chosen that revenge. John Lambert hadn't been kind to her either, and they were both so stubborn there was no talking sense into either of them about their feud. So Jane had looked for other ways to help her father. The King, with a bit of gentle nudging from Jane, had repaid John Lambert for his loans with a gift of 2,000 acres in the West Country, confiscated from the Lancastrian Courtenay family. Jane's father had started to find himself enjoying his new manors in Devon and Somerset, enough to want more. He needed Jane right where she was. So Jane carried on from one carefree day to the next, doing one small favour here and another insignificant kindness there, going hawking or staying at home playing cards with her guests, without worrying too much about tomorrow. Edward would give John Lambert a knighthood soon. And whatever happened, she thought, God would provide for her.

But Isabel – there was no reason for her to wait. And Jane had an instinct that there was more to Isabel's trips west so many times a year than the agonisingly slow progress of the silk-weaving venture really justified.

Part of it Jane understood. It was obvious Isabel wanted time away from that old dragon Alice Claver, who as far as Jane could see still treated her clever, competent, loyal ex-apprentice with the kind of suspicious mistrust not

210

even a thief deserved. Jane was delighted to help deceive the stout old brute by pretending Isabel was with her whenever Isabel asked her to. But she couldn't help hoping there was more to the trips than that. She wanted them to mean there was a love story somewhere in Isabel's life.

That was why, the last time Edward had spent the night with her, she'd hit on the French gowns alteration idea. She'd broached it at just the right moment, too: after she'd teased him, when he'd pushed the blankets of her bed away and revealed his increasingly well-upholstered stomach, and she'd put her head happily on it and her bare arms around it and whispered, mischievously, 'still a fine figure of a man!' – which he was, considering he'd turned forty and enjoyed his pleasures so flamboyantly – and he'd laughed until his gut rippled, and grinned down at her in his indulgent way, and pulled her back up to him. It was in the middle of the kiss that followed that she'd realised what she needed to ask – to get Isabel all the free time away she could need.

Jane looked with satisfaction at her sister, who was talking with such animation now to dear old Will. 'I've told them I'm going to spend Friday nights at the silk house from now on,' Isabel was telling him, at the rattlesnake speed she favoured when she was excited, 'so I'll be right next door. We could have dinner at the tavern, often; and perhaps even eat together in the mornings, if you can spare the time, before I come back to London. I'll be taking the boat, for now; no horses yet; it's too early to hire servants, until we know when the silk teams will be here; I don't want to take yours too often . . .'

There was a bit of colour in Isabel's usually pale cheeks, Jane thought; but nothing to suggest anything more than excitement at the idea of actually sleeping at the silk house – which must make the idea of the silk-weaving venture seem more real for her. Nothing to suggest a hidden love.

She smiled wistfully at them. She didn't mind the possibility that Isabel might be hiding something from her; not if it made her happy. If Isabel did turn out to have a secret in Westminster, Jane thought, trusting in God to make everything come right in His own time, she'd tell her sister about it whenever the moment was right.

Goffredo hadn't come back by Passiontide. Nor had Dickon. But Isabel's pleasant new routine of weekly visits to the Princess, dinners at the Red Pale with Will Caxton and Friday night stays at the silk house was well enough established for her to have grown used even to the place's lonely night-time creaks and scuttlings.

She couldn't go for the usual fitting on Good Friday itself, so, unusually, she went the following Tuesday instead, 9 April, once the churches were glorious with flowers and the Lenten shrouds thrown back and people with roast lamb in their stomachs had lost the meatless scratchiness of March and got roses in their cheeks instead.

She hardly noticed the balminess of the breeze. She let the river slip by unwatched. She was happily preoccupied with the task ahead: discussing with the Princess the placement of tassels and the commissioning of new laces and points for a pair of crimson damask sleeves embroidered with fleurs-de-lys, which would also need unpicking and reworking. With white roses, perhaps?

It was only as she got off the boat at Westminster that she realised something was wrong.

There were more people out and about than usual – all sorts: men-at-arms, housewives, monks – and there was an air of panic about them. Rushing about like ants whose home has been trodden on, she thought curiously. What's got into them?

Then the bells began. Abbey bells. One booming,

gloomy note, over and over again. It went right through her head.

Half-deafened, full of a misery she didn't yet understand, she trotted into the gatehouse to ask. There was a fat woman outside, holding a grocery basket, sobbing.

The gatekeeper's hat was off. He looked frightened.

'Someone's died,' Isabel said: a kind of question.

The man crossed himself and shivered. 'God rest his soul. He only had a cold,' he mumbled confusedly.

'Who?' Isabel snapped. But even as she asked she realised she knew; and with the knowledge came dread at all the unknown possibilities this death might bring – a dread so intense that she almost burst into tears like the fat housewife outside. By the time the gatekeeper had composed himself enough to mutter two words – 'The King' – Isabel was on her way out.

She had to get back to London. Jane would need her.

10

'All I can say', panted Anne Pratte, half-running along beside Isabel – who had nodded curtly when she'd seen the white-headed silkwoman hovering by the Ludgate jetty, but hadn't slowed down, because she was trying to avoid acknowledging that Anne Pratte was waiting specially for her even if no other explanation was likely; because she didn't want to get caught up with the Catte Street women now; because she wanted to get to Jane's as quickly as possible – 'is thank the good Lord that Goffredo isn't going to be back for a while with his people. Because this is not the time. Not at all the time. Now, do slow down a bit, dear, would you? I'm all out of breath.'

Isabel sighed and stopped. Anne Pratte's little chest was heaving so much she'd put a frail claw of a hand to her throat. But it didn't make Isabel soften as much as she was meant to. She knew Anne Pratte was using her fluffiness as a weapon. Alice Claver must have sent her out to bring Isabel home. 'I can't come home with you now,' Isabel said firmly, though less firmly than she'd meant to. 'I have to go to Jane.'

Her heart was pounding. She'd spent the entire trip back imagining Jane, alone in her room, listening to the bells; with her future gone, with no one to turn to, no one to talk to, no one to tell her what was happening. Imagining Jane's pain made her feel dizzy. Bereft.

She had to shout above all the other voices, and the bells. There were bells ringing everywhere, the same slow one-note lament being bashed out from every belfry, so loud and discordant and ominous you could go mad from it. No one had known the King was ill, but now everyone was whispering. He'd caught a cold fishing. He'd had a fit thinking about the King of France. His death brought utter shock. It was pandemonium everywhere you looked: markets closing hours ahead of time; shutters going up against the midday sun on the windows of houses; youths scurrying home under mounds of bolts and bags and bundles of goods; a crowd of citizens shouting at St Paul's Yard, some in their ill-fitting military harness, with straps hanging loose and bellies hanging out; and every church doorway up Ludgate Hill a smaller buzz of panic and people. No one able to see whether this news would rupture the delicate webs of agreements they'd made of their peaceable lives; everyone fearing the worst.

Anne Pratte's face fell. She looked piteous. 'Have the apprentices closed down the shops?' Isabel asked. Reluctantly, Anne Pratte nodded. 'Is everything properly shuttered and boarded?' Isabel asked. Anne Pratte nodded, even more reluctantly. 'Are all the girls in and is there supper for everyone?' Another woebegone nod. 'Well, then, you'll be fine. You've got it all in hand. Go back. I'll come as soon as I can,' Isabel said.

'But, dear, you can't wander round on your own in all this,' Anne Pratte quavered. 'Alice would never forgive me if I let any harm come to you.' She stopped as if struck by an idea. 'I know!' she exclaimed brightly. 'I'll come with you.'

'No,' Isabel said.

Anne Pratte gave her a birdlike, considering stare. Isabel stared levelly back. The Catte Street women would, once they stopped panicking, probably want to know how Jane was faring, she thought. Isabel smiled down at Anne Pratte, but firmly. 'Tell Alice I'll be back in an hour,' she said.

They'd reached Old Jewry. Isabel banged on Jane's door, only half-listening to Anne Pratte's meek 'All right, then, dear,' and retreating footsteps. But, as she was let into the courtyard and turned to hand the boy her reins, she realised Anne Pratte was going no further than the Prattes' own home over the road, to wait out Isabel's visit.

Jane was sitting in her great hall, on a stool, up against the edge of the window, leaning her cheek on the leaded panes, still in bright skirts, watching the crowds.

She didn't get up when her eyes fell on Isabel. But she raised her head. The leading had imprinted her cheek with a red lattice of diamond marks. She must have been there for hours, ever since the bells began.

Jane smiled vaguely. 'Just like that,' she said. She clicked her fingers, then looked surprised at them for making their loud sharp sound. 'Gone.'

It was unbearable. Isabel rushed to her, enfolding Jane's unresisting limpness in her own arms. They swayed together like that for a while; for long enough that Isabel noticed the first raindrops begin to batter against the glass; for long enough for her to realise Jane was still staring over her shoulder through the window; for long enough for her to realise Jane wasn't going to cry.

'Look at them,' Jane said. 'Running about. Everyone so scared.' She was still smiling. Her voice was hollow. 'But no one knowing what to be scared of.'

216

Isabel didn't know how to be of comfort. After a pause, she pulled up a stool and sat down.

'How can I help?' she asked. But Jane only said, kindly, but as though from a great distance: 'You mustn't worry about me, Isabel. I don't need anything. I've been lucky.'

'But do you have money?' Isabel asked. She knew the house was Jane's, and that Jane had an allowance, but she'd never thought about the mechanics of it. If the King was dead, would it stop?

Jane shook her head as if she didn't want to think of such things now. 'I'm fine, honestly. I'm quite rich, I think. I have rents, shops, I don't even know what. Father administers it all; he set it up so I'd never have to worry; he pays my allowance.' She laughed, plucking at her rings. 'He's always said how bad Edward is with money,' she added. She opened her eyes wide at what she'd said, but didn't stumble or sob as she corrected herself: 'Was.'

'What will you do?' Isabel asked, trying to force Jane to acknowledge the reality of King Edward being gone; of being left alone here: to organise herself for an uncertain future in some new way. 'Do you want to stay with me?' But she knew as she said it that that was a bad idea. Alice Claver wouldn't be able to behave. Perhaps Jane should go for a while to their father's, in Somerset?

Jane only shook her head. 'Why would I go away?' she said blankly. 'There are memories here, in everything I touch and see. This is my home. Where would I go?'

There was a bang at the door. Footsteps.

Jane was up off her stool and running across the room.

From the shadows out of sight, beyond the doorway, Isabel heard Jane's voice cry, 'I thought you'd never come!' and a deep voice she thought she knew from somewhere answer with a murmur of comfort.

She sat absolutely still on her stool, hardly daring to breathe.

When Jane came back into the room, Isabel noticed tears glistening on her face. Not enough to blotch her skin or make her ugly; just a couple of dewdrops on her cheeks and squeezing from her green eyes. But she looked relieved; less frozen. And behind her was Lord Hastings – razor-cheekboned, straight-nosed, bare-headed and tousled from the ride; with his dripping hat in his hand and his long, dark eyebrows making a single slash of a line across his forehead. He still looked young; unlike the King he'd stayed slim and fighting fit. It took Isabel a second or two to notice that the dead King's best friend had his arm around Jane's waist.

Hastings nodded at Isabel with a glimmer of acceptance that came close to a smile. She'd always liked his straightforwardness. 'Mistress Claver,' he said, by way of greeting.

She nodded back. Avoided Jane's eye. 'My lord,' she answered, with all the poise she could manage; then, neutrally, to Jane's shoulder, aware of Jane's hand settling on Will Hastings' arm on Jane's waist; of the moist, hungry look in her sister's eyes: 'I should get back to Catte Street. My old ladies need me.'

She was astonished when Jane's lips began to twitch. 'I think you'll find Anne Pratte outside,' she said, not unkindly. 'She's been sitting at her window watching us ever since you got here. Look at her. Eating us up. She's waiting for you. She's worried.'

Isabel glanced over at the window as she backed towards the door. It was true. There was a shadow in the window of the house opposite. Jane had guessed it was Anne Pratte; she was more observant than Isabel even now. Why had Isabel thought she'd need protecting?

She didn't have to turn round as she left the room to know Jane was already kissing Lord Hastings.

*   *   *

218

'Oh there you are, dear,' Anne Pratte said cosily, as Isabel trudged miserably out to the wet street. She looked supremely unconcerned by the coincidence of being there as Isabel emerged. She had a bundle in her hand and a piece of sacking over her head. 'We can walk back together, then. I've just been picking up a few things from home . . .'

Isabel sighed and took the bundle. Her mind was churning with so many new thoughts that there was no space for annoyance. But she wasn't letting Anne Pratte have her own way in everything. When the older woman asked, casually, as they began to move forwards, side by side, both heads under the sacking, 'Wasn't that Lord Hastings going into your sister's house?' Isabel pretended not to hear.

She walked on, feeling her clothes get wetter, ignoring the rain funnelling down the frayed threads edging the sack and dripping into her eyes. But she was aware of Anne Pratte's sideways looks.

'You look shocked,' she heard the thin little voice say. She walked on. 'Don't be.' She kept walking. 'She needs a new protector.' Isabel carried on walking, as if she hadn't heard the voice, wondering why the raindrops on her face felt hot and salty.

'Girls your age usually don't understand. You didn't grow up in the war; how can you? But she's no fool,' Anne Pratte was saying, almost as if she were talking to herself. Gradually, without looking, Isabel found herself listening. 'I understand her. I'm old; and all us old people grew up with fear. When the war was on you could be swallowed up by the unknown at any moment, and you never forgot it. I was a grown-up girl the year you were born; when King Henry's garrison in the Tower turned their guns on us to force London to be Lancastrian. Of course it turned us Yorkist instead. To a man. To a woman.

219

We'd had enough: ships not coming in; the courts full of bully boys; the roads full of robbers. So we all came out to fight for the Duke of York. My old father was one of the men blockading the Tower. And when the French Queen brought her army to the gates – they were north-erners; people said they howled instead of talking, like the hounds of Hell – my father was one of the Londoners who went out and told them we weren't opening the gates to that woman. No one knew what would happen. It was terrifying; but not like giving in to the war had been before. We weren't just waiting for death any more; we were doing something. It was them who gave up in the end, not us: the North men and the French Queen. They went away. We won – the little people of London. That's how brave we were. And when the Duke of York came with his army at the end of the summer, we let him in. We chose him. That's how we ended up with good King Edward, God rest his soul, and all these years of peace and prosperity we've enjoyed till now.' She crossed herself. 'And it's how I know about being afraid unless you act to protect yourself.'

Isabel stole a glance at Anne Pratte. The little old woman's face was as calm as her voice; but her eyes were strangely full of fire. 'I was never supposed to be a silk-woman, you know,' Anne Pratte added unexpectedly. 'My father had me down for a nunnery – the Minories. But then my sister died. Alice, she was called; she got hit by the wildfire they started pelting us with. The Lancastrians. It stuck to her arm, stuck and burned. You couldn't wash it off. We tried, but water only made it burn harder. I'll never forget the way she screamed. All night long. It was after she died, God rest her, that my father went out and started helping the men at the Tower. They got the garrison commander in the end: Lord Scales. Caught him trying to escape down the Thames disguised as a woman. The boatmen recognised him. They left his body at St Mary Overy. My father took us to see. Stab wounds everywhere. Flies. People spitting. My mother spat. I was the only child they had left. So he sent me to be an apprentice at John Large's instead of a bride of Christ. And I married William.' She smiled, but there was sadness in her face. 'And I've been happy with him.'

She added: 'They say war is like the wind. It brings on the storm clouds, but it brings the silver linings too. You feel more alive in the shadow of death. You seize your chances; you don't think twice. And things change so fast that, even if everything you thought you had disappears just like that, other dreams come true. If you're quick on your feet.

'Your Jane's quick on her feet,' she finished, slipping an arm through Isabel's. 'She's always had a kind heart. She's helped you with your dreams. All of us. Maybe this is her time to have her dreams come true.'

Isabel's head nodded rhythmically as she walked, eyes still fixed ahead; finding the warmth of Anne Pratte's arm a comfort. Thinking about dreams coming true.

William Hastings closed his eyes for a moment, shutting out everything but Jane's mouth gently on his chest and her long hair under his mouth, the astonishing sensation of skin on skin; his arms around her; the quiet that no one now had a right to break.

He'd galloped here all the way from Westminster, his men lost behind him. He was drenched in sweat when he walked through her door, pacing and flashing with the memories of the morning. He hadn't said a word as he'd carried her upstairs. But he hadn't needed to. It was the moment they'd both waited years for.

He opened his eyes. She was still there, soft as swan down.

Not a dream, then, he thought with a brief return of the humour that had deserted him earlier. But that meant the rest of what had happened wasn't just a nightmare either.

He sat bolt upright, abruptly, bringing her up with him so she was straddling him again, so one of his hands brushed her white-peach thigh, so her hair fell over his shoulders. She made a little sound; somewhere between indrawn breath and giggle. But the eyes she turned on him were serious.

'What is it?' Jane was murmuring now, giving his lips butterfly kisses. She smelt of flowers. 'What are you thinking?'

It was all flooding back now: why he was here. He clenched jaw and fists; trying to keep down the tide of fury, or fear, it made no difference which, that was rising in his throat.

The King was dead – the King he'd shared so many battlefields and beds and mistresses and misfortunes with, the red hazes of war and lust, since long before Edward was a king or hoped to be, since Will Hastings, a not very rich distant cousin, had first been made his boyhood gentleman in waiting. His dearest friend.

Worse. Edward's death threatened the peace which had held for twelve years.

The Prince of Wales – the new King Edward V – was only twelve years old, not a good age for kingship at the best of times. The boy was at Ludlow, where his separate court on the Welsh border was headquartered. What with all the solemn Masses they'd have to get through in every town they passed, it would take them weeks to get here. And, until he reached London, the younger Edward would remain in the clutches of his tutor, Earl Rivers, that sly, prayerful, perfumed man of letters, with his almond eyes and suspiciously elegant turn of phrase: Queen Elizabeth's brother – and a Woodville.

222

Woodvilles had already insinuated themselves into every nook and cranny at court. They'd crept in behind their Queen, like spiders or scorpions. From now on, they'd be greedier still. They'd want complete control of the new King, who was young and weak and easily influenced; whose blood ran in their veins.

That could lead only to one thing: a deadly struggle between the relatives of the Queen and the relatives of the King – England's true nobility.

Hastings was the only one of the King's men in London. And the entire loathsome swarm of Woodvilles, led by his old enemy Dorset, was here, coming after him. He'd be as loyal to the new King as he'd been to the old; but what if the new King was in the sway of the Woodville Dorset, who wanted him dead? He thought: 'I'm in danger,' then realised he must have said it out loud. Jane was staring at him. He squeezed her shoulders, added, while trying to keep panic out of his voice: 'Considerable danger.'

'What do you mean?' she whispered.

'Woodvilles,' he replied, getting up, squeezing his hands hard over his eyes as if that would stopper up his panic.

Hastings had only called the Council session that morning for administrative purposes: to organise how to bury one king and crown the next. But as soon as he'd seen the smug Woodville eyes at the table, glittering in the knowledge that they weren't just unwanted in-laws any more, but the new King's blood relatives, he'd sensed trouble. Dorset's were most openly full of fight. But even fat little Dr Morton, who these days was Dowager Queen Elizabeth Woodville's creature, had strutted to his seat with an impertinent grin. Morton hated Hastings and didn't bother to hide it. Morton would never forget that it would have been Hastings' job to find him guilty of treason after the Warwick rebellion, when Morton had been caught on the losing

223

Lancastrian side. Luckily for Morton, he'd somehow escaped from the Tower and saved himself; and he'd remade himself since as a Woodville fancier. Hastings had thought, looking grimly at the blob of wobbling malice in priest's robes in front of him: I should have finished him faster. Another mistake.

Hastings had asked Council to name Richard, Duke of Gloucester as Protector of England until Edward turned fifteen and could rule in his own right. That would have been right. Dickon was the boy's uncle; the senior prince of the York blood.

But they'd said no. They'd voted instead for some sort of regency council – controlled by Woodvilles, naturally.

When Hastings kept his temper, Dorset, unnervingly, began to stare at him. Jutting his jaw out. Leaning forward over clenched hands. Trying to stare Hastings down; the stare of a man with death in mind; holding the eye-lock for so long Hastings had thought he might pull out a sword then and there.

All Dorset actually said was: 'Now let's set a date for the coronation.' Then, still eyeballing Hastings: 'I propose midsummer. St John's Eve.'

'We can't decide that,' Hastings objected. 'Not without Gloucester.'

But Dorset had only glittered malice back at him. Hastings thought the one-time country squire might actually have been pleased to be given the chance to sneer out his ill-bred impertinence. He'd curled his lips back and said, biting off each word: 'We are quite important enough to take decisions without the King's uncle.'

Now Jane was in front of him, peeling his hands off his eyes. He was surprised to find how tight his muscles were clamped.

He told Jane: 'Dorset wants to control the King; and he wants my blood.'

224

She murmured, uneasily. But she'd chosen him, not Dorset; he could trust her.

He went on: 'I shouted at him in Council. I told him he was insolent and vicious. I said the Woodvilles' blood was too base to rule England. And I walked out.'

Her eyes opened wide.

Hastings didn't even tell her the worst. He'd been full of rage when he'd slammed the door on the Council meeting. But he'd only felt the prickle of real danger when, in the antechamber, a scrivener quietly showed him the order Dorset had wanted a fair copy of. The document – which Dorset planned to sign, 'half-brother to the King' – authorised Sir Edward Woodville to take the royal fleet to sea. If a Woodville seized control of the fleet, Hastings would be cut off from his power base at Calais. He'd be lost. 'Thank you,' he said to the sweating scribe. He tore up Dorset's page and dictated his own counter-order to the fleet – *Don't leave port*. The man scuttled back to his desk with Hastings' coin in his hand and a mixture of relief and fear in his eyes. Hastings waited, fiddling with his sword. He signed. Then he took the fastest horse he could, at a gallop, to London to be near the port.

He'd come here because Jane was here; but he also knew, if he were honest, that he hadn't wanted to go to his own house on Paul's Wharf. Even the idea of it made him feel trapped; made his flesh creep. He'd sent his retinue there. He was safer with Jane.

But those weren't thoughts to share. All he said was: 'I can't fight all of them. I'm alone. I need to send word to Dickon.'

She must feel as alone against enemies without Edward as he did; as willing to jump at shadows. He gazed at her, wishing he could shut the world out and stay here with her forever. The sight of her made him feel suddenly old: tired of office, tired of soldiering, tired of caring, tired of the treachery that seemed to shadow anyone born to bear arms. They said there was no good to be found in the service classes; but he'd found the merchants of the staple at Calais to be honest and congenial sorts. And there was no one like Jane. Hastings' wife, long dead now, had been just a marriage: a girl with good bloodlines and £400 a year, the fifth sister of the Earl of Warwick – a way for him to become Edward's first cousin by marriage. He hardly remembered her. She hadn't had hair that shimmered like spun gold, or looked at him with happy emerald eyes. She'd never sung like an angel. Made jokes that amused without hurting. Laughed like a goddess; danced like a lark on the wing. Nor had the other women. Just Jane, his second spring. He wouldn't have been unhappy if Fate had made him the humblest of merchants, he thought, if that had meant he could have married her and been free, for good, of the shadow of the sword.

Softly, Jane said: 'I'll find you paper and pen.' Her voice was steady. He took strength from it. She handed him his linen; slipped hers on too. 'You can write your letter now.'

Isabel woke in the night.

The dread that had woken her wouldn't go away.

She got up. Lit a candle from the embers of her fire. Her fear took shape.

With the King dead, what would happen to the silk-weaving contract? And the house?

Her mind flew north, to wherever Dickon was. If only he were here. If only he could advise her.

Biting her lip, she dropped to her knees.

Isabel went to see Jane early in the morning. Anne Pratte told her to – 'She'll want to see you,' she said, without a hint of the leer that would have made Isabel refuse – and walked with Isabel to Old Jewry again.

Once they were out of the house, Isabel asked, as plainly as she could: 'Is our contract with the King still valid now he's dead?'

Anne Pratte reacted equally calmly. 'We don't know,' she replied, looking ahead. 'Alice thinks not.'

So they'd talked about it already, Isabel thought, with unwilling admiration. There were still things she could learn from them; they had the experience she didn't of living in turmoil.

She felt Anne Pratte's claw of a hand on her arm. 'But no one will stop paying yet,' the soft little voice went on. 'Everything will just go on as it is, out of inertia. And once things get settled the new way, if they don't go our way, you've got your relation with Princess Elizabeth now. You can ask her to help. She's the King's sister: that's got to count for something.'

Isabel persisted: 'What if Goffredo's already on his way?'

'Alice wrote to him yesterday; told him not to hurry until things are more settled,' Anne said, with none of the despair Isabel was feeling showing in her voice. 'We'll know better once everyone stops running round like a bunch of headless chickens.' She squeezed Isabel's arm. 'Have faith,' she said. 'I'm always telling you that. And don't think about it now; there's too much else to worry about.'

Isabel nodded, partly reassured by Anne's confidence, more by the private faith she was placing in Dickon. Anyway, Anne was right: she could do nothing about it now.

Making an effort to put it out of her mind, she looked around. There were too many people in the streets. Even if the markets were open, a lot of people were, like herself and Anne, not at work; instead they were sorting things out so they could face some event they hadn't foreseen if

227

it came suddenly upon them. There was an air of purpose in the wet streets: the concentration of minds of house-holders thinking what they could eat if there was no fresh food for sale; how many pickled eggs were left from Lent; how much dried fish; how much firewood; how much flour?

Joan Woulbarowe, humping a bag of kindling back to her room, stopped for long enough to hiss at them: 'Can you believe it? They say the Woodvilles went into the King's bedchamber while he was still lying dead on the bed and stole all his money and jewels. The Marquess of Dorset. Filthy carrion.'

'All I can say is let's hope the Duke of Gloucester gets here before there's any more of that,' Anne Pratte said sententiously. 'He's our best hope now. He's straight, at least. And properly royal. It's high time someone banged all their heads together and set things straight.' But Joan had already dived off down a dank alley with her load. Only Isabel – whose night-time prayers had been for news that Dickon was on his way south – was left to hear. And she said nothing. She just looked hastily away, in case Anne Pratte's sharp eyes saw the hope that Dickon's name awoke in her heart.

Jane's door opened before Isabel even had time to knock. Jane, dressed but with her head bare, looking pale, drew her sister quickly inside. 'I'm so happy to see you,' she murmured, and Isabel saw her eyes were full of honey before Jane put her arms around her sister in a tight embrace. 'Thank you for coming back.'

Jane clung to her. 'Don't think badly of me,' her voice said, from Isabel's shoulder, through a hot cloud of hair. 'I've always loved him. It's mad; but I'm so happy.'

Isabel kissed the messy beauty of that hair. 'I under-stand,' she whispered.

Jane looked up through it, shyly. 'Do you?' she said. She must have seen forgiveness. Then, 'Come in,' she added in a more ordinary voice. 'Will Hastings is here.'

He was eating bread and cheese in the great hall. His buckler was propped up against the bench. He put his food aside, got up and bowed when he saw Isabel. He was thinner than she remembered, with a silvering at the temples she hadn't noticed yesterday. But he didn't have the look of anger on him that she'd seen yesterday; the look that might also have been fear.

'Mistress Claver,' he said formally.

'My lord,' she said formally back; but her eyes were signalling her acceptance of the sight of him at her sister's table. 'Please – eat.'

Then he grinned at her; a return to the straightforwardness she'd liked in him before. Still standing, he picked up his hunk of bread and bit into it again.

Jane had woken Hastings up when she slid back into bed at dawn. 'Your man's been,' she said. 'I gave him your letter. He had this for you.'

It was the letter he'd hoped for from Dickon, promising loyal support for Edward's son and back-up for himself. It calmed him; banished his terror; made him himself again.

Now, looking at Jane's sister – that oddity, the girl who looked almost as pretty as his love but whose mind was a merchant's counting-house – he found he was able to smile.

'I've just had word from His Grace of Gloucester,' he told her, his words muffled by his mouthful. 'He's holding a memorial Mass for His Majesty at York now. He'll be on the road again this afternoon. He's moving south.'

He was pleased to see her put a hand to the table, as if to steady herself; to see the sharpness of relief on her face. She'd tell people. She'd spread the word in the City.

He said, faster now: 'It will take him a while to get to London; there are a lot of cities to pass through and a lot of Masses to say. But he's sworn loyalty to the new King. He's written to Council to say he'd swear loyalty, if God forbid it should ever be needed, even to a girl ruler. That should calm the crowds here.'

The Princess was frozen inside the cloth-of-silver gown her mother had decided she should wear for her brother's coronation. She hadn't said a word since Isabel arrived. She wasn't even looking at Isabel, who was kneeling before her setting her hem. But Isabel knew her ways better now, and didn't feel humiliated by being ignored. The Princess was staring through the window, to where her mother, thin and tense in black velvet, was conferring, soundlessly, with the Marquess of Dorset. Isabel sneaked a look at him too. He was still as honey-blond as Jane, but he looked as anxious and angry as Hastings had last night.

They're not in grief. They're terrified, Isabel thought. Looking up at the Princess, she also thought, no wonder she's so quiet; those two are enough to give anyone nightmares.

'Your Highness,' she said, 'they're saying in London that the Duke of Gloucester has sworn loyalty to His Majesty your brother.'

She wanted to reassure the troubled little soul she guessed at behind those blank eyes.

She went on: 'They say he's even pledged that, if God forbid His Majesty your brother were to die, he would swear loyalty to you if you were to inherit the throne.'

She held her breath.

Slowly, Elizabeth looked down. For a moment, Isabel was appalled by the utter coldness she saw in that young face. She'd been mad to open her mouth. She'd be asked to leave, just when she might really need the Princess. She'd spoiled everything.

Then she realised the Princess was crying. Her face wasn't moving. But there were gleaming trails running down her cheeks.

In a choking voice, the Princess said: 'But Her Majesty my mother hates the Duke of Gloucester. She says he wants to destroy her and all her blood. Her brothers. My brothers. Me.'

Isabel didn't know how to answer, she was so astonished. Was that really what the child was so scared of? Dickon? She took hold of the limp little royal hand in front of her eyes and muttered, 'There, there', and, 'Nothing bad will happen', and, after a while, when nothing terrible had happened to her, 'What people are saying is that the Duke will set everything straight.'

Eventually her confidence transmitted itself. She felt an answering pressure from the hand she was holding. Elizabeth swallowed, and sought her eyes. 'Is that really what they're saying?' the Princess asked in a whisper. Then: 'Is that what you believe?'

Isabel nodded, with relief prickling and bubbling through her. She hadn't spoiled everything, after all; the Princess was actually opening up to her. Elizabeth began shaking her head, though Isabel couldn't tell whether she was indicating disbelief or was just unsure how to remove the tears from her face. Quietly, Isabel passed her a rag. The new King's sister wiped her face and blew her nose. Gradually, the tears stopped.

Isabel had one more task in Westminster. On her way home, she slipped into St Stephen's chapel and joined the rest of the muddy worshippers queuing up to prostrate themselves before the embalmed King's coffin. They were still muttering about how Dorset had stolen his jewels

231

and money on his deathbed. Perhaps it was true. She looked into Edward's upturned face, wiped of its lazy charm, with the handsome features now as meaningless as a statue's. She wondered at its uncanny stillness. Thank you, she thought, kissing the ground; not thanking the slab of flesh here but the live King she remembered – the man whose grace towards merchants had been translated, in her particular case, into almost unimaginable generosity. Praying that Edward's generous contract with her would be honoured by his son. Praying for Dickon to get here quickly and make her silk dream safe for the future. Then, just praying for Dickon to get here.

In the days that followed, Isabel's confidence that Dickon would come and make everything all right seemed to spread to other people.

The King was buried quickly (his body wasn't well enough preserved to wait until the new King, or the Duke of Gloucester, made their separate entrances to London). The markets went back to work as usual. Apart from an early rumour that the Woodvilles had tried to seize the navy, it seemed even the courtiers were suspending their feud, while waiting for normality to return in the shape of a new King.

The only tears Isabel still saw for the dead King after that were the surreptitious ones shed by the Princess at later fittings, while her coronation gown was adjusted. Isabel was gentle with Elizabeth; she might need her soon. 'Get your grief out, you'll feel better,' she'd murmur, while the Princess stood, ramrod-straight, as salt water flowed from her eyes.

There was summer in the air. Londoners were reassured enough to dance at the maypole on May Day. Isabel and Alice and the Prattes walked through the crowded streets, licking pork fat off their fingers, watching the dancers, and listening to the hopeful talk. The King will be here any day now. The Duke will be here any day. We'll have a coronation before the month is out. Have faith.

11

So strong a hold had the idea taken that the Duke of Gloucester was the kingdom's best chance of safety and order in the transition of power ahead, that the gatemen at Westminster didn't even look worried, the morning after May Day, by the story they were telling. A crowd of gate-house visitors were listening as Isabel walked in off the boat.

While most of the country had been innocently dancing at the maypole, the Duke of Gloucester had swiftly marched his army cross-country – and captured the King. Gloucester and his friend the Duke of Buckingham had arrested the two Woodville uncles travelling with the King. They'd announced that Earl Rivers and Richard Grey had been plotting their murder. The Woodvilles and the King's chamberlain, Thomas Vaughan, were being sent to Pontefract under armed guard.

'He's a man of action, the Duke of Gloucester,' the guard said admiringly. 'No nonsense about him.'

His sidekick said: 'Time to take all those Woodville heads off, if you ask me. Did you hear about Dorset, just going and helping himself from the King's casket before the man was even dead?' He drew a finger happily across his throat. There was a general murmur of approval.

The head guard leaned over to Isabel, who was still trying to take the story in. 'So I don't know what you're here for, Missis, not today,' he said, enjoying her look of confusion. 'You don't think your Princess is still in there, do you?' He shook his head with gusto. 'Oh no . . . her mum's much too fly. She's a Woodville, isn't she? She was off over the road to the Abbey and sanctuary, children and all, as soon as she heard. In the middle of the night. A right old upheaval it was too.'

Isabel walked towards the twin towers of the Abbey with her head spinning.

She didn't know what to make of it. Her doubts and fears came rushing back. Could it be right? Had Dickon really been in danger of being murdered? What was he up to?

It was easier, for now, to concentrate on what she could do here. Queen Elizabeth Woodville would be at the Abbot's house, where she'd lived in sanctuary once before, during the Warwick rebellion, while her husband was in hiding overseas. The Queen had given birth to her son Edward in that house; the boy who was now king. Princess Elizabeth might even remember being a toddler cooped up there in voluntary captivity. How frightening it must be to be back.

It was unlikely the panicking Woodvilles had taken Elizabeth's coronation robe with them as they fled across Westminster. It was more than unlikely that the Princess would want a fitting now. But all those quiet tears the Princess had been shedding since her father died had left their mark on Isabel's heart. Even if there was no work she could do, she thought, she should at least go to her royal client and offer comfort.

She was dreading seeing the fear on the girl's face, though. So it was a relief, as she turned the next corner, to see the more familiar form of Will Caxton in the distance. He was listening to a market woman, who was gesticulating excitedly as she talked; then, nodding his head up and down, clearly alarmed, he bought all the bread in her basket and began to shovel it into the already bulging leather sack on his shoulder. She quickened her pace; was surprised to realise how fast her heart was beating; and half-shouted, 'Will.'

Breathlessly, he fell into step beside her, half-trotting to keep up. 'Have you heard?' he said. His eyes were round. 'Earl Rivers. My best client. A prisoner.'

She darted a look at him. She hadn't realised he'd see it like that. Of course he would.

'They'll kill him, won't they?' Caxton said, lost in his own worry. 'Gloucester will.'

Isabel said, falteringly: 'But Rivers was going to murder the Duke of Gloucester . . . they say . . .'

'They say,' Caxton spat. 'Gloucester says, you mean. But he would, wouldn't he?'

That wasn't at all what she wanted to hear. Not from Will, whose advice she always asked; whose judgement she trusted. It crystallised her vague disquiet into a definite shape. Feeling sick inside, she stopped walking. She stared at him, and said, 'You think it's a lie?'

'I think he's got murder in mind,' Caxton replied, as if surprised she'd even bother to ask. 'Of course he has. Why wouldn't he? He's an ambitious, bloodthirsty brute. Always has been. And there's no one to stop him now.'

She shook her head.

Caxton looked hard at her; she could see his alarm turning to anger. 'Look, I know everyone's been carrying on recently as if he's the Messiah made flesh,' he said. 'Though God knows why. But you're not that stupid. You know as well as I do what he is. Who do you think murdered the Duke of Clarence? And old King Henry?'

She shook her head again, refusing to acknowledge his words – those were old rumours he was repeating, nothing more – but feeling the panic inside her flex and bite.

Caxton said, doggedly: 'He'll kill Rivers, I'm telling you. And now he's got the King in his clutches, who's to say he won't kill him too?'

Feeling so anguished she could hardly control her tongue, she mumbled, thickly, 'No', and 'You're wrong, I'm sure you are.'

Will Caxton drew himself up: a tall, stringy angel of righteousness. He said: 'Forgive me, my dear, but how can you be sure?'

To Isabel's astonished horror, she felt her own eyes fill with tears and her shoulders start to shake. She put her hands over her eyes. 'Because I know him,' she whimpered through her tears. 'And I know he's not . . . not . . .' Then the sobs engulfed her so she couldn't go on. But Will Caxton had quick reflexes for an elderly man. Before she knew where she was, before she'd even had time to take in the brief look of utter surprise in his eyes, he had his arms around her, and a kerchief at her face, and was murmuring, 'Don't cry, now', and 'No wonder, our nerves are all on edge', and, as he steered her gently into the tavern at the roadside, 'What do you mean, you *know* him?'

Will Caxton didn't say anything for a while after she'd stumbled it all out, through a storm of sobs: the snatched meetings; Dickon's fiercely practical good nature; the straight-as-a-die honesty of him. Will just sat with an arm around her and clicked his tongue. After a while, the torrent subsided. She sniffed, and wiped her eyes and nose.

When she finally dared look up, through puffy eyes, he was gazing at her with a half-smile on his lips and his head rocking, very gently, up and down. 'Oh, you Lambert sisters,' he murmured ruefully. 'You kill with a glance, both of you, don't you?'

'I shouldn't have said anything,' she muttered, with her heart racing again as the foolishness of what she'd done sank in. 'You won't tell Alice, will you? Or Jane?'

He shook his head. There was a great kindness on his face; a look like love.

Even though a part of her felt horribly embarrassed, she realised her confusion was mixed with relief. Will wasn't judging her harshly. And she'd been so lonely with her private thoughts about Dickon. It was good to have a friend she could trust.

'I'd been trying so hard not to think the things you were saying; trying to have faith,' she said, excusing herself. Then: 'I know you're almost always right, Will. But I so want you to be wrong, just this once. You understand, don't you?'

Will looked at her serious face. He nodded. 'I made a fool of myself once, long ago, by questioning your judgement,' he said comfortably. 'I was wrong then. So I'm going to trust you now on this; try to share your faith. Let's just both hope you're right.'

Hastings was enough of a soldier not to betray his shock at what was in the letter the Mayor of London was showing him.

He knew Edmund Shaa well. The sleek goldsmith had worked with him on the new coinage. Hastings trusted him. He just wasn't sure he could trust his own judgement of the words dancing in front of him, or the danger he felt all around.

The letter was from Dickon to the City of London's leaders. It said Dickon and the King were on their way to London.

'They're on their way to London,' Hastings said, more

calmly than he felt, putting the paper down. He'd noticed the inconsistency in it; perhaps Shaa hadn't. Perhaps he could keep it to himself, while he thought out what it meant, and what best to do.

Shaa's jowl quivered. 'But the letter comes from Northampton, while the arrests yesterday were made closer to hand, at Stony Stratford,' he said, bowing with unctuous merchant politeness, but refusing to be fobbed off. 'Which raises the question, is he really coming to London? He's moving the King backwards, not forwards.'

There was a long pause.

Shaa persisted: 'Do you think the Duke might be trying to seize the throne?'

No, Hastings thought.

It was impossible to tell. He didn't want to agree. Yet everything pointed to that.

If Dickon were mounting a coup, Hastings would have to choose between his old friend and master's son, now the rightful King, and his old friend and master's brother. Fighting for a child King amounted to suicide. He didn't want to die. He had Jane. But it was nevertheless his duty to choose the child over Dickon.

Reluctantly, he lifted his eyes so Shaa could see his fear. He said: 'I don't know.'

Isabel could almost smell the children's fear. All six royal offspring from the Palace – Elizabeth, her four younger sisters, the nurse sitting on a stool holding three-year-old Brigid, and dark-haired, wide-eyed Richard, the ten-year-old Duke of York – had been crammed into a small parlour looking on to a dark kitchen courtyard since before dawn. They'd had nothing to do but think and stare down at scullions and rubbish for hours. There were cups and scraps of food left uncleared on the table, as if no one had remembered to send a servant to them in the upheaval.

Some tight little fingers must have shredded that fringe on the edge of one of the luxurious cushions on the floor.

Their eyes all turned towards Isabel when she was ushered in, and followed her wordlessly across the room. Two small girls came out from behind a hanging. They stood, limp-armed and expressionless, and stared with big O eyes as she shifted herself around them to reach their older sister. Princess Elizabeth, sitting at the bench by the window, was gawping at her too.

Very slowly, as if she didn't know what to do, the eldest Princess got up. Isabel put down her sewing basket and dropped into a deep bow, murmuring, 'Your Highness', trying to keep the pity out of her voice. They were all so helpless.

'I know you won't want me to work today,' Isabel went on, since no one else seemed to be saying anything, 'but I couldn't just go home without seeing you . . .'

Princess Elizabeth said, almost apologetically, 'There was no time to bring the gown.' She was twisting her hands. She looked miserably afraid. But she was trying to be correct. 'We'll send for it tomorrow. Once we've been settled in here.'

'Well, never mind about that for now,' Isabel said, as reassuringly as she could. 'Shall we do something else today?'

Her sewing basket was full of odds and ends of stuff: silk, linen, threads, scraps. She opened it. The smaller girls crept closer. Prince Richard went on sitting on the floor, playing bones by himself, or half-playing them, rattling and rattling them in his hand without actually throwing them, and staring at her with a blank face.

'We could make some dolls with what I've got in here,' Isabel said, and the circle closed in a little tighter. 'I could leave them with you . . . it's a bit empty in here, isn't it?'

By the time she left, an hour later, she'd got the children

to make three rough stuffed bodies and sewn faces and skirts on for them. They looked relieved to have something to do with themselves at last; but they still hardly said a word.

It was only when the younger girls had taken two of the finished dolls and were quietly making them dance with each other, and even smiling a little, that the boy finally got up and walked over to Isabel. She was still sitting cross-legged on the floor by her basket, tidying it up before taking her leave, not sure whether she'd helped.

Little Richard put a shy hand on her arm. 'We don't know where my brother is,' he piped. 'Please . . . have you heard anything new?'

She quailed before the intensity of their stares.

Princess Elizabeth said, with that same distant, stunned, apologetic note, as if she were explaining an impertinence: 'We don't hear anything in here. We're so cut off.'

One of the smaller girls gabbled, looking appalled at herself, 'They just woke us up and told us we were in danger, and rushed us over here. In the dark. In our night-shirts.'

Now they were all rushing to speak.

'They said it was our uncle . . .'

'The Duke of Gloucester . . .'

'And that he'd arrested our other uncles . . .'

'Earl Rivers . . .'

'And marched our brother Edward off . . .'

'No one knew where . . .'

'But what are they saying now?'

They had puppy eyes; melting and pleading.

But there was nothing new she could honestly tell them that would comfort them, except what she'd heard at the gatehouse: that their brother Edward was on his way to London, escorted by the Duke.

They nodded in silence. They didn't ask again about their Woodville uncles.

'Have faith,' Isabel said, almost pleading with the little boy whose hand was still on her arm and whose eyes were so hungrily on her. 'Your uncle Gloucester is a good man. Everyone in London believes that. And no one doubts he'll do the right thing. He'll bring your brother safely back to you . . . for his coronation . . . so try not to worry.'

The boy nodded again, still more solemnly. Isabel didn't know whether he believed her; or whether she believed herself.

She couldn't bear their eyes any more. She scrambled to her feet. She felt the child's hand slide off her arm. She picked up the third doll, still lying on the table, and gave it to him to hold instead. Perhaps that would comfort him.

'Thank you,' he said. But when she turned around for a last glance back at them from the doorway, she saw he'd put the doll down and gone back to his patch of floor. He was rattling his set of knucklebones in his hand, as he must have been doing all day, and staring into space.

But the next news was good. She and Will Caxton were on their anxious way to Vespers at the Abbey just an hour or two later when they heard the crier.

'The King and the Duke are at St Albans!' the man was yelling, clanging his bell. St Albans: just thirty miles from London. 'The King will enter London tomorrow!'

There was a tightening of attention from the thin crowd stopping to listen. A first ragged cheer. A ripple of applause. The whisper spread, like fire over a field of stubble.

'There,' Will Caxton muttered in her ear. 'It looks like you were right.'

'O ye of little faith,' Isabel breathed back. There'd been nothing to fear, after all. The Princesses would go back to the Palace. There'd be a coronation. Angels were singing in her head.

They went to the Red Pale to eat. She was too relieved to be hungry, even before the innkeeper's son, who served their beef stew, gave her the message. 'A man just gave me a penny to tell you the blacksmith will be passing through at first light,' he sang out.

Isabel felt Will Caxton's speculative eyes on her. 'Well, the house needs new fire-irons!' she protested, staring at her boots and not admitting anything. But she knew he'd guessed this to be word from Dickon. She couldn't stop herself blushing, or beaming.

She loved this empty room with its pale walls bathed in dawn light: the colour of happiness.

'What's been happening?' she whispered between kisses. 'I've been so worried.'

Dickon was pulling off her kirtle. 'Later,' he muttered. 'It's been too long.'

Even afterwards, when he'd sat up and wrapped the sheet around himself and started to talk, he was glitter-eyed and full of restless energy; grinning as though he'd managed to work some unexpected miracle.

'I knew everything would be all right once you got here,' she muttered, gratefully kissing his hands; then, noticing the engrained black tracery of lines on them, laughing and pushing them away. 'Though it's true I've never seen you so dirty.'

He barked out a hard laugh. 'Well, it's been tough. No time for lavender baths. I'm exhausted,' he grinned, as if knowing his manner contradicted his words, 'and the boy's half-dead with fatigue too. We've done a lot of riding.'

He softened. 'He's a good boy, though. He soldiers on.'

He was up already. Dancing about, looking for the clothes he'd thrown off. Picking crumpled things up.

Tossing hers back down. She'd never seen him in mid-campaign; with his fighting self at the fore, with his blood up. His excitement made him almost a stranger.

'They said Earl Rivers and his brother were planning to kill you . . .' Isabel said, fixing him with her eyes, trying to make him stop and concentrate on her for a moment. She took a deep breath. She wouldn't be able to put that conversation with Will Caxton out of her head unless she knew for sure. 'Was it true?'

She got a bright stare back as he picked up the right garment. 'Bloody Woodville vermin,' he agreed cheerfully, diving into his undershirt. His voice came out of it, muffled. 'They were after me, all right. Going to cut me down at the meeting at Stony Stratford, apparently.' His head popped out. 'But Rivers' man came over to us. Told us everything. So we moved first.'

Dickon nodded his head firmly. He reached for his doublet and stuck his arms in: 'Hastings says they were out for his blood too. Even tried to commandeer the fleet. They should've known that would never work. Of course he got word. He's popular.'

She breathed out in relief. She believed him. 'But Hastings was worried for a while,' she said, stretching happily back on the cushions. 'I could see it in his eyes.'

He didn't seem to have noticed her doubt, or its passing. He hardly seemed to be listening. His mind was on what lay ahead; he was nodding her up. Rushing. 'Come,' he said briskly. 'I can't stay. Nor can you. So up with you.'

He sat down to pull up his hose. She'd put her linen on and was standing fastening her kirtle when, suddenly, he looked up at her. His gaze was piercing. He was nodding, with amusement in his eyes. 'Aha . . . You've been seeing Hastings, have you?' he asked merrily. 'I wondered who Jane Shore would have picked as her next protector.'

244

She laughed. After all this: a moment of normality. It was wonderful to have him back.

He stood up, tugging at the fabric of his garments. 'And what's become of Dorset?' he asked, in the same bantering tone. 'Disappointed, is he?'

But he must know the answer to that, she thought, with another little stab of anxiety. She said: 'He's with the Queen. They've taken sanctuary at the Abbey. Didn't you know?'

He nodded, vaguely, but she could see his attention was more on tying his sleeves than on her. 'I'll do those,' she said, and began fastening the ribbons. She needed his attention. There was so much she needed to ask him, and he was going to go away. 'Dickon,' she said urgently as she tied. 'You have to do something about those children in sanctuary. They're so scared. Tell them Edward's safe. Get them to come out.'

He nodded. 'I'm going to see her now,' he said, looking at her hands on his shoulders. 'The Queen. Calm her down. She panicked. Stupid. But we all know what she's like.'

Isabel reached for the other sleeve and slipped it on his arm, trying to smile with him. But the thought that Queen Elizabeth Woodville had had good reason to be alarmed when both her brothers were arrested crept into her resistant mind all the same. She tried to put it out of her head.

There was still the most important question to ask.

Balancing on the mattress, she nuzzled his neck, ran her tongue along his jawline.

'Dickon,' she said, a little ashamed of the wheedling note creeping into her voice, 'the thing I've been next most worried about, after you, was my contract. The silk house. The weavers. I know you have too much to think about now. But once everything is settled . . . when you have time . . . will you ask Edward to honour it, on the same terms?'

He nodded, and put his arms around her shoulders. For a moment he stood very still with her, and the look in his eyes was the gentle one she knew. 'You don't need to worry,' he murmured, so low she could hardly hear: a velvet whisper. 'You'll never need to worry.'

She didn't want this moment to end. It was the first real peace she'd known for weeks. But, quietly but firmly, he moved her back. Turned away. Reached for his buckler, with muscles taut as wire again. He was speaking, but over his shoulder as he picked up his last possessions, with his eyes darting over the floor and bed to make sure he hadn't forgotten anything. 'I'll be staying at Crosby's Place for a couple of nights once we're in London . . . With Edward . . . It's going to take a few days for them to get the state apartments ready for him at the Tower. But after that . . .'

He turned back to her from the doorway. Met her eyes. Raised one eyebrow. Grinned. Blew a light-hearted kiss. 'I'll see you here.'

He was about to go, when a last thought seemed to come to him. A slight wrinkle appeared on his brow; a tone of mild surprise crept into his voice.

'What did Hastings have to be worried about, anyway?' he said. Then he was gone.

Isabel went back to the Woodville sanctuary a little later that morning, too, before taking the boat home. She had a story prepared for the guards about having left behind some of her work. She wanted to be sure that the children were either calmer or already leaving to go back to the Palace, now their mother had talked to Dickon.

The Queen and her family were still at the Abbot's house, though someone had found more embroidering for the little girls to do, and Princess Elizabeth was sitting at the window quietly reading her prayer book. She could see little Richard's legs under the hanging. He must be playing knucklebones there. He didn't come out. The girls all looked searchingly at her as soon as they saw a new face – making Isabel blushingly aware of the happiness she couldn't help showing after being with Dickon, and of the stubble-scratched pinkness of her cheeks. But they didn't come creeping closer, hoping for comfort. They were busy. Isabel sensed that they were less worried than yesterday.

'We can't come out,' the Princess said, answering Isabel's inquiring look. 'Her Majesty my mother still doesn't trust him.'

But her voice was calm. The younger children went on with their sewing, and watched.

'But . . .' Isabel stammered.

'We're staying here,' the Princess said. She was shrugging.

Then she did a strange thing. She looked at Isabel, very carefully, through narrowed eyes. And, once she'd satisfied herself of whatever she was thinking through, she leaned forward, challenging Isabel with suddenly lively eyes, and pulled a face. A gargoyle grimace: eyebrows pulled up and lower eyelids down with her fingers, tongue stuck out.

Isabel began to laugh at the sheer cheek of the Princess mocking her mother. She felt honoured to have been trusted with that glimpse of childish rebellion, and relieved that the children's spirits were so much higher, whatever fears the Queen still harboured. The Princess blanked her face again. She said, as sombrely as if she'd never made herself so monstrous: 'Her Majesty my mother says so.'

*　　*　　*

Hastings sat with Jane in her bower of roses long after the sun set; till after the curfew bell had broken off the clanging peals of relief from every church in town. 'I worried too much,' Hastings said, leaning back on the bench and stretching out his long legs. One arm was around Jane's shoulders. Out there with the birds and gnats and fruit trees, for the first time in years, he felt perfectly at peace. 'I should have known Dickon was to be trusted. I should have had more faith.'

She ran her hand through his hair.

'He hasn't put a foot wrong,' Hastings exulted, enjoying the feel of her fingers on his scalp. Every muscle in his body was relaxing after all those days clenched for action; he would sleep tonight. 'He's changed us from government by the Queen's kin to government by the King's with no more bloodshed than you'd get from a cut finger.'

She kissed him. He loved the look of trust in her eyes.

When Lord Stanley's messenger banged at the door at midnight, Hastings' first thought, looking down through the glass, then back at Jane's perfectly peaceful sleep, curled up in the moonlight, was to send the man away. But it was midnight. It must be important.

He opened the window. A melodious low voice began to mutter Stanley's message. He listened, incredulously. Stanley wanted to tell him he'd had a nightmare. It was an omen, the man was explaining. Hastings should leave town with his master now.

Hastings only realised he'd raised his own voice when he saw Jane lift her head sleepily towards him. He'd been snarling: 'What do you mean, a nightmare?' But he didn't want to frighten Jane. And it was almost funny. It was funny. He laughed and lowered his voice. 'Tell him not to be so superstitious,' he said, more gently. 'I'm not going anywhere.'

'What was that?' Jane whispered, snuggling back into his chest. From out there in the silence, he could hear the unearthly bark of a fox. He thought, impatiently, why is Stanley still so jittery? The man had woken up in terror, it seemed, after dreaming that he and Hastings were being chased by a boar. A white boar; Dickon's emblem; and a white boar drenched in blood. But experience had just proved they'd been wrong to mistrust Dickon. Stanley should have woken up from his nightmare and dealt with his own fears, without pestering Hastings. He put his brown arms around Jane's white shoulders. He thought: nothing matters except this.

'It was nothing,' he said softly.

She was already asleep.

Chess

12

Friday 13th

Another shout woke Hastings into a hot morning. He'd
ignored the sounds of servants about their business in the
house, the wafts of fish stew, the sun streaming into the
room through bed-curtains he'd forgotten to close. But
he couldn't ignore the cheerful voice yelling from the street:
'Hey! Slugabed! My Lord Hastings! Stir yourself! Hey!'

Jane groaned and tightened against him. 'Is that the
time?' she whispered, but showed no sign of opening her
eyes. He disentangled himself, stood up and stretched
lazily, enjoying his freedom to look at her for as long as
he wanted, disregarding the voice, which was still caterwauling away outside, for a moment longer.

He knew that voice. It was Howard's son, Thomas. He
must want to walk to Council together.

Without bothering to hide his nakedness – if Thomas
Howard knew to find him here, he'd know why, and
Hastings was proud of that – he went to the window and
waved. Young Howard was leaning against a tree trunk.
There were green shadows in his hair.

'All right,' Hastings called, resigning himself to spending

this glorious morning niggling over the details of the coronation next month. He wasn't in a mood for committee squabbles, personally. The boy could wear purple sacking as far as he was concerned, now he knew they'd be getting him to the church on time. But he was sure Morton and Dorset would have a long list of points they'd insist be discussed, just to show Gloucester – who, they'd voted yesterday, in a belated climb-down he'd had the restraint not to gloat about, could, after all, be sole Protector – how attentive they were to protocol. 'That's enough yelling. I'll be down in a minute.'

He pulled on yesterday's linen. It would be fine. He should make proper arrangements soon, though; get some clothes sent here. He dipped his hands in the pitcher of water, sloshed a cold shock of it on his face. It was pure spring water. Jane didn't stint herself. He drank some from his cupped hands. Ran wet hands through his hair to smooth it down; leaned down to kiss Jane's shoulder, which glowed out of the nest of sheets like a ripe peach. Mine forever, he thought; and wondered if he'd dare marry her.

Well, he didn't have to decide now. He could just enjoy the golden summer's day. He was whistling as he got to the bottom of the stairs.

They sauntered companionably through the streets, side by side, Hastings still whistling, young Howard still grinning. Hastings could see the townsfolk in their flapping gowns smiling at the sight of them. And why not? These two noblemen without a care in the world were living, walking proof that London was safe.

'Father Paul,' he called merrily at the priest gliding towards him on Tower Street; Jane's confessor from St Thomas of Acre. The man's pudding of a face broke into a smile. He changed course; crossed the road towards them to greet them.

'Come on,' Hastings heard Howard say at his side, 'you don't need a priest yet.' And he threw back his head and roared with laughter.

Hastings laughed with the younger man, who this morning looked the spitting image of his father as Hastings had first known him – fresh cheeks, bright eyes, a hay-mop of hair. He let himself be led on.

But he did stop to greet his poursuivant. He liked the sight of his own black and silver livery on the man's back, against the glitter of silver on dark water at Tower Wharf. And he wanted to squint up at the Palace. In this light, today, even that great pile of threat didn't look as forbid-ding as usual. 'Sir Thomas; my lord Hastings,' the man said, turning away from the barrels he'd been inspecting on the quayside to sweep them a deep bow. Hastings hoped they were the extra supplies of wine he'd ordered for his household to celebrate the King's arrival with.

'How are you this morning, Robert?' Hastings asked affectionately, taking no notice of Howard fidgeting at his side. He could wait. They were early. And Hastings' brave fighting men deserved the best, always.

Robert grinned back: 'All the better for seeing all this, sir. And you?'

Hastings drew in a deep lungful of glittering air, taking in the whiff of river dankness, the ropes like rat tails, the creaking of wood on water; thinking with grim pleasure of the Woodville prisoners at Pontefract, who were to be executed that day. 'Me?' he replied exultantly. 'I've never been better.'

The others were already inside, scuffing their feet on the floor like schoolboys waiting for class. Not many of them; there was another coronation meeting for the other half of Council at Westminster, chaired by Bishop Russell. The Woodvilles were there; the only people here were Archbishop Rotherham, the disgusting slug Morton, the

Duke of Buckingham, and Lord Stanley, who was embarrassed enough now by the foolish night message he'd sent to be avoiding Hastings' eye.

Well, it was understandable he might have panicked, Hastings thought forgivingly; after all, Stanley had more than most to worry about. It couldn't be easy being married to that object of perpetual suspicion, the last Lancastrian princess, however deep Margaret Beaufort chose to bury herself in the countryside. No wonder the man's nerve had broken.

He strode over to Stanley and clapped him on the back. 'Thomas,' he said; and, when the other man turned baggy, anxious eyes towards him, he winked. Then he bowed low to Buckingham, who wasn't a man to make an enemy of; who had been with Dickon on his dash across England to take the King from the Woodvilles; who, last year, had been the lord to pronounce Parliament's death sentence on the Duke of Clarence; a man whose hard eagle features never relaxed. Hastings even nodded at Morton.

Hastings was the first to rise to his feet when he heard footsteps in the corridor.

'My Lord Protector,' he said, bowing deep as Dickon walked in, taking pleasure at letting the title he'd fought for Dickon to get rolled off his tongue now; enjoying the tight smile he glimpsed on Morton's fat little face too.

Dickon stopped in front of Hastings. Held his gaze for a second, with that stillness he'd always had. Then the Lord Protector whom Hastings had helped to create lifted the corners of his mouth into a half-smile, and nodded. 'My lord,' he said lightly. Hastings read that as a careful acknowledgement of his loyalty.

Dickon nodded at Morton and Stanley too; keeping things even. He'd always been a diplomat. Then he said to the group, just as lightly: 'Could you start without me? I'll be with you in an hour,' and, without another word, left again. It was frustrating. No one wanted to spend longer on this than they needed. But, watching Morton's hand, with its list already out, ready to impress, fluttering disconsolately back down to his robe, Hastings couldn't help but smile inside.

Morton's enthusiasm for the task at hand had thoroughly annoyed them all by the time the footsteps came back. Hastings and Stanley were raising exasperated eyebrows at each other as the prelate made one long-winded proposal after another; as if he wanted to organise the whole event himself before Dickon got back to run the meeting. Rotherham had retreated into a series of patient nods of assent; Hastings thought from the man's occasional starts and blinks that he might be trying to fight the urge to doze off. Buckingham was sitting very still, looking impatiently out of the window; while young Howard, who kept glancing sideways at the Duke, was trying to do the same.

Hastings stood up with an easygoing smile of relief, ready to roll his eyes at Dickon too.

But the Protector who walked through the door this time was in no mood for laughing.

He was angry – breathing fast; walking fast; ready on his toes; full of fight. 'What', he barked out, staring round at them, one after the other, 'should be the penalty for planning to destroy me?' There was an astonished silence. 'Me, so near in blood to the King?' Another, sicker silence. 'Me, the Protector of his realm?'

Dickon's jaw was out; he was bobbing forward with every question; he was ready to go on lashing them with words unless he was answered.

Hastings recognised from the shuffling and shifting around him that the others were waiting for him to head off this unexpected rage. He'd known the Protector best for longest. He was a head taller than Dickon; so he did what he could to make himself smaller, hunching down in the inoffensive way of servants or grooms gentling horses.

'Why, my lord,' he said soothingly, 'of course they should be arrested as traitors.'

Before he could ask who had made the Protector so angry, Dickon started plucking frantically at his left arm with his right. When he couldn't roll the offending sleeve up, he ripped it. Underneath was the same scar from Scotland that Hastings had seen before – a thin white slash on dark skin, fully healed. But Dickon was staring at it with horror, as if it had changed. There was white all around the edges of his rolling eyes.

'They've withered me.' It was half-snarl, half-howl. 'They've bewitched me.'

Hastings felt a sick black rush in his gut. This was how Clarence had got at the end: the ravings about pins and dolls and poisonings. He remembered how fastidiously Dickon had raised his eyebrows at his brother's behaviour then; the regretful way he'd shaken his head. It beggared belief that cool-headed Dickon could be going the same way now.

He was so worried that he stepped forward and put his hand on the Protector's clothed arm. He pleaded: 'Dickon?', not bothering with protocol, just wanting this stranger with the familiar face to turn back into his old friend.

Dickon whirled round to him as if seeing him for the first time. There was a cunning look on the Protector's face.

'Ah,' he said, 'you don't ask who did it, do you? Ask me who. Go on,' he said, sticking his face right up against Hastings'. 'Ask me who.'

The others had gone as quiet as woodland animals

frozen before a predator. It was as if there were only the two of them left in the room.

Obediently, Hastings asked: 'Who?'

Dickon hissed back: 'The secret forces behind Queen Elizabeth Woodville and Jane Shore, that's who.'

There was a tighter hush all around. That made no sense. Everyone knew the Queen hated Jane Shore. Out of the corner of his eye, Hastings saw Rotherham cross himself.

Eyeball to eyeball, Dickon went on, in the same uncanny hiss: 'You.'

'What, me?' Hastings said. 'What?'

And suddenly the hush was over. Dickon thumped his fist on the table. Men at arms ran in. They must have been waiting outside. The room filled with sound and sweat: thumps and grunts and punches and the scrape of overturning furniture. Stanley dived under the table, but they knocked it aside and grabbed his feet and pulled him up. They got him in an armlock that made him moan and sweat. They dragged him away, and the two grey-faced, unresisting priests behind him.

Around Hastings there was a blur of flailing limbs, then nothing. He opened his eyes to find himself on the floor with the solid legs of a billman on either side of his chest. They must have hit him on the head. He hadn't seen what they'd done to Buckingham and young Howard; but both had gone. When he looked up he could see the underside of Dickon's chin at the window, and a bristle of lances. He couldn't see Dickon's eyes.

He didn't need to. The voice was enough. 'Make your peace with God, traitor,' Dickon was taunting, the wild high cry of a man on the battlefield, kindling the frenzy in the blood of the men around him with words; the kind of words best forgotten once the red haze receded: 'because I won't eat until I've seen your head off.'

Groggily he wondered if this was how he and the three Plantagenet brothers – Edward, Dickon and, back then, even George Clarence – had seemed to Henry VI's son after Tewkesbury, when they'd closed in on him for the kill. After Edward had hit the prisoner across his smooth boy-cheek with a gauntlet, and they'd backed him up against the canvas tent wall and knocked him down and cut and kicked him a few times; just playing. After Edward had pushed the rest of them away for a moment to lift the still resisting mess of flesh from the floor; to yell, 'How dare you come and make war in England?' into the ripped ear of the last Lancastrian prince. After he'd dropped him again and turned away; when they came back with their feet and fists and hot breath – a many-headed animal with eyes full of death.

There was no time now to think of Jane or the appalled knowledge in Stanley's eyes when the soldiers had come in; the mute accusation: we should have run. He had to ask God's forgiveness for all those battles; for the times his own eyes had been full of death. But when he felt the rough hands start hauling him over the flags to the green outside, and realised what they were going to do, he stopped thinking he had time to pray either. His soldier's instinct took over. He fought. Punched and kicked and jostled and bashed at them with his knees and elbows and head, with every ounce of strength in him, with grass and earth in his mouth and terror rising in his gorge, as they dragged him on to the tree stump that would do quite well as an executioner's block and yanked his head down. His chin bristled on wood. They kicked him to stop him struggling. But he was still flailing and thrashing his head from side to side as the blade flashed high above.

Jane was sewing in the rose bower. The sun was hot. Every now and then she shivered with remembered pleasure as flashes of last night came back into her mind. She was wondering whether to have the boring boiled chicken for dinner or just pick a few of the strawberries she'd seen peeking out red and delicious from the tub by the stables.

A male voice interrupted her reverie.

'Mistress Shoo-ore,' it called flirtatiously from over the wall. She recognised it as the same playful voice that had woken her that morning; the man who'd taken Will away.

Perhaps Will had finished early at Council? The idea came to her that they could go and dine at the Tumbling Bear, where they did fast-day food so deliciously. She could ask the gentleman messenger too; why not? If only she knew his name.

She put down her work.

'Do come in,' she called back, politely.

But no one did. Perhaps they hadn't heard. She didn't like to shout. So she went to the courtyard door herself and opened it with her dewy sideways smile.

The man in the street was young. He had fresh cheeks, bright eyes, and a haystack of yellow hair. He'd taken his hat off. She liked the aristocratic respect of that gesture.

'Mistress Shore,' he began.

At the same moment she said, very sweetly: 'Of course I know who you are – you came for Lord Hastings today – but I'm afraid I don't know your name.'

There was a muffled snort from somewhere behind. The young man lost his composure, looked sideways for a second. Jane looked the same way he was looking, over his shoulder. It took her a couple of seconds to make sense of what she was seeing. There were half a dozen soldiers with him, in sallets and jacks.

'I'm Sir Thomas Howard,' he replied. Automatically, he bowed; but he looked embarrassed. He went on, in a quite different voice: 'Mistress Jane Shore, I am here with

261

an order from the Lord Protector of England to arrest you.'

She stared. She almost laughed. It must be a joke, surely?

'Whatever for?' she breathed, not really scared yet. The calm of her garden was behind her. Will would be here any minute.

He blushed over the absurd words 'witchcraft' and 'treason', but he rushed them out as fiercely as if he were daring her to contradict him. There was another suppressed snort.

'I see,' she said in bewilderment. She stepped forward to look at the men: yes, they really were there. They stared insolently back. One of them grinned right into her face. Others were twitching lips; wiggling eyebrows; putting hands on hips. She saw with a sinking heart that they were the kind to enjoy a victim. It would be wiser to ignore them.

Turning back to the mortified youth who was, at least nominally, in charge of these thugs, she said, very politely and correctly: 'Sir Thomas, perhaps you could wait and explain to Lord Hastings what's going on? He will be here shortly.'

There was a silence long enough for her to realise she'd said the wrong thing. Sir Thomas looked at his feet. His face was beetroot. His men were quivering; about to explode with their joke. It was the man with the hands on his hips who answered in the end. 'Oh no he won't,' he jeered. The others tittered and whistled.

Jane knew not to ask more. Not to think more. She could almost smell the danger now. They were looking at her, as Will liked to say, with the eyes of enemies. They wanted to hurt her. She needed to keep her wits about her; think only from moment to moment. Her body went still. Keeping her breathing shallow, she fixed her eyes on Sir Thomas. He looked up. 'Very well,' she said, more calmly than she felt, and, with a straight back and not even a glance at the garden behind, she stepped out into the street. But before she could even add, 'I'm ready,' she became aware of another commotion from behind. Scuffling. 'Geddorf,' she heard one of the men say. 'Here. Stop it,' said another, and: 'Oi.'

Sir Thomas turned round. Jane turned with him. They both stared. The men-at-arms were no longer alone. They were being surrounded by women. Tough women with set, suspicious faces and arms on their hips. Women who'd been led out of the house opposite – the Prattes' house – by a solid figure with iron-grey hair and a stick. With a shock of joy she never expected to feel at this sight, Jane recognised Alice Claver.

'What in the name of God do you think you're doing, young man?' Alice Claver boomed, pushing past the suddenly quiet soldiers to Sir Thomas Howard and dealing his arm a smart thwack. 'Let go of her at once. The impertinence.'

He jumped back, letting go of Jane as he clutched his arm; giving Alice the shocked, sick look of a child caught misbehaving by its nurse. 'And don't you look at me like that either,' the silkwoman continued forbiddingly, raising her voice further and putting her own arm protectively through Jane's. Her women – there must have been twelve or more of them by now, and there were more coming, both from Anne Pratte's house and the nearby Royal Wardrobe – were directing withering looks at the men-at-arms they'd surrounded. The soldiers were scuffing their feet and looking down. Alice Claver rapped out: 'We were watching you from over the road. We could see exactly what you were up to, so don't bother denying it. I don't know what made you take it into your head that it would be all right to parade round the City of London with this gang of hoodlums, terrorising whoever takes your fancy, but let me tell you it's not. You're breaking the law.'

Jane felt almost sorry for him. 'No,' he whimpered, feeling for his purse. 'You don't understand . . . I've got an order from the Lord Protector . . . here . . .'

Alice Claver folded her arms across her chest. 'I don't want to see your piece of paper,' she said sternly. 'You know as well as I do that we don't allow bandit behaviour in the City of London. If you want to make an arrest here, you have to do it by the book. Go to the Guildhall. Ask them to send out a troop of the watch. They'll make your arrest for you if your papers are right. You can't just start walking our streets, picking people up and taking them off to God knows where. This good lady', she gestured splendidly at Jane, 'is a Freewoman of the City of London. Like us. She has her rights. We all do.' She stuck her nose pugnaciously out. She was nearly as tall as him, and twice as broad. 'And don't you forget it.'

Weakly, Sir Thomas nodded his head.

'Now,' Alice Claver finished up, scarcely drawing breath, keeping the initiative: 'I think we'd better make sure you don't make any more mistakes. Come on,' she jerked her finger towards the Guildhall. 'We'll take you there. It's just round the corner.'

The women worried the men-at-arms forward, like dogs snapping at the heels of sheep, until it seemed to everyone that it was Sir Thomas Howard's troop that was under arrest rather than Jane. Jane, so stunned by now that all she could do was stare and watch events and feet move forward, found herself flanked by Alice Claver and small, white-haired Anne Pratte. Alice Claver kept waving her stick longingly in the direction of Thomas Howard, just in front of them, as if keen to whack him again on the arm or leg.

Anne Pratte, meanwhile, was whispering advice to Jane. 'They'll have to shut you up if he's really got an order,' she muttered. 'But only in a proper city prison. And don't forget, as a Freewoman you get to choose which one.' Jane nodded blankly. 'Are you taking this in, dear?' Anne Pratte said, more sharply, then took both Jane's hands in hers, squeezed them until Jane's eyes focused, and hissed: 'Ask for Ludgate Prison!'

Which was how Jane came to be locked, not in a festering dungeon somewhere underground, but into a light, bare room over Ludgate, with the traffic that clattered in and out of the City through the western gate passing directly under her floor. Her cell was built into the stone City wall on one side but it had wooden walls on the other sides. It had a big window through which she could look down over the people coming in and walking up Ludgate Hill. She could see all the way to St Paul's. There was a thin rope attached to a hook by the window, which she could let down, so visitors who came and stood below and shouted to get her attention could reach for the swinging end and tie a bag of food onto it for her to haul up and eat, and she could let down her laundry for her friends to wash.

'Don't you worry,' Anne Pratte said encouragingly, a small figure below, after she'd made Jane winch up a bottle of beer and some bread in a bag. 'We'll be back.'

Jane watched that purposeful little back disappear up the hill and into the crowd. She didn't open the bag. She didn't do anything. It was as if she'd forgotten how. She just went on sitting, stiller than she'd ever have thought possible, looking out but not noticing the sunlight on the cathedral tower turn a richer gold, then deep red.

Isabel clip-clopped along the road to Westminster alone, in a dream so sweet that she was only vaguely aware of the dozens of soldiers out this morning, pacing one arm-span apart through the fields of tall young corn as far as the eye could see, leaving trampled trails of bleeding green behind; of the dogs sniffing and barking on their leashes. All she really saw was her interior vision of the room where she'd spent yesterday afternoon, cool and empty of everything except Dickon and the rumpled bed. She could still smell him on her. Anything being done out here, in the reality of this hot summer's morning, might as well not be happening. But she had to go to the Princess. They'd have delivered the coronation robe to her in sanctuary now. The Princess had asked for a fitting.

It was only when she got to the Abbot's house that the trails of glory began to dissipate.

There were twice as many soldiers as usual on the door: cold, unfamiliar faces. The whispers she heard, from behind her back, were in the harsh language of the North. She thought she could hear weeping through the open windows. She strained her ears when she got inside, but there was none of the usual bustle of a big household; just whispers and an uncanny silence. When Lady Elizabeth Darcey was called to see Isabel in, she saw the noblewoman's long and usually controlled face was twitching and patchy with red; her eyes swollen. 'You!' she said in uncontrollable surprise at the sight of Isabel; which was odd because Isabel had been supposed to come at this time. Lady Darcey stammered: 'I didn't think . . . well, I suppose there's no harm . . .' but before leading Isabel into the sewing parlour she drew her aside and added, 'but you should know: their Highnesses are . . . His Highness Prince Richard has gone . . .' and, to Isabel's astonishment, the other woman's face twisted into the beginning of a sob.

Daringly, Isabel put a hand on Lady Elizabeth's arm and was rewarded with a sudden, grateful look as Lady Elizabeth swallowed and recomposed her face. They stood like that for a minute, as if the noblewoman was furtively drawing comfort from her warm hand. Then Lady Elizabeth moved just out of her reach. 'Her Highness will be pleased to see you,' she said, almost back to her brittle usual self, 'Come', and darted off down the corridor so fast that Isabel almost had to run to keep up.

The princesses had all been crying.

The eyes Elizabeth turned on Isabel were so red and puffy she could hardly see out. There wasn't even a trace of coldness in her today. She and her sisters pulled Isabel to the table and sat her down as if she were one of them. Elizabeth whispered the story.

The Duke of Buckingham had just been, with Lord Howard, Archbishop Bourchier of Canterbury and the Lord Chancellor, Bishop Russell. They'd scared Queen Elizabeth Woodville into giving up her younger son. They said little Richard, the Duke of York, should be with his brother Edward, who was moving into the state apartments in the Tower ahead of the coronation. Edward would be bored on his own. They gave Queen Elizabeth Woodville a moment to say her goodbyes. Then they took him away.

'They had such frightening eyes,' one of the little girls said numbly. It set the others off.

'My mother says they hate us.'

'My brother was crying. He tried not to but we heard him all the way down the corridor.'

'He didn't even take his game.'

Helplessly, Isabel patted small hands and shoulders and looked at the polished knucklebones they were showing her, the game Richard had left behind. The lords who had come were all Dickon's men, and she knew them to be as loyal to him as Lord Hastings. They would mean the little boy no harm, any more than Dickon did. But she could so easily imagine how their intent faces and hurried demeanour would have terrified the children.

She murmured: 'You poor things', and, 'I can see you were scared.' They nodded earnestly; fixed eyes as round as as red platters on her. Gently, she added, 'But, you know, they're right. Edward would be lonely if he didn't have anyone to play with.'

They looked uncertain.

'Why can't we see Edward here?' one of the little redheads asked. 'Why won't they let him come to us?'

'My mother says our uncle Gloucester has taken him prisoner.'

'And now Richard too.'

'She says we'll never see either of them again.'

'And our uncle Dorset has gone away too.'

'He's our half-brother really; but we call him uncle.'

'And Brigid's nurse says she's heard they're going to execute our other Woodville uncles today.'

'In Pontefract.'

'And then they'll come to get us.'

'And murder us in our beds.'

Little Brigid, who'd been doing her best to follow the conversation, understood that perfectly. She burst into loud wails. The others just stared at her. They weren't used to looking after themselves or each other. Where was the nurse? Isabel wondered. Finally, reluctantly – what could she be expected to know about babies? – she picked the weeping child up herself and sat her on her knee. Brigid burrowed at her ribs, still sobbing.

'Hush now,' Isabel said, trying to sound soothing, but suddenly rattled herself. 'Hush.'

She thought: It's all their mother's fault. Of course Queen Elizabeth Woodville would feel frightened and alone. But, she thought, it was still wrong for the self-made queen to make assumptions that everyone else was motivated by the same greedy thoughts she would probably have had herself if she'd been in Dickon's position. And it was wrong to terrify her children with these nightmarish expectations.

268

Blaming the Queen calmed Isabel down. Once the little girl's sobs had faded to sniffles, Isabel told her, kindly but firmly, 'It's only because you're here that you can't see your brother. He's got to stay in London in the King's apartments now he's King. Your mother's been just as scared as you, and while we didn't know where he was she thought coming here was the best way to keep you safe. That was a wise thing for her to think. But it's all over now. We know Edward's safe. There's no reason for you to be scared any more. Your mother will see that soon enough. And then you'll be out too, and at the Palace again, and going with Richard to see Edward crowned King.'

She was talking to Brigid, but all the princesses were hanging on her words. She thought their panic was ebbing. She noticed Elizabeth look down for a second when she spoke of Edward's coronation. There was a flash of what Isabel thought might be envy in her eyes – but that was positive, too, she thought; a sign of normal feelings returning.

There was someone hiding in the silk house.

Isabel knew as soon as she let herself in, to check briefly on its state, brushing through the waist-high cow-parsley at her door. It was shut-up and cobwebby. Will Caxton's maid couldn't have been here since the unrest started. But there was a table inside already; two benches; buckets and brooms and bowls in the kitchen, ready for the new inhabitants; and, in the workroom, the half-assembled pieces of loom propped up all along the inner wall, covered in sacking. She knew there were piles of mattresses and blankets upstairs – the basics, ready for Goffredo's teams. All she could hear was the two flies buzzing peaceably backwards and forwards near the dark window. But she could feel the breathing.

'Who's there?' she called, with her heart thumping and flesh creeping. The quality of the silence changed. If there was someone there, they must be listening.

For a moment she wondered whether to run to Will's house and get back-up. Then she steeled herself. She wasn't going to let them know she was scared of shadows. She might be imagining it. Leaving the front door open, she walked very quickly into the kitchen.

The back door to the yard was open too. There was a man in the shadow behind it. He was tall but very quiet; sweating in a dark cloak; ready for flight if her voice meant enemies. He was so still.

It was Dorset.

She stopped dead.

He'd shoved his hands inside her gown once. Sneering and forcing his mouth on hers. She didn't want to be alone with him. She wouldn't easily forget the insult in his eyes.

But there was only fear in his eyes now.

'Are you alone?' he whispered, from the safety of his doorway. She nodded, from hers.

'What are you doing here?' she muttered. 'In my house?'

He must have realised at last that she thought he might be going to try again to tumble her. He shut his eyes, snorted: 'Ach. Not *that*.' Then, cunningly, as if realising an attempt at charm would be politic in these circumstances, 'I didn't mean to scare you.'

She waited, watching him carefully. Keeping her distance.

But she remembered now. One of the little princesses had said uncle Dorset had gone. She should have paid more attention. If he'd run away from sanctuary, he'd be fair game for anyone trying to arrest him. And Dickon's lords had been with the Queen today, taking the boy. They must have realised he'd gone. There'd been soldiers with Northern voices and dogs trampling through the cornfields round Westminster by mid-morning. She understood now. They were hunting the Woodville Marquess down. They wanted to kill him.

'I'm in danger,' he said. 'You've got to help me.'

'How did you find me?' she countered suspiciously. 'Here?'

No one knew about this house. Did they?

'Jane said . . .' Dorset replied, rumpling boyish hair, giving her his most appealing look.

Her eyes narrowed. Jane. How dare she?

'. . . that if I ever needed to get a message to her urgently to give it to Will Caxton, for you to take back to London. She said you had a house nearby. I asked. And some German artisan said it was this one.'

She breathed out.

'But why are you still here?' she asked, still coldly but with calm returning. 'Why didn't you just give Caxton your message and go?'

His handsome mouth curled briefly in a how-can-you-be-so-stupid sneer. Then, remembering where he was and why he was here, he blanked his face again.

'Because I heard the crier,' he said in a very patient voice. And he added, staring into her eyes as if trying to suck knowledge out of her: 'Is Jane safe?'

'Jane?' she said stupidly.

'You didn't hear the herald, did you,' he said – not a question. He shook his head. She shook hers. There was a pause. She could see he didn't know how to frame whatever it was he needed to tell her.

There was a bugle blast from the Red Pale out in front of the house. He looked terrified again for a second, then his face cleared. 'There,' he said quietly. 'He's come here. Listen for yourself.'

He took her by the arm – she hardly even shuddered

271

at his touch any more; she recognised that something altogether different from her memory of this man was happening today – and led her towards the noise. They stood just inside the closed shutters, hidden from the listeners coming out of their houses all around.

The proclamation had begun; but it took Isabel a while to make sense of it. The man's voice seemed to be saying that Lord Hastings had plotted to kill the dukes of Gloucester and Buckingham and seize the king. It seemed to be saying that Lord Hastings had led the late King Edward IV into debauchery.

And it was saying, very clearly now, that Mistress Shore, with whom Lord Hastings lay by night, was of his secret counsel in heinous treason. The iron band was tightening on Isabel's gut. She could hardly breathe.

'Ungracious living brought him to an unhappy end,' the voice shouted. The horn blew another flamboyant fanfare. Hooves moved off. They could hear the uncertain ripple of conversation from the listeners.

Dorset whispered: 'You see. They must have killed him. So what have they done to her?'

She bowed her head. She couldn't think. She couldn't believe this. 'I don't understand,' she whispered. But when he said, impatiently, 'Gloucester is seizing power,' she only nodded. She knew that too, really. Dickon had raised his game. Nothing else made sense.

There was nothing for it but to help Dorset get to London. She couldn't leave him.

Her mind was racing now, uselessly, since she knew she had to stifle all thoughts but a list of her most immediate needs. She borrowed a stained work smock and half a dozen copies of Earl Rivers' curial from Will Caxton's workshop – the foreign foreman didn't seem to mind, just nodded when she smiled and waved and said, slowly enough for him to understand, that she'd return every-thing tomorrow. She dirtied the Woodville Marquess's handsome face and made him grime up his clean finger-nails. Luckily he too had the wordless urgency of a man who will do whatever is needed, at once, to save himself. She put his expensive cloak and his sword in a big rough sack on her saddle; put herself up on her horse and tried not to heed her pounding heartbeat as they set out. She got Dorset to bow his head and put the books under one arm. 'You're a German printer; you don't speak English,' was all she said to him, and he nodded obedi-ently. She got him to lead her, on foot, out of the gate, past the sweating soldiers in the fields, past the dogs, along the riverside strand, past the bishops' fortresses, along the caked mud of Fleet Street, to London. She tried to think of nothing more alarming than the birds fluttering up from the battered fields, the white fleece scudding along overhead. A part of her felt safe enough; after all, she'd spent a year walking the familiar streets of the Mercery unrecognised by all the grand mercers she'd grown up among, just because she'd started wearing the humble drab of the district's poor throwsters and shepsters. Dorset's disguise was working just as well now. No one looked at them, even Davey at the Westminster gate, who'd averted his eyes as studiously as if she'd become the vilest of lepers. No one was interested in the dirty, broken silhouette that Dorset had become. Still, she'd never been so happy to see the Fleet Bridge and Ludgate looming up ahead. Every jolt of horseflesh under her, every breath she'd taken, had reminded her of how tight her jaw was clenched; how tense her arms and back.

There was a knot of silkwomen standing around inside the safety of the London wall. Familiar faces: Joan Woulbarowe and Agnes Brundyssch and Isabel Fremely. Isabel was momentarily startled to see even Joan

Woulbarowe's former mistress, the throwster Katherine Dore – who hated her ex-apprentice and had spent years trying to get the courts of London to punish Joan for leaving her service – standing lean and tall and intimidating in the whispering group.

'Look,' Joan Woulbarowe said, seeing Isabel, running up, taking her arm. Not, for once, displaying her black teeth in her doggy smile; instead looking purposeful and urgent. She didn't even waste a glance on the shabby man leading Isabel's horse, but the moment of contact set Isabel's heart racing with terror.

'Not now,' she said coldly, hardening her face, and rode on.

Joan stood aside. 'But Mistress Claver said,' Isabel heard her wail, with defeat in her voice. Well, Alice Claver could wait. Joan would give up; she had no more fight in her than a whipped dog. But the voice behind went on calling. Instead of trailing forlornly away it rose in volume. 'Jane's up there!' it cried.

Isabel turned in the saddle. Dorset, head down, was still urging the horse forward.

It wasn't just Joan. All the silkwomen were staring at her with anxious eyes, and pointing up at the wall; to where the cells of Ludgate jail were built in, above the gate. And they were all calling, contorting their faces in their need for her to understand, as loudly as they dared, hissing in what they must think were whispers: 'Jane!'

Isabel squinted up at the wall. She couldn't see anyone at a cell window. The fingers on her reins were slippery. She could feel her breath and heart. She nodded back at them. 'An hour,' she called, as the horse and Dorset carried on walking.

They turned without speaking into the courtyard at Catte Street. He shut the gate and looked up at her. There was a glitter of satisfaction in his eyes. She felt it too.

It was good to be behind a wall and off the street. But they both knew it was only the first step.

Isabel already had the first glimmer of an idea of what to do with him next. But she needed Alice Claver's approval.

'Come on,' she said. 'Behind me.' And she strode through the house with her follower, looking into the great hall, the parlours, the storeroom, the herb garden, and even upstairs into the bedchambers, looking for Alice; suddenly wanting to see those broad shoulders and that down-to-earth face, with its ready scowl and its rare bursts of jollity, more than she'd ever thought she could.

The relief of seeing Alice's and Anne Pratte's heads bent over a bag in one of the larders was almost more than she could bear. She let out a breath, feeling the emotion she'd been keeping at bay wash through her; wondering if she was going to cry.

'Alice,' she said, and her voice was strangely small and unsteady. 'Anne.'

They looked up; and she saw in their hungry eyes that they felt the same tumult, even before they both dropped what they were doing and rushed to her with their arms open. It only lasted a second, the wobbly embrace that followed. Alice Claver caught herself swaying in it and pulled away, leaving Anne Pratte holding Isabel's hand as if she'd never let go and staring up at her in soft delight. But Alice Claver couldn't quite stop; she went on awkwardly patting Isabel's back as she growled, 'We were worried'. Isabel even thought she saw a gleam of wet on that lined cheek.

There was a cough behind her. 'We have a guest,' Isabel said, gathering her wits, surprised she could have forgotten Dorset. He was standing awkwardly in the doorway, clearly not sure whether to go on hunching over his books like an old man but doing it anyway, to be on the safe side.

The silkwomen rose to the occasion with aplomb. No exaggerated respect, no bobs and bows; that wasn't their way, and wouldn't have been even if they'd been admirers of the Woodvilles. But, once Isabel had explained, they willingly set out bread and cold pork and the leftover dish of greens they hadn't touched at dinner and a couple of tankards of weak ale, and, while Dorset fell on the food like a starving man and Isabel picked at it without really eating, and talked, in a voice higher and faster than usual, they listened.

Alice looked at Dorset with no particular warmth. He was an extra problem she had no relish for solving. 'So what do you plan to do next, young man?' she asked, and noted his bewildered shrug with a pursing of her own lips. But she'd already thought of the answer, and, to Isabel's private joy, it was the same answer she herself had thought of earlier.

'You'd better', Alice Claver pronounced briskly, 'join William's travelling party.'

William Pratte was going to Bruges for the fair. As well as representing English merchants – an official mission for the Guildhall – he was going to unofficially stand in for Alice and do some of the buying she'd normally do there herself at this time of year. She'd decided not to this year in case Goffredo returned early.

Anne Pratte's eyes sparkled. Isabel sometimes thought she didn't understand fear. 'You could be his Flemish secretary,' she said, playing with the idea. 'William can lend you a set of clothes.' She stressed the word 'lend' – you didn't want to let noblemen make the mistake they were so prone to, of thinking you wanted to just give your possessions to them. 'We'll sort that out; make you look right. But you'd better wear that smock you've got on to come home with me now. We don't want any nosy questions.'

Gratitude swept through Isabel. They were taking charge of him. She was suddenly bone tired. She wanted nothing more than to go to sleep. Thinking could wait.

Alice Claver was addressing the Marquess sternly as she ushered him to the door, practically pushing him forward. 'Now you take that bag please . . . you're younger and stronger than Mistress Pratte here . . . who is doing you a great service today, as you'll appreciate . . . and for God's sake when you get outside don't forget at any time that you're supposed to be a foreigner. Don't start talking to people, whatever you do. Just look humble and say nothing. Look humble. Can you remember that?'

Yawning, drooping on her bench, Isabel thought: Well, she's always liked taking people down a peg or two. Isabel couldn't find it in her to feel too sorry for Dorset. He hadn't even bothered to thank her for getting him out of Westminster and into safe hands. And he hadn't stopped to spare a thought for Jane, either, even though he'd spent all those years publicly sighing for love of her – almost as long as Lord Hastings had.

Isabel jolted upright. Lord Hastings, she thought. And, with fear flooding into her: Jane. Before she knew it, she was on her feet again, flying towards the door to find Alice.

They went to Jane's house first. 'Before we know where we are they'll be helping themselves to her things,' Alice Claver said sagely. 'We might as well safeguard what we can.'

The empty house was a treasure trove of beautiful trinkets and pictures and textiles. Isabel looked round as if to memorise it all, realising she might never see it again. But they took only jewels and linen and a book of hours and two skirts in modest colours, slipping their armfuls of booty over the road to the back stable at Anne Pratte's house which had been empty since a horse that had gone lame had been sold. They made Jane a food bag from her own kitchen. Isabel could see some of the early strawberries her sister loved peeping out of a tub by the stable; she picked a few and put them in a pewter mug, topped with leaves to keep them in. Alice – grimly cutting cheese and cured meat into big coarse slabs that Jane would never eat, and taking half of the great loaf the cook had left on the table before he'd vanished to the safety of Anne Pratte's – laughed, not very sympathetically, at Isabel's whimsy. 'You'd be better off checking what other valuables there are,' she said. 'Hasn't she got a money box?'

She did have one: a lovely carved oakwood casket, which Isabel saw, when she opened it, was painted inside with pictures of a knight and his lady who had the faces of Jane and Lord Hastings. She'd thought it was heavy, and now she saw why. It was stuffed to the brim with gold coins. 'There, you see,' Alice Claver said, materialising behind her, with hands on hips, 'she'll thank you more for getting that out of the way than for picking her strawberries. There must be hundreds of pounds in there.'

They lugged it over the road together, panting with the weight of it. They'd been going to come back for the food, but at the last minute Isabel had slung the bag over her shoulder. It was just as well. Before they'd even settled the casket in a dark corner and covered it with mouldy hay, they heard the horses clopping quietly up to stop outside Jane's gate, the jangle of harness and the creak of leather masking the whispers. 'You see?' Alice Claver muttered triumphantly. 'They'll have stripped it bare by morning.'

The two of them walked onto the street, looking straight ahead, acting, like everyone else on Old Jewry, as though the men in leather jackets and metal helmets swarming into Jane's house didn't exist. Alice Claver held her head very high and kept a pointed look of disgust on her face until they'd swept round the corner into Cheapside. Isabel's food bag was too heavy and lopsided for her to maintain the same hauteur. Also, she was too curious; she couldn't resist sneaking a sideways look. She didn't know the young gentleman issuing soldiers with sacks before they went in, but she recognised him at once as the villain from Alice's story. He was tall, fresh-faced and innocent-looking, with freckles and a shock of straw-coloured hair, and he was smiling.

She didn't expect them to, but the men at Ludgate let Isabel upstairs with her bag of food and clothes. They were family men, with tired, kindly faces, and they looked sorry for her. 'We're looking after her, don't you worry,' the bald one said when he first saw Isabel's provisions. But then he glanced round, saw his mate nod, and quietly opened the door to the stairs. 'Come on,' he said, jerking a thumb upwards. 'Quick.'

Jane was sitting on the bench staring at the reddish light on St Paul's. She didn't turn round when the door opened. Isabel was touched to see a little posy of flowers on the window. 'It's me,' she whispered, not wanting to shock her sister. The man shut the door behind her as Jane raised haggard, empty eyes, then stumbled up and into an embrace – the kind of incredulous embrace in which every move and breath and slope of the other person's shoulder is proof that your worst nightmares haven't, after all, yet come true.

When they partly disentangled themselves and sat down side by side, with their knees brushing against each other and their hands clasped together and their eyes fastened on each other's faces, Isabel couldn't begin to think what needed to be said. Then she looked down and saw the knot of silkwomen still standing there, grinning soppily at the two heads reunited in the window. That might be enough for now.

'Look,' she whispered; and Jane stared down at them, not understanding.

'Are they . . . ?' she murmured eventually, with a glimmer of something like hope.

'They've been there all day,' Isabel said gently. 'Ever since they stopped the soldiers taking you away.'

Jane went on staring then raised a tentative hand. There was a murmur, then a few hands waving back from the shadows. Jane managed a melancholy smile. 'My army,' she said in a small voice, before the tears came.

She'd heard the heralds. She knew Hastings was dead. After a while, when her tears had settled into a steady flow down a wet face, but when she could listen again, Isabel told her what little more Alice and Anne had gleaned on the streets: about how the Council meeting had turned into a blood-letting; about how Sir Thomas Howard had slipped away from the melee to arrest Jane, while the Duke of Buckingham had gone to Westminster to take little Prince Richard, the Duke of York, from the Woodvilles in sanctuary there. Jane's expression was passive, her head bowed into a supporting hand. From time to time she nodded. Every now and then she flinched.

She only looked down and shrugged helplessly at the idea of the charges against her. Witchcraft – what was there to say?

'We all know it's absurd,' Isabel babbled; trying to shut out her picture of Dickon yesterday, naked, with his head thrown back laughing, 'everyone knows that . . . it must be a mistake . . . the Guildhall is going to raise it with Council, William Pratte says; they're going to insist that City Freemen and Freewomen can't be treated like this . . . it's not as bad as it looks . . . You'll be out of here very soon . . . We'll find a way.' She knew these were faint hopes. Jane had been imprisoned because of something Hastings had been thought guilty enough of to die for. Jane smiled sadly and sighed and said nothing.

Yet she livened up at the news that Dorset was free and on the run – though only enough to look anxious at the idea of him trying to leave the country. 'Make sure he has money,' she said, with her eyes darting around the walls as if trying to work out how to make that happen. She squeezed Isabel's hands. 'I've got money. In my box at home. Give him fifty pounds if he needs it. You will, won't you?'

The door was already opening. The time was up. 'I promise,' Isabel said, and threw herself into her sister's arms and clung to that fugitive smell of rosewater and sunshine. The man behind was shuffling in an embarrassed way. He was too polite to interrupt.

'I don't want to get you into trouble,' Jane said, breaking away, turning to her jailer. Even in this cell, in this bad light, she was beautiful. 'Thank you for letting my sister in.' And Isabel saw his lines soften in response into an adoring, black-toothed smile.

'It's not right,' he muttered to Isabel on the stairwell, 'and no one thinks it is. A lovely, sweet-natured lady like that. A witch, indeed. The only reason she's in here is politics. It's Them Up There fighting for the gubbins, like pigs at a trough, isn't it? Not her.' Defiantly, he banged open the door and let Isabel out, gesturing at the silk-women on the cobbles. 'I don't care who hears me, either. We all know what's really going on.'

The yawning pit in Isabel's stomach didn't stop her flinging herself on her bed and sleeping the sleep of the dead as soon as she got home. But she woke up in the middle of the night to find herself sitting up, with her teeth grinding and her eyes staring through the darkness.

281

It wasn't just the thought of Jane in her prison cell that had woken her in this panic. It wasn't just the crazed scurrying of the day that had finished; rushing from one catastrophe to the next, dealing with each one as it arose, with no time to think. It was what Dorset had said in the morning, the words she'd been refusing ever since to let her mind dwell on. Dickon was seizing power. It was the only explanation that made any sense. He must be going to try and make himself king. Lord Hastings was dead. The little King and Prince Richard were in his control. There'd be no one to stop him.

She thought: Queen Elizabeth Woodville might have been right after all not to leave sanctuary. She almost started worrying about the royal children. But there was too much else to worry about. She kept that door in her mind shut.

She couldn't believe it. She went through every moment of her time with Dickon yesterday. There had been no sign, no sign. He'd laughed at the idea of Jane and Hastings together. He'd laughed at the idea of Dorset being disappointed. Something must have come up since he'd seen her; something that changed everything. She'd have known if he had something like this on his mind, wouldn't she? He'd have told her. He'd have hinted. He'd have spared Jane, at least. What did Jane have to do with any of this?

Then she thought, remembering his rush to go, remembering the jerky, excited way he'd been moving and talking, his lack of attention: Would he?

And, with a shame that made her cheeks burn and her stomach clutch, she thought: Why would he think I cared about sparing Jane, when I've always said such hard things about her? When he might easily think I hate her?

The more she agonised the less she understood, until her mind filled with a jumble of bright still images that didn't fit together. Dickon laughing. Dorset's terrified

282

breathing when the herald's horn blew. Jane, smelling of innocent rosewater, sighing in her cell. Jane's house being emptied by a young, smiling blond man with soldiers.

And, gradually, a small, sick, hateful thought came to the surface. *She might easily not have known.* What did she really know about Dickon, after all? A smell; the taste of his skin; a set of gestures; a glint of eyes. She'd thought it was a meeting of minds. But she knew nothing that would let her be sure how he might behave in his public life, while he did whatever he considered necessary to protect himself and his kin. Nothing except the street talk everyone knew. That he was a good ruler of the North and a good soldier. The rumours that he'd done various small cruel acts to the widows and mothers of Lancastrians who couldn't fight back (but nothing worse than other lords did). The foolish street talk, what she'd always thought foolish street talk, about him murdering his brother and old King Henry in the Tower. She'd thought she knew the man within; thought they were kindred spirits. But if this was the reality, the Dickon she knew was a distorted shadow, unknowably, unguessably unlike the prince the world was seeing.

The darkness that came over her then was so bleak, so overwhelming, that she drew into a tight crouch of agony, arms squeezing knees, eyes squeezing shut, feeling her face contort with the dryness of the pain. Trying to push away each memory of his body as the agony broke over her in another tidal wave of blackness: each low laugh in her ear; each slippery feel of skin on skin; the deep touch that turned a hand on her elbow or a touch on the back of her neck into a caress; the way he'd roll his body up onto one elbow to look at her and run a gentle hand through her hair, afterwards, while they talked.

She knew already what it meant to have realised this. There would be no more of it. No more winks at the door of the Red Pale; no more sly doffings of hats through windows. No more intoxicating expectation; no more giggles as they flew up the stairs to be reunited. No more joy.

The sense of loss made her breathless. But what made her more breathless still was the thought that, if he'd been planning all this yesterday, which he almost certainly must have been, he must have known it would mean the end of Isabel's trust. He must have thought it would be their last time together. He must have decided it didn't matter.

No one in the Claver household paid any attention to Isabel's ravaged face or silence in the morning. She was grateful, if not altogether surprised. There was so much else going on that there was no time for talk. Alice Claver only nodded absentmindedly when Isabel said, in a controlled voice, 'There's no point in my going to Westminster for a while, is there?' She couldn't bear the idea of facing Princess Elizabeth and her sisters, and seeing the mute accusation in their eyes – you were wrong – and there'd be no question of sewing coronation gowns now. And Dickon wasn't there.

'You'll want to go and see your sister today,' Alice said. 'She'll need new linen. And you tell her I'm going to the Mayor about her, with William; I want this sorted out before William leaves.'

By noon, when she went to the Guildhall with the bag of fifty gold coins she'd counted out for Dorset, Alice and William had already made their petition to the Mayor, asking him to negotiate Jane's release. They were standing in the street waiting for her. It clearly hadn't gone well. Alice was fuming. She said they'd been interrupted by a gentleman from the Duke of Buckingham's household with advance word of what the Duke planned to tell the Guildhall at the beginning of next week about the events of the previous day. So, squashed into a corner of the Mayor's table by the Duke's delegation, they'd heard the whole speech. 'And you'd be hard put to imagine a more disgraceful set of slanders,' Alice snorted. 'When I think how we all went out into the streets and fought for the Yorks, all those years ago; endangering life and limb. The whole of London: Yorkist to a man. When I think of my son . . .' She stopped for a moment; crossed herself; then, in a smaller voice, added, 'and your husband', and, almost apologetically, met Isabel's eye. Taking a deep breath, and getting back to her strident form, she finished: 'All I can say is: it wasn't for this.'

'What does the speech say?' Isabel asked, strangely warmed by that reluctant aside.

Alice went so red Isabel thought she might have a fit. It was William Pratte who began hesitantly to paraphrase. The speech accused the late King Edward of being a womaniser, he said. It was such a strange accusation that despite herself Isabel almost laughed. 'Well, that's true enough,' she said. 'But what does it have to do with any of this?'

Alice snapped, 'For no woman was there anywhere, young or old, poor or rich, whom he set eye on, but that he would importunately pursue his appetite and have her, to the great destruction of many a good woman.'

Isabel stared; not because of the older woman's fluency in quotation, but because of the malice of the thought behind it. 'They're trying to blacken King Edward's memory,' William Pratte said, shaking his head. Like most people, he was too cautious to name whomever he thought responsible: the words 'the Duke of Gloucester' had not passed his lips. But he added: 'His own blood. Edward was the only good King we've ever known.'

'And then it went', Alice stormed on, in her own stream of thought, 'something to the effect that he "paid more attention to Shore's wife, a vile and abominable strumpet, than to all the lords in England, except those who made her their protector".'

'Hastings?' Isabel queried.

'And Dorset,' William Pratte reminded her quietly.

After that, Alice and William had given up and slunk out. There was no point in staying near the Mayor. They weren't going to get anywhere for now. 'I wouldn't altogether give up hope, though,' William Pratte said thoughtfully. They looked quickly up; William was their statesman. He went on: 'I'd say they're realising they won't get anywhere with this idea they've been floating – accusing Jane and Lord Hastings of plotting to cast spells on Richard. It's already obvious no one's going to believe it. Not here; where people know her. It's too stupid. So they'll have to let it drop. But they'll look fools if they just let her walk free. So they'll have to keep her in jail for a bit; and I'd guess they'll go on denouncing her as a whore for a while too. It's an easy enough way to tell the people that whoever becomes king next will be less prone to vicious living than the King we've just buried – to make them look good.' He paused; said defiantly: 'God rest King Edward's soul. I'd say the Mayor will be minded to help Jane, once things quieten down,' he added, more practically. 'I could see the look in his eyes. I know him. He won't willingly let a Freewoman be dragged into all this.'

In his eyes, Isabel could see the doggedness of every merchant forced to live cheek by jowl with his lords, men who lived by the sword and didn't fear dying by the sword in pursuit of their ambitions. She sensed the resentment of every Londoner who knew that his peaceable markets and streets and churches just filled up the spaces between the looming city fortresses the lords maintained among all that merchant industry; who was able to do nothing but shrug and lock up his house whenever those lords felt the urge to march through the gates of the City with their armies of horsemen, alien beings in armour and weapons, who might, at any moment, take it into their heads to turn violent. Seeing the stubborn frown lines between his eyes, she could believe the Mayor would share these Londoners' feelings enough to do his best to keep Jane safe.

'I'm still going to have to go to Bruges,' William Pratte said. 'Especially now, with Dorset to get rid of. You and Jane are going to have to see this through without me. But my advice is: wait a week or so; get my lawyer involved; then go back to the Mayor.'

The coup gathered pace. The merchants' delegation setting off for Bruges delayed their departure until Sunday afternoon, on the strong advice of the Mayor, who thought it would be politic for them to hear the sermon to be preached at Paul's Cross outside the Cathedral.

It was a blustery day under curdled yellow skies. There was a vast crowd, muttering and anxious; sullen-looking people waiting to hear the excuses of the powerful for an upheaval they suspected could only damage them, looking for clues as to how their own lives would get worse. Isabel, Alice and Anne Pratte walked there with the merchant delegation William Pratte would be taking to Bruges later. Knowing there would be many eyes on Isabel, Anne Pratte prudently took it upon herself to link arms with the handsome young Flemish clerk in sombre tunic and leggings, whose face was cast down; whose shoulders were nervously hunched. But he couldn't stop raising his eyes at his first sight of Isabel and smiling slightly; and she had to make a conscious effort not to bow her head in acknowledgement and mutter, 'my lord'.

She waited until the bodies were so densely packed

around the pulpit that no one could possibly see, then wedged herself next to him and said, into his ear, 'from Jane, for your travels', and slipped the money bag into his hand. She could see from Dorset's face that he was feeling the bag with his fingers; realising it contained coins; realising too that Jane had been thinking about providing for his needs even while she was locked up at Ludgate. His eyes widened.

'Thank you,' he mouthed. Then: 'Thank her for me.'

She eased; after all, perhaps he wasn't quite as selfish and ungrateful as she'd thought. Then, after a long internal reflection, which she could see had reached its conclusion from the new resolve dawning in his beautiful eyes: 'Or can you help me thank her myself?'

She shook her head in alarm. Then, feeling she'd been hasty – he was well-disguised now, after all – slowly nodded. 'What time do you set off?' she asked. The delegation was to take ship for Coventry later that day. 'We could walk you down to her window after this. You could wave. She'd see you. She'd like that. Would you have time?'

There was no time for more than a nod; the crowd was stirring. Isabel could hardly see the preacher climbing into the pulpit; at first she could only half-hear the shouted words that began to emanate from it. Then, as the gasps and murmurs all around her got louder, she could hardly hear at all.

But she heard enough.

The preacher was saying that England was ruled by a bastard. Most of the rest of the royal family were illegitimate too. Years of vicious living had so corrupted the blood royal that there was scarcely a man standing worthy of wearing the crown of England.

'Bastard slips shall take no root!' he yelled, and the wind carried that shout to Isabel.

It was too stupefying to take in at once. How had they all so suddenly come to be bastards? Some people as bewildered as she was began obediently yelling the slogan back. Others angrily shushed them. They wanted to hear the reasoning behind this extraordinary claim.

Now the voice was explaining. King Edward's already scandalous secret marriage to Queen Elizabeth Woodville had been invalid, it said. The grossly promiscuous old King had been secretly betrothed even before that, to Lady Eleanor Butler; and that first betrothal had been binding enough to make any later marriages null and void. It meant that Queen Elizabeth Woodville had never truly been Queen of England, and her children were not fit to be known as princes and princesses. Little King Edward, in the state apartments at the Tower awaiting his coronation, was no more King Edward V than his brother was worthy of the title Prince Richard. They were Edward Bastard and Richard Bastard.

'Edward Bastard!' a few voices cried back. But not many.

Hundreds of indrawn breaths made a new hush as the preacher swept on to still more shocking claims. It wasn't just the new king who was a bastard, he said. Old King Edward had been one too. So had his brother, the Duke of Clarence. Their mother, the old Duchess of York, had been unfaithful to their father while he was off campaigning in France. Her first two sons – tall, strapping, golden men – had not been the blood of the small, spare, sharp-featured, black-haired Duke, even if they'd called him father.

'I can see what's coming next,' Alice Claver's voice muttered disgustedly, behind Isabel.

So could the rest of the crowd. When the preacher yelled his triumphant finale into the wind – 'Only Richard, Duke of Gloucester, is the rightful son of his father!' –

there were no more gasps or shudders, just a sense of anticlimax. Just a few voices calling out, 'Richard Gloucester!' and 'God Save King Richard!' almost experimentally, over the cautious talk between friends and family members and neighbours, while the rest of the assembly began to eddy away home. There were glum faces everywhere.

So Isabel was surprised when she glanced up at Dorset, to see him grinning. He straightened his face hastily. But his eyes glinted at her with a furtive shadow of the same amusement and explained his thought. 'I wouldn't like to be in Richard Gloucester's shoes when his mother gets hold of him,' he whispered, shaking his head. 'Casting aspersions on her honour. She's the fiercest woman in Christendom. It's her Neville blood. She makes even my aunt look timid. It wouldn't be worth being king if Proud Cis wanted your blood.'

Unwillingly, Isabel found herself starting to like Dorset.

'Ssh,' she said reprovingly, but she let her eyes laugh with him. Then she whispered: 'After Bruges, where are you going to go?' She could tell Jane later.

'Britanny,' he said. He'd obviously thought this out. 'To Henry Tudor.'

She stared.

She'd heard of Henry Tudor; but only just. He was the Earl of Richmond, and a Lancastrian of sorts; he and his Tudor uncle Jasper had raised Wales for mad old King Henry VI thirteen years earlier, during the Earl of Warwick's brief restoration of the Lancastrian king. She knew Henry Tudor was the son, from an early marriage, of Lady Margaret Beaufort, the last Lancastrian princess, who was now the wife of Thomas, Lord Stanley, who in turn had been old King Edward's Lord Steward. She knew all about them, because they were the kind of lords you had to know about in business. She knew Lady Margaret

Beaufort had often been at King Edward's court and sometimes carried Queen Elizabeth Woodville's train, though she was still viewed with suspicion as the last of the rival royal line. She knew Lord Stanley's son had married a Woodville niece. But all she knew about Henry Tudor was that he'd escaped to Britanny after Warwick's attempt at king-making had failed years ago, and stayed there; some people said almost as a prisoner of the Duke of Britanny. He was no one. Why go to him?

Dorset smiled a little sadly at her bafflement. 'There's no one else left,' he said.

She nodded. How helpless they all were. They stood for a long moment under the bilious sky, blown by the wind, jostled by the thinning crowd. His hand was on her arm; for a moment she could imagine the strength he seemed to have gained flowing into her now the worst had happened and he'd survived. 'God speed,' she said. 'Be safe.'

And she cut off his muttered thanks to put him into the care of Anne Pratte, and arrange with her that the traveller would walk down to Ludgate to say his hurried goodbyes to Jane. There was no time for more.

On the next afternoon, Isabel met the lawyer that William Pratte sent. When the man walked into Alice's storeroom, stooping to get through the door – he was taller than most of the people who came into this place of women – she found herself staring. Hadn't this happened before?

'Don't I know you?' she asked, suddenly uncertain.

He smiled and bowed. 'Of course,' he answered. 'I drew up your apprenticeship agreement.' And at the cheerful glitter in his hazel eyes all the memories of her girlhood came flooding back: Elizabeth Marchpane giggling and calling the colour of those eyes topaz; Anne Hagour calling them manticore. Later, Alice Claver snarling at him to hurry up and cross out part of the agreement he'd drawn up; his even-tempered acquiescence. He was one of the Lynom boys. Grown up now, more solidly muscled, with the angelic blond hair that the girls had all sighed over now darker and less fine, but with the same amused look she remembered from before. It was reassuring to think Jane's fate would be in the hands of Robert Lynom.

He didn't waste time on small talk. He expressed regret for Jane's imprisonment. 'You must be very worried. But,' he added straightforwardly, 'I think there's a reasonable chance we can make a deal with the new administration – and get her out of jail altogether. After the coronation. I've spoken to the Mayor about it. He's quite clear that this is what we should work for. And we don't think it will be impossible to get all the charges dropped. We already have an informal agreement that the witchcraft allegation won't be pursued. This case has become an embarrassment to the authorities. Even', he paused delicately; no one knew these days quite how to refer to Dickon, 'to his Majesty.'

'You've talked to the Mayor?' she asked, impressed by his clear, direct way of talking. Listening to him felt like seeing sunlight break through clouds. 'Already?'

He grinned. 'No point in wasting time,' he answered, 'when we know what we want.'

The change of power was inevitable now. Everyone did what they had to do.

On Monday, the Duke of Buckingham denounced old King Edward's morals to the Guildhall, saying that he had ruled England for years by oppression and self-will.

Members of a parliament that would not meet for another year also gathered to write a petition. The petition echoed the Duke of Buckingham's speech. The parliamentarians denounced the dead king as a satyr whose depravity had

292

made every good woman and maiden dread being ravished and defouled. They said Edward IV's marriage to Elizabeth Woodville had been secret and illegal – and sorcerous to boot. They said any children born from that marriage were bastards. Like the Duke, they begged Richard of Gloucester to take the throne.

On Tuesday, the Duke of Buckingham, Lord Howard, the Mayor and aldermen formed a delegation and visited the Duke of Gloucester to ask him to become king.

On Wednesday, Richard of Gloucester was proclaimed King of England. Isabel wasn't at Paul's Cross when the proclamation was read out, but Anne Pratte relayed every detail. The coronation was set for 6 July.

A boy came into the seld stall where Anne was telling her story. He muttered at Isabel, touched his hat and left.

'What was that?' Anne Pratte asked.

'Oh, nothing,' Isabel said; she knew she must look sullen, 'just a firewood delivery at the silk house. I can't go.'

'Well, you'll have to start going to Westminster again soon, you know. I can't imagine Queen Elizabeth Woodville not finding a way through this and getting herself back to court; she's too ambitious not to try, at least; and you don't want to lose the Princess,' Anne Pratte urged.

'Elizabeth Bastard,' Isabel said emptily. She shook her head. Then, seeing the silkwoman's reproving look: 'All right. Tomorrow.'

'You lied to me,' she grated, shuddering backwards against the bolted door. She pushed Dickon away. But she was uncomfortably aware that she'd let him bundle her up the rough stairs and start to kiss her as soon as they were inside the door. She'd never see Dickon again. She'd known that before she came; she was trying to cling to the knowledge now. But she'd wanted to feel the touch of his body against hers, just for a moment, just one more time.

He laughed. Took a few paces back and sat down on the bed. Patted the place beside him; delaying tactics. Then, when she didn't come to him, he raised his arms in a parody of innocence. 'I did not lie,' he said, very definitely. But she could see he was uneasy.

She wouldn't get caught up in Jesuitry. Her eyes bored into his. 'You should have said.'

'Said what?' he hedged. There was a half-smile on his lips. She couldn't tell whether it signified anxiety or indifference, or even triumph, but whichever it was it was enough to make her lose her temper. She had her father's blood in her, all right.

Her hands were on her hips, and suddenly she was hissing, as if cursing him: 'That you were getting up from this bed to arrest my sister and kill her lover and hunt down my lord Dorset and steal Prince Richard from his mother to God knows where. What do you think?'

To her horror, Isabel felt her voice thicken and break. 'She's my sister, Dickon,' she muttered, looking hastily down to hide the hot tears coming to her eyes.

There was a silence.

When she finally dared peep up through hot, wet, angry eyes, she saw, with dread, that he was angry too. He was standing up, like her. Staring back. His jaw was out.

'Pull yourself together,' he said coldly. 'This isn't about your sister, for God's sake.'

He took a breath. She felt him consciously loosen his muscles.

'This is an affair of state,' he began, in a more emollient tone. 'We all have to submit . . .'

But she couldn't listen. She broke in, with furious passion: 'It *is* about my sister! How can you say it's not? You've shut her up in Ludgate jail! I've been there; I've seen her!'

294

'What do you care?' he snapped back. 'You've always hated her. Suddenly you're her protector?'

She fell silent; twisted her fingers. She didn't know what to say.

Then, ignoring his last words, she summoned up her last flickers of righteous anger. 'You're calling her a whore and your brother a womaniser – but you're here, meeting me. Aren't I a whore, too, then? And aren't you a womaniser, too – and a hypocrite into the bargain?'

'Look,' he said quietly, 'Isabel. Let's start again.'

Unwillingly, she looked up. 'I'm not a hypocrite,' he said with rough calm; holding her eyes with his. 'If you're talking about my being in this room with you, it's you who always said that what happened in this room was separate from ordinary life. You can't change the rules now, just because you feel like it.'

It stung her. He was right, about that at least. 'And if you're talking about . . .' he gave her a look that was aggressive and wary in equal measures as he thought of the right word, 'outside, what's been happening outside, then for God's sake stop being a fool. It doesn't suit you.'

He stood up, with the vague threat that was part of his every movement. 'This is just reality, Isabel,' he said. 'You have to do everything you can for your blood. It's what I've always said; what I've always done. You've known me for long enough to know that.'

'But you . . .' She stuttered, so wrong-footed now she couldn't get her words out.

He swept on. 'You've been doing it too; protecting your blood. Hiding traitors for Jane Shore's sake.' She went still. 'Don't think I don't hear talk from the City, too,' he said, an aside, nodding at her shock with a chilly smile. Then he went on: 'So you should understand. I'm just doing what I have to do to secure my dynasty.'

She stammered something, but even she couldn't say

what. He ignored it; kept his eyes boring into hers. He was talking more persuasively now, carrying her along with his argument.

'You must see how important this is. Those children are illegitimate. There's no doubt about that. The Bishop of Bath and Wells says so; and he was the priest before whom Edward promised to marry Eleanor Butler. He's kept his peace for years – maybe because of the allowance Edward paid him, who can say? – but now both Edward and the hush money are gone, and his conscience has finally made him speak out. There's nothing for me to do but to deal with the consequences. God knows I didn't ask for this.'

She took a step into the room. Still mistrustful, but at least willing to hear him out.

'You can't have a child bastard on the throne of England. It would be a blasphemy in the eyes of God and a crime in the eyes of man,' he went on, drawing her closer; visibly growing in confidence as she went on listening. 'It's bad enough having a child King, with every great lord in the land eyeing him and wondering whether his own blood isn't bluer and his own army bigger and if it mightn't be worth trying to seize power. But once the child's known to be a bastard, it would be anarchy. You'd have civil war again before you could blink. You'd have Lancastrians creeping back from overseas; enemies crawling in from everywhere. And hasn't enough English blood been shed already, in enough wars no one wanted? For the sake of my country . . . for the sake of my family honour . . . I had no choice.'

Isabel wanted to be convinced. But this wasn't enough.

Flatly, she said: 'But you called your brother a bastard too. You shamed *his* memory. There was no need for that.'

Flatly, he replied: 'There was. It's true.'

She looked as sceptical as she dared.

But he went on, in the same flat, everyday voice: 'We've

296

always known it in the family. My father was away fighting in France for a year before Edward was born.'

She was still taunting him with her hard eyes; but he didn't seem to care.

'Work it out,' he added harshly. 'It only takes nine months.'

In the uneasy silence that followed, Isabel thought: He seems so sure.

She didn't even ask him why he'd never accused Edward of being a bastard while he was still alive. Why would he, back then, when Edward was King, and the best, safest King in living memory into the bargain; and when Edward was happy to make over to his brother the entire North of England for himself? If he was telling the truth now, the lie would have been in the past; but she could see why he'd have been tempted to keep quiet until now. 'Once I'd started truth-telling, there was no reason not to tell all the truths,' Dickon went on, as if agreeing with her unspoken judgement. 'It makes things clearer.'

Then he sighed, and bleakness shivered over his face like the North wind.

'But I knew Hastings would never accept the truth about Edward,' he added. 'He'd spent his life serving him. I knew he'd fight me to get Edward's boy the crown.' He looked sadder still. 'So I did what I had to . . . He was my friend, but I had no choice . . .'

The distance between them had diminished; had she gone on creeping towards him? He took a last step forward to stand before her, head bowed, eyes on hers. She could feel his breath on her cheek. She meant to ask about Rivers, or Grey; people were saying he'd had the princesses' Woodville uncles executed this week too. But somehow she didn't.

'I want you to understand,' he said, very softly. 'I don't harm the innocent. You know me. You know that. The boys are safe; my nephews. So is your sister, if it comes to that.' She caught her breath. 'I'd never hurt a woman. She'll come to no harm, I promise.'

'But you accused her of witchcraft,' she muttered faintly, trying to fight the longing to fall into his arms. 'Jane. She could burn for that. And you can't possibly think it's true.'

He shook his head. 'It's just what the crowd needed to hear, to know it's serious. She won't be tried as a witch,' he whispered. 'Trust me.' But his eyes shifted away. As if aware that he'd shown weakness by admitting to a lie, he added irritably: 'Look, it's the same thing you did when you stole your father's apprentices – you were showing you meant business. Don't be so prissy. You know exactly why I did it.'

Isabel didn't want to be distracted into defending herself over that. It was true, she'd felt triumphant at gaining the ascendancy, as well as guilty, after hiring away John Lambert's staff and seeing her father leave London, bewildered and beaten. Perhaps Dickon had been striving for the same effect when he'd had Jane denounced as a sorceress. Perhaps he felt guilty too.

All she said, looking imploringly at him, was: 'But why Jane? Why mix her up in all this at all? You said it yourself. She's got nothing to do with it. It's not about her.'

He shrugged. She thought he might be surprised she kept coming back to Jane.

His voice got lighter. It made her cheeks burn again to see he couldn't take Jane Shore's plight seriously; she didn't want to think about why. He said: 'Because people need a clear idea of who's ruling them. They know Edward was a lady's man; now they can see that wasn't such a good thing. Jane Shore behind bars has been an illustration everyone can understand. It shows them: from now on, we live by the rules.'

His voice was still quiet; but determined. 'My rules,' he said. She blinked.

'People like to complicate things, but I'm a very simple man,' he said, and he looked at her as straightforwardly as he ever had. 'These are just the things you have to do to make sure the things you need to happen do happen. Not always nice, but necessary. You can't be a king and a parfit gentil knight at the same time.'

His face was inches away; looming over hers. His hand brushed her shoulder. She couldn't live in a world where his hand would never touch her shoulder again. Her body seemed to be drawing towards his. There was nothing her mind could do about it.

She felt her body strain towards him. Held it in check. He murmured: 'No one wants more war. I had to stop the factions . . . the plots. I want to be King of a land at peace.'

There was a terrible sincerity on his face. He was looking intently into her eyes. She could see how important it was to him that she should believe him; and a part of her was, unwillingly, grateful that he so wanted her approval. But by then she was so full of contradictory desires – with the urges to shout and slap giving way again to the longing to fall into his arms and do without words altogether – that the only phrase he'd spoken that she remembered was, 'I want to be King.'

'Trust me,' he breathed.

She didn't. However familiar his face, and her feelings, she knew she was looking into the eyes of someone who'd become a stranger. Yet that didn't stop her wanting him.

They stood very close, arms by their sides, not touching.

When she went on not moving, he muttered, and she thought she detected a note of pleading: 'You know I'm the only safety this land can hope for; and I've been doing the best I can to keep the peace. You must know that;

from your own perspective if nothing else. Think about it. Your Goffredo's coming back; you know your weaving venture will be safe if I'm on the throne. Every other entrepreneur in London will be making the same calculation.' He gave her a bright stare; a challenge. 'Without me, who knows?'

If Goffredo ever does come, Isabel thought hopelessly. There had been no word from the Venetian since all this started. What Dickon was saying now was true enough. But it still sounded like a bargain with the devil – a bribe. Accept me, or go under.

Still, she could make bargains too, she thought, glimpsing a way to regain her peace of mind. Stepping back, but gently, she said: 'All right, but let Jane go.' Every fibre of her being wanted to stay; she was astonished at the iron willpower pulling her away. 'She's served the purpose you wanted, hasn't she?'

There was surprise on his face; but reluctant admiration too. His head began nodding – a tiny movement. That half-smile came back to his lips. She stopped in the doorway. 'I'll come back here next week, at the same time,' she added, more calmly than she felt. 'But only if Jane's free.'

Isabel didn't want to visit Will Caxton at the Red Pale today; she didn't dare look in his eyes after telling him that she was Dickon's lover. He'd be frantic with worry that Dickon had imprisoned Jane. He might even, unbearably, want her to admit her judgement had been as addled by love as she privately knew it to be. So she kept away.

Still, she felt more self-possessed as she walked to the Abbot's house. Making her demand that Jane be set free had given her at least a frail hope to cling to. If there'd been any truth in Dickon's litany of self-justification and excuses, he'd surely see sense and get Jane released from prison. That would be something.

Her hope wasn't enough to help her face the five pairs of eyes in the princesses' parlour.

She could see at once they'd learned new facts that frightened them. Perhaps they'd found out that their Woodville uncles, Earl Rivers and Sir Thomas Grey, were dead. Perhaps they'd heard that Lord Hastings' servants had tried to visit princes Edward and Richard at the Tower, but had been turned away.

It didn't take long for her to understand how they'd started to find out more, either. It was Elizabeth who was putting the questions this time, not the little girls with their lisping voices and terrified pink-rimmed rabbit eyes. Elizabeth had stopped being reluctant to be seen to beg for information. In her dangerous position, she must have realised she needed to know everything she could – just to survive. She must have started asking every servant and passing priest what was happening. Princess Elizabeth had got thinner in the past week. She was very pale, too, but it suited her; her cheekbones were becoming as elegant as her mother's. And she was wheedling rumours out of Isabel this morning with all the expert cunning of a market woman.

'They *have* killed my mother's brothers,' she said quietly, drawing Isabel in and sitting her down on the bench; making a flattering point of paying attention to the silk-woman's comfort. There was no sign of the coronation dress. It must have been shut away in a chest somewhere. 'My mother's confessor told us.'

Isabel nodded. She crossed herself. 'God rest their souls,' she said carefully; not knowing, in the confusion of these times, what would constitute treason; worried even that banality might. 'I'd heard too. I'm sorry for your grief.'

301

The Princess paused; then, very softly, while Isabel was still full of pity, she asked: 'Perhaps you know – is there any news in London of *our* brothers?'

Isabel glanced up to the window ledge, where little Richard's game of knucklebones was still waiting for his return, gathering dust. Isabel didn't want to deceive Princess Elizabeth. She and her sisters must be afraid men would come for them too. It was natural for the princesses to try to find out all they could, and plan their defences accordingly. So, haltingly, Isabel told them that the Princes hadn't been seen playing outside the royal apartments at the Tower in the past few days, and that Lord Hastings' men had been turned away when they'd tried to pay a visit. There was tavern talk about rescuing them. She told Elizabeth that too. She kept quiet about the other piece of tavern gossip doing the rounds: that the boys had been murdered.

'I'm sorry not to have better news,' she finished, to the girls' quietly bowed heads. 'They've probably just been moved to a different apartment.'

They must know that was a false hope. But the younger girls nodded earnestly as if they really wanted to believe it; and even Elizabeth looked grateful to Isabel for trying.

It wrung Isabel's heart. There had to be something she could say that would represent genuinely good news for them. Then she realised what. 'I've heard', she found herself saying, 'that your uncle Dorset is safe.'

She thought, as she spoke: Why am I doing this? I'd do better to keep quiet. Then, defiantly: If Dickon's heard that Dorset's got away abroad from listening to City talk, why shouldn't I know? 'Overseas,' she added. 'No one knows how.' Five pairs of eyes, blazing with hope, begged for more. 'I don't know if it's true, of course,' she continued, 'it's just what they're saying in the markets. But they're saying he's gone to Britanny. To Henry Tudor.'

They sat very quietly, hardly daring to breathe, taking that in. But Isabel was briefly aware of a gleam of satisfaction in Princess Elizabeth's eyes – the same satisfaction she'd have felt herself, digging out a nugget of street knowledge that could be of value soon.

She sat on the boat, painfully remembering the quiet room she'd walked out of, repeating to herself: If Dickon lets Jane out, it will prove he's telling the truth. And if he tells the truth about that, why would I doubt everything else? If Dickon lets Jane out, I'll be able to go back next week.

Hope was so cruel. It brought wisps of more innocent moments with Dickon back into her mind. Stories she knew half of, through him; whose endings she still longed to hear.

Only a few weeks ago they'd been on a boat like this, together, wondering whether Dickon would have to go to France to fight Edward's war. That story had been broken off forever, she thought, and relief mixed itself up in her agonising nostalgia. There'd be no French war for a while now. Thank God. She let her mind meander on. There'd been the story of the dying nephew, too. What had happened to him? In that other life just a few weeks ago, Dickon had been hiring doctors to go north to treat little George Neville. He'd been so worried about the boy's health. If George Neville died, Dickon's land-holdings would be compromised. His son wouldn't inherit. He'd have to beg the King for help.

What had happened after that? Had the boy died? Perhaps he had. How worried Dickon would have been when King Edward died too, right at the same time, Isabel thought, with sudden compassion – if the King's death had come just when Dickon most needed his brother's help to keep his lands together. He must have felt as panicked as she had about her silk-weaving house. He'd been far away in the North; he'd been only the uncle of the new King-to-be, whom he hardly knew; and the boy had seemed so safely in the hands of his other uncles, the Woodvilles, whom he loved; and they hated Dickon . . . Dickon couldn't have had faith that the boy-king Edward would have helped him.

She reined herself in. Why was she fretting about this? The likeliest outcome was that the Neville child had recovered weeks ago, she thought briskly. Dickon probably hadn't given that illness another moment's thought. If the boy had got better, Dickon certainly wouldn't have gone on panicking over how to hold together his estates when King Edward died. She was just indulging in a fantasy that would suggest she and Dickon had been in the same vulnerable position, between kings. She should stop daydreaming.

Sternly, she told herself: It's just another story that's stopped mattering. Dickon is King now; what does he care about the Duke of Gloucester's estates in the North? Leaving some Godforsaken moors to his son? His son will inherit something better: a crown.

She sat up straighter in the boat. She was trying not to start thinking about Dickon in a boat like this, last time – unlacing her under the cloak and laughing.

She stopped herself. She couldn't, yet. Everything was still too uncertain. He'd have to release Jane before she could even begin to hope.

Isabel couldn't think what the racket was as she walked into the Claver house at Catte Street. The voices sounded too deep for the silkwomen, the footsteps too sturdy.

It was only when she got into the great hall that she saw. A dozen strangers were crammed in, staring round in frank curiosity at Alice and Anne and the hangings, and helping themselves hungrily from the platters the kitchen boy was hurriedly handing round. Men and women both, all with black curls and lustrous eyes; all indescribably filthy. She couldn't catch a word they were saying.

There were trunks and bags everywhere.

It was only when she saw the bowl of pomegranates that she began to guess. She looked round. He had more grey hair than before but his dark-brown eyes, liquid and long-lashed as ever, were on her with just the same playful devotion she remembered. He was unfurling his cloak with a flourish. 'What a fool I am to have arrrrived on a Friday; no meat!' he was saying, in his flamboyant way – the cheerful, carefree way that had been hers, all of theirs, before Friday 13th. It seemed another life. His warmth was infectious. She flung herself into his arms in front of all of them, grinned over his shoulder at Alice with a cheekiness she'd almost forgotten, and cried: 'Goffredo!'

If Goffredo's return was a good omen, there was better to come. They let Jane out on the Sunday night, but first they made her publicly repent of her sins. She had to walk barefoot through the City, carrying a lighted taper. And she was allowed to wear nothing more than a kirtle.

If the crowds that gathered to watch her pass, praying in her circle of light, were supposed to jeer and snicker and jostle and try to pull up her skirt and peer down her shift and hurl rotten fruit and dog turds and cobblestones at the whore in nothing but her linen, to enjoy the sight of her delicate white coverings and skin turning mottled and discoloured, to have fun watching her flinch and cry out in pain, they were a disappointment.

Instead, the audience fell silent and stared at her beauty. She was one of them; a Londoner. Some even prayed with her.

Perhaps they'd had their fill of blood at the executions the day before, when four ordinary London citizens – strangers who'd got talking in a tavern, like everyone else was doing, about where the two princes, last seen in the Tower, could have disappeared to, and then, somehow, found themselves plotting a rescue – had been beheaded on Tower Hill. All that William Davy, Robert Russe, John Smith and Stephen Ireland actually seemed to have done was set fires in different parts of London. People said that must have been just the first step in the plan; while the garrison was away putting out the fires, they said, the men would have crept in and snatched the princes. No one quite knew. But no one really believed in such a cack-handed plan. No one escaped from the Tower, especially not in a rescue organised by four drunken tavern bruisers.

Then again, according to another rumour in the taverns, Bishop Morton, who'd been arrested when Hastings had been killed, had just escaped from the Tower a second time, fat and short and red-faced though he was. So perhaps it was possible. Or perhaps any small act of dis-loyalty became possible – even turning a blind eye to a plump prisoner waddling out of the world's stoutest fortress – when you didn't believe in your King.

Jane's jailors at Ludgate were certainly happy enough when Isabel and Alice Claver and Anne Pratte, flanked by a quietly triumphant crowd of silkwomen, picked up their prisoner. It was just after nightfall. Jane was waiting for them, in a quiet dove-grey gown over the kirtle she'd walked through London in. It was still as snowy white as they'd delivered it the previous day. She was praying when they came for her; she'd prayed more in her days at Ludgate than Isabel remembered her ever having done before. She was calm as she got up to go. She gave the three men in the gate lodge gifts of all the sweetmeats she'd been brought, divided evenly; she shook each one's hand and thanked them for their patience with her visitors, in a huskier, more tired voice than usual, but with loving looks.

Isabel gave the head gateman a little bag of coins as they left. 'A thank-you to all of you for all your kindness,' she murmured; and she was touched to see his rheumy eyes fill.

He said gruffly: 'Glad to see her out of here. It wasn't right. But it'll be lonely without her. We were just getting used to the crowds.' He was still harrumphing sentimentally and blowing his nose as the procession of women set off.

Isabel thought John Lambert should have come to London for his daughter's release. She'd noticed, with scorn, that although her father had written to Jane at Ludgate prison, he'd cautiously sent the letters to Catte Street rather than to the jail; he wasn't the type to want to be too closely associated, in public, with an enemy of the King. She'd even suggested Jane ask him to come and show support. But Jane had just laughed forgivingly whenever Isabel complained about their father's cowardice: 'But he's right, Isabel; he has to be careful.'

Jane wasn't laughing now. She was looking ahead, not meeting any eyes. 'I so want to get home,' she said. 'Away from people staring.'

'We're staying tonight at Catte Street,' Isabel reminded her gently. Perhaps Jane hadn't understood before that her own house had been shut up, ransacked and confiscated?

Jane paused, as if thinking; then nodded. 'Catte Street,' she acquiesced, with blank eyes.

They put her to bed in Isabel's room. She was pliant, yielding, and remote. She said nothing except a faint 'good night' to Alice and Anne. But when Isabel, the last to leave, was about to draw the bedcurtains and slip away

307

with her candle, Jane pleaded, 'Stay with me a while', and Isabel, happy to see a flicker of life in her sister's eyes at last, not wanting to leave her alone in a strange place with her disturbing memories, put down her candle and sat down on the blankets, taking Jane's hands.

'They haven't finished with me, have they?' Jane said faintly. 'They told me . . . *there* . . . That there was word I'd have to be interrogated again. By the King's Solicitor.'

She was clinging to Isabel's hands, and there was anguish in her eyes.

Isabel didn't like the way her sister's eyes made her feel.

She'd been saving her news to tell Jane once she'd slept, but perhaps now would be the right time to reassure her. This was the best thing Robert Lynom had done yet. 'Yes, but,' she said cheerfully, 'can you guess who the new King's Solicitor is?'

Jane shook her head. 'I don't know anyone now,' she whispered; and Isabel felt guiltier still for having tried to play guessing games with her.

'Thomas Lynom,' she replied gently. 'Robert's twin. A friend.' And she watched the slow answering smile spread across Jane's face; and sat with her until she fell asleep.

She would see Dickon again.

Jane was changed – wounded, quiet, prayerful – but at least she was free. Dickon had kept his word. She could see him. The thought filled her with joy; it was all she could do to keep it from her sister, who spent her days dozing in the bed they were sharing again, like children.

Isabel even managed to meet Will Caxton's eyes when the wiry printer came to call. He'd brought a little posy for Jane. He'd scrubbed most of the blue stains off his hands. His bony, freckled face was a study in anxious solicitousness. 'She's got so thin,' he kept saying, after she'd come downstairs for a few minutes to thank him.

'So pale.' Alice and Anne fed him and wouldn't leave his side, so there was no real danger of unwanted confidences. But Isabel was grateful for his delicacy anyway; in the one moment she had been left alone with him, and he'd raised frank eyes to hers, he'd just patted her hand and said, 'You must have been so worried,' and then, with great kindness, 'you couldn't possibly have thought this would happen. You mustn't blame yourself.'

There were five days till Friday.

On Monday the contracts were given out for the vestments for King Richard III's forthcoming coronation. After an hour of frantic pushing and shoving at Old Jewry, waiting for news of who would be assigned which task, peace descended on the markets. The mercers who'd got contracts retired to their workshops with satisfied looks on their faces to sew and cut and embroider round the clock. The others vanished indoors to hide their disappointment. The House of Claver, represented in the crush by Isabel, did well. There was one commission to supply cloth for the Queen's train. And Anne Pratte was asked, personally, to make three mantle laces of purple silk with tassels and buttons of the same stuff, mixed with Venetian gold thread, and another set of white rather than purple – one for the King and one for the Queen.

Walking home, letting herself take pleasure in the moment, feeling proud of her business's well-deserved reputation, Isabel happened upon one of the London Italians walking out of St Thomas of Acre. It was Dr Gigli, portly and quivering in black velvet.

'Ah, it is Mistress Claver,' he said suavely. 'I see from your face you have done well with the contracts.'

She smiled and bowed, remembering that Dr Gigli was the physician who'd gone north with Dickon to treat his sickly nephew.

'Yes, we've been honoured twice over,' she replied, with

carefully measured professional boastfulness. 'What a compliment to our silkwomen.'

He nodded and beamed back, asking with great charm for details.

Once the Claver commissions had been discussed to their mutual satisfaction, she turned to go. Then, as if suddenly remembering something, she added casually: 'You've been travelling, I understand? You must be just back from Middleham?'

Dr Gigli bowed. He was too much of a politician to look surprised at her knowledge. But he looked regretful as he raised his head. 'A while ago now,' he said. 'Two weeks.'

'I hope your patient is restored to good health?' she asked solicitously. 'Young George Neville . . .'

Dr Gigli lowered his head again. 'Regrettably . . .' he murmured. He crossed himself.

So the boy had died. Isabel listened carefully. Dr Gigli had thought his patient had nothing worse than an ague. He'd cupped him and prescribed a special diet, and young George Neville's condition had seemed to improve. Until the evening when George Neville's fever came back with a vengeance. He'd passed away by dawn.

'My lord Gloucester must have been distressed,' Isabel said sympathetically.

'Ah . . . but he did not hear at once . . . he was already on his way to London by the time it happened,' Dr Gigli replied, like her, not quite calling Dickon 'His Majesty'. There were no agreed names yet for the turmoil of the past few weeks. 'I had to break the news to him here, myself, at Crosby's Place, once I'd reached London. And that was only last Thursday . . . the day before . . .' He hesitated; felt for the right phrase to describe the day of the change of power. Then he gave up, said helplessly, 'all *that*', and waved his fat ringed hands instead. 'He was distressed, of course. The boy was his blood, after all. But he had pressing affairs of state to consider too. When I heard, the next day . . .' he gestured again, 'about . . . all *that* . . . I understood why he'd been in such haste.'

There was the beginning of a frown on Dr Gigli's well-padded brow. Something must have worried him about the way Dickon had received the news he'd have broken so diplomatically. But he composed himself. Smoothed down his black velvet over his paunch and smiled a full, superb smile in Isabel's direction. 'It was a long journey,' he added, then yawned magnificently, 'and I am still a little travel-weary. Forgive me.'

With all the smiles and ceremoniousness she could muster, Isabel bowed him on his way.

But the doubt he hadn't wanted to discuss dragged at her fragile new happiness. Like Dr Gigli, she didn't want to think about what the story might mean. She hurried home, not giving herself time to wonder.

On Tuesday morning a merry Goffredo took his Italian teams to Westminster, on foot. Their trunks and bags were going by river, but so many foreigners would attract attention on the wherries. It was safer to walk. Isabel was to join them at the silk house on Friday night. 'We will cook you a magnificent dinner, *cara*,' Goffredo promised.

For the rest of Tuesday and through Wednesday and Thursday, Isabel worked with Anne Pratte on the royal mantle laces for the coronation. 'It will do you good to do something normal,' Anne Pratte said, firmly, giving her the white set for the Queen. Isabel would rather have made the purple set Dickon was to wear. But she submitted. It was something to do, to keep her from her thoughts. And Friday was almost here.

There was a palfrey tethered outside the Red Pale. She only really believed he'd be in the room once she'd seen it. She tiptoed upstairs, suddenly as quiet and shy as an innocent. He was sitting on the bed, reading his Book of Hours. He hadn't seen her. She looked at him for a moment without moving. She didn't deserve this much happiness.

A floorboard creaked. He looked up. She could see in the lightening of his eyes that he'd doubted she'd come. Hesitantly, she said: 'I'm here.'

He opened his arms. She ran to him.

She lost herself for what seemed like hours in the beauty of their lovemaking. She didn't want to stop. There was too much sadness in her heart. She didn't want to let it out.

'What are you thinking?' he murmured into her ear, when it was over, putting an arm over her chest. He was smiling, lazily. He didn't have to go yet. There was time for more.

She kissed him very tenderly on the mouth. She knew she had to ask. But a dreamy melancholy was settling on her even before she did. She knew the answer he'd give, too.

'When did you find out George Neville was dead?' she whispered.

She could imagine it so well. Dr Gigli mournfully bowing and scraping as he made his announcement. Dickon's mind, razor-sharp, racing ahead to how his own Northern lands were compromised by the child's death. So full of the troubles facing him that he could hardly bring himself to acknowledge the fat Italian. Then realising he had another young nephew in his hands, right here and now. Realising there might be a quicker, more effective way of shoring up his position than struggling through layers of Woodvilles to beg for his royal nephew's help. Thinking: Wouldn't it be easier just to grab the big prize and stop bothering about the details?

Dickon's eyes flickered. He knew she knew. Without moving, he said: 'The day before . . .' Even he didn't know what to call the day he'd seized power. He hesitated. She nodded. It was just as she'd thought.

He added hastily, 'but that's not why.'

But his eyes told a different story. They both knew it.

They went on staring at each other. Aeons passed. I should go, she thought. Everything he's told me has been a lie. Everything I suspected was true. He murdered Hastings deliberately, so he could steal power. Disgraced Jane. Maybe murdered his nephews too.

But she knew she wouldn't go. And he knew too.

So there was no point in recriminations. The sadness in her eyes, and his, wasn't farewell. It was an acknowledgement, on his part, of crimes he'd committed for power; and, on her part, that she didn't care what he'd done as long as he was there. They were grieving, together, for the one victim of his coup on her heart: their lost innocence.

When she did, finally, get up and begin dressing, he watched from the bed.

'Will you come back?' he said, and his voice was humble.

Gently, she nodded. She'd looked into the depths of his soul. She hadn't found it in her to recoil. How could she say no now?

Instead, hating the terrible joy she could feel crackling through her, she just muttered 'Friday', and slipped out into the burning summer afternoon.

13

'Health and wealth and happiness to us all!' Alice Claver declaimed, making up in volume for what her voice lacked in clarity, and every cup in the room was raised to her in wobbly candlelight. There was a whisper of translation; then smiles.

It had taken till the end of summer, but the workshop was up and running. The dormitories were full. The cookpots in the kitchen were bubbling with warm foreign-scented herbs now the harvest was in and Michaelmas approaching. No one in London had found the Clavers out as they spirited the Italians away downriver. And none of the neighbours in Westminster thought anything much of the new machines whirring next to Will Caxton's, or the new foreigners groping their uncertain way round the streets. Thank God for Will Caxton, Alice thought, not for the first time.

The machines astonished her. Goffredo had risen magnificently to the occasion. As well as the looms, he'd also brought the two devices they'd talked about last year, the machines she'd heard were gaining popularity in Venice

314

and saved untold amounts of labour. Both were giant wooden frames suspended from the ceiling. One contraption, if you wound it, could draw up dozens of strands of silk at once straight from the boiled silkworm cocoons and throw them, and another could reel dozens of thrown or twisted threads together ready for use. She'd never seen anything like either of them.

But Alice loved the looms best. Loved watching as Gasparino's brother strung the first one up with its spider's web of subtle grey and tan warps and tan and grey wefts; or as Gasparino's thin dark hands flew between the complicated arrangements of strings and threads and bobbins, lifting, pushing, combing, until the cloth began to glow and flow with fantasy foliage. Gasparino and Alvise and Marino and their families couldn't yet speak enough English to explain themselves except through signs, so Goffredo helped. 'For this pattern', he told Alice, who was always hungry for explanations, 'you need three paired main warps and one binding warp; the main warps are a mixture of tan and grey silk, and we've used tan silk alone for the binding warp. The main wefts are the same mixture of grey and tan silk; and the pattern weft is pure tan silk.'

Alice nodded, fiercely trying to absorb the weave detail she didn't need to learn for herself, just because she so loved the way the cloth came out. All she really needed to know was that Gasparino's family was teaching one group of apprentices to make damasks; that Marino was in charge of lampas, and that Alvise was showing the third group the secrets of velvet. Isabel had chosen the Londoners for their deft fingers and, almost as importantly, their lack of family: Joan Woulbarowe ('Silkbarowe now!' the fool kept lisping excitedly through her black teeth); Katherine Arnold, who without parents in the business or capital to set herself up had been a servant in the silk business all her life; the throwster widows Agnes

Brundyssch and Isabel Fremely, who wanted a change and a better-paid skill; and, of course, John Lambert's one-time best employees, Jane Cotford, from Derby, Mary Fleet, from Southwark, and Ellen, the widow of William Lovell, a vintner fallen on hard times. Alice sighed; she knew that the most practical way to behave would be just to let Jane Cotford and Ellen Lovell fret about the technicalities of how to pattern the velvet – whether to void it right down to its satin ground, have the pile cut or uncut, or work with cut pile of two or three different heights to add interest and complexity to the pattern; or how many warp face satin threads you needed for the ground before the interruption; or the ratio of pile warp ends to main warp ends. All Alice needed to do was marvel like a child at her dream coming true – to stare at the flying hands and muse, So this is how it happens. But it was the stubborn child in her that wanted to grab the shuttle and clack the frames and start learning to weave beauty for herself.

This dinner had been Isabel's idea. They couldn't get an Italian priest to bless the house, she'd argued, since he'd only go back and blab to the Lombard merchants; but they could all dine together as an extended family. Eat the Venetians' basilic-scented salads. Make the new families and the new apprentices feel part of a home. And have them show their talents to Alice and Anne and William, who only came occasionally to Westminster, and left Isabel and Goffredo to manage the house, and to Will Caxton, who supported them in spirit by dropping in at all hours from his house next door. Isabel had said: 'It needn't be expensive. A couple of chickens and a piece of beef and some salads and a couple of fruit pies. It would be a symbol. A new start.' Quite right. Isabel was a good girl. She hadn't started off that way, maybe; but this was what a good training did for a girl.

But where was Isabel? Alice looked at the darkness falling – not still in sanctuary with the Princesses, surely? She tutted. It was all very well working her fingers to the bone, as the girl was doing now the weavers were here at last: rising before dawn, staying more than half the week in Westminster, and pulling off some big contracts in London, too, on the few days she spent there. But she should still have been here when she had guests waiting. When she hadn't seen Alice and Anne all week. She should have hurried. It was a question of respect. There were still a few rough edges to knock off the girl.

Isabel came into the room, patting at her hair. They'd started without her.

One of the Italians was plucking slowly at a lute and the rest were dancing the basse dance. Alice Claver, rather drunk, was whispering to William Pratte at the table. Anne Pratte was coming back from the loom room, looking impressed. Joan Woulbarowe was partnering Gasparino's brother Andrea, dancing quite nicely. The other thin, wispy, spinster silkwomen had paired up with Lombard men too. It was lucky for them that there were only three wives among the incomers.

With relief, Isabel realised no one seemed to be angry at her late arrival.

But her heart went on beating too fast.

She shouldn't have met Dickon today, with this party to come to afterwards. It took her hours, after each meeting now, to stop feeling shamed and dirty; to stop shying away from people, unable to stop herself believing they'd smell the rank sweat of the sheets – proof of her guilt. The lingering guilt she lived with all day long had stopped her inviting Jane here at all; Jane, whose new fragility looked to Isabel like innocence; whose gentle, grateful eyes she found so hard to meet. With the scent of damnation still on her now, she wasn't yet ready to chat to Alice as if nothing was the matter.

Alice didn't see her, lingering in the shadows. But Will Caxton's eyes lit up at the sight of her; so did Goffredo's. She smiled but turned down both their offers to dance. She'd got shy of even the casual intimacy of the dance floor; even with these old friends. She told herself she was saying no because Will, whom she'd been avoiding, might ask her frankly whether she'd gone on meeting Dickon, and because Goffredo might try and pull her into a flirtation that was only half a joke. But she knew the truth. By choosing to make Dickon's love, and her acceptance of what he was, the centre of her reality, she couldn't but distance herself from the other people she loved. They had to be distant shadows to her if he was to be real; there was no other way. She had to be with Dickon. She couldn't let anyone else guess how the shame inside her was staining her soul. Still, she was relieved to sit quietly down with Will and Goffredo at the side of the table, and let them talk while she composed herself.

Isabel couldn't hear what William Pratte and Alice were muttering at the top of the table. But she could guess from their defiant, childishly naughty expressions. Now it was actually happening, they were rattled beyond belief by their own cheek in setting up this business. The silkwomen had petitioned parliament so often, throughout Alice's working life, to stop the Italian merchants who traded in London from importing the worked silk goods that London silkwomen already made so beautifully, so there could be no damaging foreign competition. The last petition, which had become law only last year, had brought in fines not just for any Italian merchants who imported wrought goods but even for any Londoner foolhardy enough to buy from them. Isabel should know: she'd written in the new clause herself after seeing Queen Elizabeth Woodville carrying an Italian-made purse. The trade truce with the Italians that had evolved over time was this: Italians made the whole cloths and exported them either to trade fairs at Bruges and Antwerp or directly to London; while Londoners cut and sewed the cloths and worked the silk threads imported alongside. But the Claver venture was now breaking every rule on which that compromise was based.

Isabel could imagine how frightening it must be to take this dangerous step, after a lifetime of keeping in with the sophisticated alien merchants who used their London shops to supply Alice and William and every other big mercer in town with the letters of credit they needed to buy whole silk cloths abroad, and to sell a few of the finest silk cloths directly, over the shop counter, to lesser merchants who couldn't afford their own trade in the Low Countries. The Lombards were the heart of the silk trade. And the Lombards would destroy them if they found out about this before the apprentices were trained. After that, it would be too late. The Londoners would have the knowledge.

Even for Isabel, who had spent so much less time being respectful to Italians, it was unnerving. She thought of the rich Lombards at the Lucchese chapel at St Thomas of Acre: all those tall men with hook noses and velvet cloaks and dark dagger stares, the ones the street boys hissed at if they dared for keeping the best of the English trade for themselves and seducing the wives of English mercers into the bargain. Mancini. Bonvisi. The Borromei bankers of Milan. The Conterini of Venice. And Jacopo Salviati of Florence, doing so well now that the rival Medici bankers had closed their shop and their former representative, Gherardo Canigiani, had married a London mercer's widow and started calling himself Gerard. Isabel wasn't quite like the youths who'd mutter, 'whoreson foreigners!' after them – though only once the Italians were safely out of earshot and wouldn't turn back for a fight. Yet she had as much nervous respect as they did for the power that those expensive cloaks and formal manners and slightly sinister eyes represented.

Still, she thought, turning her mind away from the danger, trying to stop her mind racing, trying to feel calm. In for a penny, in for a pound. It would all be worth it if it worked. It wasn't just that they'd be powerful and rich beyond their wildest dreams, though more money and power were always welcome. The truly important thing was that the English would be at the heart of the trade if they could make their own cloths, and the Claver house – a house of women – at the heart of the English trade; and she, Isabel, at the heart of the Claver house.

If she was at the heart of everything, she told herself, she could protect the silkwomen.

She could form them into a legal guild; she could force the Mercers to recognise them; or she could separate them from the Mercers altogether. The Mercers had spent years firmly co-opting all small groups of men doing almost-mercer trades such as vestment-making, and forcing them to pay their dues to the Mercers' guild. The Mercers' guild was one of the biggest and most powerful in London, along with the princes of fish and wine at the Fishmongers' and Vintners' guilds. But the liverymen in blue velvet had been indulgent with the silkwomen they were allied with. They'd let them organise themselves almost as a guild of their own for as long as anyone could remember, taking apprentices for money, drawing up their own contracts, sometimes even trading independently of their men. They'd had to; so many of the silkwomen were their own wives, after all, and might chase them round the kitchen with the soup ladle if crossed.

So the silkwomen didn't have to pay for their privileges. They were left alone. And they were almost a force to be reckoned with. But, because they were unrecognised by law as an industry in their own right, they still had to go cap in hand to their mercer contacts – the indulgent William Pratte if they were lucky, or the less indulgent John Lambert if they weren't – to negotiate with the outside world. They couldn't hire lawyers as a group, or press an argument with the king or parliament, except through the indulgence of mercers who supported them. They couldn't earn the freedom of the City as silkwomen unless they had a father or husband who'd endorse their request to be Freewomen. They couldn't even hold an annual dinner like the men did. They lived in the shadows. Isabel had fretted over the injustice of it ever since she first clashed with her father. Her business skills were as sharply honed as his; there was a whole younger generation of men like the Lynoms ready to back the silkwomen, and once she'd pulled off a big commercial coup like this silk-weaving project, surely no mercers would dare refuse formal recognition to silkwomen?

And, once she'd done so much good, surely she could allow herself to stop feeling so guilty?

She caught herself; dreaming again. The important thing now was to stay calm; avoid getting rattled; take one step at a time. She was managing it all so far. Having Alice and the Prattes see the Italian workers today, for instance. Tomorrow, visiting the Princess and sewing in her new laces for the violet silk gown. After that, snatching another hour with Dickon on the way back. Then innocently chatting with Will Caxton at his gate about her time with the Princess. It was all possible, if you kept your head. It could all work.

Goffredo was dancing with Joan Woulbarowe. The party was getting noisy. Caxton played servant, pouring wine into Isabel's cup. Then he leaned forward, under cover of the yelps and singing on the floor. 'I never know how to ask,' he said nervously, 'about . . .' he hesitated, 'what you once told me.'

She looked away. But he'd been bound to ask about Dickon sooner or later.

'Forgive me,' he said, cringing. But she couldn't leave it like that; leave him wondering, and watching, when she was meeting Dickon right under his nose. So she plucked up her courage and looked him straight in the eye.

'The important thing is to learn from our mistakes, isn't it?' she said, not quite lying, but deliberately creating the impression that what they were talking about was firmly in the past. 'I'm not proud of what I did.'

She saw the relief brighten his eyes. 'Yes,' he said, thinking he understood, 'of course. After what he did to Jane, you couldn't carry on as you were.' He patted her hand. 'I respect you for that,' he said warmly. 'I won't mention it again.'

She wasn't proud of herself then, either. Will Caxton was a decent, straightforward man. But he had to be deceived. She thought, without remorse: one step at a time.

14

The Princess's peaky white face, which could be as still as marble, was full of life today. Isabel hadn't seen her so excited in the whole five months since Queen Elizabeth Woodville's daughters had shut themselves up in their voluntary prison.

Elizabeth's eyebrows were lifted high and alert. She clearly couldn't wait for Lady Elizabeth Darcey to leave them alone. Isabel found it mildly alarming.

One of the choices Isabel had had to make while making her peace with Dickon was to refine her attitude to the disinherited children of King Edward. She couldn't allow herself any more of the pity that she'd felt so strongly at the start. Once she'd understood that Dickon must have stolen the royal status that was rightfully theirs, she'd necessarily become complicit. She'd had to harden her heart to the princesses.

So now, although she knew it was selfish to hope that Princess Elizabeth's expression wasn't the first sign of more upheaval that might spread into her own life – just when things were getting back into a routine – that was what she found herself hoping anyway.

She went to the sewing box in the corner. They'd stopped

trying to get her to alter dresses. There was so little point in sanctuary. All you could do while you were hiding from the world was to try not to look too frowsty and hope for better times when you got outside. So, for three hours every Friday morning, Isabel and the Princess had started turning an unwanted French wedding gown of figured white damask with pearls into two sets of white cloths for the altar of the Virgin in the Abbey – a thank-you to the Abbot for keeping the Woodville females safe. Isabel had designed the embroidery: trees of red roses and red lilies on each set, along with a far more complex embroidery for the Princess, who had so much more time on her hands: an image of the Assumption of the Virgin.

Elizabeth felt at ease with Isabel; they'd spent so many hours together, quietly sewing. But the younger princesses no longer joined them. They'd sensed the change in Isabel, and found something else to do with their time. They'd stopped hoping she might bring news. No one had had any news of the Princes since the summer. Isabel had told them what Dickon had told her to tell them: that the word in the markets was that they'd been quietly moved out of London, for their own safety. Perhaps they hadn't believed that, any more than Isabel did. ('They're in East Anglia,' Dickon had told Isabel, 'though you needn't tell Elizabeth that; with a man of mine who has sons their ages. Practising their archery.' And he'd laughed; but he hadn't met her eyes.) Isabel didn't even ask about what people really thought had become of the boys when she was in London these days. She didn't like to think of them. She tried not to look at the knucklebones, still on the window ledge, waiting for Richard's return.

Isabel picked up her piece of white damask. She threaded a needle. She sat under the window, facing the fire, and turned her back on the falling leaves and the rain. No more storms, she prayed.

Elizabeth sat down next to her and picked up her own cloth. She began to sew as if nothing had changed. But Isabel noticed that Lady Darcey gave her charge a slightly longer look than usual before closing the door on them, leaving the guards outside.

The two needles flashed quietly. Then Princess Elizabeth put her sewing down. 'I know I can trust you,' she said.

Isabel nodded without committing herself.

She waited.

Elizabeth said, enigmatically: 'My mother is discussing a marriage for me.'

Isabel didn't think there would be many marriage prospects open to a girl now known, officially, as Elizabeth Bastard. She lifted one eyebrow a fraction on her humbly lowered face.

'With the mother of the Earl of Richmond,' Elizabeth whispered.

Isabel was aware of the Princess's slightly protruding eyes fixed on her at the same time as realising she had no idea of how to react. The Earl of Richmond was Henry Tudor, the new Lancastrian leader; the exile in Brittany. Surely Princess Elizabeth could never marry Henry Tudor unless the present King of England, who would never allow such a match, were dead? No one had ever before confessed to her that they were contemplating an act of treason.

She kept her face tilted down; raised the second eyebrow. As slowly and coolly as she could manage, she raised just her eyes, too, to Elizabeth's face.

Why are you telling me this? Isabel's eyes silently beseeched her. But the Princess didn't notice. She'd had no hope for so long. Now she was full of this possible escape.

The more Isabel heard the less she liked it. It was a full-blown plot.

Queen Elizabeth Woodville had been approached with the idea of the marriage by the Duke of Buckingham, who'd sent a messenger; and he in turn had been approached by Henry Tudor's mother on the road to Shrewsbury (Lady Margaret Beaufort was, as she innocently explained, going to pray at the shrine of the virgin at Worcester).

The idea, at the beginning, had been to resuscitate a marriage plan for Elizabeth and Henry of Richmond that had first been vaguely raised a year earlier, with old King Edward, after Elizabeth's French marriage had fallen through: a harmless plan that would allow Henry Tudor back to England, return some of his forfeit estates, and let him live quietly in Wales, on his father's ancestral lands, with his Plantagenet bride.

But it hadn't taken long for the Dowager Queen, Lady Margaret and the Duke of Buckingham to realise that the new King Richard was even less likely than his brother to welcome the last Lancastrian imp home. If they hadn't realised that themselves, it was soon borne in on them once they admitted a fourth person to their counsels: Dr Morton, the Bishop of Ely, the wiliest man in England: a man to spot and iron out the shortcomings in any plot, a man to go for the jugular.

Isabel had heard plenty of talk about Dr Morton. Lord Hastings had loathed him. Morton had been arrested when Hastings was beheaded. People had said in the summer that he'd somehow escaped from the Tower. But that turned out to be wrong. His friends at Oxford University had lobbied so hard for him to be set free that Dickon had released him into the personal care of the Duke of Buckingham – a dear friend; the man who'd helped Dickon stop the Woodvilles and take control of Edward Bastard.

At the time, Isabel had thought Dickon's idea of quietly giving the prisoner to Buckingham to lock up in the depths of Wales was foolproof enough. But now, as the Princess talked, she realised what a dangerous mistake it had been.

Dickon hadn't thought the rotund little Bishop of Ely would be any trouble at all for the tall, terrifying Duke, especially if the two of them were holed up together in remote Brecknock Castle. But he hadn't thought enough about Morton's bright little eyes, burning out of his red slab of a face; about his knack for a well-turned joke and a bark of laughter; about the energy and cynicism with which the Bishop would turn his talent for talking to saving himself. It hadn't occurred to him that Harry Buckingham, who had only ever known other tall, tight tornadoes of aristocratic power like himself and was scarcely ever seen off a horse's back or unarmed, might be so surprised and fascinated by the prelate's steady stream of sly conversation that, for the first time in his life, he would feel he almost understood what it was to fall in love. That was the miracle Dr Morton seemed to have achieved. He'd talked his jailer round – making him change sides, and turn to the Woodvilles and Lancastrians.

Now Morton was involved, the nature of the plan had changed. He opened the two mothers' eyes to bigger opportunities. There was no more talk of persuading King Richard to allow Princess Elizabeth to marry Henry Tudor. King Richard only figured in the current version of the plan as a corpse. Morton's idea was that Henry would invade England, seize the throne, kill King Richard, rescue Elizabeth and marry her.

'Easy,' Isabel said expressionlessly.

The Princess paused and gave her the slightly worried look of a raconteur who fears the audience is not getting the point of the story.

Isabel smiled, to put the Princess's mind at rest. But

behind her smile she was thinking: I don't want a new King. I don't want any more unrest. I don't want to hide inside my house for weeks, behind bars and shutters, drinking rainwater, listening for footsteps; I don't want my old folk terrified half to death by Kentish looters. And I certainly don't want to have to beg for a new licence for the silk house from a new King – a stranger – when everything has got so far. I want things to stay as they are.

Loudest of all, her heart was screaming: I don't want a King who's not Dickon. She was remembering him warm against her, before he'd set off on his latest travels, pulling her to him at the tavern window to look at the full moon rising, and saying, very quietly, in a voice that sent shivers down her back while her waist and ribs and shoulders were warmed against his flesh: 'This is what I do when we're apart. I come out and look at the full moon and think of you, wherever you are. You don't feel so far away if I can think you're looking at the same moon.'

She shook herself. 'Well, so . . . what's he like, your future husband?' she said, trying to look and sound warmer without saying anything overtly treasonous; who knew what the Princess might take it into her head to blurt out about this conversation at some later date?

Elizabeth shrugged. 'Don't know,' she said calmly. 'Bad teeth, thin hair: that's what people say. It's not for me to ask. My mother would think anyone a good catch if they had a chance of being King of England . . . I just obey.'

She said it with complete acceptance. There was even a hint of rueful laughter in her eyes when she looked at Isabel again; as if she knew Isabel was secretly counting the beads of her own memories of Dickon, and giving thanks for each one, and feeling blessed to have been born, not with Elizabeth's royal blood flowing in her veins, but with all the possibilities of freedom and damnation open to her. As if the Princess, for a moment, had become older and wiser than her confidante.

'They're planning to move on St Luke's Day,' Isabel said clearly. It was important to get the detail right. 'October the eighteenth. Risings all over southeast England. Kentishmen attacking London. The Duke of Buckingham bringing an army of Welshmen across the Severn. A West Country army meeting him. Then both armies going to meet Henry Tudor, who'll be landing in Devon with five thousand soldiers from Britanny. Then all of them marching east to engage you.'

Dickon had covered his face with his hands and turned his back when she'd first said his friend Buckingham was planning to betray him. There'd been a groan from inside the rumpled linen, where his head was. But she'd gone on talking to his one exposed shoulder, with its beloved tawny skin. Feeling righteous. Something had to be done.

He'd turned back round when she'd started giving the military details, though. She'd felt the alert flash of his eyes; sensed his mind fixing on her. He couldn't have expected her to know this. Now he was eating her up with his stare, weighing every word, almost smiling. When she finished, he did smile. But all he said was: 'You'd have made a good soldier.' And they lay in silence for a while, thinking their thoughts.

She hadn't had a qualm in the end.

After she'd left the Princess, she'd gone back to the silk house to think. She'd sat distractedly for a while, watching Joan Woulbarowe grinning rather prettily at her Lombard, Gasparino's brother Andrea, pulling down her lips to cover her bad teeth, as the first shaky pattern began to appear in the damask they were working on together, and giggling delightedly when the darker, younger man murmured Italian back at her, of which Isabel could only make out basic words, '*Benon, benon,*' but perhaps Joan had already grasped more of the language. Or perhaps she just liked the seductive tone of voice. Isabel thought: Do I protect the Princess's secret? Or do I protect these people? My people?

The answer had been too obvious to worry over. You had to look after your own. It wasn't as hard as she'd thought it might be to betray the Princess's trust.

Dickon sat up in the bed. The straw in the mattress was fresh and soft and smelled of summer. He was going to make light of it to her.

'Well, what do you think?' he said, his voice higher than usual. 'Could they win?'

He kept his eyes turned away.

'I'm no soldier,' she said helplessly.

'You're my most honest adviser.'

He waited.

She said, doubtfully, thinking of all those armies blundering around different parts of the West Country, trying to meet up. 'Well, it seems . . . messy.'

She didn't think the armies would beat Dickon's. Not by themselves. But what if ordinary people were pleased enough at the idea of getting rid of this king that they joined the enemy armies? There was so much talk, so many people who suspected Dickon had stolen the crown, insulted his mother's honour, killed his nephews, and who disliked him for it.

He nodded, as if he understood the thought she was hesitating over. The hardness that had always been a possibility in his face was suddenly visible again, in lines round his cheeks and eyes. He was making plans; moving troops in his mind.

She could see he wouldn't let himself be harmed. What worried her now was the harm he might do while he was making himself safe. She said, hastily: 'Dickon.' And when he looked at her, with eyes that were somewhere else, she added, as if the fog she lived in had suddenly cleared: 'Please. Whatever you do, don't hurt the Princess.'

He didn't answer straight away. She wished she could know what was on his mind. He kissed her forehead and her heart turned over. 'Of course,' he said, more gently than she'd expected. 'Elizabeth's not to blame. I'd never hurt her.' After a pause, he added: 'I wouldn't harm any of my kin. And I'd never kill a woman. You know that.'

London only heard the story of how the October rebellion was put down with delays, in dribs and drabs, in taverns and markets, from messengers and heralds, pedlars and gossips, as bitter autumn rain stripped leaves from the trees and life from the streets.

The rain stopped the Duke of Buckingham's army, as if God were on King Richard's side. A storm blew Henry Tudor's little fleet to the wrong place. He never landed. Prudently, he sailed back to Britanny. The various West Country uprisings fizzled out without joining up. Buckingham was caught at Salisbury and beheaded.

Lady Darcey was present at Isabel's next few sewing sessions. Isabel avoided the Princess's pink eyes, feeling the dislike that comes naturally for someone you've wronged. The uprising was not mentioned. Three needles flashed in silence. The King was away in the West Country for weeks, cleaning up.

No one harmed Princess Elizabeth or her mother or sisters. Dickon had told the truth about that, at least. None of the street talk even associated them with the foiled plot. People on the street just wondered why the King hadn't done something worse to Lady Margaret Beaufort, Henry Tudor's mother, who was known to have been raising money in the City for the uprising. She was under house arrest, but her jailer was her husband, Lord Stanley. There was no accounting for it, they shrugged; she'd only try again. They weren't softened by the King's softness.

The person most frightened by the talk of armies, as far as Isabel could see, was Jane. She'd got out of bed at last, and recovered her health enough to go to church every morning and have her daily interrogations conducted, in Alice's great hall, by the King's Solicitor. Thomas Lynom might be a royal bureaucrat, but he seemed a friendly enough man, with his brother's kindly eyes and good bones. He raised his hat to Isabel and passed the time of day affably enough with her whenever they passed in the hall, and she sensed he was well-disposed towards Jane. But when the invasion talk started, Jane, very quiet by day, began grinding her teeth and crying out in her sleep at night. Her thin fingers pulled at things. Whenever Isabel stayed in London, sharing a bed with Jane, she noticed boxes with their silk hinges broken; ripped cushions with their stuffing pulled half out. But she didn't ask Jane what was troubling her. She couldn't. It wasn't her place, if Jane hadn't confided in her. Isabel stifled the hurt she might have felt that Jane hadn't done so. She'd hoped that they might become closer, but perhaps it was as well they hadn't. Isabel didn't trust herself with other people's secrets any more. Her sister might just say something she'd feel compelled to tell Dickon.

But Isabel listened. And one day, as she left the house for the Guildhall, where she was to represent the Clavers at a meeting with Low Countries merchants, through the open door of the great hall she overheard Jane's new, thin, weak voice. 'I'm so afraid,' her sister was saying, and she sounded on the verge of tears. 'I have nightmares about soldiers . . . I wake up in the night thinking they're coming for me.'

There was a comforting male rumble.

'But I'm a sitting target,' Jane said, her voice going higher before it did break into sobs. 'And it would be so easy for him to do it again. Blame me for all this. Call me a witch. Make a public example of me . . . I'm so afraid, so afraid . . .'

Isabel slipped out. She didn't want to hear any more.

She didn't hurry back; she didn't want to have to face Jane's terror. But when she did slip in to dinner, late, everything had changed. Alice and Anne weren't the only people at the table, methodically shoving food into their mouths. Thomas Lynom was there too, sitting beside Jane, and there were flowers on the table, and Jane, who'd hardly eaten a thing for days, was looking at her interrogator with shining eyes as he put bits of game pie in her mouth and murmured, to approving laughs from the silkwomen, 'Now, eat up, do; you look like a dying bird; it's time we fattened you up.'

Jane got up when she saw her sister. Shyly, she smiled. 'Isabel,' she said, and Isabel was astonished to see her sister's eyes start batting up and down, in that charmingly flirtatious way she'd had before, from the hands in her lap to Isabel's face. 'I have something to tell you . . .'

Isabel guessed what was coming as soon as she glanced at Thomas, who was blushing to the roots of his dark-blond hair, looking a fool but too happy to care.

'We're going to marry at the end of the month. I'm going to move to the country,' Jane murmured breathily, and her eyes, as clear as summer skies, invited Isabel to celebrate her joy.

For the first time in a long time, Isabel found herself bursting out laughing. Alice was guffawing, too; and Isabel was able to meet her mistress's relieved eyes and share the moment. She needn't have worried about Jane, after all. Jane hadn't lost her resilience, any more than she'd lost her old knack of casting spells over men. But marrying her interrogator; now that was a masterstroke. Whatever was Dickon going to say?

She didn't care. It would be all right now Jane was going to be all right. She couldn't believe Dickon would punish her sister for falling in love. So she rushed to her sister and Thomas; embraced them both; let her gratitude to her sister's unexpected saviour shine on her face. Still, she couldn't quite stop herself dissembling. She didn't say any of the things she'd actually been thinking. Instead, with a light laugh that didn't altogether hide her sympathy for the oldest fool for love she knew, she just asked: 'Whatever will poor Will Caxton say?'

15

Isabel had never felt the need to be cautious with her lover before he was King. But now Dickon dreamed of invading armies coming to get him, and his dreams pursued him into his waking life. He had early-warning patrols man the cliffs of England's southern coasts with torches and ponies, watching for ships from Britanny. The new King preferred sleeping in Nottingham, in the middle of England, to Westminster and London; he said he'd be better able to muster his Northern armies from the Midlands when the enemy came.

Isabel saw him less than she had before. In the South, he slept fitfully. He startled awake if he heard a mouse scuttling or a floorboard creaking in the night. He woke, pale and dazed, with anxiety lines etched across his forehead that Isabel couldn't smooth away.

But he could still be cheerful – reckless, even – when the mood took him.

When Isabel told him that the interrogator he'd sent to correct Jane Shore and show her the error of her sinful ways had fallen in love with her instead, he laughed.

He laughed so much he had to sit down on the bed and hold his sides. He laughed till he had tears in his eyes, and rolling down his cheeks, and the tension lines marking his face had vanished. 'What a woman,' he wheezed. 'I take my hat off to her. She never gives up, does she?'

There was a glint of real admiration in his wet eyes.

He laughed even more when Isabel said Thomas Lynom was agonising over a letter to him, to ask his permission to marry.

'Well, I did tell him to make an honest woman of the King's whore,' he gulped, 'but I never intended him to take me so literally.'

She'd been planning to beg him not to punish Thomas or his betrothed. She hadn't expected this stormy amusement.

'So will you, might you,' she breathed, encouraged, 'say yes?'

He had to struggle to get enough air in his lungs to reply. He took a couple of deep breaths; closed his eyes. But even when his body stopped shaking with merriment, he couldn't take the impish grin off his face.

Trying to compose himself, he said ruefully, 'Well, I'll have to talk to my errant servant, of course. But once I'm certain that there's no talking him out of this foolishness – and I can see already that there won't be – I don't see any alternative but to let him have his head.'

Then he went back to chuckling. Slowly, Isabel began to grin too.

It was a quiet winter wedding – just the couple and the Claver family at the church door – but it gave Isabel hope.

She'd lived all year with the loneliness of shame. If Dickon had murdered for power, and she knew it but couldn't stop loving him, she was guilty by association. Her punishment was to be cut off from intimacy with the friends she no longer felt honest with.

But now a new idea took root in Isabel's heart. Perhaps Dickon's crimes weren't as unforgivable as she'd thought them at first. If she could only explain them all to herself, satisfactorily, then perhaps, after all, she could forgive herself for forgiving him.

Whatever he'd done during that grab for power, she was beginning to believe again that Dickon wasn't cruel at heart. He couldn't be, could he, now he'd set Jane free and resignedly laughed off her marriage? He'd let Lady Margaret Beaufort off lightly for the Tudor rebellion, too; and he'd left the Woodville women untouched.

He hadn't been wrong to get rid of the Woodville uncles, either. They'd wanted to kill him. He'd said so.

It was only when she came to the death of Lord Hastings that Isabel's heart sank, or when she remembered little Prince Richard's thin, warm little arm under her hand, as soft and vulnerable as a bird's; his frightened child's eyes on her.

She wanted to believe he and his brother were being brought up incognito in the Suffolk countryside, as Dickon said. She wanted to believe Lord Hastings had done . . . something.

It stretched belief. But when she couldn't bring herself to have faith, she told herself instead that she couldn't hope to understand the temptation that the possibility of royal power must have represented to someone so close to the crown; that if she didn't know, she couldn't judge. And sometimes she so nearly succeeded in believing what she was telling herself that she felt something close to peace of mind stealing back into her heart.

Jane and Thomas Lynom arrived in London in early April, a year into Dickon's reign. It was the first time they'd left their new manor house at Sutton. Alice Claver prepared a feast.

The Lynoms, husband and wife, were already at Catte Street when Isabel walked in: the centre of attention, both smiling radiantly, both as golden as summer apricots, being plied with wine and refreshments after their morning's ride.

Jane had stopped wearing nun-like greys and browns since she married, but she hadn't gone back to her old peacock finery either. Today she was wearing a fine, yet modest, patterned damask robe in tans and browns and greys. The sprays of foliage shone as she moved, yet so discreetly that even Alice Claver couldn't really disapprove. 'Being a country gentlewoman seems to be suiting you,' Alice Claver barked, glaring down at Jane's hands, which were conspicuously un-roughened by her new rustic life; but, despite the snap in the mistress of the house's gruff voice, they all knew that, somehow, Jane had sneaked herself into Alice Claver's heart. So no one worried.

'How well you look, my dear,' William Pratte said affectionately, deftly stepping past Will Caxton to embrace the bride. Caxton had glued himself to Jane since he arrived, fussing and grinning like a devoted dog refusing to be parted from its long-lost mistress. He'd hardly said a word to Thomas Lynom; but the young husband was taking the prickliness of Jane's long-term admirer in good part.

'More beautiful than ever,' declaimed Goffredo, with something of his old flirtatiousness. Goffredo had been very quiet recently. Since the Londoners and Venetians at the silk house had learned enough of each other's languages to talk properly, it had emerged that Goffredo had had a wife in Venice for twenty years, but had never mentioned her to Alice Claver and her friends. The childless wife had been carried off last spring by a bout of fever, so he was now, officially, a widower at last. But Alice and Anne were teasing him so brutally about his lengthy, half-joking flirtation with Isabel that he'd stopped daring to answer

338

back or proposing almost light-heartedly to her several times a day. 'A woman in every port,' they'd cackle to each other; or, 'You know the punishment for bigamy is eternal damnation, don't you?' And poor Goffredo's eyes would flicker and his smile would grow uncertain. Isabel was partly relieved that he was fighting shy of her, as a result, but she missed Goffredo's old exuberance too. So she was happy to see a more cheerful gleam in his eyes now.

'Yes; you're blooming, dear,' Anne Pratte said from just behind her husband. Isabel noticed Thomas give Anne Pratte a single quiet look and Anne Pratte smiled innocently back before she lowered her eyes. But no one else noticed, because Robert Lynom walked in at that moment. He'd become a friend as well as their lawyer; he'd even been entrusted with the secret of the silk-weaving venture at Westminster, with much significant lowering of voices and tapping of noses on Anne Pratte's part. So there were more embraces and joy and long blond limbs clapping each other on the back, and deep brotherly voices booming affectionately at each other.

They all settled at table and, while the goose was carved up and the pies and vegetable dishes sampled, Thomas, who, as the husband of a formerly treasonable person, had been tickled to be appointed to a royal commission investigating other treasonable persons in Essex, told stories about his work. The King had just given him another manor, at Colmworth in Bedfordshire, for his pains; he and Jane were on their way to visit it for the first time. There was a possibility he'd be transferred again to run a section of the elaborate, expensive new coastal defences. 'I seem to count as an honorary Northerner these days, luckily,' he said comfortably, not quite mocking a monarch who so distrusted the Southern gentry that he'd started importing hundreds of sheriffs and other officials to run the administration of the South. 'I had no idea when I went to work in York five years ago what a good choice I was making.'

He was so comfortable, Thomas Lynom; so at ease. So unlike Dickon.

How cosy everything has become here; how calm, Isabel thought gratefully.

When Jane, putting a hand on her husband's arm, said shyly: 'Thomas and I have news', and there was a burst of excited chatter about when the Lynom baby would be born and what it should be called, Isabel let herself be swept up as much as everyone else by the hope lighting up the table. She raised her glass: 'To new beginnings,' she said, 'for all of us.' And they all laughed and banged the table with their hands, while Thomas Lynom blushed and kissed his wife.

Isabel's happiness flickered and faded when she and Will Caxton landed at Westminster, towards evening, and heard bells.

Someone was dead.

She saw the alarm in Will's eyes. Her heart was thudding. Without a word, they half-walked, half-ran through the mournful din to the nearest tavern to find out who. The tavern was called the White Boar, like Dickon's badge. Inside, there was a heaving ant-heap of turmoil.

'It's a sign from God,' a stout elderly woman in tight black was saying, crossing herself. 'It must be.'

The monk she was with nodded. He had the same snub nose and pig cheeks as her, and was near the bottom of a tankard of ale. He drained it before replying, with foam on his face and gloomy relish in his rough voice: 'Mmm. A year to the day. Struck down by the Good Lord in His righteous anger. It's the only explanation.'

Staring at them, Isabel thought, stupidly, slowly: it's the

ninth of April. It took her a moment to remember what had happened last April ninth. Then she did. It was the day King Edward had died. The day she'd first heard this head-splitting clangour of bells.

When the fear came, it was like drowning in black water. She gasped with it. Dickon?

'But who is dead?' Will Caxton was asking.

'The Prince of Wales,' the monk said. 'The boy.'

'God rest his soul,' Will whispered, crossing himself. She crossed herself too, but the sensation sweeping through her limbs was the sweetest relief imaginable. It was only when she looked up, and found a whole circle of bystanders turning astonished eyes on her, that she realised what she'd been muttering as her hand moved: 'Thank God.'

Will said: 'She means, she was afraid you might be talking about the King.' He spoke quickly and protectively, before the surprise turned to hostility. She nodded.

'But this is worse,' the White Boar's innkeeper called out, hands full of tankards, wiping the sweat from his forehead onto a forearm. The crowd nodded, and there were rumbles of 'wickedness' and 'divine punishment'. 'There are no other children. No heirs. No daughters. Hardly a nephew left alive. He says they're all bastards, doesn't he? We all know what that means for us. When he dies, we get more war. And my question is: What bloody good is a living king to any of us if his dynasty's dead?'

'They say the Queen's gone mad with it,' Anne Pratte said. 'Grief.'

Alice sighed gustily. Their needles flashed in rhythm.

'Anne, really,' William Pratte remonstrated.

There was only one legitimate York heir left. King Edward's children were bastards. The Duke of Clarence's son was barred from the throne because his father had died a traitor. That left a cousin: John de la Pole, the Earl of Lincoln. Another nine-year-old.

'The King, too,' Anne Pratte went remorselessly on. 'They say he bangs his head against the wall and tears his hair out. In handfuls.'

Isabel winced inside. 'Anne,' William Pratte said.

She fixed him with a cold look. 'I don't know why you're being so squeamish about this, dear,' she said. 'It's not as if I'm just gossiping. I'm not calling it God's punishment, whatever anyone else says. I just say we have a right to worry. They say there are three hundred rebel lords in Britanny now. They will have been waiting for something like this. How long will it take them to start making trouble? And what will become of us then?'

It was a rhetorical question. They'd told Isabel often enough exactly what would become of them if there was war again: the contracts vanishing, the foreigners too, the wine fleet stopping, food prices rising, crazy war taxes, the law courts clogging up with unheard cases, the roads filling up with brigands, the seas filling up with pirates. She knew the answer. But they'd lived it. She could see the fear in their eyes.

Isabel didn't expect to see Dickon soon. The body had to be buried; the kingdom's defences shored up. She'd wait.

But he came. She was out in the little garden, picking gillyflowers for the table, feeling the sun on her back, knowing that tonight would be full moon, when she heard the low whistle from behind the hedge. She hadn't even noticed the fall of hooves until then. She went to the gate to see who could be whistling her out.

'You,' she said; feeling a great slow breath of happiness fill her, somehow not surprised after all.

He looked dusty from the road and marked by his pain

– thinner, somehow shrunken, with dark under the eyes and sadness dragging at his face.

They hadn't ever spoken on the street. It was too over-looked, too public. Their tacit agreement was that once she saw his horse, she'd slip over the road and up the tavern's back stairs to find him in the room. If she was careful, no one need ever see her.

But he did speak now, under the windows that might be full of eyes, as if he didn't care any more who saw him. He dismounted and walked straight to her, before even tethering the horse, so that human and animal faces came at her together over the gate. He kissed her in a sour cloud of horse sweat and leather; a strangely nostalgic, uncertain kiss.

When they drew apart, she said, a little frightened by this new simplicity: 'I've been so sad for you.'

He said, with that unearthly calm that never seemed to desert him: 'Can you imagine how much I loved him?', and she nodded. If her imagination could conjure up no greater love than the bittersweet pleasure she was feeling here, now, at being with Dickon, at being needed in this moment, it would be enough. Eyes on eyes: a long silence. She never wanted to look away. 'You can't know how much I've missed you,' he said, and her heart turned over. 'I know I can trust you. Come and talk.'

She was still holding the gillyflowers. She opened the gate and walked straight over the road, behind him, to the Red Pale's back door.

The pale walls and the straw still held a memory of happi-ness. But now she was fully clothed and holding the hand of a man hunched on a mattress in dusty clothes who'd said he needed her but hardly seemed to know she was there. Who was talking about pain, as if to himself. She was watching a ravaged living face appear to age before her eyes as he described the radiance his dead child had lost. The slight fever; the rash; the lethargic tears. Nothing. A brief bad dream. But Edward had been dead by morning.

She could imagine how Dickon would have held his sorrow in. Using his miraculously deep, reassuring voice to calm others; being dignified, prosaic and practical. But shutting himself away in prayer, or taking himself off for the fierce lonely gallops he loved, trying not to give way to emotion however much he wanted to howl out his grief.

'There was a silkwoman who worked for us once,' she whispered, her eyes swimming with pity, hoping he would not guess how full her heart was with its own muted radiance at being here, chosen, talking with this man about things so close to his heart. 'Her little boy died. She just disappeared. They didn't find her for a week. She'd gone right out to the woods and dug herself into a foxhole. As if she was trying to bury herself. They dug her up and brought her back, but she didn't want to come. She kept saying, "Let me die, let me die." They said she'd gone mad; put her in Bethlem for three months. She's never been right since . . .' She stopped. 'But you; you've been strong.'

Dickon looked straight at her for the first time since they'd shut the door. He was so tired his face was grey. There was grey in his hair too. He crunched his hands together until his knuckles cracked.

'You know,' he said. 'Don't you? What Anne's been like.'

His wife; the Queen of England. She flinched, but he didn't seem to notice. He went on talking. Anne Neville wanted to die. She couldn't eat. She couldn't sleep. Her bones stuck out and her eyes stuck out. She howled and tore down draperies. She fell down stairs; slashed at her wrists; beat her head against walls. There were no other children.

Hollowly he said: 'It's as if she's possessed. I can't be

with her. I can't let her go either.' Isabel made herself small and still and said nothing. His face was twitching. He went on urgently, a whisper with a suppressed howl in it: 'She wants to die. But I can't let her. She remembers Edward like I do.'

What comfort could she offer? She squeezed at his dry hand; he squeezed hers back. He sat in silence for a while. He composed himself; fingered the crucifix he'd taken off and laid on the floor as he entered the room; muttered a prayer. It wasn't his usual crucifix. It was smaller and more delicate, decorated with a single chip of ruby. He caught her looking at it. Uncomfortably, he said: 'It's his. Edward's.' Then: 'Was Edward's.' He didn't look at her as he went on, 'They're expecting me. I have to go.'

She watched the full moon come up, alone, before letting herself out to cross the road home. She took the wilted gillyflowers.

Will Caxton looked out of an upstairs window as her gate creaked. He was in his nightshirt, stretching and smiling while he reached for his shutters. 'You're out late,' he said.

She held up the flowers. He was too far away and, even in the moonlight, it was too dark for him to see how faded they'd got. He'd think she'd been out picking them at night, maybe.

He nodded. 'They're pretty,' he said kindly; then, 'Isn't it beautiful out tonight? This magical light. I love the full moon. Don't you?'

Liking Will Caxton, Isabel said, 'I do.' As she padded up the path and lifted the latch to her own door, she added, 'Though sometimes it seems sad. So pale and quiet.'

With Will's murmur still in her ears, Isabel stopped just inside the door. She could hear the usual evening dancing and music and hubbub coming from behind the closed doors opposite. Perhaps, in a while, she'd join the weavers.

There was so much sadness in the world. Dickon was in grief. But he'd brought his grief to her; no one else. When she thought of that, she could bear anything. She might even dance.

'Did you see boxes outside?' Princess Elizabeth said; and her voice seemed to have got faster and sharper. 'Have they started taking them away yet?'

Isabel shook her head. 'Boxes . . .' She was baffled. Elizabeth had been so quiet, so correct, so hopeless since the failure of Henry Tudor's rebellion; as if the life had been snuffed out of her.

'We're going,' the Princess said impatiently, as if Isabel were being slow. 'Home. Back to the Palace. To court. Didn't you know?'

More kindly, she added: 'It's been chaos in our bedchambers for hours; packing and folding and pinning and I don't know what. Chests everywhere. I thought you'd have seen some outside already.'

Elizabeth was starting to share the cream-and-copper beauty of her mother. Her face had points: cheekbones and a straight, neat nose. Her father's small mouth had become a pretty Cupid's bow on her. And there was a glow about her that Isabel hadn't seen before.

'But . . . why?' Isabel asked, in the end. She couldn't think how to phrase the question more delicately. Prudently, she added: 'If I may ask?'

The Princess didn't mind answering. 'Because of the letter,' she said, sitting down on a cushion, invitingly patting the stool next to her. 'My mother feels safer now.'

'Letter?' Isabel repeated. She was beginning to feel she really was getting stupid. What letter could possibly persuade Dowager Queen Elizabeth Woodville to leave sanctuary?

'From my brother,' the Princess said, in the slow voice

of one dealing gently with the simple-minded, and, when Isabel continued to stare blankly at her: 'Richard. You know him. You saw him, didn't you? Here, before they took him off?'

A letter from one of the vanished Princes. Isabel's head swam. So they really were alive. She sat down rather suddenly, full of a greater tenderness for Dickon than she'd ever known. She hadn't thought till now that it would be possible for her to love him more than she already did, and this extra tide of happiness, sweeping away the doubts she hadn't wanted to have, restoring the innocence she'd lost, took her by surprise. He'd told the truth. She should have known. She should have trusted him.

'Oh,' she said.

The Princess was laughing at her stunned look. But the Princess had had longer to get over the shock. 'Yes,' Elizabeth said, as happy and relaxed as an ordinary girl. 'He wrote to us. Just like that. All those months of being so scared, and now,' a softness stole across her royal face, 'it turns out that there's been nothing to fear all along.'

Men came. Two chests were dumped on the floor. Isabel packed the altar cloths into sacking covers and sewed them carefully into parcels. She made separate sacking packets for the pearls and red and green silk threads and the Venice gold, and sewed them onto the biggest of the main parcels. And then she packed each rough parcel into the chests, between layers of straw to stop them being crushed. And all the time she worked, she smiled. And all the time she worked, the Princess sat on her cushion and talked.

'They left London last October . . . my uncle said they'd be safer away . . . Suffolk . . . Little Gipping . . . Very remote . . . they're in good health, at least Richard is, but he says Edward's been ill . . . they're with a family . . .

other boys . . . Tyrrell . . . they ride . . . get about . . . the servants don't know who they are . . . they call them "Lord Edward" and "Lord Richard" . . . which isn't bad; better than 'Edward Bastard' anyway . . . I suppose I'm going to have to get used to being 'Elizabeth Bastard' myself . . . but at least I'll be back at court again, not cooped up in here . . . It's funny, isn't it; we're only moving over the road, really, a few hundred yards, but everything changes once you cross the road, everything . . . There won't be dancing for a few months, though; because of the mourning. I didn't know my cousin Edward . . . though I'm sad, of course . . . We won't get the same apartments but they'll be good ones . . . I'll be able to ride again . . . Do you think it's time to start work on my wedding gown? Because perhaps I'll be able to make a good marriage now, after all. Live happily ever after.'

Isabel let it wash over her, enjoying it, enjoying the flash of her needle, light-headed with her private relief. But when the Princess began to talk about marrying, she did look up.

'Not Henry Tudor?' she asked, trying to make a shared joke of him. The Princess laughed, a light, brittle, social laugh. But she didn't offer a name. All she said was, 'ah', and there was an enigmatic look on her face as she played with the crucifix round her neck; then: 'It would be foolish to make the same mistake twice, wouldn't it?'

It was only on her way out of the Abbot's house that Isabel realised what had troubled her most about that moment. Elizabeth's crucifix was decorated with a single small ruby. It was the double of the one Dickon had been carrying the previous night.

Dickon's eyes were as empty as last time. But they made love. He didn't speak, just drew in a deep breath of need at the sight of her, closed his eyes and put his lips to hers.

Even when they were tumbled breathlessly on the bed together, sated, he didn't smile or break his silence. But he went on holding her so close, so hard, that she could feel his heart beat and sense the depth of the loneliness he was trying to escape. It was enough.

'I worry for you,' she whispered. He kissed her, but she thought it might be to stop her talking. She felt he might just want to feel her skin on his today, not words. She'd do whatever he needed. She relaxed against his body; kissed his chest with butterfly kisses; willed him to find his eyes closing. Then she remembered the letter; and couldn't stop herself voicing her gratitude.

'Elizabeth . . .' she whispered – she couldn't call her either 'Princess' or 'Bastard' with Dickon – 'Elizabeth was so happy with the letter from her brother.'

He might have brought the letter himself. But he only grunted. He kept his eyes shut.

'I am too,' she breathed. 'Thank you.'

She'd kept faith. She'd had doubts; but the darkness was fading.

As she settled herself blissfully against him, she looked at the ground where his crucifix lay. It was the usual big one with sapphires. The dead child's cross had gone.

She lay with one cheek on Dickon's chest, staring down at the shadows on the floor.

She didn't know why, or what had changed. But she was no longer feeling happy.

Love

16

When she asked about the crucifix, Dickon just sighed.

'It's the same one,' he said wearily, pulling himself up and buckling on his sword belt. 'I gave it to Elizabeth to remember him by.'

But Elizabeth had said she'd hardly known her cousin. Why would she want his cross?

Isabel went on looking at Dickon. He frowned. 'They were cousins,' he said evasively.

She didn't look away.

As irritably as if she were interrogating him and forcing a confession, Dickon added: 'And I've been wondering about her as a possible wife. If Anne were to die.'

She stared.

Defensively, he said: 'Well, it would stop Henry Tudor trying to marry her. She'd get a crown, even as a bastard. It would stop her mother wanting revenge on me. It would make sense.'

Then, into the silence, he snapped: 'For God's sake. Stop looking at me like that.'

But she couldn't. She couldn't even summon up the strength to pick up the sheet that had fallen away from her nakedness. She just went on sitting in the rumpled bed, with her chin on her knees and pale red hair flaming round her eyes, staring.

She'd accepted everything till now. She'd lived with her fears. She'd heard the stories about Hastings being dragged kicking and screaming from the Council chamber and spread-eagled across a tree stump to be beheaded, while Dickon watched. She'd shut her mind to them.

But this felt worse. It was betrayal. She couldn't say yes to this. She couldn't let him love another woman; and she couldn't believe his only motive, if he were thinking of marrying Elizabeth, would be forming a good alliance.

She couldn't shut her mind to the thought of his fastening that cross round Elizabeth's long neck.

Mastering himself, he sat down again. Put his hand on hers. 'Look,' he said, but she sensed that his gentleness masked impatience. 'My son is dead; my wife is dying. It's my duty to think about this. I need an heir. This would be an alliance, that's all.'

She said nothing. She was ashes inside. Had he only really come to London this time to see Elizabeth; to make marriage plans with her?

'Elizabeth's a child,' he said, as if that would comfort her. 'I don't love her.'

She said nothing.

He said: 'I have to go.' He was leaving for Nottingham and the North tomorrow.

She nodded.

He kissed her cheek before he went.

It would be weeks before he got back: the end of summer. She wouldn't even think about what he'd said. She couldn't. She threw herself even harder into her work.

She and Goffredo bought in weaving materials for the Italian teams, going at different times to the London markets and being careful to vary their suppliers. The slightly wobbly lengths of luminous cloth on the looms were getting bigger. It wouldn't be more than a few months before the silk-women could weave without guidance from the Italians. Soon they'd need to start planning how to announce the existence of the workshop at the Guildhall; from next spring, once the Mercery allowed them to trade, they'd be able to start making sales.

In London, where she went on Sundays to spend half of her week with the old women, she also made deals in the selds; wrote her sales into Alice's ledgers; joined the older women to entertain their clients; and went to the Guildhall with Alice and William Pratte. No one else had Isabel's eye for truth and falsehood, even Alice; Isabel was in constant demand on the commission, checking imported silk cloths for frauds. The Mercers relied on her ability to open up a length of damask and, after feeling it and looking at it by the light of the window, pronounce it either properly finished or badly worked in places, or inconsistent, or with warps too thin and however many pounds light of the weft threads it would have needed to make it tighter; or, having sniffed a suspect cloth, to say it had been artificially thickened, by a fraudulent exporter, with paste.

She remembered every foreign regulation, too, better than any clerk. When the foreign importer jumped angrily from his chair, shouting, 'But it is perfectly honest to use *gomma*!' it was Isabel who knew, and replied without hesitation, that while you could use it honestly in light cloths, such as sandals and satins, to make the colours shine and give consistency, the Venetian government had made the use of paste in any heavy *parangon* cloths illegal in 1457 and had enforced the regulation strictly ever since. London followed Venice's direction. There would be nothing for the importer to do but take his cloth and flounce away.

They were saying in the markets that the Queen was dying and the King was being punished for his sins. But the Claver profits were up.

'You're a marvel; you work so hard,' Robert Lynom said. 'But don't you ever want to enjoy yourself? Go and stay with Jane. She's lonely; Thomas is always away these days raising troops for the King.'

She shook her head. 'Too much to do here,' she said briskly.

If she went to the country, how could she be at Westminster?

Isabel stayed up late at Westminster on her three days a week there. At the silk house she made the silk weavers teach her the rudiments of their craft by day and danced with the Lombards at night, very fast, very late.

Once a week she walked to the Palace to the big bright apartment overlooking the river, where Princess Elizabeth now busied herself with hunts and preparations for the dances that would start again at the end of the summer. The Princess didn't want to finish the altar vestments that reminded her of those endless miserable months of sanctuary. They'd been sent off to the City for finishing. But she and her sisters did want dancing gowns. Isabel took a profitable commission from Lady Darcey, and subcontracted the job in the Mercery. Her patience with the princesses was paying dividends. Alice would be pleased.

But that was no longer the reason Isabel came. She came to torment herself by looking at Elizabeth from under her eyelashes: measuring the smoothness of the Princess's sixteen-year-old skin and the tiny waist and the slim neck and the white hands and the prominent eyes that she'd once thought ugly but which now seemed to glow with secrets. She tried not to think of the fine lines around her own eyes; the pale streaks in her hair. But she couldn't stop herself asking: How could Dickon not love this niece?

'That's a beautiful cross,' she said, on one knee, pinning.

Elizabeth looked down her thin nose, squinting towards it. 'My cousin's,' she said quietly, 'God rest his soul. His Majesty gave it to me.' But she didn't offer any more information.

Fishing for more, Isabel ventured, 'How relieved you must be that His Majesty is so well-disposed to your family . . .' But the Princess only nodded, with a remote half-smile. She'd learned caution. It was a long time since she'd confided in Isabel.

If only more people were more cautious, Isabel thought angrily, catching up with her servant.

'Speta, Dotor Gigli! Drio de vu! Vienlo a Mesa?' Joan Woulbarowe was joyfully trilling. She was looking prettier these days than she had in all the years Isabel had known her. She'd lost her neglected air. Her hair was dressed under her kerchief and her lips were full and pink and her eyes were gleaming, and there was a pretty gold heart on a red ribbon round her neck. The other Westminster silkwomen spent their evenings putting bets on how long it would take timid little Andrea di Costanzo to pluck up the courage to ask his brother Gasparino to ask Goffredo to ask Alice Claver to allow him to marry Joan Woulbarowe at the end of her initial two-year silk training contract. No one expected him to rush, but everyone knew he'd do it eventually.

Still, happy or not, Joan Woulbarowe would always be a fool, Isabel thought severely, as she emerged blinking into the summer sun from the dark mouth of St Thomas of Acre behind the fat doctor who'd been worshipping at the Italian chapel. What did Joan think she was doing, wandering round the City on a Sunday morning, warbling away in her fluent bad Italian to Lombards and drawing attention to herself? She was supposed to stay out of harm's way at Westminster.

Isabel caught up and tapped Joan Woulbarowe on the shoulder, interrupting whatever cheerful comment she'd been making to the Italian. Dr Gigli was a priest and medical man, not a merchant, so there was less immediate danger that Joan's sudden display of knowledge of Italian would cause any market gossip, but it was best to send Joan on her way quickly in any case.

Joan looked startled – though, Isabel thought grimly, not half-guilty enough at her own indiscretion.

'Did you have a message for Mistress Claver, Joan?' Isabel said, flashing a warning with her eyes.

'Oh, no, Mistress Isabel,' Joan answered innocently, 'I was just going to visit my Auntie Rose in Lad Lane. She's broken her ankle. She likes to see me on a Sunday.'

Isabel sighed. 'Well, run along,' she said, and Joan fluttered anxious, uncomprehending eyes at her before turning away.

'*Bexon' ndar caxa*,' she said politely to Dr Gigli, bobbing as she went. '*Ah, la vita l'è na fraxe interóta. S-ciào vostro*,' he replied, equally courteously.

Isabel stood uncertainly, watching. Dr Gigli stayed where he was, too, watching Joan's back recede. 'It is a long time I do not see Joan,' he said with warmth. 'Her aunt used to work in my house.'

Isabel smiled in a 'very-interesting-but-I-must-rush' way, but the plump Italian with the intrigued expression wasn't letting her go that easily. He turned his pot belly her way.

'She has been learning Italian, I see.'

Isabel quailed inside. But she put a confiding, knowing, slightly leering look on her face. 'She's in love,' she said.

'So I've heard.' He nodded, up and down, up and down, so that his double chins wobbled into one another. Gaining confidence – it was so nearly the truth of why Joan was learning Italian – she embroidered her story by adding, 'with a Lucchese, they say', at the same time as Dr Gigli said something himself.

She only realised what he'd been saying, and how definitely he'd been saying it, when it was too late: 'With a Venetian, I can hear. She's talking Venetian.'

'*El maestro de léngoa pì sicuro xe l'uso,*' he added thoughtfully. 'Usage is the best teacher of language.'

Isabel cursed herself. Why hadn't she shut up? She was more of a fool than Joan. She smiled wider and shook her head innocently. 'Oh, I wouldn't know. A Lucchese – that's just what I heard,' she gabbled, aware she was sounding foolish. 'But maybe a Venetian. I won't contradict you. I expect you can tell, can't you? Different accents, words . . .'

He was looking at her again now, squinting against the sun. 'There are not so many Venetians in London,' he said consideringly. 'Just the Conterini and their people. And me. And your friend Goffredo D'Amico, of course.' Isabel nodded, politely, desperate to move away. 'Although,' he added, 'there is always talk of others.'

'I must go,' she said, simpering uneasily.

'Perhaps you've heard the rumours yourself? That King Edward wrote a licence for Italians to teach silk weaving here? Venetians? Signor Mancini has been saying for years that he heard that at court, from the scrivener of', he crossed himself, 'the late Lord Hastings.'

She looked down. He gestured up at St Thomas', still smiling. 'Since your servant speaks my language so well, you may know the Venetian saying yourself: *La mé religion xe sercar la verità 'nte la vita e la vita 'nte la verità.* My religion is to seek out truth in life and life in truth.'

359

She shook her head, trying to keep the smile on her face.

'We also say,' he continued urbanely, *'Juteme a capir quel che ve digo e ve lo speigarò mejo*: help me to understand what I am saying, and I will explain it better.'

He held her gaze. She looked blankly back. 'There's even a rumour that your Signore D'Amico has been importing looms from Venice,' he added. His chins rippled again. 'Not that there's any sign of any such thing actually happening. Still, you know what we Venetians are like – we love gossip. What would life be without a good rumour, eh!'

And he threw back his head and bellowed with laughter. Isabel laughed too; bowed and walked away, still smiling prettily. It was only when she turned off Cheapside to walk through the market that she saw Dr Gigli still standing outside the church. He wasn't laughing any more, but he was still looking her way.

But she put Dr Gigli out of her mind when she got back to the quiet of Westminster. He was so far away. And she had too much else to worry about.

What she'd found herself thinking about, most of every day and even in the night, when she woke up, tossing and turning, was how to get the Princess to discuss Dickon. She'd find something out that way, at least, wouldn't she? She'd thought of so many ways to get that conversation going; but they all seemed contrived.

She knew – felt – there was something going on. The whispers she overheard, through half-closed bedchamber doors at the Princess's Palace rooms, were quick and intent. She just couldn't tell if they were connected with Dickon. Once she heard a doubtful mutter of, 'You'd think ten drops of laudanum a day would fell an ox,' before the Princess came out to the parlour to greet her.

It had been a female voice speaking, though so low-pitched she couldn't be sure it had been the Princess's; but what could those words mean? Dowager Elizabeth Woodville had taken to flashing in and out of the fittings, inspecting Isabel's sewing with her old queenly demeanour, breathing through a nose which, though beautiful, always had the white flecks of suppressed anger in it. She was waiting for something.

Isabel was tacking on a sleeve lace, miserably aware of Elizabeth's elegant column of a neck just a few inches away, when she finally plucked up courage to find out more.

'Your lovely crucifix . . . your gift from His Majesty,' she murmured, and Elizabeth fluttered a hand towards it: a lovely hand with white, smooth skin, glittering with rings.

'. . . It reminds me of what I've heard people saying . . .' Isabel went on, and she was aware of Elizabeth's sharpening of attention without needing to look up.

'. . . about His Majesty's intentions if, God forbid, God takes Her Majesty the Queen to Himself . . .'

Elizabeth said nothing, but her narrow nostrils flared white; how like her mother she'd become.

Isabel blurted: 'They're saying he might take it into his head to marry you next.'

She was miserably aware that she hadn't got her opening gambit right, even before she saw Elizabeth's green eyes move down to fix consideringly on her own lowered head. There was a flicker of what she thought might be amusement on the Princess's face.

Gently, Elizabeth said: 'You seem to be taking a great interest in his intentions . . .' And she raised one eyebrow and let the faintest of smiles come onto her lips.

Isabel widened her eyes, hoping she looked innocent rather than alarmed. The Princess's tone was cooler and more knowing than she'd anticipated. 'Oh no,' she muttered hastily, 'I just thought . . . you'd . . . appreciate being forewarned.'

The Princess nodded. 'Thank you,' she said, ending the conversation.

Isabel's mouth was so dry it felt as though she'd been eating ashes. Had the Princess become so sharply aware of another woman's interest in Dickon because she too was in love? Isabel stepped around her client to begin working on the laces for the other shoulder, and as she moved she noticed Elizabeth's hand flutter back up to the red winking eye of the cross round her neck.

Winter set in early that year. By the first Friday in September, the wind outside was already heavy with the rot of wet leaves and the threat of snow; inside the Palace, the smell of fish frying in the kitchens hung in the air.

The word was the King was on his way south.

Isabel and the princesses were putting together the finished sections of the altarpiece that Isabel had had made up in the City and brought back. Dowager Elizabeth Woodville was going to offer the cloths to the Abbot, who'd afforded her so much hospitality, as a Christmas gift of thanks.

Elizabeth hadn't settled to the work. She was restless. When she'd seen the silkwoman walk in, she'd just nodded and flown off to her sisters' bedchambers – the chambers all opened on to the same reception room – chirruping at them from the doorways to come out and finish the work they'd started. Then she'd called to Isabel: 'I have a letter to finish; I'll join you shortly,' and vanished.

Isabel was left alone with the younger girls, who didn't much like the idea of sewing up panels they were only pretending to have embroidered themselves, but who at least hadn't altogether lost the habit of confiding. So she sewed. They talked. She listened.

362

'Our mother is so happy to be back at court . . .'

'She's even started writing to Uncle Dorset . . .'

'He's her son . . . our half-brother . . . her favourite, we think . . . she misses him . . .'

'She's told him it's quite safe here now, after all . . .'

'She wants him to desert Henry Tudor . . .'

'And come home . . .'

'And he's thinking about it . . .'

'It's miserable in Britanny, he says . . .'

'Cold and tense . . .'

'So he says he might come . . .'

'And we're wondering if he'll be here by Christmas.'

She smiled, for their happiness but also for the shiver of hope in her own heart. Perhaps that was what all the whispering and letters whisked away when she got too close had been about all along; perhaps the plotting had been as innocent as these children's stories; perhaps there'd been no reason for her to worry. The Queen wasn't dead, for all the gloomy rumours in the markets. Dickon didn't need a new wife. The Queen would get better. The rebels would creep back from abroad, like Dorset. He'd regain his old confidence; get over his grief; lose his fears. She just needed to keep faith.

The children got bored before the work was done. One by one they lisped their excuses and went back to their rooms. Isabel carried on sewing, alone, feeling more peaceful than she had all summer. She just needed faith, she thought; everything would be all right. Have faith, she found herself whispering, in time with her stitches. Have faith.

A shadow moved nearby. Male footsteps stopped a few paces away. She didn't recognise them; it must be a servant. She didn't look up.

The footsteps moved quietly away. It wasn't a servant. The man had spurs that clinked. Looking past her needle at the ground, she saw mud on his boots. The spurs were golden.

With a shock, she realised whose boots these were. This was how they'd first met, wasn't it? In a church, by candle-light, with the spurs glinting.

There was a silence the length of a held breath. He'd always had the gift of stillness.

Her first instinct, before she even looked up, was to surrender to the tide of happiness flooding over her. She'd been waiting for months to feel his hand on the curve of her back again; the deep, comforting, heel-of-the-hand caress she'd made her life. Concern on his thin, dark face, in his narrow eyes, which needn't be hard. The silken bass voice murmuring, 'I've missed you.' And now he was here.

The things she hadn't realised she'd been planning to say all summer were on her lips now. She'd say: 'I'm sorry.' She'd say: 'I took no account of your grief.' She'd say: 'I reacted wrongly,' and: 'I will always love you.' They never talked of love. She'd say anything to make it right.

The weight she'd been carrying for so long was miracu-lously rising from her shoulders. Everything could be mended, she thought blissfully: everything. She looked up.

But none of what she'd imagined happened.

When their eyes did meet, she found him poised, taut and still and dark as ever. But his expression was guarded. His eyes were hooded. There wasn't even a ghost of a smile on his lips. She thought: he's embarrassed. She realised, hotly: embarrassed I'm here.

She realised: He's come to see Elizabeth first.

He bowed slightly. She'd never seen him in court clothes; in smooth-fitting hose; in a beautifully cut, black velvet tunic with gold embroidery and a jewelled crucifix swinging from it; in an elaborate mulberry hat. He didn't remove the hat.

'Good day,' he said quietly, but his eyes slid away.

'You're here,' she said. It sounded stupid. But she didn't understand. Why hadn't he sent her a message?

He looked around at all the open doorways. Nodded, rather sadly.

'To see the lady Elizabeth,' he said, in the kind of firm but gentle voice people use when breaking bad news.

Beseechingly, she put a hand out; her eyes were so full of heat and wetness she could hardly see him. She couldn't bear it.

He caught the hand. Clasped it in both his. 'Isabel,' he muttered; and when she somehow managed to open her eyes and look piteously up at him, stripped of every shred of pride and self-respect she'd ever laid claim to, she saw pain in his eyes too.

'I was coming to you, too,' he whispered indecisively. 'Truly.' She could see he didn't know how to placate her – not here, where anyone might come in at any time.

But he hadn't come to her first. Her mind kept coming back to that. He always came to the Red Pale before the Palace. The only reason he could have to avoid meeting her this time was that he did intend to marry Elizabeth – and, worse, that he loved Elizabeth – and didn't want to have to explain himself to Isabel. Isabel knew him too well to be deceived. He must have realised she'd see through him if he tried to lie.

Nothing else made sense.

'It's not that I don't want . . .' he whispered. He was having trouble getting the next word out. His teeth were clenched. He shut his eyes. '. . . you.' He squeezed her hand till she thought her bones would break. 'You know I do. But I need this.'

There was no time for more. Low though their voices were, Elizabeth had heard something. She came dancing out through her doorway with sunshine on her white-peach

365

cheeks and, with more charm than decorum, half-ran over the flagstones towards her uncle.

Hastily, Dickon dropped Isabel's hand at the first sound from the bedchamber. Then he turned to his niece and clasped her hands instead. As he bowed to her, Isabel saw the look he gave Elizabeth – a look of utter, devoted enchantment; nothing like the amused way his eyes crinkled at her. Then it was gone, while he swept his hat down, revealing the rumpled black hair that Isabel wanted, more than ever before, to run her fingers through; the head she knew, in that instant, she'd never touch again.

The Princess fluttered; looking beautiful. Turning uncertainly towards Isabel, whose presence she'd just remembered. 'This is my . . . embroiderer . . . Mistress Claver,' she murmured to him, as if drawing his attention to the presence of a servant. 'His Majesty,' she added, over Isabel's head.

'Your Majesty,' she said, head down, so no one could see her clenching her teeth. 'I was just leaving.'

'No,' the Princess said politely, 'please stay. Don't hurry. Finish the work before you go.' She turned to Dickon, and slipped her arm through his. Dully, Isabel watched the two arms, one black, one a gleaming blue-green, twine together. 'I was hoping His Majesty might take me for a stroll anyway . . . ?'

He bowed again and walked his niece out. Neither of them looked back. The Princess was giggling in a breathy, girlish way. His head was bowed towards her.

Isabel sat and listened to their footsteps recede until all she could hear was the beat of her own heart. She was remembering those two arms touching each other. She was staring at the roses and pearls on the altar cloth, but her eyes weren't focused; she could only see a vague whiteness, the colour of clouds and shrouds. She could still feel herself breathing, strangely calm. But she didn't understand how that could be, since her life had just ended.

No one else was there, so, methodically, obsessively, Isabel searched the rooms for more proof. It didn't take long. Elizabeth had left a letter out, only half-finished, in her private room.

Like a spy, Isabel scanned the page. The Princess had been writing to the Duke of Norfolk – Lord Howard's new title, a reward for helping Dickon take power last year.

In the letter, the Princess asked the Duke of Norfolk 'to be a mediator for me to the King, on behalf of the marriage propounded between us'.

The Princess called Dickon 'my only joy and maker in this world'.

The Princess wrote that she was the King's, in heart and thought.

The Princess had stopped and scratched out the last line of her draft. But Isabel could still make out what was underneath the petulant stabs of ink. The words Princess Elizabeth had thought better of writing had been: 'Winter is on us already, and I fear the Queen will never die.'

Feeling blanketed in an otherworldly white cloud, Isabel walked back to the Red Pale, wondering at how ordinary her rhythmic footfalls sounded, how steady her breathing.

'Forget him,' Will Caxton kept saying. 'We all make mistakes. Put it behind you. Let it go.' She could feel his hands patting ineffectually at her heaving shoulders. She could feel the rough wood of his kitchen table against her cheek. He seemed to have been saying the same thing for hours, and his voice was harder than his hands.

'I can't,' she snivelled or howled by turns, hating her weakness. She couldn't imagine a life without Dickon. What would be left?

Seriously, Caxton said: 'You must. Don't think you can play Jane to his Edward and not be scarred. He's not Edward. Edward might have been a sensualist; but he had a good heart, at least. He honestly loved Jane.'

Isabel was too flayed inside to feel the anger she should at being compared with Jane. She shouldn't have told Will that Dickon had never said he loved her; had never given her gifts. Perhaps that was why Will looked angry; he was such a soft man. He thought love should be hearts and flowers and frolics. He couldn't imagine it being the need she felt.

She just muttered, defiantly: 'But I don't want trou-badours and trinkets. That's not why . . . I'm not like Jane. I didn't want a king. He wasn't a king when I met him. I didn't even know who he was. He was just a man; one who showed me how to think; how to plan for success. When I had nothing else; when I was just an apprentice; when my father turned me away; I thought, all the time, for years, what would *he* do in my posi-tion? I modelled myself on him . . .' she sniffed. 'And if I lose him, and that, I'd lose what I've made myself. What would be left?'

Will said, impatiently, 'But you're not making sense. So what if he taught you chess? You're certainly not thinking strategically now. You're blinding yourself to your own needs. You're letting him hurt you. You're refusing to see the truth: that even if you love him, he's cold. Corrupt. Rotten to the core. You must know that. Don't let him corrupt you too.'

She shook her head, desperate to defend Dickon. 'But he's not,' she stammered. 'People say he's wicked. But he's not.'

The shadows from the candle flame lent Caxton's gentle features the sternness of an avenging angel. 'Look,' he said, 'this isn't the worst thing he's done, by a long way. I can see it would hurt you to find out he's fixing up a marriage to the niece he calls a bastard before his wife's even dead. But why are you so much more upset about this than anything else? You can't have just forgotten the rest, surely? Putting your sister in prison. Murdering her lover. Stealing the throne. Killing his nephews.'

'But he didn't, he didn't,' she sobbed defiantly. 'They're alive.'

Very gently, he said, 'How do you know?'

'Because the Princess told me.'

'And how does she know?'

'Because she got a letter from her brother. It's what made her come out of sanctuary.'

'And who delivered the letter to her?' Caxton asked.

Dickon. She didn't bother saying the word. She could see Will knew.

He nodded, as if she'd proved his point. 'You see,' he said kindly. 'If you believe that, he's corrupted you already.'

Caxton found a scrap of compassion for the Princess. 'She'd want to believe it – her mother too – because their only chance of becoming royal again is if she marries his crown. But you're better than that; there's no need for you to believe a lie. Try and think clearly. It makes no sense to break your heart over whether he's fallen in love with your Princess. What you should be worrying about is what he wants from you. He's never loved you; he just needed someone to approve of all his schemes and games and manoeuvrings for power; someone to make him feel he's not wicked. He is. He didn't even care enough about you not to persecute your sister when it suited him. Can't you see?'

'But,' she sobbed. It was all true; Will was right; Dickon's darkness was eating away at her. But she didn't care, as long as she could see him. Sometimes; somehow. 'He's all I have.'

That made Will angry. He stopped patting her shoulders. He stood up, pushing his stool back. He grabbed her wrists and pulled her up too. The pale eyes looking into hers were furious. She flinched.

'He's not all you have,' Caxton said loudly and quickly. 'That's nonsense. Nonsense. You're the heir to one of the best silk businesses in London. You have your weavers to look after. And you have us, to look after you. There's a lot in your life. Don't forget it.'

It would never be enough without Dickon.

But when Will saw the shame in Isabel's eyes at that thought, he stopped shaking her. He dropped her wrists and let her go back to her hopeless sobbing. She cried herself out.

In the end, in the quiet, he shook his own head. 'It's like a sickness, what you've got, isn't it?' he said. His voice was sad; but cold, too. 'Go home. Think about what I'm saying, Isabel. It's madness for you to love that man. Don't let him destroy you.'

There was frost on the bushes. The looms were just falling silent when she pushed her own door open. She could hear voices. Joan Woulbarowe's Andrea looked up and grinned. He was a wizened nut of a man. His teeth were as black as his bride's.

'Look, Mistress,' he said, beckoning her over. 'It is going very well. This cloth,' he pointed at the loom he'd been examining, where Joan sat bathed in evening light over a blue-green woven marvel of flowers and birds, 'is the first we can be proud to sell.'

Isabel couldn't focus on the cloth. It reminded her of the Princess's sleeve, rubbing against Dickon's arm. She thought she might be sick if she looked. So she smiled. It was a pale, grim excuse of a smile, but it cost her more effort than she'd have thought possible. 'Good,' she said faintly, feeling proud to be trying. 'Good. Good.'

'I am going to finish it with a gold thread in the selvage,' he said importantly, 'and the Claver seal. We can put it in the storehouse, ready for trading. God willing we will have twenty or thirty of this quality ready for sale by Passiontide.'

She said, 'Good. Good,' a few more times, then stopped.

He looked curiously at her. 'I believe we are about to be very successful,' he said.

She mumbled, 'Good', again.

He stared. 'Mistress Claver,' he said, 'are you feeling well?'

She could feel shivers down her back; aches in her arms and legs. What was she doing in this dark little house, with its walls swaying drunkenly in and out, with this dark little man she hardly knew?

'Not very well,' she muttered. 'I think . . . a chill coming on . . . lie down.'

He beckoned to Joan and Agnes, who hurried forward. Anxiously they bundled Isabel upstairs to the women's room, loosened her robe, and covered her with all the blankets they could find. Someone brought her broth.

She lay glassy-eyed, feeling far away from the bustle, wondering why she'd wanted this – why she'd ever thought weaving silk mattered, or that she'd be happy if she made this business work – when now she understood, with sickening simplicity, that happiness was somewhere quite different; somewhere she'd never go again.

17

It was Goffredo who fetched her back to London the next day. He came towards the end of most weeks anyway, talked over his team's progress, and took part in a hearty Lombard dinner. But as soon as he arrived on that December Saturday and heard Isabel was unwell, he was up the ladder and poking his head through the trapdoor and rushing over to poke his head through her curtains too.

She heard Will's voice downstairs, saying, carefully but anxiously, 'a chill . . . she's run down . . .' Will would never enter a woman's bedroom the way Goffredo was now doing – striding decisively in and taking charge. Will would be too embarrassed; and he was angry with her, in his quiet way.

She was glad it wasn't Will coming in now. She couldn't face him yet. She'd confided in him, but he'd only added to her guilt and shame; she wouldn't be able to look him in the eye until she'd thought how to do as he'd suggested. She needed to think. She was surprised at how relieved she felt to see the worry and affection on Goffredo's powerful features. Goffredo would cope with everything for her now. She could relax.

He did. He fretted with the sheets for a minute or two,

twitching at things, clearing away bowls and water jugs, plumping up her cushions. She lay limply and watched him. Then he twinkled at her from his laughter-lined eyes, and pinched her cheeks. 'We need to get some colour back in these,' he said briskly. Then he kissed her pinched cheeks. He did it chastely and with great kindness.

'You've been working too hard for too long, *cara*,' he said gently. 'We've all been telling you. You need a proper rest. I'm going to get them to bring you some food up now; and then, when you've eaten, we'll wrap you up warm and take you home to Alice.'

They sat in the wherry, with his arm protectively around her and his cloak around them both. There was snow in the air and black in the water. She was slumped into him; too tired to sit up straight and quietly enjoying his strength and warmth.

'You should marry me, you know,' he said. 'Joking apart. It's time someone looked after you.'

She was feverish. She let herself think about it. Running the weaving business with Goffredo, openly, from the house in Westminster; in a few months, once they'd registered at the Guildhall and proved they had goods of acceptable quality, defying the Italians and selling cloths in the selds and at the Prince's Wardrobe. Talking over the day's business together. He'd always be laughing, whatever they were doing. Dropping by to see Will Caxton, the neighbour, her friend again; taking the wherry to London on Sundays to spend the day with Alice and the Prattes. Goffredo was old but kind and funny and, now she came to look at him properly, for the first time in years, still handsome. She couldn't yet imagine making love with him, although she was trying, but at least the idea didn't appal her. She probably could. And she'd never care for Goffredo so much that it hurt.

It was time, after all. She'd be twenty-eight in a few months. The business would be registered. They could stop living a secret. Perhaps her life could be this simple. She could be Isabel Lambert Claver D'Amico, running a weavers' workshop in Westminster with her husband. It would be the same life, almost. She had to at least try to think about it. It might have been what God intended all along.

But it would be utterly different, too: life without Dickon. She'd never listen out for hooves or boys with messages. The tavern over the road would be just that again – a tavern. The Red Pale's upstairs room would be just the place the D'Amicos sent overflow guests to sleep in. She'd forget that its plaster and straw and honey sunlight had once meant happiness.

She sighed. The misery came back; the tears too. She wouldn't forget. 'You're probably right,' she snivelled into Goffredo's strong ribcage, grateful for his strength. Her head was pounding. 'About marrying.'

She didn't want to hurt his feelings by crying. She didn't know whether he'd take that as a possible yes or a probable no. She didn't even know which she meant. She didn't know what had got into her. But he just clicked his tongue and said soothingly: 'Don't even think about it now. Later; when you're better. Let's get you well first.'

The idea of marrying Goffredo went on bobbing up in Isabel's mind for weeks afterwards. While she lay blacked out in her bed in Catte Street, with the old women bringing her hot drinks and warming-pans and tucking her up; while a muted, expectant Christmas was observed; while she rode, in the last days of December, to Sutton on Derwent with a nervous Thomas Lynom, to wait with the astonishingly swollen Jane for her child to be born. During the blood and shouting and panic of the birth. Afterwards,

374

while she watched her sister hold her baby, a wrinkled girl, and noticed the tenderness in Jane's eyes and voice, a love that turned her bruised eyes and limp sweaty hair and pale skin and bloody linen and flabby stomach back into beauty.

Julyan had just a few fine strands of hair on her head. She had hypnotic round eyes: nothing like Jane's green colour, a paler blue than Thomas's. But she already had the beautiful profile of her father: a short straight nose, high cheekbones, perfect proportions, a generous mouth. When Thomas held her, he was transformed too.

I could do this too, Isabel would think. Perhaps. She kept experimenting with the thought, trying to find ways of healing herself of the gritty, grinding pain she carried with her. It didn't stop the blackness altogether to imagine herself married to Goffredo, holding a baby, being a merchant's wife. But it helped. It lightened her mood, at least, until it was no worse than a cheerless grey. If she did it, then later, much later, after a year, after five, perhaps ten, although she knew she'd never find happiness, she might at least find peace.

The Londoners all came for Candlemas; they were going to take Isabel back to London with them after the holy day. Jane was churched the day before the guests arrived, on 1 February, a month after the birth, so she could receive visitors again.

By then, Isabel wanted to go home. She'd had time to recover. She'd had time to reflect, too, though instead of taking Will's advice and trying to reason herself out of what she felt for Dickon, she'd just tried to convince herself she felt nothing. In Jane's house it was easy enough to make herself think she'd shut down the secret part of herself that dreamed and breathed Dickon; in Jane's house she slept heavily and woke up joyless but calm. But the idleness of her country existence was beginning to bore her. She told herself: I need to be busy. She was longing to talk about work. She wanted to get back to the weavers.

She'd persuaded herself everyone would only want to talk about the weaving project. So she was surprised by the adoring stares, the hush. Even from Alice Claver.

At least Goffredo looked at Isabel long enough to say, 'How thin you've got.' But she must have looked almost normal because no one else did anything but stare at Julyan. Even after the visitors' gifts were admired, after the baby's feeding and sleeping habits had been discussed, after the parents' happiness had been commented on and praise given to their choice of name, after the mystic of Norwich, Alice and William and Anne and Goffredo still had to be nudged into mentioning the workshop.

Isabel asked Alice directly: 'So when is the registration hearing at the Guildhall?' and Alice, rocking the baby, looked up absentmindedly, then back down to where tiny fingers were curling fiercely around her thumb.

'Right after Lady Day,' she said; then, almost whispering, 'when my Thomas was born, I couldn't believe those tiny fingers.'

Late March; seven weeks or so away. Isabel tried to catch Goffredo's eye, but he was also staring down as if he was about to devour the little scrap of flesh in her soft linen wrapping, flexing her toes. 'Goffredo,' she said, and he looked up. 'How many cloths will be ready by Lady Day?'

'Oh,' he said, 'enough. Thirty?'

He wanted to go on playing with the baby again. 'Goffredo,' she said patiently, and he looked up again, a little guilty. He said, trying to satisfy her properly this time with a thorough answer:

'If we stock them at Alice's shops; if we price them attractively, say half the sale price of Italian cloths, they'll

376

probably shift fast. Say they take till midsummer – St John's Eve. Three months. We can have thirty more ready by then.'

She nodded, longing to feel brisk and businesslike and in charge of something again. 'And we can start taking on more apprentices once we're registered, too. Get all the looms you've brought working.'

'Twenty looms; we've been talking about taking on fourteen more women,' he agreed, concentrating on plans with her, not on the baby. 'As soon as we have the registration,' he added, 'so we can recruit without worrying about the Conterini and Salviati.'

He was looking enthusiastic now; his warmth for the dream they'd all cherished for so long was there on his face again. She sighed with relief: Goffredo, her partner. Willing to humour her even though they both knew she was, childishly, suddenly jealous of her sister's newborn. He was a good man. He'd probably be a good husband too.

Isabel had thought she wanted to be off. A bleak impatience to get home sustained her through the long, jerky clip-clop back down the Great North Road. But when she saw Moorgate looming up ahead, beyond the butts and the vegetable gardens, and the City rooftops behind, she began to remember what her dread had felt like. Her holiday from heartbreak was over now. She couldn't lie in bed, pretending to be ill, refusing to face reality. She'd have to go back to work. To the selds; the Guildhall; the silk house.

She had a headache like a punch in the eyes. She didn't want to see the tapestries in her room, the expensive bedcurtains, the embroidered cushions, the patterns, the gay splashes of lilady and mulberry and applebloom, the scents of lavender and rose. She wanted straw and plain plaster; but, if she was sensible, she'd never have that again.

It was only once she'd walked into that familiar, dusty, claustrophobic bedroom at Catte Street, and been overwhelmed by how overstuffed it was with pillows and memories, that she realised that now she'd also have to go back to sewing for the Princess.

Go to Westminster. Face Will Caxton's eyes. Go to the Palace. Where Dickon might be.

The thought didn't make her weep. She was past that. But she went to the window and stood with her cheek against the cool glass and metal. Burning. Gulping in air.

'Now,' a familiar voice boomed behind her, and Alice Claver swept into the room, without knocking, a tornado trailing draperies. 'There's something I want to ask you.'

Isabel closed her eyes. It was too much. She couldn't face Alice as well as these feelings.

'Another of these boys has just come,' Alice was saying, and her clever eyes were looking carefully into Isabel's. 'With a message about firewood.'

Isabel opened her eyes.

'What do you mean, another?' she asked, too quickly.

Alice nodded to herself, two or three times, as if her own question had been answered.

'There've been a couple, over the winter,' Alice said. 'While you've been ill, and away. Which is odd, wouldn't you say? Since we all know Will Caxton's cook buys the firewood, not you.'

Isabel hung her head. She was ashamed to meet Alice Claver's eyes. She didn't know what to say. Nor did she want Alice to see the joy coursing through her, as fierce and stinging as if there was acquavitae in her veins. He'd sent for her. He'd sent for her.

Alice sat heavily down on the bed. She patted the place next to her for Isabel.

'I'm not going to try to ferret it out of you, you know,' Alice said gruffly. 'But I'd be a fool not to know what's going on.'

Isabel felt hot blood staining her face and neck; but there was relief mixed up in her agony of embarrassment. Alice nodded again. 'There,' Isabel's mistress said, in a not unfriendly voice. 'I was right. I'm not just an old fool, am I?'

Isabel even managed to answer. 'You were never a fool,' she got out, with reluctant admiration.

'I wasn't always old, either,' Alice said energetically. 'And there's nothing I don't know about girls getting their hearts broken.'

She spread her big hands out, put one on each large thigh, and leaned comfortably if inelegantly forward. There was a nostalgic look in her eyes. 'You won't have heard this from Caxton or Anne or William, but back when we were apprenticed to Master Large, right here in this house . . .' she began, with gusto.

The voices inside Isabel's head were still singing. 'Dickon sent for me; he sent for me.'

But she turned her face towards Alice Claver, and set herself to listen.

'. . . I didn't know what had hit me,' Alice Claver was saying, and her big red face was gentler than Isabel had ever seen it. 'The master himself, kissing me . . . It was madness, of course. Where could it go, with the mistress in the house too, watching him like a hawk, and the other apprentices with me at every moment of the day and night? There wasn't even any*where* for us to go to be together. We had the odd scuffle in a store cupboard. Sometimes we'd manage to meet on a street corner. And I think we once took a walk round Moorfields. Stupid, really. But there was a whole year when it was Heaven and Hell rolled into one. I couldn't think of anything else. I was like a thing possessed.'

She looked ruefully at Isabel. Then she snorted with laughter. 'But do you know what?' she added. 'Once I'd got over it, I couldn't think what had got into me for so long. He was just a fat old man with a bald patch. A dear old thing.'

It was extraordinary enough to grab Isabel's full attention. She could hardly believe what she was hearing. She'd never once heard Alice Claver talk like this, or about this; or the others, come to that. They couldn't ever have known.

Drawing closer, wondering what Alice Claver must have looked like before she got so broad and red-faced; trying, and almost managing, to imagine her a slip of a thing, kissing someone in a store cupboard, Isabel asked softly: 'But how did you get over it?'

'Work,' Alice Claver replied, with a snap of lips. 'Of course. It's the only way. He sent me to Antwerp for the fair. Richard went too. We spent a month there. Worked like dogs. I was much too busy to be pining for love. We did our first big deal there. The most exciting moment of my life. Made . . . the other thing . . . seem plain foolishness; which it had been. We went out celebrating. Betrothed before I knew where I was.'

She shifted one of her beefy hands on to Isabel's leg and gave it a firm pat.

'It's time we got you back to work too,' Alice said heartily. 'There's going to be a lot to do between now and Lady Day if we're to get the registration through in good order.'

Isabel nodded eagerly. She was full of energy again; she'd be going to Westminster, maybe as soon as tomorrow. She was so touched by Alice's opening of her heart that she felt dishonest to be thinking the way she was; but in her heart of hearts she knew that the first thing she'd do when she got there would be to find a way to see Dickon.

'But,' Alice went on, patting Isabel's leg even harder – almost a slap – 'I don't think you're well enough to go traipsing off to Westminster for half the week just yet.' She looked hard at Isabel; and Isabel realised the older silkwoman was one step ahead of her again. Alice had guessed exactly what was on her mind.

'Goffredo can handle things at the silk house until the registration,' Alice said briskly. 'And I'm going to send word to your Lady Darcey, too, that you're still convalescing – you were really ill, you know; we were worried. You're not up to Palace jaunts yet.'

Isabel opened her mouth, then closed it. She could see Alice wouldn't brook dissent.

She didn't mind. She'd do this for Alice. She'd bide her time when it came to Dickon. There'd be a moment soon enough. She had the strength and endurance for anything, as long as she could have hope.

The silkwoman heaved herself up and clapped Isabel on the shoulder. 'We need you in London right now. We'll think again about letting you go back to Westminster – later. Once we've got through Lady Day.' Despite her gruff words, there was a very soft look in her eye as she swept off towards the corridor.

The thirty silk cloths were brought to Alice's house a week before Lady Day, ironed flat and stored carefully inside a chest. The cloths, each marked with the Claver seal and the gold thread through the selvage, were stowed safely in an anteroom in the warmth of the silk storeroom at Catte Street when the summons to the Guildhall came.

The letter was for Goffredo – a demand to present himself at the City government centre tomorrow. It was delivered to Catte Street, even though everyone knew Goffredo always put up at the Prattes'. Alice opened it – it was her house, after all – and, once she'd read it, sent it round to Goffredo. It wasn't for her to worry, yet; if a problem arose she had faith that the Guildhall would always come to the right decision. But she had no idea why the City government would want to see Goffredo now. They were all curious.

Goffredo was at Catte Street within an hour, looking baffled.

'Have they brought the registration hearing forward?' he said. 'Is that it?'

'It can't be that,' Alice Claver replied. 'Or we'd all be called. This is just for you. You aren't in any trouble over any other business, are you? Short weights, behind on your documents? Problems with cargoes?'

He shook his head. 'Nothing,' he said. 'Of course.'

The Prattes came later. But they didn't know anything either. William Pratte had given up most of his Guildhall committees, except the venturers' one on trade overseas. He hadn't heard of any reason why the Mayor would want to interview Goffredo. Anne hadn't heard anything in the selds.

It was worrying, all the same. Especially now, with the registration hearing so close.

Isabel said: 'The letter came here. Perhaps we should all go tomorrow?'

Goffredo looked grateful. But William Pratte cautiously shook his head.

Isabel went anyway, without telling the others. It seemed right. She waited in the street for Goffredo the next morning. He turned up outside the Guildhall in his best dark velvets, washed and shaved, with only a tic in his jaw giving away his nervousness.

His eyes widened when he saw her. '*Cara Isabella,*' he said gently.

'Well, I was free this morning,' she muttered,

embarrassed by her own gesture. She linked her blue silk arm through his black velvet one, as if they were a real couple, and stepped quickly forward.

She gasped when she entered the chamber. It was hot. Packed. Full of shifting bodies and eyes. It looked as though every liveryman in London was there – except William Pratte and Will Caxton. She could even see her father, with his noble profile and his eager smile, standing right behind the new Mayor, William Stokker – a draper. John Lambert must have come to London specially. How had the Prattes not known?

Goffredo glanced at her. Neither of them understood.

They sat at the table on the dais, on one side of the Mayor and his men, watched by many dozens of eyes.

Then another delegation walked through the door opposite. The men who sat down at the other end of the table were all in black velvet. They had dark skins and dark hair and strong features and expensive jewels. And they were familiar. She'd seen them pray at the Lucchese chapel at St Thomas of Acre. She knew some of their names. Dr Gigli. Jacopo Salviati himself, towering over the rest. Two young men from the Conterini great place in Botolph Lane. And two others whose names she didn't know, but who she recognised from the markets: more merchant strangers from Italy.

'Keep calm,' she whispered to Goffredo, whose eyes were flickering from one Lombard face to another.

'This is a trap,' Goffredo whispered back. 'We've walked right into it.'

It wasn't an Italian who presented the case against Goffredo. It was a minor merchant from Southampton called John Burdean, a badly put together sack of a man, full of spit and resentment. Isabel could see from the way his and Goffredo's eyes narrowed when they saw each other that they must have once done business together, and fallen out.

The blood was pounding so loudly in her head that she could hardly hear what John Burdean was saying. Concentrate, she told herself, and locked her eyes on Master Burdean's angry paunch and bony legs and thin, hard voice. She couldn't meet his eyes.

He seemed to be saying Goffredo owed him money. Large sums. Debts stretching back years; money even Isabel could tell Goffredo couldn't really owe in full, because some of the purported debts had allegedly been contracted in Southampton at times when Isabel knew Goffredo to have been in Venice.

But the Italians were nodding as if they had checked these charges among themselves and found them true. Now one Lombard after another was standing up to add a charge. Goffredo had stolen a silk damask cloth from the Conterini warehouse and fraudulently sold it to John Burdean, telling him it was a cloth he'd imported himself. Goffredo had trespassed in the Salviati shop with intent to steal again.

They're making the whole thing up, Isabel realised. They've dug up some nasty little man with a grudge; and they're using him to smear Goffredo's name. If there are doubts about Goffredo, he won't be able to operate in London any more. And we'll have trouble registering the weaving business next week. They don't know how far we've come; how near we are to registering. But they're trying to close us down before we begin.

The thought made her angry, but only for a moment. Then she felt her breathing getting tighter and more controlled; her mind beginning to work out responses. The Lombards weren't going to win so easily.

Each Lombard accusation was followed by more buzzing and whispering. The merchants of London didn't know whether to be surprised or angry. D'Amico didn't look an out-and-out villain, after all; most people in the room had done business with him and didn't recall being cheated. Then again, you could never tell with Lombards. They were sly. D'Amico had stooped low to steal from his own kind, in a foreign land. Who could say what other crimes had gone undetected? Their faces darkened.

The Mayor was standing up. 'Having heard the charges brought against you,' he was saying, and Goffredo, strangely white for someone so sallow, was swaying in his chair. 'In the circumstances,' the Mayor was saying, 'I have no alternative but to place you,' he paused before the foreign name, then went roundly on, 'you, George D'Amico,' and Goffredo flinched, 'under arrest, pending a full investigation and trial.'

The Italians allowed themselves small smiles. John Burdean was sweating. He grinned and wiped his hands on his legs. He stood up as if it were all over, then sat down again. The London merchants muttered and waited. The Mayor was talking again; saying, 'Your right to trade in this city is suspended until further notice; your goods are impounded and must be handed in. You may continue to reside at the home of William Pratte but must report daily to the Guildhall . . .'

Isabel wanted to whisper to Goffredo, but she couldn't get him to meet her eye. He was frozen. She touched his arm to get his attention. Still staring down at his hands, he muttered: 'They've got us. They moved first. They've got us.' Then a gabble of Italian and a flash of eyes. She didn't want to know what it meant. It wouldn't be helpful.

'Goffredo,' she whispered, wishing Robert Lynom were there too, 'can I answer?'

He looked puzzled. 'Them?' he hissed. 'Fight them?'

She nodded briskly; she'd take that as permission, she decided.

'Your Honours,' she called loudly as the Mayor wound up, and the room went quiet. The eyes were all on her now. Among them she was aware of her father's look of horror. Taking a deep breath, hearing her voice tremble, she went on: 'Speaking on behalf of Master D'Amico, who is the most trusted foreign trading partner of the House of Claver, which I represent, I want to draw the attention of the worshipful company to certain facts about Master D'Amico's business that have not been mentioned by any of the speakers so far – and may shed light on the allegations made in this room today . . .'

The real reason Goffredo D'Amico was in the dock today, she told them, was not because he'd cheated John Burdean or the London Lombards. She paused, waiting for the eddy of interest to subside. It wasn't so hard once she'd started. She was scared, but exhilarated too.

'Your Honours. Master D'Amico has cooperated with the House of Claver in bringing to the City of London a group of Venetian silk weavers,' she announced, with her heart racing. 'These weavers have been teaching English craftswomen how to weave cloths of damask, velvets, cloth of gold and silver and other cloths of silk,' – she paused, and looked Dr Gigli straight in the eye – 'for the past two years.'

There were gasps at this. There were murmurs of 'two years!' and 'silk weaving!' and 'in London!' and 'where?'. She felt excitement all around. She couldn't stop to see where the gasps had come from; but she hoped some might have been from dismayed Lombard mouths.

'The training is nearly complete. Very soon,' she went on, 'our English weavers – London women – will be producing and selling whole silk cloths as lovely, as accomplished – and as valuable – as anything made in Venice or Florence.'

Was that something like a cheer? She ignored it. She said:

'So important is this work for England, and for the City of London in particular, that the King himself supports it. The weavers and their pupils are housed and provided for by the high command of His Majesty; from the royal purse. His Majesty understands, as well as you will all understand, how crucial acquiring this new skill is for England – how it will enhance English trade and boost English prestige . . .'

She looked round, and fixed the impassive Lombards with a steely eye. 'In fact, your Honours,' she went on, 'the only losers from the transfer of knowledge Master D'Amico has made possible will be the other merchant strangers of London. We Londoners may soon start thinking their Venetian and Florentine and Sienese and Lucchese cloths are too expensive – or coarse – or ugly – compared with London's own homemade silk cloths. The merchant strangers you see before you – our honoured Lombard guests – are going to have to work much harder than before to make the same profits from selling us their silk cloths.' There was definitely a cheer in the air now; her audience was getting her drift all right. 'No wonder they're smarting, your Honours,' she finished. 'No wonder they're angry with Master D'Amico.'

She smiled, and a wave of hoots and laughs and gasps and claps broke over the room. The crowd was with her. Goffredo was standing tall. The Italians did not smile.

From out of the corner of her eye, she noticed her father's face. There was astonished respect on it, something she'd longed for years to see. She only wished she had time to enjoy it, now it was there. But she had to keep thinking.

After a whispered consultation with the men around him, the Mayor leaned forward.

'Are you suggesting, Mistress Claver,' he said distantly, 'that the actions of debt and trespass taken out against Master D'Amico today are', he wrinkled his nose, 'false?'

Isabel stood tall. Her cheeks were pink. Her voice rang out loud and proud. 'I am, your Honour,' she answered, and was aware of another sudden buzz of talk, and some frankly vicious looks from the Italian end of the table. She also noticed Goffredo, staring at her with admiration; shaking his head ruefully at her impudence; beginning to grin. He'd kiss his hand at her in a minute. She liked him so much that she nearly laughed.

Triumphantly, she went on: 'I'm no lawyer, your Honour. But I believe Master D'Amico and his lawyer, Master Robert Lynom, will contact you shortly to ask for a corpus cum causa to be directed to the Sheriff of London. We want the motives of the plaintiffs in this case investigated. And we want all charges against Master D'Amico dropped.'

Isabel and Goffredo were nearly mobbed on the way back to Catte Street. Everyone in the Mercery wanted to know more about the mystery weavers.

'Soon,' Isabel said calmly in answer to all the questions, nudging the beaming Goffredo through the crowd. 'We will have more to tell you soon.'

When her own father appeared, she dropped a deep curtsey and kissed his hand, as a daughter should. She didn't ask what had brought him back to London for the Guildhall meeting. He didn't explain. But when he said, a little hesitantly, 'So, you've set up a weaving venture . . . ?' and paused, hoping for a dutiful filial answer, she only nodded her head sideways at Goffredo and said, as she had to the others, 'Soon; we'll have more to tell you soon.' But she put a hand on his arm – that soft, beseeching movement Jane used so often, to convey helpless goodwill – and added, 'I promise,' and then, 'dear Father.' And she was surprised to see a timid look of pleasure in his eyes.

She couldn't say more. She wasn't sure it was wise to let the Italian merchants know quite how close the Clavers were to succeeding. The news was out now; telling had got a reprieve for Goffredo while the Lombards' claim and his counter-claim were looked into. Registering the weaving business together would still be impossible till the Mayor was satisfied Goffredo was honest; but at least she'd created a mood of sympathy for him, and raised the question of what the other Lombards were really up to. If all else failed, she could go to the King for justice. She thought she'd get it, whatever else came between her and Dickon. Yet the thought of approaching him made her quail. She didn't want to let it into her mind yet. She thought the Clavers could win by themselves.

Still, she thought, it would be prudent to choke off any more talk for now. She moved off, linking arms with Goffredo so they could step through the crowd together.

'You're not', Goffredo said, with the broadest of smiles, squeezing her arm with his, 'afraid of gossip? About you and me?'

She grinned. She could hardly remember feeling this on top of life. Everything seemed easy all of a sudden. 'No,' she said, deciding what would come next on the spur of the moment. 'Why? Everyone thinks we'll marry anyway, sooner or later. This is only what they've been expecting. It makes sense.' Not quite believing she meant it, he laughed incredulously, then, when she didn't laugh back, tried to pull her to him. Gently, she pushed his chest. She went on: 'Not now. We can talk after all this is over.'

She'd forgotten the painful longing for a while, when she'd been on her feet addressing the Mayor. She'd been floating; her feet hardly touching the ground; her mind and mouth full of inspiration. But the pain came back as her breathing slowed down; as the front door creaked open and they stepped back into the familiar gloom of inside. Her unglamorous, tiring, dull pain: an ache, her patient hope, endlessly deferred.

She sat and said nothing while Goffredo – who was full of inspiration and excitement himself now, waving his arms and talking nineteen to the dozen – told and retold the story of the ambush for Alice and Anne and William. 'You should have heard Isabel,' he said. 'I cut a pitiful figure at first. But she was magnificent.'

'You didn't,' she said, 'you were braver than I could have been. Dignified. You didn't flinch once. You kept your head.' But she cut short the rest of his generous praise. She didn't look at the quiet hurt in his eyes, though she admired the manful way he banished it. She didn't want to sit up late and eat and talk. 'I'm not hungry,' she said. 'I'm tired. It's been a long day.'

She dreamed she was in the tavern room. It was empty except for the unmade bed. The sheets smelled of Dickon. Then she saw he was there, after all. Asleep: a dark shoulder; rumpled black hair. Suddenly she was honey and sunlight. She tiptoed to the bed. She was going to kiss his forehead, very tenderly. The first thing he'd see when his eyes opened would be her.

She woke up as she leaned towards him. She didn't know where she was or what had changed. When she realised she was at Catte Street, alone, she cried. It was worse to have dreamed of happiness, but woken up, than not to have had the dream at all. No one saw or heard her cry. The house was asleep. It was dark. The full moon had set.

If Isabel woke up to the understanding that loving Dickon meant she'd never be able to bring herself to marry

Goffredo, or anyone else, the others woke up with nerves. Alice called the Prattes and Goffredo to Catte Street. 'We must be very careful from now on,' she said sternly. 'More careful. They'll be watching us like hawks.'

Anne Pratte breathed out through her teeth. She said: 'Ooh! It still gives me goose bumps to think how close they came yesterday to shutting us down.'

She always sounded as though she were enjoying herself. Alice ignored her. 'They'll be looking for the workshop,' Alice went on, looking into one face after another. 'It's not going to be that hard to find. That's what we need to shut down.'

William Pratte nodded. 'You're right,' he said, sounding relieved. 'We should stop till we have the registration sorted out. We have the first cloths ready. Let's dismantle the looms. Get the weavers out of Westminster. Lie low until all this blows over.'

Working out how to quietly vanish, then reappear, was harder than it seemed. The elaborate plan Anne Pratte proposed began with Isabel going to Westminster, as she'd done every Thursday before her illness, to spend the night in the house before her Friday session with the Princess.

Alice shook her head. Isabel said falteringly: 'But I've been ill. It's months since I've been to the Palace. They won't be expecting me.' She was suddenly scared of being swept up again in that other world, when all this was so urgent.

'You're better now,' Anne Pratte said firmly, ignoring Alice's mute warnings. 'Who's going to believe you're still convalescing after what you did today? The whole City will be talking about it. It's time to start again. The Princess is your best patron. You shouldn't lose her.'

Reluctantly, Alice nodded. It had taken Isabel a while to recognise this, but she usually let Anne Pratte decide what should happen at moments of crisis.

Anne went on setting out her plan. As soon as Isabel reached the house on Thursday evening, she was to tell the silk teams they were going on holiday. She'd leave them on Friday morning, taking apart the looms and stacking them against the walls. She'd go to the Palace; return to the house; and spend Friday night at Westminster.

The others, meanwhile, would leave London one by one and make their separate ways to Westminster on Friday: Alice and Anne by boat; William by road; Goffredo, later, by a different boat. If asked, they'd say they were invited to a Friday dinner at Will Caxton's. Once at Westminster, they would supervise the packing. Alice and Anne would load the valuable silk thread supplies onto William's horse, ready to take back to London. Everyone would be waiting to leave when Isabel finished at the Palace on Friday afternoon.

They'd have a bite to eat together at the house, then they'd split up. Will Caxton could ride William's horse and the silk supplies back to London before curfew. The two old ladies could go back by boat to show their faces in the Mercery the next day, as usual. Meanwhile, Goffredo and William would walk the silk weavers downriver to Chelsea, stay the night at the inn there, and be off by road for Jane's house by dawn. Once the weavers were settled in Hertfordshire, the two men could return to London. Goffredo would be in plenty of time for his Guildhall appeal.

Isabel would come back to London on Saturday morning. The weavers would stay away until they knew Goffredo had been cleared and the business formally recognised and registered at the Guildhall.

Any snoopers who found the Westminster house before that would see nothing more than meaningless bits of wooden frame propped against the walls and Will Caxton's foreign print workers next door, gabbling at them in their murderous foreign tongues.

Isabel nodded. She didn't respond to Goffredo's smiles and nods and hand-squeezes. She hadn't shaken off the heaviness of waking up from her dream. She was hardly thinking about the evacuation. Now she was definitely going, the thought of Westminster, and the Palace, was blotting everything else out again. She was dreading having to see Princess Elizabeth. But she was also hoping, with a raw desperation that felt as miraculous as life returning, that she might manage to run into Dickon.

She could hear Alice saying, in that booming voice that always got her noticed in crowds, 'The important thing is to be inconspicuous.' The voice seemed very far away.

She couldn't be in Westminster and not see Dickon. As she passed through the gatehouse and the corridors and the changes of guard, she so wanted him to appear spontaneously before her that her desire began to seem, even to her, like a kind of magic: a spell, an incantation, pulling him back to her. He must come; he must.

But when she did see him, leaving the Princess's rooms while she was still waiting to go in, it felt as impossible as a dream.

She smiled dreamily.

'Dickon,' she whispered.

He hadn't been looking. He was already vanishing down the stone corridor, like the wind. But he whirled round when he heard her voice.

For a moment they looked at each other without moving.

There were guards behind her, loaded down with the parts of a jewelled gown, staring stiffly ahead.

He drew her into the window. He didn't take his tired eyes off hers. There was wonder in them; and, she thought gladly, gratitude; hunger. He was paper-white, she saw. Worry, or fear, had gouged scars across his face.

'I thought . . .' he began in a whisper. 'I thought you'd gone for good.'

She could feel his hand on her arm. It made her glow with joy. She shook her head.

She saw a hope she hadn't dared expect come into his face.

He looked back at the guards. Their presence clearly bothered him.

'Can I see you?' he muttered. 'Later?'

It was what she'd wanted for so long. Quickly, she nodded. Then she remembered.

'Not after this,' she muttered. They'd be packing up at the silk house this afternoon. There'd be pandemonium. They'd all notice if she just vanished.

Evacuating the silk house suddenly seemed just an irritating chore; an obstacle to what she really needed to do. She sighed, thinking frantically.

But once they'd gone . . . Her face cleared. She could.

'Late,' she breathed.

He nodded, and turned on his heel.

'Are you really all right?' the Princess asked, not unkindly. 'You still don't look well.'

She'd never commented before on how Isabel looked. Why would a Princess notice her servants' complexions, after all, or the smudges under their eyes?

Isabel felt exposed by that speculative sea-green gaze. It made her feel soiled and old. She shrugged off the question, strengthening herself with the knowledge that tonight she'd be with Dickon. 'Yes,' she said as firmly as she could, through the pins in her mouth. 'I'm better.'

The Princess herself was beautiful today. Strawberry-gold hair, pink lips, warmth in her cheeks, lightness in the movement of waist and white fingers. As if she'd been gilded with happiness; as if she'd grown up enough to know the shape her life would take, and was satisfied with it.

When Isabel had come in, the Princess immediately had work for her. She'd opened a box and taken out three emeralds and a stiff piece of green cloth of gold. They'd been a gift, she said. She'd been keeping them for Isabel. She wanted her to make a purse.

And, it seemed, she was in a mood to talk.

'I've often thought about you, this winter,' she said.

Isabel lowered her head.

The Princess's voice went gently on: 'Since I realised you were right.'

She fell silent. Isabel said blurrily, through her pins and pursestrings: 'About what?'

'About the King, wanting to marry me if his wife dies. You were right. He does.'

Isabel looked up.

She was disconcerted to find the Princess's eyes on her. Princess Elizabeth's head was nodding and she was smiling, as if she knew the idea of that marriage would be of interest.

'All this', the Princess smiled down, pointing at the precious materials, with what Isabel thought might be a glint of triumph, 'is a gift from him; he wants me to keep his letters with me at all times . . .'

The thought that came to Isabel now was hateful: Princess Elizabeth couldn't know about her and Dickon, could she? This watchful intensity couldn't mean – Dickon wouldn't have told?

'My mother is delighted,' the Princess said, with composure. 'Of course.' Then she let a shadow cross the smooth perfection of her brow. 'Though naturally my own conscience won't let me even contemplate such a thing while the Queen is alive,' she added. She crossed herself virtuously. She was still smiling a little.

'Because it seems to me that the Queen's will to live must be much stronger than any of us realise,' Elizabeth went on, with her eyes boring harder than ever into Isabel's above her smile. 'She's so weak . . . Yet she's hung on for so long . . . even with all the laudanum they give her, poor thing.'

I'm not better, after all, Isabel thought, feeling as paralysed as a rabbit staring at the fox advancing on it with open jaws. It wasn't enough to sense danger, unless you reacted. But she couldn't work out how Elizabeth expected her to respond.

'Laudanum?' she repeated, stupidly.

But Elizabeth only shook her head (though her smile deepened, as though she'd caught a fish on her line). 'I probably shouldn't even have mentioned it,' she said sweetly. 'Though it does worry me. Huge doses . . . enough to knock out a grown man, let alone the walking skeleton they say she's become. But they say she goes wild without it. And I suppose the doctors probably do know best . . .'

And she lapsed into a pink and white and gold silence.

Isabel's head was spinning. She'd been away too long. She'd lost her old knack for teasing the one strand of truth out of a confused rumour; she wasn't sure any more that she knew how to tell reality from a web of lies.

So she went quiet too; she sewed and thought. Why would the Princess be hinting that the Queen was being poisoned? Why take that risk, when it would be so easy, and tempting, for Isabel to pass on the word in the City, and spread a devastating rumour that could stop the marriage the Princess must be relying on? The only real reason Isabel could think of was that the Princess wanted to warn her off Dickon: to plant the idea in Isabel's head that Dickon was too dangerous for a humble silkwoman to handle.

She was almost encouraged by that conclusion. If the

Princess felt so urgently that she needed to frighten Isabel off, she couldn't have been laughing cruelly with Dickon over Dickon's grubby affair with a merchant woman from the City. She must have a sense that Isabel had a claim on Dickon's heart, too; that, common though she was, she might be a rival. But she'd have had that thought alone – without any help from Dickon.

Isabel squared her jaw. Well, she wouldn't be scared away.

The silence continued until the end of the appointed sewing hour. Isabel got up and began to pack away her bag, with the three emeralds folded inside the valuable cloth. She couldn't be late tonight.

But the Princess didn't let her go straight away. Instead, she said, as if it was something she'd been musing on all the while, 'I feel so sorry for her . . . Queen Anne Neville.' And her eyes were caressing Isabel; inviting her to stay.

Isabel hadn't ever felt sorry for Queen Anne Neville. But she was used to feeling matter-of-fact about Dickon's wife; she'd so often heard him say, a little dismissively, 'It's a good marriage. It's made me rich', that she'd never felt the need for real jealousy. And the daughter of the Earl of Warwick wasn't the kind of person you did feel sorry for if you were a merchant. She was too rich; too remote.

But something about the Princess's murmurings today made Isabel able to see the Queen as a tragic, helpless victim of many misfortunes. Her father's rebellion against the King had failed. Her first husband, a Lancastrian prince, had been killed. She'd been kidnapped by Dickon's brother Clarence to stop Dickon marrying her. Her son had died. She'd hardly seen her husband for years. And now he was waiting for her death.

'He did love her at first,' the Princess was murmuring. 'He told me so.'

Elizabeth paused to let Isabel absorb that blow.

'He'd grown up with her, after all . . . When she ran away from Clarence, he came to London to find her.'

London. Dickon had never told Isabel this story. But she could tell when it would have been: the most important moment in her own life, when everything had changed forever. When she'd been fourteen and had first come across Dickon, praying at St Martin-le-Grand church on an April morning, with King Edward's army at the gates of London. When she'd still thought he was just a gentleman from the army. He'd been wearing black, with no insignia – the anonymous way he liked to travel. He'd bought her dinner at a tavern at Aldersgate, outside the familiar Mercery – the Bush, she thought it had been called. He'd eaten pork and said she should marry Thomas Claver. He'd said he was going to make a marriage that would be in his family's interests; she remembered that too. But what she remembered best was that she'd known she loved him before he'd said two words. Even now, it was a memory she treasured. Uneasily she thought: I never found out exactly why he was in London, by himself, two days before the army came in.

She'd leave in a minute. Alice would wait. Isabel had to hear the Princess out first.

'He searched every sanctuary in London,' the girlish voice of the Princess was saying.

Isabel remembered now – they'd said back then that the sanctuary at St Martin-le-Grand was packed with Yorkists, waiting for King Edward to come. Thousands of them; not just at St Martin's, but in every other sanctuary in London too.

Had Dickon really been looking for Anne Neville?

The Princess said: 'He got more and more desperate. She didn't seem to be anywhere. He found her by chance in the end – in a tavern on Aldersgate, scrubbing out pans.'

Isabel felt as though her breathing had stopped.

Aldersgate. 'The Bush . . .' she muttered, and the Princess nodded. 'A name like that.'

'He says it seemed like a miracle,' the Princess added sentimentally. 'It was almost dark. It was coming on to rain. But he ran to the church down the road with her and found a priest, and married her then and there. They spent the night in the tavern where he'd found her. By the time my father's army came into London a day or two later, they were man and wife and there was nothing anyone could do about it.'

Isabel felt sorry for her own fourteen-year-old self, swooning over how Dickon's hand had felt on her back, over how close he'd stood, over how nearly he'd kissed her. Believing her and Dickon's shared destiny was being revealed to her, while all along he'd been paying a priest to marry him to someone else. Someone he'd told this girl, years later, who he'd loved. It was almost funny. Isabel hadn't counted, even back then.

'It's a lovely story, isn't it?' the Princess whispered.

Isabel swayed. 'Lovely,' she replied faintly. Then, 'You know, you were right. I don't feel well.'

She hurried through the thickening afternoon towards the silk house. They'd be worried. They'd be waiting. She was so late. She'd stopped noticing the time. She didn't know any more what she was thinking or feeling. All she could think of was what happened when a silk cloth got so old and brittle and thin that the lavender you tried to preserve it with stopped working. The way it disintegrated into shards and dust.

It was chilly already. There was a touch of river fog in the air. She thought she could smell burning, as if people were lighting fires even before darkness fell. She shivered. Behind the Almonry she could see smoke drifting up from the dancing orange of what must be a bonfire.

399

She looked harder. It was too big for a bonfire. There was too much noise. She started to walk faster.

She knew the sounds of a mob.

She turned the corner. She already knew it was her house on fire. She was close enough to see the flames crackling and raging now, rushing under eaves and tiles, blossoming shockingly through windows. And she was close enough to see the shadows dancing round in the smoke too. Terrifying strangers. Londoners, not Lombards, by their voices; or nearly Londoners; they had the rough rasp of the river villages out east in their throats. They were smashing windows. Waving sticks. Jeering at the flickering, twisting human shapes that you could half make out inside the windows: 'Whoreson Lombards' and 'Thought you could lick the fat off our beards, did you?' and 'Well, we'll fry the fat off yours.'

She crossed herself. Everyone she loved was in that house.

She made her legs move. Ran for the tavern. But before she could throw herself through the doors and yell for help they burst open of their own accord and more men came rushing into the confused shadows. They brought a pocket of clear air with them. She saw the innkeeper. She saw a dozen patrolmen in sallets. A couple of them had buckets. A couple had ropes. Most had sticks. Then the stinging smoke enveloped them all again, and there was just grunting, and shouting, and the slap and clang of leather and metal and wood and flesh connecting, and the hum of prayer in her head.

She stood in the shadow of the tavern, crying and shivering and coughing.

It was only when the biggest crash of all lit the sky with a glorious shower of sparks, as two halves of a roof split and reared up into the darkness – and frightened her into screaming – that she realised she wasn't alone with a howling mob.

There was a rush of legs; then arms on her back. She screamed again and jumped back, flailing her arms, before she heard.

'Isabel,' the voice was yelling back, 'you're safe.'

There was a blackened face staring into hers: white eyes; a white mouth opening and shutting. It took a while to realise whose it was. Then she collapsed against Will Caxton's blotchy tunic and felt stringy arms holding her up as her legs gave way.

18

Isabel huddled with Caxton and his foreman Wynkyn and the other Dutchmen inside the empty tavern, listening to the shouting as the sky went slowly black.

The rioters looked a sorry enough bunch once they were tied together and herded into the drinking room. They were wet and puffy-eyed and bloody-mouthed and shaking. A dozen low-lifes. One was a wherryman. Two others were dockers for the Conterini. They all stank of ale. They'd got enough money from somewhere earlier on to go on a drinking spree. They admitted nothing.

There was nothing that could be done about Caxton's house. There was a wind. They had to pull down the frame to stop the fire spreading. He helped. They all helped. He was strangely calm. He said: 'Not till my press is out.' Four of the Germans brought his press and boxes of type out and put them inside the tavern before they began yanking on the ropes.

There was nothing that could be done about Isabel's house either, even hours later when the flames started to die down. The burned rafters went on glowing; bits of rubble falling; smoke mixing with the mist coming down. The crackling went on too.

'We have to get them out,' Isabel kept saying. 'The others.' She could hear herself saying it. She wondered why. It was so obvious no one could be alive in there. 'We have to get them out.'

'Too dangerous,' they told her gently, and, 'They're dead.' They were going to take the wreckage down in the morning, if they could, and recover the bodies.

In the end she let them put her to bed. Hamo the innkeeper gave them all a place to stay. He sat up himself to keep guard on the embers of Isabel's house. She didn't get Dickon's room, but an unfamiliar set of walls. She was grateful for that. It had pale plain plaster and a straw-filled mattress too. All the rooms did. And this one smelled of smoke.

She'd forgotten she'd been going to meet Dickon here tonight. But he came to her in her dreams.

She dreamed he was lying on the bed asleep. She was going to tiptoe up to his side and lean over the bed and wake him with a kiss.

Except she couldn't. There was no time. She had to go to a funeral. She had to get to London before the Italians did; but the boatmen weren't in their boats. She thought they must be downstairs drinking, but no one would listen. And anyway, there was another head next to Dickon's on the pillow: a woman's head, a tangle of long red hair.

The drizzle by dawn put out the embers. She woke up to the sound of men grunting outside and the shift of rubble. She couldn't look at what they'd be finding. Suddenly desperate for company, she fled downstairs as she was, rumpled, with her eyes full of dust and her hair wild. But the tavern hall was empty, piled up with the trays of type and the half-undone pieces of Will Caxton's press. It was cold, too, in this grey light, with the door open to get rid of the smoke, but with the draught blowing more ash and more of that smell that made your eyes sting into a room that was already full of ghosts.

She'd sat under the tavern arches with Dickon. When they'd just met, for a second time, when her tongue seemed to be stuck to the roof of her mouth. When he was trying to teach her chess. Before he kissed her. Her memories were so vivid that the grey shadow stooping over an untouched loaf seemed unreal by comparison. But the shadow was at the next table, looking up anxiously at Isabel out of wild sooty eyes. She said, with a rush of tenderness: 'Will.'

'Don't go outside, Isabel,' he quavered, trying to be protective. 'I don't want you to see.'

She shook her head gratefully and busied herself with knife and board, cutting bread.

'They want us to identify the prisoners,' he said. She passed him some bread.

'We should say they work for the Conterini,' he added. 'Shouldn't we?'

Deliberately she cut another slice for herself. It wouldn't do to be too weak to think straight. No point in tears. She should eat something. And yes, she could imagine the pair of them doing and saying those things before they took the bodies of their friends back to London and organised their funerals. But none of it would do any good.

She didn't need to be a soothsayer to know what would happen when this affray went to the Guildhall. The City would waver and grumble but make peace; men like her father would wring their hands and argue against offending the foreign merchants who were so important to London's economy. They might have been excited about London-made silk cloths a few days ago, when the merchandise was about to come on the market and the Clavers were about to be powerful; but they wouldn't do anything to protect the interests of dead women with a dead industry against the powerful living Lombards. They'd be scared. It was the nature of merchants.

But Isabel would need to get justice for Alice and Anne and William and Goffredo and all the weavers whose bodies were out there. She'd need the help of men of the sword. The Claver house had been under contract to the King. She thought: I need Dickon.

But he hadn't come. She hadn't thought she could feel any bleaker. Her eyes stung.

'I've got to wash,' she muttered, and fled out and up the back staircase. She was too ashamed to let Will Caxton see her cry for Dickon now. She didn't go to the room she'd slept in. Her feet took her instead to the door at the end of the corridor. Dickon's door.

She opened it and slipped inside.

She was expecting nothing better than emptiness; a place to be alone; the cold comfort of memory. But Dickon was there, standing at the window in slept-in clothes, looking with vague eyes at the men digging where the burned-out house had been.

Gratitude swept through her; a great simplicity of love. She said: 'You came,' and moved her weary limbs towards him. She was so tired. But he was here to comfort her.

Then he raised his eyes to her. And she saw they were empty.

He hadn't noticed what he was looking at outside. He wasn't even seeing the disarray of her dress.

He said, in a hollow, unearthly voice she'd never heard before: 'Anne has died.' And he rushed forward, a dark wind, to sweep her up in his arms.

He wanted her to comfort him. He buried his head in her shoulder. She heard his muffled voice saying, disjointedly: 'I couldn't bear it . . . when I got the message. She's been dead two nights . . . I came to you . . . I have to go back . . . the bells . . . they'll have to ring the bells . . .'

His head was so heavy. She stood straight under its weight; almost having to hold him up. She looked down at the black hair she'd always loved. Now she felt only numbness.

The people she really loved were out there, dead.

She'd let herself get caught up once too often in Dickon's web; sat too late with the Princess, listening to her hints about Dickon; lost herself trying to puzzle out what either of them might really want from her, or each other. If she'd got here an hour earlier, as she'd promised Alice, the silk house might have been empty by the time the men with their torches came. She'd sacrificed Alice Claver to that woman; this man.

She raised Dickon's head. He let it go on hanging heavy in her hands. He still wanted her support. But she couldn't give it. Not to a man who'd said he'd never hurt a woman, but let his doctors slip his wife murderous doses of laudanum. He might only be here now to display his grief so Isabel would naively spread word of it in London later. He might only have arranged this meeting with her after he'd heard news of his wife's death. How could she tell what might really be on his mind? There'd been so many lies, so many tangles, so many manoeuvres. And a man who couldn't stop manoeuvring couldn't feel the simplicity of love. He'd never said he loved her. He didn't know truth. He wasn't the man to get justice for Alice.

The grey light outside was brightening. Isabel blinked, as if waking up at last.

'Why are you weeping for your wife?' she whispered. 'When you poisoned her.'

He shook his head, but weakly. She didn't believe him. Gently, she pushed him away.

'Go to your new wife,' she said.

She stopped in the doorway, and turned round. He was standing very still; looking disbelievingly at her. She said, 'I have always loved you,' for the first and last time.

She reached the bottom of the stairs and felt the quiet daylight on her skin. Will Caxton would be waiting.

'I thought . . . I was so worried,' Will mumbled, wrapping his bony arms tight around her. He was clinging to her like a mother to a child who's been lost and found. 'When you rushed off like that . . .'

'I'm all right, Will,' she said. He held her a little further away and looked curiously at her. He must have been reassured by whatever he saw.

Isabel was surprised at how composed she felt.

She hadn't lost quite everything. Will Caxton was still alive. She had Jane and her family. And she had thirty cloths at Catte Street to remember the weavers by. Velvets as soft as fur; damasks whose patterns of birds and lilies and flowers and leaves shimmered like moonlight. The last cloth Joan Woulbarowe wove had been the colours of summer: blue and green and gold.

She'd started just by loving the beauty of the silk. She'd got lost in the more dangerous dream of the power it might bring. She should have stayed making beauty out of silk.

There would be no more cloths now.

She'd have to get justice for her friends, and herself, on her own.

Still, she knew exactly where to begin.

A picture of Dickon flashed into Isabel's mind, sitting in this tavern hall, long ago, with a chess piece in his hand. He was grinning wolfishly, like he used to; he was saying, 'The aim of the game is to kill the king.' It had been his idea to teach her to play by his rules. That had amused him once. Isabel wasn't a chess player, or a fighter.

She would never have any weapon but her tongue. But she knew that was a good enough weapon for what she had in mind. She was a Londoner, raised in the markets, where every merchant's worth was measured in gossip, valued in words. She knew how easily people could be destroyed by a rumour.

She didn't have time for much talk as she and Will Caxton trudged round Westminster, formally identifying rioters, then trudged round London, filing depositions at the Guildhall with awkward officials who didn't want to take them – 'What can the servants of a draper Mayor possibly understand about this?' Will Caxton said angrily as they came out. Then they went to St Thomas of Acre to arrange for the bodies to be buried and chantry priests to be hired to sing masses for the souls of the dead.

But Isabel spoke to a few friends along the way.

She didn't tell many people that Princess Elizabeth thought the King had poisoned the Queen so he could marry her.

She didn't have to. It only took a few wagging tongues.

The innkeeper's wife said: 'I wouldn't put it past him. He did away with her brothers, didn't he? Poor little mites. That girl's at his mercy. She must be terrified.'

Katherine Dore said: 'It can't be by chance that God took his son from him. I'm sure of that. Do you remember how they used to say he murdered Clarence? Drowned him in a barrel of drink in the Tower. And didn't Anne once tell us she'd heard that he kidnapped Lady Oxford and stole her house and land?'

Isabel's father came to Catte Street at once to pay his respects. To Isabel's touched surprise, he held her hand. He looked as distressed for her as if he loved her, which perhaps he did. He invited her to stay for as long as she wanted with him in Somerset. He kept searching her face for visible signs of her distress and seeming surprised by

408

her brittle energy. When she told him of the rumour, he said wisely: 'Ah . . . Never trust a man who calls his mother a whore. There's always been bad talk about him. He was at the Tower on the night poor King Henry died, wasn't he? That's what they say.'

And everyone she'd spoken to had a bright-eyed, busy look in their eyes as they rushed off about their daily business, keen to spread the word.

By the time the entire Mercers' Company and their families packed into St Thomas of Acre on Sunday – not for the funerals yet (the bodies were still being assembled, ready to be moved to London) and not even to see the Italians' faces (the Lombards had found reasons to be in Southampton for a while, attending to their shipping contracts), just to watch Isabel and Will Caxton walk in, dignified in their black – all anyone was talking about was Isabel's rumour about the royal poisoning.

19

Isabel didn't cry when they were loading up the coffins Hamo the innkeeper had ordered for her into the farm carts he'd found to take her cargo to London. She didn't look at the charred wreckage next to the Red Pale while she was settling up with him; just kept her gaze on his big slab of a face. His eyes weren't as bright and twinkling as usual. They were cloudy with sympathy, and he kept hushing himself and patting her shoulder. He was a kind man. She probably wouldn't see him again. She thought he might be expecting her to look sadder. She didn't care.

Will Caxton had retreated to the Prattes' house in Old Jewry as soon as the arrangements were made. He'd said he was tired, but she thought he didn't want to let tears overwhelm him in front of her while she was so dry-eyed. Perhaps he was just shy about his emotions; although she thought he might still be angry with her. He would never forgive her now for letting him see that she'd once thought Alice and Anne and William less important than loving Dickon. She wished she could tell him she was free; she wished she could cry with him, but she couldn't.

She didn't cry when they laid out the coffins in the hall

410

at Catte Street. She nearly laughed when she saw the cart men's faces, hesitating over whether to open the lids. She could see from their expressions that the bodies inside were too terrible to linger over. She knew they weren't all recognisable. Those of Goffredo and one of the weavers had not been found at all; there would be empty coffins. 'Leave them open,' she said. She opened her purse, and took out more coins, and sent them to the kitchen for food.

It would be Lady Day tomorrow, she thought, lighting wax tapers at the head of each coffin, averting her eyes, going to and from the storeroom to fetch more as she ran out. Twenty-two coffins. Twenty-two lids. Twenty-two winding sheets. Lady Day: spring already in the chilly evening air. The quarter day; a new year. She didn't want to finish that thought; to have to try and imagine new beginnings. She had so much still to do. She caught her breath. She hadn't remembered to cancel her appointment at the Guildhall for the registration hearing; it had been for the day after Lady Day. She let the breath out; made a conscious effort to relax. The appointment didn't matter any more. It wouldn't do to worry. She needed to keep a clear head for the job to hand now: the bodies. There were no other women in the house. She had to do it. But she couldn't bring herself to start looking in the coffins. All she could think of was the sheets. With so much linen already sent off to Westminster when the weavers came, would there be enough in the house?

She didn't even cry when she heard the first knock on the door. Or when silkwomen she hardly knew began shuffling in, offering to help prepare the bodies for burial. Or when, before she knew it, the room was gentle with female voices humming spinning songs together; lifting buckets; rhythmically pulling apart strips of cloth for winding. There weren't enough sheets; they'd make do.

She hovered. Hummed along. It was the first time since it had happened that she'd been surrounded by so much womanly industry. She wondered why she felt so empty. Then she realised. She had nothing left to do.

'You sit down there, love,' someone told her. She knew that rasping voice: Rose Trapp. 'Go on. You look done in. I don't want you looking in them coffins. And I've done my poor Joan. I'll do your folk for you too if you like.'

She nodded. She was so grateful, and so tired. But she couldn't sit down.

Instead, she put her arm through Rose Trapp's and led her out of the room, down the corridor, to the dark store-room where, she now remembered, the weavers' thirty cloths were stored. Rose Trapp didn't ask questions. She just held the light, which lit her face from below, turning her cheery wrinkles into a witch's mask of shadows. Isabel opened the chest. She picked up a careless armful of preciousness. It didn't matter now if the cloths got crumpled. Not where they were going.

She took the light in her free hand. 'You take the rest,' she said, and Rose Trapp scooped them up. The cloths glimmered between those swollen old fingers: spun sky and sea and moonbeams, the wild, tamed and civilised. Rose Trapp's face softened in their reflection. Unexpectedly, she said: 'Like liquid gold, aren't they.'

They smiled at each other over the flickering light. They both understood the magic.

But then Rose Trapp did ask a question: 'What are you going to do with them?' Her voice was abrupt, as if she was waking up from a spell and had come to her senses. Isabel saw the suspicion cross the old woman's face.

'Use the cloths as winding sheets, of course,' she said defiantly. 'Bury them with them.'

Rose Trapp's face went sullen.

Isabel said: 'Weaving those cloths killed them. And it was my fault. I want to give them a good send-off. I have to. It's a mark of respect . . . my apology.'

She could hear the pleading note in her own voice.

But Rose Trapp was still shaking her head. 'What's the point of that?' she said roughly. 'It won't help them, being dressed like kings and queens to meet their Maker. It won't bring them back, will it now?'

Isabel sank onto a stool, with the silks rustling around her. Rose knelt next to her, puffing a little as she squatted down. She put a comforting arm around Isabel, and her cloths shimmered away into a forgotten heap on the ground.

'You want to look out for the living, not the dead, Mistress Isabel,' Rose rasped, but there was kindness in her voice and on her wizened face. 'That's what your Mistress Claver would want, not some show to make you feel better. You've got four apprentices in this house; girls who are too scared to come out of their rooms; girls who don't know what to do with themselves or what will become of them next. That's who you should be thinking of. You've got to make provision for them. And there are plenty of other people you could help. The Mercery is full of honest young women without a penny to their names. Women who can't marry or set up a business because they're too poor. Women who've lost their relatives and are facing old age alone. Me, for instance. You know that.'

She stopped and patted Isabel's shoulder, apparently realising it had begun to heave. 'Now don't go crying on that silk and leaving stains on it,' Rose Trapp added in a hoarse whisper. 'You won't get half the price for it . . . if it's spoiled . . . when you sell.'

The old woman stood up, took the cloths and began to fold them back into their chest. Isabel put her hands over her face and abandoned herself to her tears.

413

When they got back to the great hall, it was Rose who broke through the buzzing of voices. She'd brought one of the cloths with her.

'Girls,' she croaked. 'We're going to want you back on Monday. After the funerals. We're going to sell these silk cloths at Mistress Claver's stalls. We're going to need help.'

Isabel nodded obediently, as unsurprised as if she'd agreed this with Rose beforehand. She'd muffled her tears, but she was so full of grief that she could only be dimly aware of the awe that was stealing into the room: the whispers, the lover's touches as the women drew close to the cloth in the colours of the summer about to come that had been Joan Woulbarowe's last work.

When they were finished, when every corpse had been washed and sprinkled with a mixture of rue and rosemary and rose petals, and every still form covered in linen, even their poor blackened faces, the women left as quietly as they'd come. They touched her as they went: on the arm, on the shoulder. Rose Trapp shut the last cloth back in its chest. Then she sat with Isabel and held her while she wept, while the candles and the logs burned down, until there was silence.

Isabel could hear ragged breathing. It was nearly dawn. The last candle was guttering. For a moment it seemed to her that she was fifteen again, sitting in this hall over another corpse, her husband's, watching a younger Alice Claver's face twitch with a mother's grief. Alice was muttering to herself about Thomas when he was little. How he'd howled with laughter when she'd swung him round in her arms. How she should have made more time. But it was already too late for those regrets.

Isabel got up from her stool. It was Rose Trapp snoring in the corner this time.

414

She could still make out her mother-in-law's familiar bulk, in its coffin, underneath the casing of cloth.

'Goodbye,' she whispered, a little experimentally; trying to believe men would come in an hour and nail the lid down over Alice's stillness – over her face – and take the box away. Trying to imagine the quiet rush of panic she'd suppress when that happened. Or what the house would be like without Alice's gruff voice and thump of a walk. Tonight.

She couldn't, any more than she could touch or kiss any of the scented human-sized cocoons on the floor, lost hopes, about to be buried. She felt the beginning of something terrible inside her. But she pinched her fingers hard into her eyes. There was no time now.

The coffins went into the darkness first, a long line of them, wobbling into the church above the thin legs of apprentices. Other boys' faces flickered behind their torches and tapers.

She went next. Then Will Caxton, with the marks of weeping on his face. Then Rose Trapp.

She thought the only other mourners might be the printers. But others came out of the crowds and joined her shuffle to the altar. Her father. Jane. Thomas Lynom. Robert Lynom. A few of the silkwomen, though many more hung respectfully back, too shy to be sure whether they counted as bereaved.

She ignored the eyes. Stuck her chin in the air while the coffins were laid down, with the occasional bump and thump and sweating pallbearer's groan breaking the quiet. She would be calm; dignified.

She had one more thing to do before she could grieve.

So she was almost surprised at the pain, when it came.

'It's bad,' Robert Lynom said kindly. 'I know.'

It had been his arm on her back in church when she

415

was crouching forward, giving herself up utterly to the agony, curling herself into it. His arm holding her up when she stumbled on the way to the graves. His kerchief, then his chest, she'd buried her face in.

Robert Lynom had half-carried her up the Catte Street stairs afterwards, disregarding Rose Trapp's anguished flapping at the height of his elbow and Will Caxton's ineffectual flapping somewhere behind. 'Let's not worry too much about etiquette right now,' he'd said reassuringly to Rose, 'this is just easier for me', and Rose Trapp had subsided into watchful silence. He'd laid Isabel on the bed, still in her gown. 'Rest,' he'd said, putting a big cool hand on her hot head. For a while, there'd just been Rose Trapp in the solar with her, muttering what words of comfort she could, with gnarled hands fussing over laces and hooks as she eased off headdress and gown and kirtle. And then there was just Isabel, in her pale linen, and the coiling, roiling, heaving inside her. Hot eyes. Something steaming on the table. A white sky at the window. And a meagre comfort in the clump of boots downstairs; mourners at the meal Will Caxton had paid his own thirty marks for.

Will and his men were going back to Westminster later. He'd been apologetic about it; but she'd seen the estrangement in his eyes. He didn't think he'd find comfort in being with Isabel. He couldn't wait to get busy; get away from the pointless pain of memory. He'd got timber and tools ordered. They'd start rebuilding his house in the morning.

Tomorrow she would sell the cloths. After that, she'd be alone.

She thought about that for a while. Imagined the white silences, broken only by the two new kitchen men she hardly knew. Days with Alice's apprentices, four pink-faced girls from the provinces whom she'd kept apart from for fear they'd find out too much.

She didn't want to be alone.

She was still frozen into a kind of calm when she first realised that. But she could feel the fear coming, a great wave of it, rushing at her, about to break.

Then, instead, she heard footsteps. Robert Lynom's unhurried tread on the stairs.

Relief at the prospect of his sensible company brought her back to reality. The fear would wait. Her hands flew to her face for a moment – a reflex action, as if she were about to flirtatiously pat skin and hair back to something like normality. Then she stopped, and even the stopping was a new kind of relief. There was no point. She was past caring. Robert knew. She didn't need to worry with him.

The only thing he could sit on was a tiny stool. He was much too big for it, even curled up with one ankle on the other knee and his big clean hands composedly on the crossed leg. She smiled weakly, and wasn't sure herself whether it was because of him cramped comically on that stool or just because his presence made some of her cares drop away.

Without being asked, he'd ensured she wouldn't be alone. Jane had had to rush back to her baby after church, he said; Julyan was ill after the journey. But he didn't think it was anything serious. The Thomas Lynoms were staying with him (it was familiar territory, after all; he'd bought Jane's confiscated house at Old Jewry, just round the corner). But, all being well, Jane wanted to bring the baby, and the nurse, later, and stay with Isabel instead, as long as Isabel felt up to the commotion. 'They'll bring their own linen,' he said. 'I have plenty.' He'd even thought of that.

She nodded, too grateful to speak. He'd done more. He'd taken it on himself to pay Rose to stay at the house for a few months, too, he said. Rose could run the household; stop the kitchen men getting carried away; do the marketing. He hoped she didn't mind.

'You've had bad luck,' he was saying now; each word a certainty. 'You don't deserve it.'

She nodded, feeling stronger.

'It won't last,' he said. 'The bad luck; it will pass.' And his strong face was so full of conviction that she almost believed him.

He looked thoughtfully down at her. 'Do you mind if I say something now that goes beyond my calling as your lawyer?' he went on, sounding, for the first time she could remember, a little hesitant. She nodded him on.

'It's this. There's more to life than trading silk,' he said carefully. 'You don't have to spend your days between Cheapside and Soper Lane and Hosiers Lane and Pissing Lane, living cheek by jowl with crowds of other people doing exactly what you do and trying to beat them at it, making it your business to know every detail of their business and private lives while you try to stop them finding out about yours. It's a small place, the Mercery. There's a world outside. I haven't regretted getting out. Nor has Thomas. Nor has Jane. You've given it your all, Isabel. But there might be more for you in life too.'

There was compassion in his voice now. Her eyes asked the question: 'What?'

He spread his hands, palms up. 'Happiness. Peace.'

Perhaps her face closed at that. At any rate, he drew back, shaking his head as if mildly surprised that he'd gone so far. In something much more like his usual down-to-earth lawyer's tones, he said: 'You don't need to worry about money, whatever you decide to do. You have more than enough. Alice has left you a very profitable business. You have the lease on this house. You own the goods in the storeroom; you have contracts, contacts and apprentices. You can keep things just as they are if you want.

You know the business backwards. I would imagine you'll be very successful. But it wouldn't do any harm to remember you could also sell. Retire. Even think of marrying and having children. You have choices.'

He stood up. 'Think about it,' he said. 'And now, get some sleep.'

She'd dreaded the empty darkness of the coming night, the creaks and scuttles in the silence. But it wasn't going to be like that after all. She had choices. Her blankets felt warm. She snuggled drowsily into them and fell asleep listening to his footsteps on the stairs.

The calm that Robert Lynom's common sense had brought Isabel sustained her through the silent loneliness of the next dawn.

Rose Trapp mustered the four apprentices and the others who trooped in at the back door at first light. They didn't stop to eat. They had a purposeful look in their eyes: the look of women being given an unexpected chance in life and eager to seize it in both hands. Rose Trapp had told them half the proceeds of the sale would go to providing a memorial for Alice and Anne; the other half would be used to give dowries and seed capital for deserving silk-women, and they would be among the first candidates. Two of the four girls Alice had brought down from Derby as apprentices – Annie and Janie, blonde, round-faced sisters – came up to Isabel as Rose supervised the packing of the silk cloths in rough bags, and, silently, nervously, pressed her hand. She nodded, suddenly more grateful than she knew to Rose Trapp; wondering how she hadn't realised for herself that Alice would think it important to set these girls up in life.

Alice's familiar stall was empty. Rose Trapp supervised the laying out of the cloths. Isabel watched in silence at first. She felt numb; she'd be numb until all this was over.

419

But after a while she shook herself and mustered her reserves of strength. She owed it to Alice Claver to make this sale a success.

She noticed that Rose Trapp was taking great pains to have her Joan's lovely cloth advantageously displayed at the top of the pile, folding and curving it so its summer colours glowed. It was clear that the old woman wanted that cloth to sell for the best price of all. She must hope the proceeds of that sale might be given to her, to fund her own lonely old age.

'Rose,' Isabel said. Her voice sounded loud in the silence. The old woman looked up, almost guiltily, caught out in her hope.

'That cloth is the most beautiful of all of them,' Isabel said. 'Isn't it?' No one would deny that Joan's cloth was a masterpiece. Once the market opened to customers, she knew it would go for a good price: twenty pounds, maybe, or even more – enough for an old woman in a tenement room to live on, frugally, for the rest of her days.

'So you're right to display it like that,' she went on. 'Give it pride of place.'

Rose Trapp waited warily, with the dumb patience of the poor, who can't hope for much and whose small hopes are so often disappointed. Her gnarled hand touched a corner of the green and gold and blue cloth, as if she were memorising its lustrousness; as if she feared that even this might be about to be snatched away from her.

'It's yours,' Isabel said reassuringly, and saw the veiny claw relax. 'I know that. But I'd like to offer to buy it from you. I'll make you a good price. Let's leave it out on display for now; it will help draw in the crowds. But don't let it go for less than' – she paused; thought how much would make Joan Woulbarowe's old aunt financially secure without making her feel Isabel was offering her charity – 'fifty pounds,' she finished – a price verging on the fantastical – and watched the joy come into those cloudy blue eyes. 'I'll match any offer up to that.'

Rose nodded, lowering her eyes. She was whistling under her breath as she finished setting out cloths and coins.

The word had gone round. Within minutes of the opening bell, the little shop was crowded with visitors eager to see the silk cloths woven by their own London kind. Isabel and Rose had the silkwomen stand round the sides, keeping the throng back; letting in only one or two representatives of the wealthy at a time to feel and discuss the qualities of the cloths, the choice of warp and weft, the number of threads per inch, the weight and thickness of gold thread, the grace of pattern and colour; moving towards a possible purchase. The excited voices of those still waiting grew so loud they had to raise their voices to be heard.

At one point, Isabel shivered. She looked up to see Dr Gigli's fat black velvet paunch only inches away, through the little sales area's window. He was watching her steadily, intently, and nodding his head as if memorising an enemy's surprising strength. The malevolence in his eyes made her flesh creep. But she raised her head proudly, met his gaze, and smiled. He looked away. He'd gone the next time she looked up.

After that, Isabel forgot herself and her troubles in the rush. It was her honey voice they all wanted to hear; her knowledge of an industry they'd all have liked to learn that drew them in. She talked; persuaded; charmed. And she enjoyed the clink of coins falling into Rose Trapp's bag.

John Lambert came and bought a length of tan-and-grey brocade. He'd brought cash. 'We should have gone into business together, after all,' he said.

She kissed him and pressed his hands, aware that he'd come as close as he could to apologising, and grateful for it; acknowledging, equally silently, how hard it must have been for him to come back to this market today after he'd been squeezed out of the City; remembering, with a shock of shame, how she'd helped squeeze him out by hiring away his workers. She said: 'I'm sorry we didn't, too.'

Isabel just shook her head and smiled and politely refused to answer questions about how the fire had started that had destroyed her workshop and killed so many of her colleagues. The only time her flushed, smiling face clouded was when would-be buyers offered prices for Joan Woulbarowe's cloth. 'Not for sale,' she said briefly; and, nodding regretfully, the clients moved on to examine the next cloths in the pile.

By the time the crowd thinned and Isabel drew breath and looked round long enough to realise other silk traders were already packing up their stalls, all thirty cloths were sold or pledged. When Rose Trapp lifted the bulging bag of coins from the cash purchases, there was an almost comical look of wonder in her eyes at how much they'd fetched.

It was done. Everything was gone. Isabel's euphoria vanished too. Suddenly she was desperately tired. Her feet hurt from standing. Her face hurt from smiling. She didn't want to be here, with people looking at her. She needed to get away from the eyes.

'Here,' Rose Trapp said, as if she knew, pressing the bag and the pile of bills of sale into Isabel's hands. 'The girls will clear up and wrap up your cloth. I'm taking you home.'

It was the sight of the bills of sale that forced Isabel to recognise reality.

She'd made her last sale in the Mercery. She couldn't, after all, go on operating the Claver silk business. She didn't, after all, have choices. She'd have to sell up.

She walked home, ignoring Rose Trapp, staring at the bills of sale, feeling dazed. The documents in her hand were innocent enough – simple pledges to pay her, at her house in London, by the end of the month, for the single silk cloth being contracted for. But they were also a reminder of the paperwork she needed to make the whole-sale, international end of her business work – which she'd never get into place again. She needed to go to the trade fairs of the Low Countries a couple of times a year to buy silk cloths to sell on in London. And, to do that, she needed the banking services of one of the powerful London Lombard families – a wealthy Italian who would write letters of credit, like these bills of sale but for much larger sums, with which she could make purchases abroad. But she'd seen the hatred in Dr Gigli's eyes. She knew no London Italian would underwrite her now, or ever again. And she couldn't buy without money.

She could still try to fight for justice at the Guildhall – get the Italians responsible for the fire named and punished, so that others who came afterwards would lend to her again. But she knew in advance how hopeless that would be.

Her mind darted desperately from faint hope to fading possibility.

She still had half a year's supply of silks in the store-house, she thought. She could go on trading with them for a while, and hope things would right themselves of their own accord and the Italians would forget their animosity. But she knew even as she clung to that thought that it wouldn't save her. City people were cautious, but they were merciless once they smelled defeat on someone. She'd seen her father cling too long to his City existence, after he lost his aldermanship; she'd seen him battered by lawsuits, a target for opportunists and raiders like herself, before he'd finally accepted defeat and retired to the country. It would be more dignified to go now with her good name intact.

Or, just possibly, she thought, she could sell up and start again later in partnership with her father – using the House of Claver's money to finance a renewed House of Lambert fronted by John Lambert, to whom the Italians might lend.

She sighed. Tried and failed to imagine talking over new strategies with her father. He'd never agree to following up any of her ideas. They'd only fight.

She shook her head. In the morning she'd tell Robert Lynom that she'd decided to sell.

She was so tired.

20

It was well into the morning when Isabel woke up. Rose Trapp was sitting on the stool by her window, hunched up in the threadbare brown gown she always wore. She had some sewing in her hands. She wasn't sewing, though, just gazing out. The sky was a promising pale blue, shot with silvery wisps. But Isabel didn't think the old woman was looking at the clouds. She thought she was listening. Isabel could hear loud street talk.

Rose Trapp looked round and saw Isabel's eyes on hers. She looked guilty.

'Did you have a nice rest, dear?' she said quickly. 'You look a bit better, I must say. You were as white as death last night. I was worried. Your sister's here, and the baby. I put them in Mistress Claver's bed last night; I hope that's all right. She's brought a load of linen. Everything's fine. Everyone's fine. Now, you just stay put. I'll run and tell her you're awake. And I'll bring you a bite to eat in a bit.'

Rose Trapp stood up. Why was she gabbling, as if she had something to hide?

Anxiously, Isabel said: 'What are they saying out there?' and nodded at the window.

Rose Trapp looked hunted. 'Don't you worry, dear,' she wheezed. 'Everything's fine.'

'Tell me,' Isabel said faintly.

'Oh, just some nonsense . . . There's always something, isn't there? To be honest, I can't make it out myself,' Rose Trapp lied unconvincingly.

'Tell me,' Isabel said; but she was slipping back into sleep as she spoke.

When she woke up next, Jane was with her. The baby, in her basket, was at Jane's feet. Jane was sewing. But, like Rose Trapp the other time, Jane wasn't paying attention to her work. She'd turned her eyes to the window. She was listening.

'What are they saying?' Isabel asked. Her voice seemed loud.

Startled, Jane turned towards her sister. Her eyes softened. 'Oh . . . you're awake . . . and you look so much better . . . Thank God.'

Then she looked out again, and her sigh of relief turned into a different kind of sigh.

'It's terrible out there. There's a crowd on the street the whole time. I've stopped going out, especially with the baby. They're so angry. It scares me what they might do . . .'

Jane caught Isabel's blank stare. She shook her head. 'Didn't you know?' she said tenderly. 'They think the King poisoned the Queen.'

Jane leaned forward and put a hand on the blanket mound made by Isabel's knee. 'Come and stay with me at Sutton,' she muttered pleadingly. 'Please, Isabel. Leave Robert to handle everything here. Let's get out of London. I'm scared.'

She was nodding her head encouragingly; hoping she could make Isabel nod hers back, like a reflection, without even realising Jane was tricking her into happiness.

There was nothing Isabel would have liked more than to be running through a meadow, with buttercups in the grass and her hems sodden with dew. But not yet. She still had to talk to Robert: make sure he understood the need to find new apprenticeships for the four girls; make sure he knew how she wanted the fund for silkwomen to be run.

The King called a meeting at the hall of the Knights of St John at Clerkenwell the next day at noon to address Mayor Stokker and the citizens of London.

The room was packed, and buzzing. There'd never been an occasion like this. There was only one thing King Richard could be going to talk about – his marriage plans.

Jane and Isabel and Robert Lynom squeezed between the liverymen in their furred robes of office and wives in their finest silks. There were apothecaries and armourers and bakers and barbers and basketmakers and blacksmiths and brasiers and brewers and butchers and carpenters and chandlers and cordwainers and curriers and cutlers and dentists and dyers and farriers and fishmongers and girdlers and goldsmiths and loriners and masons and mercers and needlemakers and patternmakers and plasterers and plumbers and poulters and saddlers and salters and skinners and surgeons and upholders and vintners and weavers and wheelwrights and woolmen. There were a few silkwomen too, around the edges of the room: the ones with fathers or husbands whose status guaranteed them entry to this hall; or the few, like Isabel, who were registered as femmes soles, responsible for their debts. They'd tell the others what happened later.

When Dickon walked in, almost alone, with an entourage of three men bobbing anxiously behind, the crowd bowed and bobbed and fell silent.

427

You couldn't fault his bravery. He was pale, so pale. His lips were tight. But he was composed.

He came straight to the point. 'Since the death of my beloved wife, Anne, a week ago,' he said clearly, 'you, the worshipful citizens of London, have naturally been concerned by an ugly rumour. That I had already chosen as my next wife Elizabeth, the niece of my brother Edward. And that I was hastening the death of the Queen of England to bring this new marriage about.'

There was a rush of indrawn breath. A note of reluctant admiration in the whispering. Who'd have expected the King to talk so straight?

'I'm here to tell you – that rumour is false,' Dickon went on.

Hubbub. He didn't mind. He knew how to talk to a crowd. He nodded and waited out the noise. Then he gestured for quiet with downturned hands.

'I am not – have never been – could never be – glad of my wife's death,' the King said. He crossed himself.

Most of the audience crossed themselves too. The man in black velvet before them was so pale; so clearly in grief.

'And,' he paused, to be sure there was complete silence, 'I have never – intended – to marry – my niece.'

Liar, Isabel thought savagely. But she was unsettled to hear more than a few satisfied grunts from around her.

'He's got guts, that's for sure,' a man in the crowd said behind her as the merchants began pushing for the door. 'But I still say he killed her.'

Isabel kept quiet. She was hugging one last memory of Dickon to herself.

She'd felt numb at the sight of him, or she'd thought she had. No shock, no pain; just a coldness in her heart. She told herself: he's a stranger to me; always has been. Still, she hadn't been able to stop herself catching his eye as he looked around the hall before leaving. She'd held his gaze until he'd turned away. But she'd seen the acknowledgement of defeat in his face. He'd lost. He'd lied, and he knew she knew. That was enough. She wanted to get away.

'Tomorrow,' she said, turning to Jane. 'Let's leave London tomorrow.'

She was packing. She was wondering at the foggy emptiness inside her. It took her a while even to notice the scuffle at the door. Then Will Caxton burst into her room. She realised he'd just torn past Rose Trapp, ignoring her agonised cry of, 'Here, you can't just burst in! On a lady! She's not even dressed proper!' She looked down in mild surprise – it was true, she was only in her kirtle; she'd been going to change gowns. Will was gulping in air as if he'd ridden at a gallop, or run, all the way from the Red Pale. He rushed straight to Isabel's side and began shaking her shoulders. He was indescribably dirty. There was earth and ash caked into his nails and eyes and clothes. His last few sandy hairs were rumpled up. His caved-in face was red and sweaty. There was a wild gleam in his eye.

'Will!' she exclaimed, dropping the linen she'd been packing into her trunk. She didn't understand. If he was too excited even to notice the impropriety of his behaviour, he couldn't have come to make his peace with her.

'I came myself . . .' he panted. 'fetch you . . . important . . . take you back . . . hurry now.'

She stared.

His impatience was making him stutter. 'Goffredo, they've found Goffredo,' he finally got out. She was rushing into her gown even before he said: 'A-a-a-alive.'

But Goffredo was only just alive. They'd found him that morning in the collapsed cellar of the silk house. The ruins had shifted overnight; the cellar roof had caved in, leaving an open pit. When the print workers looked down to see if there was anything they could salvage, they saw feet in the pit. A beam had fallen over Goffredo's legs.

He was unconscious. Only his hands were burned, but his legs were smashed and he'd been down there for more than a week. They put him on a plank and carried him to the tavern. Hamo called in a surgeon and a priest.

The surgeon had cut away his clothes and washed him and splinted his legs by the time Isabel and Will half-fell off their horse and dashed inside. The priest was muttering the last rites over a knobbly mound in white.

Hamo, standing in a corner, watching, looked sombre when he saw Will and Isabel. 'The surgeon's coming back with a poultice,' he muttered. 'But . . .' He shook his head.

The terrible burning hope in Will's eyes flickered. Goffredo was his last friend from the old days. He let air slowly out of his lungs, with a piteous noise he didn't seem aware of.

He knelt next to the priest. 'Thirty years I've known you,' Isabel could hear Will mutter; a prayer as fervent as any priest's Latin. 'Thirty years.' There were tears on his cheeks.

Isabel knelt next to him. They were in Dickon's room, she noticed, without minding.

She leaned forward and looked into Goffredo's gashed, bruised mash of a face. There was nowhere she could safely touch that bloody mask. She started muttering her own prayers, too, but she didn't think he'd survive the night. She was saying goodbye.

'You should go,' Hamo said quietly. 'Your people are waiting. There's nothing to hope for here.'

She nodded.

Will looked up from beside the bed. Blindly, he nodded too. He'd thought this rescue would turn out well; but it wasn't going to. She thought: He doesn't want me here, watching Goffredo die.

'He'll let you know,' Hamo said, 'when . . .'

His face said: When there's a burial to come back for. She nodded. She couldn't speak.

She knelt by Goffredo once more. She wouldn't have another chance. 'I used to think this room was the colour of happiness,' she whispered, wishing she could at least touch his oozing hands. 'But it was the wrong kind of happiness. I wish I'd chosen yours.'

21

The merciful fog came down over Isabel again at Sutton. London and the past seemed so far away that Isabel's grief for her lost friends could be contained within a comforting timetable of moments of wistfulness, unfocused eyes in a church candle flame, the comfort in the chantry priest's mumble of prayers. That would do, for now. She knew the real pain was there; waiting until she was ready.

It was important to do the right things, in the right order. She wrote to the Princess, a short letter explaining there'd been a tragedy in her family and that she would be returning to London later in the year to sell up. She'd return the Princess's goods – three emeralds and a piece of green cloth of gold – as soon as she wound up her affairs. But she couldn't complete the commission, or go on sewing for her.

She didn't think of Dickon. Her heart was empty.

She didn't hear from Will Caxton. There was no reply to the two letters she wrote, asking for news of his new house and of Goffredo. In this new, numb, passive mood, she accepted the loss of the printer with the same vague sadness she felt about everything else. He's buried Goffredo

432

and not wanted to ask me, she realised. He can't make his peace with me now they're all gone. What's done is done. Perhaps he was right to think I didn't value my real friends enough while I still had them.

She thought she was numb because she was so idle; caught between worlds.

She knew she was idle because, as spring turned into summer, Jane took to bringing Isabel with her on her rounds of her household, and Jane was always busy now. Jane spent her days running the brewing of beer in the brewhouse and the baking of bread in the bakehouse and the production of butter and cheese and eggs in the dairy. She supervised the home farm and the spinning of wool from the sheep and the weaving of woollens and the making of clothes. She checked on the apples and pears and quinces in the orchard, and the vines growing against the side of the house. She watched her bees gather nectar from a flower garden filled with marguerites and early roses and lavender bushes just coming into bloom. She tended her herbs, which she used both for medicine and cooking; overseeing the planting of vegetable and salad shoots, grown from seed earlier in the year. She watched the baby melons fattening.

Jane chose the meals, did the marketing, and coordinated her underlings. She charmed the gardeners and labourers and dairymaids and brewers and bakers and cooks and spit boys and servants whose work she oversaw into doing their best. She settled disputes. She hired and fired. She was a businesswoman on a surprisingly impressive scale. When Thomas was away, she was even supposed to deal with legal disputes and draw up wills.

'How did you learn all this?' Isabel asked. Jane had never before done anything more demanding than play the lute and shuffle her pack of cards and look beautiful. The new, bustling, aproned, unflappable, pink-cheeked Jane with dozens of keys at her belt laughed, remembering. 'Mistress Lynom, of course,' she said briskly. 'She came from Dorset to teach me. She was brought up there; she's a gentleman's daughter. She's a terror. Still, it isn't so hard. I enjoy it.'

'But you were always the lazy one.'

'This is nothing,' Jane said, and her cheeks went pinker still. 'It's quiet now. You should see what it's like in autumn. I couldn't believe how busy we were then, when we were killing pigs and salting down meat and curing bacon and smoking out the bees for the honey and making candles and boiling up berries for the jam – as well as all this.'

She leaned forward. Put her hand, rougher now, on Isabel's arm. Smiled, as though she wanted to draw a confidence out of her sister. 'Perhaps, once you've sold up, you'll be doing all this too . . . see for yourself . . . I know Robert's ready to settle down . . .'

Jane was dropping hints almost every day about Robert, who, in London, was organising the sale of Isabel's inheritance. But Isabel only blinked. She couldn't think of Robert. Not yet.

Avoiding a direct reply about Robert, Isabel said: 'But you used to spend your days lolling round on silk cushions, and going hawking . . . Don't you miss all that?'

Jane shook her head. 'Oh no,' she said firmly. 'I just didn't know then how bored I was.'

On the hot August day when Robert finally came to collect her to ride to London and sign the documents selling Alice's effects to the various buyers he'd found, he brought the first news Isabel had had in months of Dickon.

'You won't have heard it here, but London's full of the

434

talk. They say Henry Tudor's invaded again; they say his army's marching on the King's garrison at Nottingham.'

Isabel couldn't really take in the idea of armies. Nottingham was so far away. Her mind was on matters closer at hand. She'd tried not to think of this day coming for so long; she'd dreaded the trip to London and the memories it would awaken. But now Robert was actually here, and it was beginning, she found her worries receding. He was so matter-of-fact. He was good-looking, too. She'd forgotten how elegantly chiselled his features were, under that look of calm amusement; she hadn't remembered his long, blond ease of movement or his kindness clearly enough.

Jane crossed herself at his news, then clucked at her daughter. Nottingham was far away from her mind, too; too remote for everyone. Julyan laughed, and pulled at Robert's hair. Robert cooed at her, catching Isabel's eye and inviting her to laugh too. There was affection in the look he flashed at his sister-in-law.

Robert was saying something about business; trying to catch Isabel's eye again. She looked up and smiled at him; he was so kind; she should be as courteous back.

'. . . and I've had a letter from Lady Darcey; she says you still have some materials here that you've promised to return to the Princess,' he said. 'She says the Princess would like you to deliver them in person on your return. If you like, we could do that on this trip?'

Isabel's heart sank. But she knew she should. 'Of course,' she said, trying to sound warm.

Jane beamed. 'Yes, do sort everything out,' she said happily. 'It's time . . .'

Isabel could predict exactly how the London trip would end. That was the beauty of the Lynoms: you knew where you stood with them. Robert would reassure her through the painful business of signing. The money would be counted out. Then, once he was sure Isabel knew where she stood in the world, and what her choices were, he would offer her his hand in marriage. Jane had already mentioned the vacant manor near her home at Sutton that Robert might be interested in buying, once he was settled. So Isabel even knew where she'd be living. All she needed to do was let her decorous future unfold.

Most people would consider it a happy ending to make a fortune, marry well, enter the gentry and live happily ever after.

But Isabel couldn't quite restrain a sigh.

She took the lead when they got to Westminster. She didn't want to go through her old streets. Robert was too sensitive to ask why she was taking this unfamiliar route. He knew they'd find a tavern somewhere along this road, too, where he could wait.

Sensing aimlessness, the horses eventually took matters into their own hands and plunged their heads into the first trough they saw. 'Let's stop,' Robert said. There was a tavern opposite. 'That'll do for us. I'll order some food while I wait for you.'

It was a sprawl of a building, with overhanging solars and big stables stretching back off the courtyard. Isabel thought she remembered it. She was almost sure she recognised the beefy innkeeper, who was up a ladder with a paintbrush, touching up the sign. The boy with him was holding a bucket of blue paint.

She didn't understand what they were doing. Her stomach was too full of butterflies at the prospect of seeing the Princess again. She didn't want to think that the Princess would know it was Isabel who'd betrayed her secret fear about the King poisoning the Queen; she didn't want Elizabeth to hate her.

Robert understood the repainting straight away. He

436

stepped forward, took off his hat, and asked the innkeeper: 'Blue?'

It was only when all other eyes were raised to the sign that hers followed. The innkeeper had painted roughly over the silhouette of a white boar that his sign had shown until an hour before – King Richard's badge – with blue paint that was still glistening and wet. There were still traces of white showing through the new blue boar's body. The innkeeper had a splodge of blue paint on his nose.

The innkeeper scratched his head; he had the grace to look a little embarrassed. 'The Earl of Oxford's badge,' he mumbled.

The Earl of Oxford: Henry Tudor's man. Robert laughed. 'You've gone over to the House of Lancaster, then,' he said, and waited.

The man wriggled uneasily on his ladder. But Robert went on looking inquiring. Finally, as if sensing this stranger wouldn't just go away, but didn't represent a threat, the innkeeper laughed too, and began getting down, leaving the sign unfinished. 'Look, I know I can't draw,' he said, picking up his ladder. 'I'm all thumbs with a paintbrush. This was the best I could come up with on the spur of the moment.'

There were no bells ringing, Isabel thought numbly. If this innkeeper wanted to paint over the traces of his earlier loyalty to King Richard and the House of York in such a hurry, with his own clumsy hands, he must have heard something. But if there was news, why weren't there any bells? Then her head cleared. The messenger would have stopped here; maybe changed horses. The innkeeper would be the first to know.

Robert cut through her slow thoughts. Still sounding no more than cheerfully interested, he said to the innkeeper: 'So there's been a battle . . .'

'Market Bosworth,' the man answered, readily enough.

'Yesterday. A rout. He's dead. They cut him down. Stripped him naked. Carried his corpse into town on a donkey.'

There was no need to ask who the innkeeper was talking about.

The man spat, but not angrily; just in quiet, all-purpose disgust, his stock-in-trade.

'God's punishment,' he added reflectively. 'It was only a matter of time.'

The bells had started pealing by the time Isabel was shown into the Princess's parlour: a cascade of joy; a new tomorrow.

Elizabeth was standing at the window, listening to the bells. She was perfectly still.

Isabel had stood outside for several minutes, relieved to be alone but for the sentries' frightened eyes while the quiet sadness of things lost forever deepened in her. She'd thought she might see a reflection of that softness in Elizabeth. She'd been almost glad they would be together in this moment, to share their loss.

But when Elizabeth did turn round, her green eyes were glittering.

She didn't mention the bells. She just said: 'Come in, come in,' without surprise, and sat down on the cushions of the window seat, patting the place next to her with something close to warmth. 'I've been hoping you'd come back. I was sad to hear of your loss.'

Isabel bowed acknowledgement. But she couldn't sit. The young woman in front of her seemed a stranger. Isabel couldn't imagine what they would talk about.

Awkwardly, Isabel nodded her head at the window, and said: 'I'm sorry for your grief now.' The words brought the beginning of shame. Even more awkwardly, she reached down for her big sewing bag and fumbled out the Princess's valuables. They were lying on top of Joan

Woulbarowe's silk cloth, which nearly filled the bag. With her eyes still down, Isabel held out the green cloth and the little purse with the emeralds.

But no one took them.

When Isabel finally looked up, she saw the Princess smiling at her, very calmly, and shaking her head. Her hands were folded in her lap.

'No, you keep them,' Elizabeth said. 'As a token of my gratitude. You've served me well.' She smiled more broadly. 'Better than you know, perhaps,' she added. 'Are you really selling up and leaving London?'

Isabel nodded. She went on holding the cloth and purse out, as if someone might still relieve her of them. She said, as if wishing her safe future into existence, 'I'm going to marry; live in Hertfordshire; at Sutton on Derwent.'

The Princess nodded once or twice.

'Well,' she said, after a while. 'It's a pity. I'd hoped you might make my wedding gown.'

The bells rang louder.

'Because it seems . . .' the Princess added quietly, 'from those bells, that Henry's won.'

She smiled again, a curved, private, self-satisfied cat-smile.

'Or that I have,' she added, and she tinkled with laughter.

Isabel stared. Demurely, the Princess explained. 'Henry Tudor pledged last Christmas Day, in front of his court, to marry me as soon as he'd defeated my uncle. He's been my betrothed, in the eyes of God, ever since.'

Isabel stuttered: 'Christmas?'

She was counting back. Yes; it was only after Christmas that the Princess had told her she was afraid the King was poisoning his wife.

She stared at Elizabeth, too astounded to speak. Was this why?

Elizabeth's green eyes glittered again. Gently, she nodded.

'Of course, I had to stop my uncle Gloucester trying to marry me in the meantime,' she added. 'The match my mother wanted . . .'

'But,' Isabel said. She was imagining Dickon's body, bloodied and stripped naked, hanging over the back of a donkey. She was remembering his velvet voice saying, long ago, 'We all end up equal in the bottom of a bag.' The pity of it overwhelmed her.

There was no point in asking directly whether the Princess had just made up the story of the poisoning. Isabel could imagine the elegant shrug; the shoulders turning away.

'But why?' she stammered instead. 'When you could have been his Queen . . . when he loved you?'

Elizabeth didn't flicker at the word love. Lightly, far too lightly, she said, 'Oh, he wanted me all right. But why would I want a husband who'd declared me a bastard? I'd never have escaped that stigma, even if he'd let me wear a crown.'

She laughed.

'Henry – now . . . Henry's different. Henry needs me. I never stopped being a royal princess in his eyes: he sees me as the senior surviving member of the House of York. And he's not so royal himself – he's just the last man left standing with a drop of Lancastrian blood in his veins. He'll be grateful to have me.' She looked dreamily up at Isabel: 'Yes, it was well worth taking the risk of waiting to be the Tudor Queen.'

She stood up. As if surprised that Isabel was still holding out the piece of gold cloth and the bag of emeralds, and not rushing to pack them back into her bag, the Princess made a pretty shooing motion with her hands. 'So take your gift; go on,' she said, a little impatiently. 'I'm grateful to you.'

440

She began walking towards the door. Isabel knew she was being dismissed. She wanted to go. She had no place in this palace. She'd never be enough of a strategist to play these games. It had taken her a long while to understand.

'What about your brothers?' Isabel asked breathlessly, trotting after the Princess. 'You said they were alive. You said you knew where they were . . .'

'Oh, they're safe enough,' Elizabeth said. She opened the door. 'Henry will never find them. It's as well for them that he won't; he'd kill them if he knew where to look.' In the uncertain sunshine, her eyes were glittering harder than diamonds. 'But I'm the first-born child of a king. It's my destiny to be Queen of England.'

The door shut. The guards moved into place as if they'd heard nothing. Feeling stunned, Isabel allowed herself to be led off down the corridor. It was only when she reached the next door that she realised her hands were still stiffly holding out the piece of cloth of gold and the bag of emeralds the Queen-to-be had given her: her reward, apparently, for the job she'd never realised she was doing. Blankly, she looked at them, then, shaking herself back into the here and now, signalled to the guards to wait, put down the workbasket on her arm, and folded the treasures carefully away.

22

It was another bright August day when Isabel came back to Westminster. She tried not to look at the burned-out space where a house had once stood beside the tavern; but she couldn't help noticing that most of the gaunt, charred timbers were already peacefully overgrown. All you could really see, so late in the summer, were the drifts of tangleweed and cow-parsley and bright meadow flowers, nodding in the breeze. She could hear the buzzing of bees. She pushed open Will Caxton's gate.

He was inside, in a knot of men wearing smudged aprons, all staring at one of his machines and scratching their heads as they talked. He had his stooped back to her. There were other men in the interior shadow beyond, sitting on stools, clicking tiny metal blocks of type. She liked the busyness of it; the quiet hum. He hadn't heard her.

She stepped forward.

He looked up. His whitish eyebrows rose. Excusing himself from his men, he walked quickly towards her. He was smiling, but she could see his eyes were wary.

'It's going well, then,' she said.

He nodded.

'You built the new house quickly.'

He nodded again.

'I've sold up,' she said. 'My business was worth quite a lot of money; the houses too.'

He waited.

'But it won't be the House of Claver any more. So I've come to talk to you about setting up a memorial for Alice and Anne. Something people will be happy to remember them by.' She clasped Will Caxton's dry hand. 'You were right, Will. They were the most important people in my life.'

He only nodded again, but she could see his shoulders relax. He sighed. Then, impulsively, he put a shy arm around her.

'You look . . . better. Calm,' he said, and she could see the old friendly light in his eye. It was time for the two of them to make peace. 'What are you going to do now?'

'Well, Robert Lynom has asked me to marry him,' she said. His eyes moved, reflecting the blue sky drifting by behind her. 'He wants to settle down near Jane and Thomas, in Hertfordshire. It's a good life. Jane's happy being a country gentlewoman. My father will be pleased.'

Will said, still squinting at the sky: 'Robert's a good man.'

Then he said: 'But won't you miss the silk?'

And then: 'Goffredo does.'

Goffredo was round the back of the house. He was sitting on a bench under an apple tree, with a stick propped up next to him, enjoying the sun. He was watching the serving boy putting down the bread at the table in front of him, and humming.

Isabel knew the chirpy tune and the bittersweet Venetian words. The weavers had danced to that song, sometimes.

Damn the loot!
I am right here, in safety,
and almost can't believe
I am.
And if I were not me?
And if I had been killed in battle?
And if I were my ghost?
That would be just great.
No, damn, ghosts don't eat.

She crept up behind him and put her hands round his eyes. She sang the last line, very quietly, into his ear: 'No, càncaro, spiriti no manga'.

Goffredo always had smelled like this: of spices and sandalwood. He didn't wriggle in panic at having his eyes covered up, as Will Caxton might have. He just turned his head, gently but firmly, until his eyes were free of her hands and he was looking up at her. 'I knew it,' he breathed, and she saw his powerful dark face – miraculously restored after the fire – was already creasing into a laugh. 'Isabel.'

'Well, I don't have to say yet,' she said, munching on a bit of cheese. 'It's a big decision. I've been a widow for years. I don't need to worry about money. I can take my time.'

Will began cutting up an apple. Goffredo was flicking his kerchief at the midges. She hadn't felt as light-hearted for months as she did now, with her Italian friend here. He'd laughed for sheer joy just before, when she'd said she'd sent Joan Woulbarowe's cloth as a gift to the Princess, with a request that she use it in her wedding wardrobe if she liked it. 'Think how thrilled Joan would have been,' he'd chortled, without a hint of sentimentality. 'Weaver to the Queen of England.' Now he was humming again.

444

'What about you?' she asked him.

Goffredo swept his arms apart in the ironic full-body shrug she remembered so well. He smiled, but he was shaking his head at the same time.

'I'm not sure,' he said ruefully, 'but I should be off. I'm well again. There's nothing for me in London any more.'

No one in London knew Goffredo was here. He didn't want the Conterini to find him. Will had kept quiet, and kept him safe. But Goffredo wanted to get back to work. 'I sit under my tree every day, and look at our friend here,' he said, stroking Will's shoulder so fondly it made Will wriggle with embarrassment. '. . . as happy as a flea with his machines and his ideas, and I envy him. I wasn't made for idleness.'

He had ideas, of course. Goffredo always had ideas. And he always waved his arms like this when he got so excited about them that his big black eyebrows started dancing.

Maybe he'd just go home to Venice. But there'd be huge fines to pay if he came back without his teams and without the Venetian government's cut from his English venture.

So, maybe Spain. The glorious old Moorish silk production there had been in decline since the Castilian Queen started turning all of Spain Catholic. The Christians and Moriscos and *conversos* who'd taken over the looms in Valencia and Barcelona only knew how to make cheap haberdashery, low-quality stuff mixed with second-choice silk and flax and cotton. Italians were moving in to compete. There were Tuscans and Ligurians in Barcelona. There was a guild of Italian velvet weavers in Valencia.

Or perhaps the Orient. Goffredo's father had been one of the Venetian merchants who used to travel the Black Sea to buy Persian silk in Tana and Trebizond and

Constantinople. That market had been closed off in Goffredo's lifetime by the Turkish conquest of Byzantium. But the silks had gone on coming west, by caravan, from Persia to Syria, bypassing the Turks. The markets of Damascus and Aleppo were booming. The profits were easy. Goffredo could make himself understood in Persian.

'Just think,' Goffredo breathed, 'I could be in Tripoli, with the sun on my back, loading up a cargo of silks lovelier than anything in Christendom . . . doing what God intended.'

His handsome eyes were glowing. Listening to him, Isabel could almost smell salt on the wind; almost hear the wood of the galleys creaking, the ropes flapping; almost see the oiled, weathered skin of the sailors.

'Silks from the Caspian,' she breathed in reply. 'Ghilan, Shiraz, Azerbaijan.'

Even saying those words made her feel alive again; gave her the sense of inspiration she remembered from the old days.

She went on, more excitedly: 'You know the ports, the people, the markets over there as well as here. You know both ends of the silk trade. Who else knows everything you do?'

She stopped. She could feel a new idea take shape. 'Goffredo,' she said, feeling dizzy with it. 'You'd know how to import silk directly, from the East to London . . . without needing to go through the authorities in Venice . . . wouldn't you?'

He was nodding. He was caught up in her excitement. His eyes were glowing.

She caught her breath; added: 'You could do it: cut out the middleman. Cut out Italy. How Alice would love that. All you'd need would be some capital.'

Out of the corner of her eye, she saw Will Caxton's head move. But she paid no attention. 'Just think of the profits,' she murmured, looking into Goffredo's eyes, feeling the corners of her mouth lift. 'If it worked.'

Goffredo was smiling back; and although his lips were saying, 'madness, sheer madness,' there was delight in his eyes and he was nodding his head.

As she watched him, a memory came unbidden to Isabel's mind. A memory of Alice Claver, lit up by a dusty sunbeam in a silkroom strewn with the glories of the East, teaching her the names of threads from Persia and Syria. Rolling the names joyfully over her tongue – *ardassa, rasbar, castrovana, safetina* – and nodding her big head as she conjured each treasure into words.

Suddenly Isabel knew what Alice would have wanted for her. It was all simpler than she would have believed possible, she realised, feeling as gloriously illuminated as if she was bathing in that same ray of sunlight. She knew what she wanted for herself, too.

There was only one possible right use for the money she'd made from Alice Claver's business. It had to go back into the silk trade. So did she; and she had to go in again with Goffredo. Setting up a new trade would be risky, and maybe dangerous. She didn't know what the East was like; she'd never travelled further than Bruges. But she could trust her own wits, and Goffredo's. They were two of a kind. She knew his memories, just as he knew hers. She knew how his mind worked. And he knew how to be happy. She'd always want to be sharing adventures with this man, enjoying the assurance of his movements and the ready way his powerful features broke up into a mischievous laugh under a great sweep of black eyebrow; laughing along with him.

She put her hand on Goffredo's. She wouldn't want a life in which his hands – lean, elegant and capable, even now their backs bore the pale marks of the fire – weren't within reach.

447

Goffredo looked at her fingers for a moment, then cupped them with his scarred second hand. He lifted her hand to his lips and kissed it. He waited; looking brightly at her, half-laughing, perhaps wondering if she'd push him away.

But Isabel was too lost in wonder at the tingle of skin brushing against skin to take away her hand. She stayed where she was, breathing in spices and sandalwood: the smell of adventure; the smell of happiness.

A quiet came on them both. But he was beginning to grin again even before Isabel spoke, as if he'd already guessed that the next thing she'd say would be: 'Take me too.'

MEDIEVAL TIMES OF YEAR

2 February: Candlemas

March 23: Spring Equinox: Lady Day/Annunciation (considered the start of the year: one of four Quarter Days)

Easter/Passiontide (30 March in 1483)

1 May: May Day

24 June: Midsummer/St John's Eve/Feast of St John the Baptist (one of four Quarter Days)

1 (or 6) August: Lammas. Christian name for the holiday, which means 'loaf-mass', since this was the day on which loaves of bread were baked from the first grain harvest and laid on the church altars as offerings. It was a day representative of 'first fruits' and early harvest.

25 September: Michaelmas (one of four Quarter Days)

1 November: All Hallows

December 25: Christmas (one of four Quarter Days)

MEDIEVAL TIMES OF PRAYER – THE HOURS

The day was another liturgical cycle. Church bells rang the hours of Divine Office. The hours begin with Vigils or Matins in the middle of the night (split into three parts, at 9 p.m., midnight, and 3 a.m.), Lauds at daybreak, then the four 'little hours': Prime (around 6 a.m.), Tierce (around 9 a.m.), Sext (around noon) and Nones (around 3 p.m.), then the evening Vespers (around 5–6 p.m.), and the final office of Compline (around 7–8 p.m.). For the monastic the true work of God (*opus dei*) was to 'pray without ceasing'. The desire to benefit from this endless prayer was what made the monasteries rich, as the nobility provided for the future welfare of their own souls by donating property to religious foundations so as to give them revenue to sustain this spiritual work.